Historical fiction

CW00496401

THE RICHARD DAVEY CHRONICLES

Needing Napoleon

Serving Shaka

Rescuing Richard

RESCUING RICHARD

Rescuing Richard

Published by The Conrad Press Ltd. in the United Kingdom 2023

Tel: +44(0)1227 472 874
www.theconradpress.com
info@theconradpress.com

ISBN 978-1-915494-55-9

Printed and bound in Great Britain by Clays Ltd, Elcograf S.p.A

Typesetting and Cover Design by The Book Typesetters
www.thebooktypesetters.com

The Conrad Press logo was designed by Maria Priestley.

RESCUING RICHARD

GARETH WILLIAMS

PREVIOUSLY...

in *The Richard Davey Chronicles*

Book One: *Needing Napoleon*

R ichard Davey is a lonely history teacher living in the present who discovers a way to travel back in time, provided he wants it to the exclusion of everything else. His life is a dead-end and his obsession with Napoleon Bonaparte, Emperor of the French, makes him the perfect candidate. He has always believed the Battle of Waterloo could have been a French victory in 1815. Now, he sets out to prove it.

Posing as an American agent, he infiltrates the French lines where he is interrogated by Emile Béraud, a career soldier and officer in Bonaparte's personal guard. He convinces Béraud he has information of great value to the emperor, and with his help, finds himself face to face with his hero. But, try as he might, he cannot persuade Napoleon to a different course of action.

He is with Bonaparte when the battle dissolves into a rout, and finds himself fleeing for Paris with the imperial entourage. He witnesses Napoleon's abdication and asks permission to accompany the former emperor into exile on St Helena, far out in the Atlantic ocean. After all, he has nowhere to go, stranded two hundred years from his old life. He begins an affair with the wife of a senior general who followed Bonaparte into exile. Richard knows Napoleon dies on the island, possibly from poisoning, in 1821 but is determined to change his fate.

Establishing links with the East India Company, Richard concocts a plan to escape the prison island. With Bonaparte disguised as a maid, accompanied by Emile Béraud, they slip away from St Helena. The merchant ship is attacked by pirates, and although they survive, Bonaparte's identity is revealed. The ship's captain sees an opportunity for fame and fortune, but before he can return the former emperor to the British, the ship is severely damaged in a storm.

Richard, Napoleon and Emile manage to turn the tables on the captain and force him to put them ashore on the southern coast of Africa.

Book Two: *Serving Shaka*

I t is June 1816. Richard and his party, which includes three former pirates, survive a lion attack before their way inland, only to be captured by local tribesmen. They are handed over to the growing power in the land, Shaka Zulu.

Aided by a mixed-race interpreter, Richard and Napoleon convince Shaka they can be of use as he builds his empire. Bonaparte dreams of supplanting Shaka while Emile, seduced by Shaka's disciplined army, volunteers.

Outmanoeuvring those who accuse them of witchcraft, Richard and Napoleon earn Shaka's trust. Napoleon despatches the former pirates with a message for his supporters. Shaka wages battle after battle, drawing more and more tribes under his control. Pleased with insights provided by Richard, drawing on his recollections of university history courses, Shaka gifts Richard a companion, Ulwazi.

Richard is conflicted about his place in Zulu society. His struggles are interrupted by the arrival, in February 1818, of two French generals loyal to Bonaparte with a supply of muskets. They are accompanied by an English missionary hoping to convert the Zulus. Shaka allows Napoleon to train a rifle company, ignoring objections from his council.

Shaka declares total war in 1818, deploying his ever-growing regiments far and wide. Richard is caught up in a battle where Bonaparte's musket company makes a valuable contribution. Emile and Richard rescue Shaka's favourite, earning his gratitude. Emile is granted permission to marry, while Richard and Napoleon are declared Zulus and appointed members of Shaka's inner council.

Richard falls for Ulwazi after a long struggle with his conscience. He resolves to accompany the French generals on the journey back to their ship on the coast in Portuguese territory. They are accompanied by the missionary whose wits have failed him in the face of the Zulus' apathetic reaction to his preaching.

It is May 1818. Richard is healthy and in love. He has never felt so comfortable in his own skin.

For Liz and Serena

sisters

Chapter One

May 1818

The Fasimba scouts chatter excitedly. Richard is at the rear of the line and cannot catch what they are saying. He steps around Daniel, who has one hand on Reverend Dalrymple's shoulder, and walks to where an agitated young Thibault is failing to communicate with their escort.

After a day's rain, a week ago, winter has returned to its habitual mild dryness. The trees are big-leaved and less densely packed here. Richard can smell rotting vegetation and sea mud. The air stirs the waxy leaves lazily. Richard tastes salt on his tongue. The sun is low in the sky, casting long shadows.

'I think we are nearly there,' he suggests to General Thibault.

Every inch an aide-de-camp, the young man whispers discreetly to General Bertrand. The marshal of France sways, arms slack at his sides. His face is yellow and flushed. Sweat beads beneath the rim of his bicorn hat. His eyes are fixed on the ground but dull.

He mumbles and Thibault leans close. Richard resents feeling guilty in the sick man's presence. 'What did he say?' he asks abruptly.

'He asks if his wife has come to meet him,' Thibault replies, his compassion obvious.

'I am sure she awaits you at the fort, General.' Richard tries to sound kind.

The young general steers Bertrand forward while Daniel guides Dalrymple, the defeated missionary. Ulwazi stands proud beneath her burden which rests on a plaited-grass ring. Her eyes are active; she is on unfamiliar territory.

The young warriors defer to the sole officer among them, a grizzled disciplinarian. He has greying temples and slack skin but his tongue is fast and his hands faster. Richard has seen him clout members of his *iviyo* or company with lightning speed when they displease him.

'We wait here,' he informs Richard, looking uncomfortable. From the start of the trip, he has kept apart from the uniformed Frenchmen, the troubled clergyman and his minder. By default, Richard has become the recipient of his reports. Ulwazi knows the man. He is a friend of Nqoboka, which explains his standoffish manner. He wants nothing to do with outside influences.

Richard nods his agreement. 'It may be many days,' he clarifies.

'We wait here,' insists the implacable old warrior.

'Will you stay with your people?' Richard asks Ulwazi carefully. He does not want to tell her what to do. Her expression is all the answer he needs. She is coming with him.

A few minutes brings the reduced party to the edge of the trees. Richard gasps. The majestic sweep of the bay frames a riot of pink and grey as the sun sets behind a mangrove-fringed horizon.

A gaggle of small boys plays in the mud beside a pair of canoes, screened by fishing nets hung from poles. Two men work meticulously, deft fingers conjuring knots wherever they are needed.

The engrossed pair do not notice the strangers emerge from the trees but one of the boys spots them. His features are crowded out by an open mouth, front teeth missing, throat vibrating in alarm.

Richard watches the other boys look up from the rock pools. They quickly add their voices, high-pitched and clear.

Lanky birds with long, precise beaks gabble as they unfurl powerful wings. Beating the air in desperation; they demand it bear them aloft. Their white feathers are ghostly against a reddening sky.

The two men do not look up until they finish their shuttle across the nets. Little arms point to the men clustered just beyond the shelter of the trees.

Lagoons glisten to the south, mangroves intertwine ahead and seagrass waves beneath the surface of the sea. There are no hills but a giant spit protects the coast from the Indian Ocean to the east.

To the north, Richard can just make out the Portuguese fort's dressed stone glowing in the febrile light.

The two fishermen usher the animated boys into canoes and push off, wiry arms stroking their paddles skilfully. Within minutes they are lost to sight around the coast.

Richard leads his modest party onto the dry fringe of mud. The sky is a riot of pink and purple now, the sea a deep blue. The grey mud gives way to stretches of sand. The waves wash gently against the shelving shore.

Richard peers at the Portuguese outpost. It looks tiny.

'How far?' he asks Daniel, trusting the fisherman's

judgement across water.

'Ten miles at least.'

Richard nods. They will have to make camp. 'We will stay close to our escort for the night, in case those fishermen return with reinforcements.'

Daniel smiles. 'Looks to be a good anchorage. No wonder the Portuguese built here.'

The next morning, Richard rises early. He has not slept well with Bertrand moaning and Dalrymple praying. Fanny is only a day's march away. He has a crick in his back and toothache. Although he says nothing, Ulwazi kneads his spine until it relaxes. He smiles his thanks but thinks he sees tears in her eyes. She moves off before he can be sure.

General Thibault joins Richard. 'The Portuguese are a conquered people, lackeys of the British, their royal family fled to their savage empire in Brazil.' His words drip contempt.

Richard does his best to disguise his annoyance. 'We need their help. It would be well to avoid antagonising them.' He looks pointedly at Marshal Bertrand, still curled up, his head tossing from side to side.

Thibault follows his gaze and colours. 'You are right. I will show them more respect than they are due.' With that, he moves off to wake Bertrand. Daniel has roused Dalrymple and is helping him eat nuts and morsels of dried meat.

The Zulu warriors remain behind the screen of trees as Richard leads the way around the curve of the bay. A substantial river forces them upstream for almost two miles to find a ford.

They break for a brief rest at noon. The fort looms larger and seems surprisingly familiar. Through his telescope, it is a tiny patch of Europe, defiant amidst tropical exuberance.

Richard traces the outward-sloping bastion and crenelations topping the walls. He spots the thrust of cannon muzzles at both visible corners. Outside the stone structure sits a scattering of huts and a large palm-thatched roof on poles. A market perhaps?

Sipping judiciously from his water, Richard takes stock of his companions. Ulwazi is wide-eyed at this unfamiliar land. Daniel gazes wistfully out to sea, towards an island broken free of the promontory. The reverend sits cross-legged, his nose buried in his bible. Thibault is trying to get some water between General Bertrand's flaking lips.

Richard is impatient to be off. Fanny Bertrand awaits; although she does not know he is coming.

The cleared ground around the fort is sandy. The huts hovering in the fort's orbit are rudimentary constructions of interlaced sticks and palm fronds. A few scrawny guinea fowl scuttle aside. A goat is on its hind legs chewing the thatch of a rickety hut. A mangy dog growls at them but slinks away when Thibault aims his foot at its thin flanks.

A face peers at them from one hut but ducks into the shadows as Richard approaches. A toddler playing with a coconut husk is swept up by a running mother wearing bright red-and-green cloth.

A shout echoes from one of the towers, '*Quem vai lá?*'

Richard speaks no Portuguese but the sentiment is obvious. General Thibault steps forward, propelling Marshal

Bertrand into view.

A greeting follows and a small, iron-studded door swings open beneath its modest portico. Shouts sound from within. Figures in uniform appear as Thibault leads Bertrand forward. Richard and Ulwazi follow the French pair with Dalrymple and Daniel behind.

A short man in a plain-brown uniform, stained with sweat but trimmed with scarlet, salutes the Frenchmen. He wears a crimson sash at his waist, tied off in a silver knot. His sabre hangs low from his hip. He is an officer. His short black boots are dusty but look well cared for.

He is flanked by a pair of NCOs in matching short brown jackets, atop brown breeches and black shoes. They both carry muskets at the shoulder. They wear black shakos topped with wilting green plumes. Their headgear bears the emblem of a bugle. Their breeches are patched and fading.

The older man, with striking blue eyes, has two yellow-lace chevrons on his right sleeve, while the younger has one. Richard thinks the first is a corporal and the second a lance-corporal.

The black-lace frogging across the officer's chest has faded to grey. His cuffs are edged by a wide gold lace. He too wears a black shako but his is trimmed with gold cord. He is poorly shaven and a stye disfigures his left eye. Nevertheless, he has a military bearing, as do the two light-infantrymen towering behind him.

All three have black hair, sallow skin, and callous eyes that study Ulwazi predatorily. Richard steps in front of her and stares at the blue-eyed NCO until he has the grace to look away.

General Thibault starts a conversation with the Portuguese officer. He is trying to be polite. He gestures towards Bertrand and then to the rest of the party. The officer nods and replies, before issuing orders to the two corporals who make off at double time.

'The captain has summoned the Bertrand family. We are assigned quarters with the officers in the block to your left.' As Thibault finishes, a vision in pale blue emerges from the furthest door. A conical skirt is finished with frills. The waistband is narrow and high, accentuating her form. Puffed sleeves complete the look. She is trailed by three children of decreasing height, and a dark-skinned maid carrying a large baby. 'That is the commandant's house,' Thibault explains. 'The captain has surrendered it to the Bertrand family.' Richard wonders if he has misheard?

'The commandant has no need of it. He is dead,' Thibault sneers, 'by his own hand, the coward! He will surely burn in hell!'

Reverend Dalrymple stumbles forward waving his bible. 'The fires of hell shall surely consume us all! There can be none but sinners in this godless place!' His voice is unnaturally high and causes Marshal Bertrand to look up.

As the general's eyes come to rest on his family they light up. Richard wonders if they are the first thing the sick man has truly seen since leaving Bulawayo?

'Fanny! Napoleon, Hortense, Henri! And of course, dear little Arthur!' His French voice croaks on the English name of his fourth child, in honour, Richard knows, of his wife's father. Arthur Dillon was an Irish officer who fought for France only to be guillotined by Republicans in 1794.

'I have so longed to be back with you all.' Bertrand's voice wavers and Thibault extends a hand to support him.

'Henri, you are unwell!' exclaims Fanny in French, her dark-honey eyes wide and wet. Her pale hands reach out as her long legs cut the space between them. Richard is transfixed by her long eyelashes. He had forgotten how compelling her porcelain face could be, even when distorted by worry. Her piled-up auburn hair cascades in curls untouched by sweat.

Fanny pays no attention to those accompanying her husband. She murmurs constantly as she takes him from Thibault and leads him towards their lodgings. Her brood flutter about her feet, basking in their father's kind smiles. Fanny has not even noticed him. Richard watches them go, trailed by the nursemaid, uncomfortable in a high-waisted floral shift.

Looking around the room allotted to him, Richard winces. He has tried ignoring the ache in his lower jaw but over the past few days it has become draining.

Ulwazi is laying out their bedding on the floor even though a cot bed sits against the far wall. Furniture is not a feature of Zulu domesticity. The sole exception being wooden headrests Richard cannot use, as he sleeps on his side.

When she is finished, Ulwazi takes his hand and pulls him insistently towards the door. 'I want to see this other world!' she pleads and he does not resist.

It is late afternoon and although the atmosphere is close, the air is a comfortable temperature. The interior of the fort is orderly, if spartan. Two accommodation blocks face each other across a parade ground.

A dog barks unseen. A servant flits from one doorway to the next and disappears. A flagpole stands, peeling white paint. The tattered flag barely stirs. It is so faded that Richard can only make out the outline of a crown topping a shield.

Steps lead to the roof of the interior buildings which acts as a parapet. The fort has a bulwark tower at each corner of its curtain wall. A pair of cannon menace at right angles from the nearest corner. A sentry mans each tower.

Ulwazi pulls Richard to the flagpole and then lets him go to grasp it in both hands. 'What kind of tree was this?' she muses. He just smiles and says nothing. She runs across the open space to the far accommodation block, her bare legs swallowing the distance. Richard estimates each exterior wall is close to one hundred yards long.

He hears voices call out to Ulwazi, in a native dialect, from the open doors of the soldiers' dormitories. He sees her head tilt as she tries to puzzle meaning from the words. A figure appears and then another. They are locally recruited soldiers.

Richard assumes they are off duty from their casual bearing. They wear ostensibly white jackets and pantaloons, edged with scarlet piping. Their lower legs and feet are bare. Each head is covered with a black cap.

Two becomes three and then four gather around Ulwazi. Uncomfortable, Richard walks across the parade ground calling her name. The soldiers duck back into their billets.

Ulwazi gives Richard a wry look and he shrugs in return. 'They were too interested in you,' he confesses weakly.

'I liked it,' she shoots back, surprising him.

He takes her by the arm and steers her up the nearest flight of steps, built against the outer wall. They climb to the parapet running around the fort. They face the sea.

A patrolling sentry steps around them, his eyes turned away. They hear waves break on the shore below. Seabirds drift overhead on the desultory breeze.

'Have you seen the ocean before?' Richard asks gently. The pain in his jaw flares but he bites down with determination.

Ulwazi nods. 'So much water, so wide.'

Richard feels a flood of affection and clasps her to him. 'Almost three-quarters of the world is covered in water,' he murmurs teasingly in her shapely ear.

She pulls away and stares into his face, scanning his features. 'It cannot be so,' she replies confidently. 'Even the largest lakes and rivers are a small portion of my homeland.' Her eyes dare him to contradict her.

A second sentry passes them. This one stares lasciviously at Ulwazi who flashes her teeth at him, eyes sparkling. He stumbles and snaps his head to the front, recovering his stride.

'How far do you think this water reaches?' He is careful with his tone.

'To the horizon is perhaps a half day's walk?' she replies whip quick and reasonable.

'There is a large island, Madagascar, seven hundred miles west, but beyond that, the sea stretches to Australia.' Distances can be hard to explain but Zulus are good with numbers. 'More than four and a half thousand miles. If a Zulu regiment covers fifty miles a day, it would take them ninety days to reach the other side, if they never stopped, day or night!'

Again, she checks his face to see if he is teasing. Apparently satisfied, she smiles up at him. 'There is much I can learn from you.' She sounds pleased. 'Tell me something else impossible!'

He smiles back. 'If you sailed south in a ship like that one at anchor,' he points at the chartered ship riding easily, stars and stripes limp at the stern, 'you would travel three thousand miles only to reach a land of intense cold. Sixty days for your unsleeping *impi*. Much of the sea is frozen into great plains and mountains of ice.'

This time she just leans against him and sighs, her eyes on the far horizon as if confirmation of his claims lies there.

Richard studies the ship at anchor. Her stern drifts into view and he can make out her home port: New Orleans. She is the spitting image of the *Arniston*, the East Indiaman he secured to whisk Napoleon Bonaparte from St Helena. The ship commanded by Captain Simpson; a man Napoleon tried to kill to cover his tracks.

He begins counting the cannon on board but keeps losing his place as the bows swing lazily. If she is anything like the *Arniston,* then she is carrying close to forty twelve-pounders, along with some smaller-calibre weapons.

When they return to their quarters, there is a brief note scratched in watery ink waiting for them.

'I am invited to dine with the officers and their guests tonight,' Richard relays to Ulwazi. The note is from the captain and written in broken English. He has signed himself 'Acting Commandant, Lourenco Marques'. Richard again wonders what drove the fort's commander to take his own life?

Ulwazi teases the fibrous paper from his grasp and studies it. She traces the pale scrawl with her index finger, lips twitching as if she can almost form the words. 'This spoke to you?' she asks eagerly. 'Why can I not hear it?'

Richard looks at her fondly. She waits patiently, so comfortably naked bar the bead kilt strung from her hips. He looks away guiltily as he considers the impending dinner. Fanny will be there!

He looks back. Ulwazi is still puzzling over the captain's invitation. She turns it over and over, quicker and quicker, as if hoping to trick it into revealing its secrets.

Richard sighs and strokes his painful jaw. 'I will teach you to make these marks and understand their meaning.'

Ulwazi throws her arms around his neck. Her sweet breath is hot in his ear, her nipples harden against his thin shirt. Her thigh rubs against his groin and he responds. His breathing grows heavy. They sink to the mats Ulwazi has laid out on the floor.

Later, a bugle sounds, waking Richard from a doze. Ulwazi squats beside him, again studying the captain's short communication. He rolls over and sits up. 'I must wash for dinner.' Ulwazi says nothing. Richard bites his lip. 'I cannot take you with me,' he says apologetically.

She looks confused. He pours water from a chipped jug into a matching bowl and buries his face in the cool water. When he surfaces, she asks, 'Why would you take me with you? This is not a matter for women.'

For a moment he stays silent, drying his face on a threadbare, musty cloth. 'The white woman you saw, General Bertrand's wife, she will be there. Her children too, I should

26

imagine.' He looks at his hands and waits for her to object.

'That was a woman? I was not sure; she was so… draped. I wondered if she was an *isangoma* who smelled the evil spirit tormenting Dalypole.' He smiles as Ulwazi mangles the missionary's name.

'But then she went to the sick Frenchman so I concluded she was an *inyanga* whose knowledge of herbs might cure him of his fever.'

Fanny, a doctor or a spirit medium? She is bewitching, certainly. He is impatient to see her, to speak with her, to see where they stand. What does he want? For Bertrand to die and leave Fanny for him? They have four children!

Ulwazi looks at him expectantly but says nothing.

'You do not mind being left alone?' He gestures around their lodgings. He can tell she senses his discomfort.

She tilts her head and looks at him slyly. 'I care not who you eat with. I have plenty of food.' She pats the bundle beside her. She sounds unperturbed.

Richard squeezes her shoulder and flees the room as his face colours.

A parade is breaking up as he emerges. Bare-legged soldiers in white jackets and pantaloons trail towards their barracks.

The light is slipping away. Night comes so fast in these latitudes, he thinks. He looks around uncertainly. Is there an officers' mess? He sees lights in the windows of the Bertrands' rooms.

He hesitates but then Daniel appears, walking with Reverend Dalrymple from the far end of the accommodation block. The missionary is well turned out, his dog-collar surprisingly bright in the swelling darkness.

Happy voices chatter as the native troops prepare supper on the other side of the fort.

'You received an invitation?' Richard asks.

Dalrymple looks confused. 'God called me!' he replies.

'We did,' confirms Daniel. 'I found a corporal who spoke some French. We managed a conversation. The meal will be in the commandant's house.'

Richard nods and the three of them head for the candlelight defying the dark. Daniel does not ask about Ulwazi.

Before they reach the threshold, the door is opened, spilling more warm light into the night. General Thibault steps out. He bows formally and gestures that they should enter.

Daniel ushers the reverend forward and follows. Richard trails them inside. The interior is warmly lit with candles behind glass and an ornate candelabra illuminates a long dining table.

The whitewashed walls are softened with mildewed wall hangings depicting Portuguese triumphs. Beneath the faded image of a sea battle, Fanny bends over, adjusting Hortense's collar while talking softly to the nearly ten-year-old Napoleon Bertrand. The boy nods solemnly, dressed in a buttoned maroon suit and black boots. His hair is long and lightly curled.

His sisters are almost overwhelmed by frills, their little faces ruddy from a recent scrubbing. Hearing voices and the closing of the door, Fanny looks up. Her eyes widen and she lets out an involuntary gasp. Richard smiles at her and makes a little bow.

Thibault is pouring himself a drink. Two Portuguese officers in their brown uniforms look over, interrupting their conversation. He ignores them. Fanny is about to speak to him. His heart hammers in his chest.

The captain strikes a knife gently against a glass. All fall silent and introductions are made.

'My name is Captain Antonio Santiago da Silva. I am pleased to welcome you all to the *Fortaleza de nossa senhora da conceicao*. You are on Portuguese soil!'

Impatiently, Richard watches Daniel seat Dalrymple in the place indicated by an attentive servant, decked out like a royal footman. The man has a dark complexion but pinched features. Richard is still standing and his host approaches, trailed by his junior officers.

'He is a mulatto,' observes the captain, noticing Richard's scrutiny. 'A half-breed. He was the commandant's man, hence his finery.' The captain sounds awkward as he glances down at his own plain uniform. 'I am proud to be less of a peacock. I wear the brown of the Portuguese *Cazadores*, our light infantry, with pride.'

The two other officers nod and smile. Unsure how to respond, Richard settles on flattery. 'Your French is very good.'

'I was captured when they invaded in 1809. I was a prisoner for almost three years. Long enough to learn the language of my enemy.' His blood up, the captain has spoken loudly and blushes as the young French general regards him coldly. 'Forgive me, this is in the past. I was liberated by the British and joined the royal court in Brazil. From there, I came to Mozambique.' Richard senses there is more to the story.

Fanny Bertrand takes her seat and all heads turn to her. 'My husband, Marshal Bertrand, is not himself. He has a fever. I have insisted he remain in bed.' Her voice is unnaturally bright. 'So, it falls to me to add my welcome to that of our Portuguese host.' She raises her glass, 'To better days!' she toasts first in French and then English.

Richard stares at her hungrily. She notices even though she avoids looking in his direction.

'It is good to see you again, Countess,' he manages in an almost steady voice. 'I did not think I should do so, after my departure from St Helena.' He sips his madeira and is delighted by the quality. The Portuguese have supplied wines to Britain for generations. No wonder they secure good vintages for themselves. Fanny inclines her head and offers him a modest smile.

Conversation flows easily as all at the table speak French, except the lieutenant. The guests ask questions and the captain furnishes replies. As he drinks steadily, his answers grow longer.

'What sort of trade occupies you here?' Thibault enquires, looking pointedly at Richard.

'There is a *feira*, a trading fair, for ivory just beyond the walls. You may have seen it?' Richard recalls the palm roof on stilts and nods as Captain da Silva continues. 'There is a network, centuries old, involving hunters and long-distance traders, Arabs and Swahili, canoe men and local rulers. But there is some agriculture and a new venture in whaling shows promise.' Their host pauses to drain his glass and gestures for another.

Before he resumes, Daniel speaks. 'Do you have many cattle? The land to the south is rich grazing. The Zulu and surrounding tribes have many head.'

Richard wonders if the Guernseyman is thinking of the Bisson brothers, his fellow indentured pirates, escaped now and returned to their island home? The younger brother, particularly, loved his cows.

The captain scowls. 'We tried many times in the early years of settlement. Every time, they sicken and die. This is a foul place for cattle. Horses too. Only local wildlife survives for long.' Aware he sounds sour; da Silva invites another enquiry.

'When was the fort built? It looks a solid affair,' Richard offers.

'It was rebuilt in stone in the 1790s when we retook this spot from the Dutch. There are few deep-water ports on this coast. We will not lose it again.'

The main course is a kind of fish stew. The captain picks at it without enthusiasm but Richard finds it delicious as do most around the table, judging by the emptying plates.

'I long for *cozido*, it is full of boiled meats and sausages, the taste of home,' Captain da Silva admits, 'my people are from the mountains,' he adds by way of further explanation.

The conversation picks up again. All three of the Bertrand children sat at table display immaculate manners and remain unheard.

Richard drinks steadily, enjoying the rich wine and the sight of Fanny. The two junior Portuguese officers talk quietly together but their eyes rove the table and its occupants.

The others discuss the interior, major Portuguese posts further north, and links with Goa on the Indian coast. Fanny talks to her children, occasionally looking across the table or laughing at a quip.

'The sailors stay on their ship for the most part,' the captain is saying in response to a question from Daniel. 'They come ashore to buy food and other things.'

Richard can imagine what those other things might be.

'There are all sorts among their crew, although the ship flies the American flag. Their captain is a Frenchman of sorts, from Louisiana.' Captain da Silva sounds disparaging. 'He visits the ivory fair, buying up almost every merchant's stock. He has metal goods, cloth and beads. He came prepared. He is also looking for slaves.'

This last observation is given no more weight than any other. Richard stiffens. 'I thought the Royal Navy patrolled these waters to disrupt the slave trade?'

Captain da Silva inclines his head, the light catching his swollen eye. Daniel spoons stew into Reverend Dalrymple's slack mouth and wipes his lips.

'We see an English ship perhaps twice a year. They come ashore and talk a great deal. Then they leave and all returns to normal.' He sounds dismissive.

'So, the Portuguese authorities do nothing to stop the trade?' Richard presses.

The captain spreads his hands and shrugs, setting the fringe of his epaulettes dancing in the flickering candlelight. 'It is not so simple. Often it is their own people who sell. Some are so desperate, they are willing.'

Richard splutters and dabs angrily at his mouth with his serviette. 'You expect me to believe that?' His voice is too loud and he is beginning to slur.

Fanny glances at him sharply. The young general shoots him a look of contempt. He wants to stop himself. He wants the meal to end so that he can get a few minutes alone with her. The disingenuous captain's face makes his hands clench into fists.

'You must understand. The rains fail. Drought grows more severe. Locusts ravage meagre crops. It is better to sell surplus population than see all go hungry.' The man's French is really very good. His face shows no sign of guilt.

Richard knows he cannot change the course of history with his outrage. He keeps his clumsy tongue behind his uneven teeth.

After a short lull, cheese is served in place of dessert. Richard empties another glass of madeira to wash down the strong, sour taste.

Coffee follows, served with flair by the liveried servant whose silent attentiveness makes Richard uncomfortable. The man's eyes are everywhere. The coffee is served black. It is strong and smooth.

'The coffee is good, yes? It used to come from our plantations in Brazil but now we grow it in Angola too,' boasts da Silva.

Richard thinks about slaves again but then looks to Fanny, encased in gauze and muslin. He takes a deep breath.

As the party breaks up, Richard tries to edge around the table towards Fanny but she is herding her three children towards a door at the end of the dining room. The sound of a baby grizzling drifts through the open door. Arthur Bertrand is awake and wants his mother.

There is nothing for it but to stumble out into the night. He does not want to return to his room. He does not want to face Ulwazi. Instead, he trips up the steps to the fort's alure, its wall-walk. He leans out and almost loses his balance as the drop looms through the embrasure.

A crescent moon casts a pallid gloss across the stone blocks. He turns away and leans against a merlon, happy to have something solid to feel. Waterloo, Paris, St Helena, Bulawayo, Lourenco Marques. What is he doing? Where is he going?

By the time he eases the door open, with the exaggerated care of drunks everywhere, Ulwazi is asleep, curled in on herself. He can only just make out her outline as his eyes adjust to the interior gloom.

He looks at the bare mattress, still tied in a roll at one end of the bed frame. He tries to unravel the knot but his fingers are clumsy so he gives up and lies down beside Ulwazi.

Chapter Two

May 1818

Richard wakes to a pounding head and a furred mouth. He rolls over on the sleeping mat. Ulwazi is not there. He is glad. He is so thirsty he fights rising nausea to get up and stagger outside.

The brightness of the morning almost knocks him off his feet. He grips the door jamb, swaying, waiting for his vision to recover. A young servant appears dressed in a pair of short, fawn trousers. Richard mimes drinking with his free hand.

The man nods and flashes teeth that put Richard's to shame. He trots ten paces and bends over a trap door abutting the wall of the accommodation block. Richard approaches, keeping one hand against the stone for support.

Peering over the crouched man's shoulder, he sees him remove the seal from a partially buried earthenware jar. Clear water fills the pottery container. It looks fresh and enticing. He licks his dry lips. The servant dips a ladle and turns, almost dropping it as he finds Richard looming over him.

The water tastes clean and is wonderfully cool. After four ladles, Richard forces himself to stop. He thanks the young man, who hangs the ladle on a hook and closes the wooden door to the water cooler before scurrying off to resume his duties.

Gradually the talk at table from the previous night returns

to his mind. Might that helpful servant actually be a slave? The Portuguese captain was at pains to lay the blame for slavery on anything but the authorities. Richard remains suspicious.

He is about to return to his room when he sees Daniel leading the befuddled missionary from the door of their shared accommodation. He raises a hand in greeting and shuffles along a route to intercept them. They meet close to a large doorway set in an architrave.

'It is a chapel,' Daniel explains. 'One of the NCOs told me of it yesterday. I thought it might do the reverend good.'

Richard pats the Guernseyman on the shoulder. 'Always thinking of others,' he comments warmly. 'Do not tell him it is a popish place of worship!'

'If I am willing to cross the threshold, raised a strict Methodist, then this high Anglican must bear it also!' Daniel replies in a serious tone.

Richard nods and follows the pair inside. The chapel is a small, whitewashed space with an arched window fitted with fogged glass. There is a smell of stale incense.

A simple altar draped in plain cloth is surmounted by a silver crucifix. A statue of Mary, resplendent in blue, her pink face looking up lovingly, kneels on a pedestal beside the door. She belongs here, Richard thinks, recalling the name of the fort, but he still stands in front of the statue, shielding Dalrymple's eyes from the sight.

Daniel steers the missionary to the single pew and settles him. Richard is surprised to find himself sitting beside the clergyman. Daniel gives him a quizzical glance but then retreats to the rear of the chapel.

Richard closes his eyes. The interior of the chapel is cool. The water he drank is doing its work.

Dalrymple is praying. The words are little more than mumbles but so familiar. Without thinking, Richard joins his voice to the missionary's slur.

'Yea, though I walk through the valley of the shadow of death, I will fear no evil: for thou art with me; thy rod and thy staff they comfort me.

'Thou preparest a table before me in the presence of mine enemies: thou anointest my head with oil; my cup runneth over.

'Surely goodness and mercy shall follow me all the days of my life: and I will dwell in the house of the Lord for ever.'

Psalm twenty-three. Richard has always loved it. The cadence of the King James version of the bible is a miracle. How can anything translated by committee make language dance so?

Richard looks at Reverend Dalrymple. Tears flood his rheumy eyes and soak his sunken cheeks. 'Time you went home, Reverend. You have done your best but this place is not ready to listen. Go, tell others what needs to be done. In a few decades there will be mission stations across the land.'

Dalrymple wipes his eyes with a shaky hand while the other clings to his bible. Now dry, his eyes are clear and regard Richard with interest. 'Thank you. I have had to travel a long way to confront the truth. This Africa has been a mirror held up to my face. I recognize the man reflected back at me. He is a hateful, puffed-up creature. He believed he could change the world because he knew the world as it should be. What arrogance! The implacable people of this land care nothing for our religion. They understand how to live in their world. Why would they let me persuade them otherwise?'

Richard has never heard the missionary sound uncertain or humble before. He reaches out a hand and places it on the veined claw grasping the bible. Then he gets up and leaves the chapel.

He is no evangelist but he must find a place for himself in this world. He does not mean Africa but the nineteenth century. Born into a peace-time democracy, he has spent his working life ensuring women receive the same educational advantages as men. Equality of opportunity was the principle he lived by in the twenty-first century.

But that was then and this is now. Women as property. Slavery. Arbitrary government. Not just in Portuguese east Africa but over almost all the world's surface. It is 1818 and he must find a way to accept that.

Ulwazi skips across the parade ground towards him. She wears a sari-style wrap of bright-cotton cloth. Wound close, the material accentuates every curve. She twirls in front of him and he cannot stop himself from smiling.

'Do you like it?' she asks.

'If you do,' he replies.

She looks crestfallen. 'I thought it made me look like your people? Someone you would want to keep.' Her voice wavers and she is suddenly vulnerable.

'You look beautiful.' He tries leaning on one version of the truth. Her smile returns nervously. 'Where did it come from?' He indicates the dress.

She points through the open gate of the fort. General Thibault is talking with Captain da Silva. 'The Frenchman bought it for me from a trader. He said I should not parade myself before the men here. That it was not... proper.' This last word causes her trouble but she constructs a phrase in Zulu that conveys social wrongdoing.

Richard understands. 'He may be right. But I would not have you change to make others happy.' He speaks without thinking.

'I do not understand. Why would I not do that which makes you happy?'

He sighs and looks around the four sides of the fort, as if trying to locate an answer. It is 1818. Ulwazi is a Zulu woman. They stand on Portuguese-controlled territory. These are facts. He cannot change them. He looks at her again. Her strong cheekbones defining her captivating face. Her head tilted slightly on one side, a furrow above her nose, one hip cocked, her whole body demanding a reply. It is 1818. He cannot change that. He has to find a way to live here.

'So long as that makes you happy too,' he offers as a compromise, willing her to accept this reply.

She shuffles her small feet and strokes the warp and weft of her garment with delicate hands. A tinkle of laughter trills between her shapely lips and her intelligent honey-gold eyes sparkle. 'I think I made you happy before dinner yesterday! That made me happy too.'

Richard blushes. For so long he resisted the ultimate intimacy with this beautiful woman. He could not accept the terms of their relationship. She is a gift from Shaka Zulu. How is that different from the slaves traded through this settlement?

She loops her arms around his neck. 'I see you remember!' she murmurs, nibbling his ear.

They are walking arm in arm towards their room when General Thibault sees them and calls out to Richard. Ulwazi smiles and indicates he should go. He squeezes her hand and walks towards the gateway. 'General Thibault, Captain da Silva,' he greets the pair.

'We are discussing offloading guns from the *Louisiana*. The captain will allow his men to help,' Thibault informs him.

Da Silva smiles ingratiatingly. Richard wonders how much gold he has demanded. 'When the cannon are ashore, I intend to see the Bertrand family on board,' Thibault adds.

Sweat pricks Richard's palms and a tick teases his left eye.

'The marshal is very ill,' the young general admits. 'The countess believes he will not survive if he remains. I agree. We have the savages as escort and the captain is prepared to lend us a company to transport the guns. We were just discussing how best to mount the cannon for the journey. The way is rough, as we both know.'

Richard cannot think of anything to say. Fanny is mere moments away but she will soon be gone. 'Excuse me, General. I must speak with the countess immediately.' Richard bows briefly and hurries across the courtyard.

He knocks impatiently at the door, not even noticing the iron studs fastening the wood. The door is opened by the local nursemaid who looks at his raised fist in surprise. He is about to lower it when she reaches out and catches it in her hand.

Looking down he sees he has broken the skin and blood is running freely. The maid ushers him in and seats him in an upright chair with cracking-leather upholstery. She is kneeling at his feet with a damp cloth when Fanny Bertrand enters and shoos her away.

Richard wraps the cloth around his abraded knuckles and stands. 'I had to see you before you leave.' He knows how feeble he sounds.

'That is most gracious of you, Mister Davey,' Fanny replies formally. It is as if she is speaking to a stranger.

'Fanny, it's like a miracle! When I heard you were here with your family, I couldn't believe it!' What is he trying to say?

She frowns at him as if he is using an unfamiliar language. 'It is not even a coincidence. As you know, wherever Napoleon Bonaparte goes, my husband is drawn to his side. Where Henri goes, I go. That is the way of it. But now my prayers are answered.' Her seductive voice falters. Her pretty, porcelain face glows in the low light.

Richard smells rancid candles but her aura banishes the stink, consuming him. She has prayed for her husband to fall ill? His heart pounds and his breathing catches. 'I have missed you so much!' He smiles awkwardly.

Fanny shakes her head, her auburn curls dancing. A severe expression stretches her face and her eyes dagger at him from beneath long lashes. 'What are you talking about?' She sounds cross and colour chases up from her neckline to shade her cheeks. 'You were an amusement on that wretched island prison.'

His eyes slip up and down her elegant body, lingering on her athletic legs, barely hinted at beneath layers of silk and muslin. He shifts one leg in front of the other, hoping she does not notice.

'My husband may have been chosen for me. I may have

resisted the match. But you forget my children. All healthy and still young enough to be saved from this madness. I intend to put as much distance as possible between my family and that insufferable, egotistical Corsican and his crazy plans for an African empire!' Deep loathing drips from every word. It is intended for Napoleon but there is enough for him too. She crosses her arms beneath her bosom and taps a foot.

He knows he has lost but cannot stop himself. 'But we had such fun together. I had never experienced anything like being with you. I was happy…'

She waves both hands in front of her face, as if warding off a wasp. 'Richard, for God's sake, stop it! You are like a child yet to master his emotions. Do not confuse lust for love, nor underestimate the pull of duty. I have seen it tug my husband this way and that. But no longer! We are leaving for a long retirement. Somewhere with salons and balls, dressmakers and good tutors for my children. Now go back to your black concubine!' With that she sweeps from the room, calling for her maid.

Richard stands in the parlour breathing in the air Fanny has just expelled. Musky lavender fills his nose. What did he want to say to her? That she should leave her husband and come with him? Where could they go? Her youngest is sixteen months old. She has four children. Does he want to become their stepfather?

He lets himself out, shutting the door behind him. He hears men haggling beyond the fort. Axes cut wood further off and monkeys screech at the calling gulls.

Ulwazi sits in the open doorway of their room. He takes one step towards her and then another.

General Thibault and Captain Guidry of the American merchant vessel argue in the shade of the officers' accommodation. Richard is leaning against the door jamb of his billet. Ulwazi is repacking her bundle with supplies secured in the market.

'The emperor will expect the very best,' Thibault insists.

'I am loyal to Bonaparte. So, believe me when I tell you it is impossible! A twelve-pounder gun weighs over two thousand pounds.'

It amuses Richard to hear the captain deploy imperial measurements in French. He is a short, squat figure with long, dark hair tumbling from below his bicorn. The hat is rimmed with gold braid matching the front of his blue tailcoat. His breeches are tan, his stockings laddered and his boots faded to grey.

'You have no limbers for the guns,' Guidry observes. 'On board, they are mounted on solid frameworks. The wheels are small affairs good for nothing but trundling on a smooth deck. There are few healthy horses or oxen to be had in this pestilential place. How many men can you call upon?'

Richard thinks of Napoleon's artillery bogged down in the mud on the morning of Waterloo. Thibault shifts from booted foot to booted foot uncomfortably. He scowls as if upset by the dust coating the black leather. 'Twenty natives and as many as Captain da Silva can spare. Perhaps thirty-five in total,' he admits reluctantly. 'But surely, if we construct rope swings, we should be able to manage?'

Captain Guidry rubs his rakish beard, as if trying to eradicate the burgeoning white hairs. 'How far?' he asks patiently.

'It took two weeks' march to get here.' Thibault looks defiant.

'Twice that to return then, even if your men are very able. You could perhaps manage two pieces but I doubt it.'

Richard is about to intervene when General Bertrand appears on his wife's arm from their apartments. 'Good morning, Thibault. Good to see you again, Captain Guidry. Thank you for your patience. It cannot have been easy keeping your men in order for so long in such a place.'

The Bonapartist merchantman looks pleased at the compliment. 'I am happy to advance the emperor's cause. That is why I try to dissuade your general here from taking twelve-pounders.'

Bertrand is pale and slick with sweat. Red rims his eyes and he is unsteady on his feet. Nevertheless, his voice is firm and calm. 'Thank you, Captain Guidry. You are quite right. My dear Thibault, you know the difficulties of the terrain. You will take whatever smaller guns are available, along with a promise that I shall despatch heavier armaments forthwith.'

Bertrand pauses. His eyes roll for a moment but then he shakes his head and continues. 'We need someone who knows this treacherous coast in detail.'

'I have heard Captain da Silva speak of Captain Owen. He commands the HMS *Leven*. He has three ships surveying these waters. It will take him years.' Guidry sounds sceptical, as if the task is beyond reach. It is clear he has no appetite himself to risk his ship inshore further south. Rounding the Cape of Good Hope at a safe distance is enough for him. His fingers ease his sword in its scabbard unconsciously, over and over again.

'We cannot alert the British to the emperor's presence. They are sure to investigate any hint of armaments being landed. Perhaps it is better to tell Bonaparte this is all that can be managed?' Bertrand sounds ineffably tired.

Thibault, as always, defers to his mentor and leads him away.

'Will you be joining the Bertrand family on their journey north?' Captain Guidry asks in a friendly tone that does not fool Richard. He scents another fare.

'No. I am tied to this land,' Richard finds himself saying. 'I never expected to be here but now, I must see what I can make of things.' He expects Guidry to press him but the captain seems perfectly satisfied.

'I understand. Captain da Silva is another seeking to make the best of things. He admitted to killing a man in a duel at the royal court in Rio de Janeiro.' This ivory-trading Bonapartist is not a man to keep secrets. 'The man was of aristocratic blood. This posting was the only option available.'

Richard nods. He deserves to be in such company. He is about to bid the captain farewell when the garrulous man starts up again. 'But that is as nothing compared to the story of the late commandant.'

The shade is pleasant. This is his life now. Fanny is leaving. Guidry is contemptible, but he is also a font of information, even if his lower decks are crammed with human cargo.

'I gather he took his own life?' Richard prompts as he eases his shoulder against the doorway.

'Indeed. He is a distant relative of the Braganzas, the royal family of Portugal. He was a member of the court when it

relocated to Brazil. I hear he made the sailors nervous.'
Captain Guidry makes a suggestive motion with his hips.
'Things were worse when they arrived. He developed a taste
for native boys, the younger the better. He was not discreet.'
Guidry attacks his pointed beard again with well-manicured
fingers.

'So, he was exiled to Mozambique?'

Captain Guidry nods. 'To a minor outpost in this
afterthought of a colony. He drank. He grew morose. He
pursued his decadent pleasures. You have seen his peacock of
a servant? A half-caste waif, abandoned by both parents. He
was one of the commandant's boys until his voice broke.
Some say it was not the commandant's hand that took his
life...' Guidry tails off as he spots Captain da Silva crossing
the parade ground with his angry eye. 'Come watch us
offload the guns for the emperor tomorrow.'

Richard accepts and the pair drift apart, leaving the fort's
commander to go about his business.

The United States merchant vessel *Louisiana* is a hive of
activity. Sailors haul ropes that squeak through pulleys, lifting
one gun and then another clear of the deck.

Richard watches from a longboat bobbing below the
bowed wall of the ship's side. He thinks of his friend,
Lieutenant Béraud, so prone to seasickness that even the
motion of this gig would upset his stomach. He shakes his
head, Emile is safely inland, serving his new regiment, the
Ama-Wombe of Shaka Zulu.

Ulwazi clings to his arm, eyes wide. She insisted on
accompanying him even though she cannot swim. Most of

the merchant sailors scrambling about the rigging are in the same boat, Richard knows.

The ship's captain watches his men at work. Although most of his guns are twelve-pounders, those being offloaded onto a raft lashed across jolly-boats are smaller. Six-pounders, Richard reckons, not from the main gun deck but the poop deck or the bow.

Pulleys squeal, ropes thrum taut and metal barrels sway threateningly as they angle out from the ship's side and are lowered towards sailors waiting below. Bare feet spread, arms raised to steady the cannon, bare-chested men call out instructions. A lookout in the rigging adds his commentary.

It is the sound of chaos and confusion but one by one, the forged weapons are laid side by side on the jury-rigged transport. As the fifth of six is offloaded, Richard's attention wanders. Ulwazi clings to his arm shivering, mesmerised by the operation and thrilled by her own audacity.

He looks at the clear sea around them, turquoise shading to green, edged close to the fort by swathes of white sand with ghostly mangroves further off. Richard hears groaning and weak cries from close to the waterline of the merchantman. He snaps at the soldiers at the oars to take them back to the fort.

The three men on the left bank dig their blades into the calm surface, while those beside them ship their oars. Once the bow has nosed around, all six men pull in time, sending the vessel skimming shoreward.

Richard thinks of the men confined to the hold, destined for plantation labour until their muscles fail and they no longer have a value. A stab of pain flares in his jaw. He holds the side of his face and wishes he was not here, not now.

In his own time, he would not hear the cries of slaves from a ship flying the American flag. In his own time, he could visit a dentist and put an end to the pain plaguing him. In his own time, he could marry Ulwazi and live with her proudly. That is what he tells himself as the crew ship their oars and hold the boat steady for them as they step onto the stone jetty.

Entering the fort by the sally-port, Richard sees Fanny ushering her brood from the chapel into their quarters. She carries Arthur swaddled in her arms. Henri, Hortense, and Napoleon are all smartly dressed in blue and white. Fanny's dress is like a crocus, a narrow yellow bell with her bonnet and wrap in lilac accents. She does not see him but he watches until the door to their apartments is shut.

'Ulwazi, what would you do if I let you go?' He looks into her intelligent, lively face and sees her firm chin jut towards him.

'What do you mean?' she asks uncertainly.

He reaches out a hand to touch her tightly curled hair, feeling the curve of her elegant skull beneath. 'If I said you did not have to return with me? You could travel with the Bertrands and see the world. You could remain here.'

He looks away as a company of soldiers form up on the parade square for inspection. Their black skin is stunning against white jackets and pantaloons. They manoeuvre to command, their actions connected if not quite synchronised. The NCO in charge shouts orders and they obey.

Nails dig into his arm and he turns from the parade. 'You don't have to stay with me.' His voice wavers as if he cannot decide how he feels. How he feels about her? How he feels about himself? He has taken every advantage of her. What else can he offer?

'You want rid of me so you can pursue the flame-haired woman with all those children? You hope her husband dies. You want to sail away.' Ulwazi has let go of him and placed her fists on her hips, confronting him, eyes blazing.

He shuffles his feet and chews the inside of his mouth to distract from the pain. It would be easy to admit it. He should admit it, even though Fanny has made it clear it will not happen.

'No, I will not sail away.'

They hear the raft being unloaded at the jetty. Two guns strike each other, sounding like a brittle bell. Men curse in a language Richard does not recognise. Gulls mock overhead as General Thibault issues plaintive orders no one seems inclined to follow.

'I have made my choices. They brought me to Shaka.' He wants to say more.

'Then why send me away? Shaka gave me to you. We share a hut.' Those last four words break Richard's resolve.

What is he doing? 'I just want you to be happy, to be free, to have a chance to live life as you wish it.' Even as he finishes, he can see his words have no meaning for her.

Her nose wrinkles and she tilts her head. Her brow is furrowed and her eyes swim with tears. She is puzzled and sad. He has done this to her. He flushes and tries to hold her but she pulls away, leaving his extended arms empty. Her lips tighten and she wipes the tears from her eyes.

She points an accusing finger at him and stamps a small foot. The gesture reminds him of the soldiers drilling behind them. 'So, you want me to choose?' she asks, her voice heavy with emotion.

Richard nods, his attempt at a smile dead on his lips.

'And you will respect that choice?' she insists. He nods again uncertainly. 'Then listen well, Richard. I choose to honour mighty Shaka's wishes. I choose to remain by your side. But if you want me to be happy, as you say, then I wish one more thing.' Richard looks expectantly at her fiery presence. Her slender muscles twitch beneath her dark-velvet skin. 'I wish to be your woman. I wish all to know it. I wish you to want me.'

Richard smiles. It is a wide, careless smile, revealing his crooked yellow teeth. His jaw throbs but he ignores it. He glances at the chapel door. Everything is clear now. He takes Ulwazi in his arms and kisses her. She is stiff and resistant for a moment but then melts against him, her lips parting. The tip of her tongue brushes his and he gasps.

A bugle sounds and the NCO dismisses his men. They hurry away, all laughter and catcalls, but Richard ignores them.

Captain da Silva sits behind his desk. His office is small but the walls are lined with timber painted a milky green. The paint is peeling as is the leather inlay of his desk. A mildewed portrait hangs behind him on the wall. A plain woman in white stares knowingly over the officer's shoulder. Her hair is piled in an improbable confection, ringlets framing her face. Her eyes are blue and bore into Richard until he looks away.

'My mother,' the captain says. 'I am a disappointment. She writes every month. Some letters arrive.' It is clear he wants to say more but he clamps his teeth together. Richard recalls Guidry telling him about da Silva's disgrace. 'I can see someone has shared my story.' There is no question in da Silva's words.

Richard wonders what gave him away. 'It is none of my affair,' he dissembles. 'Forgive me, I am sure your mother only wishes the best for her son.'

Da Silva inclines his head but his expression looks doubtful.

'I was hoping you might have a priest of some kind among your fort's company?' Richard asks.

The captain dabs at his sore eye with the edge of a delicate lace handkerchief. It comes away soiled with a yellow fluid. He scowls at it and stuffs it into the pocket of his waistcoat. Richard can see a grease mark from last night's dinner party above the pocket.

'There is a Jesuit College on Mozambique Island under a Father Rector. They have a residence at Quelimane, to the north, but they rarely reach this God-forsaken outpost. The Dominican mission is also conspicuous by its absence from Lourenco Marques. There is a priest who visits from the interior. His people are *sertanejo*, it is what we call those who venture inland. Most marry local girls and go native. They control much land and trade.'

Richard leans forward eagerly but da Silva waves him back. 'I am sorry, he has not been seen for some months. Who knows when he will appear again?' Hands spread in apology, da Silva leans back in his creaking chair.

'I need someone to administer the sacrament of matrimony,' Richard reveals awkwardly.

The captain eyes the whitewashed-stone ceiling of his office. It is punctuated by tiny stalactites where minerals and moisture combine in the humid air. 'You intend marrying your black companion?' It is not the voice of disapproval but Richard does register the officer's surprise.

'We Portuguese have been on this coast for many years. We have evolved a peculiar society. Many blacks are *chicunda*, personal slaves, but some of these wield real responsibility and live well. It is no scandal to consort with natives. Some of the most powerful families on this coast are mulatto. But to marry a full-blooded native is not our way.'

Richard squirms in his seat. He leans forward again and the captain smiles apologetically. For the first time, Richard spots a gold tooth. 'In the absence of a priest, do you have authority to perform the ceremony?'

The captain looks sympathetic. 'I have no such power. But what of your Reverend Dalrymple?'

Richard shakes his head. 'I fear it is too much to ask of him.'

Captain da Silva toys with the leather fraying from his desk top. 'There is one other man currently in Lourenco Marques who does have the authority.'

As da Silva finishes, Richard slaps his forehead. 'Of course! Captain Guidry!' He makes his excuses and escapes the gaze of da Silva's disappointed mother.

He walks around the interior perimeter of the fort but does not mount the steps to the parapet. There is a decent breeze and the fort's faded flag waves weakly. Guidry may be a Bonapartist but he is a slaver. He is also the only option within reach.

Richard stops in his tracks. Aunt Patricia's stern face hovers in the febrile air, her lips turned up at the edges in the glimmer of a smile.

'A marriage is about the pair promising themselves to each other. Don't look to me for an excuse to back out. It's taken you long enough to start living. If you need my blessing, you have it.' He can scarcely remember a time when she sounded so warm.

The following day, the Bertrand family are due to embark on the *Louisiana*. Daniel Langlois and Reverend Dalrymple have also booked passage and wait on the short jetty beneath the fort's sloping walls. Richard stands awkwardly with the pair as Captain Guidry approaches, standing amidships in *Louisiana*'s pinnace.

Richard has not revealed his intentions to anyone. The captain has barely stepped onto the stone dock when a messenger arrives. It is the Bertrands' local nursemaid. She hands Guidry the note, eyeing him suspiciously. He accepts it nonchalantly and turns away to study its contents. She stares at his back with loathing, her gentle hands clenched.

'It seems our departure is delayed,' Guidry announces. 'Marshal Bertrand is not yet well enough to travel.' He does not look displeased. 'There is still room below decks for more cargo. I have exhausted local supplies, so I will arrange an expedition into the interior. A month should be long enough to see the marshal recovered.'

He is about to step back on board the bobbing vessel when Richard reaches out a hand. 'If I might detain you for a moment, Captain? I have a request.' Guidry's face gives away nothing, so Richard adds, 'I promise you handsome remuneration for your pains.'

The captain smiles and claps Richard heartily on the back, throwing an order over his shoulder to his sailors to wait for him.

As Richard places the gold coins in Guidry's palm he shivers. He imagines the same coins handed to an Arab middleman in exchange for a shackled line of captives.

'You and your fiancée will have to come on board. I cannot conduct the ceremony on land.'

Richard eyes the door to the chapel with regret but he shrugs and agrees.

'Tomorrow, mid-morning. I shall send my pinnace. How many will be in attendance?'

Richard colours. He has not even spoken with Ulwazi. He shakes his head.

'No matter, I can send more than one boat if necessary.'

Richard shakes the captain's proffered hand reluctantly and heads for his room. He pours water and washes his hands vigorously, remembering the day he described Shaka Zulu as Pontius Pilate.

Ulwazi enters and he splashes water on his face to hide his discomfort. He dries his face on a rag and sits her on the unmade bed. He kneels in front of her and explains what he wants to do.

'You will give my family *lobola*?'

Richard agrees readily.

'And I shall grow my hair into a top knot?' He is puzzled and she smiles. 'It is the outward sign of a married woman.'

He nods enthusiastically. 'Yes, yes, to show everyone that we are married.' He manages to sound pleased while trying to banish thoughts of Fanny remaining at the fort for another month.

'Then I will happily do these things that have meaning in your world.' Her voice is bright and she fills the room with excited laughter.

Richard needs to speak with Daniel but Ulwazi detains him as he tries to stand. Her delicate hands are strong. 'A maiden wears the bead belt but when she marries, she puts on a skirt. I do not know the customs of your people. What shall I wear?'

Richard thinks of her confident nudity and looks at the cloth wrap bought for her by the prim Thibault. Then he contemplates all the sailors on the *Louisiana*. He considers asking Fanny for the loan of a dress but rejects the idea as grotesque. 'Take me to the cloth merchant,' he says finally.

It is late afternoon before Richard tracks down Daniel. He has bought a bolt of cloth for Ulwazi and she is busy transforming it into her wedding dress. He has invited da Silva to act as witness to the ceremony. Now he needs a best man.

Daniel is sitting in the shade of the fort's outer wall, facing the settlement. As always, Reverend Dalrymple is with him, his hat shading his eyes from the lowering sun as he reads the tiny print of his bible. Richard watches the defeated missionary's long forefinger turn a tissue-thin page, oblivious to his presence. Daniel smiles up at him and asks him to sit.

Settling his back against the warm stones, Richard places a

hand on the Guernseyman's shoulder. 'I have a favour to ask,' he begins.

Daniel looks at him expectantly, scratching at the scar on his left forearm. His legs bow out before him. 'What do you need?' he asks in his deep bass. They are speaking English and Daniel's accent is strong.

'A best man,' Richard replies, unable to keep his voice steady or maintain eye contact.

Daniel opens his mouth and then shuts it again. His stubbled face cracks into a smile and he hugs Richard hard between powerful arms.

'Congratulations!' He sounds genuinely pleased. 'So, you have decided to live your life?' he adds teasingly.

'Marriage is an honourable estate,' intones the clergyman without looking up from his reading, 'not by any to be entered into unadvisedly or lightly but reverently, discreetly, advisedly, soberly, and in the fear of God.' Dalrymple's voice rises and falls mellifluously.

'When do you plan to make your vows?' Daniel asks with a smile.

'Tomorrow morning on board the *Louisiana*,' Richard replies, still eyeing the absorbed cleric sitting on the other side of the fisherman.

'Captain Guidry?' asks Daniel, horror overwhelming his reserve. 'The man is devoid of principles. Think about it,' he bellows, 'you would be making your promises on a ship of shame! Innocent souls ripped from their families to be sold to the highest bidder on some far, foreign shore.' Daniel stares at him defiantly.

Richard lets his shoulders slump. He stirs the dirt with the toe of his left boot and scowls.

'I cannot do it,' Daniel concludes more softly. 'You are my friend. The girl is good for you. But this is not the way.'

'Guidry has taken my money,' Richard objects weakly.

'Wealth is worthless in the day of wrath,' Dalrymple interjects.

'Proverbs,' adds Daniel. 'Ask the Reverend Dalrymple to perform the ceremony. Hold it in the chapel.'

Richard lets out a deep breath. His body relaxes. He has not felt right from the moment he started down this path. He thought it was doubt about marrying Ulwazi but looking at the innocent question on the face of Fortescue Dalrymple, a man he once loathed, he realises the truth.

'Reverend, will you perform the marriage service for me?' His voice comes out weak and wavering but Dalrymple smiles and nods.

'A man shall leave his father and mother, and shall cleave unto his wife, and they shall be one flesh.'

Richard thinks of the car crash, the Kodachrome photo of his parents standing proudly beside their new car, and the emptiness.

'Genesis,' Daniel says quietly.

'Yes,' Richard replies with conviction.

The air begins to vibrate, the thrumming growing louder and louder. The sun's rays are shrouded by a dark cloud, moving oddly against the breeze. Myriad diamond flashes refract among the darkness of millions of insect bodies, light shining off delicate wings whirring in flight.

Inhabitants of the settlement cry out, some running towards their fields, others taking shelter in their huts.

'A swarm of locusts,' Richard shouts to Daniel.

'If thou refuse to let my people go, behold, tomorrow will I bring the locusts into thy coast!' Dalrymple recites, getting to his feet defiantly.

The swarm does not settle near the fort but turns inland and is soon lost to sight as the brightness of the late afternoon sun returns.

Richard looks around the little chapel. The single pew has been removed. The Reverend Dalrymple stands in front of the altar table patiently. Daniel Bisson pats Richard on the shoulder, then rubs his own freshly shaved chin. Captain da Silva looks on with interest. He has secured a clean waistcoat and his boots are polished to an impressive shine. He wears a brown-leather patch over his stye-infected eye. It suits him.

General Thibault is not there. Against his better judgement, aware they must travel back to Bulawayo together, Richard invited him only to be rebuffed. 'A black pagan and a mad priest! Such a rite will be an abomination before God! I cannot be party to such a debacle!' As for the Bertrand family, Richard has kept his distance.

Ulwazi is beaming at him, wrapped in Chinese silk from armpit to ankle. Richard bought the material from a Goan trader. When asked why he had such magnificent silks the man fondled his drooping moustaches and shrugged. At that moment, the liveried manservant hurried past. The trader said nothing but watched the man's receding form until it disappeared into the fort.

Ulwazi is shrouded in a flight of embroidered butterflies drifting over a sky-blue background. For a moment the swarm of locusts invades Richard's thoughts. Zulus are susceptible to omens. He has not told Ulwazi. Then she smiles, pulling him into the moment.

Richard looks at the missionary and nods decisively. The words of the Book of Common Prayer fill the small space, first in English and then translated haltingly into Zulu by Richard.

'Dearly beloved, we are gathered together here in the sight of God, and in the face of this congregation, to join this man and this woman in holy matrimony.' It is as if he is conducting his own marriage ceremony.

Afterwards, when he tries to remember, he can only recall speaking a few phrases. He insists the reverend omit any reference to obedience. Ulwazi repeats his rendering of her vows.

The Catholic Captain da Silva wipes tears from his good eye. Daniel has secured two brass rings from a sailor. Richard suspects they recently performed some task on the rigging of the *Louisiana* but he is grateful. His ring fits well but Ulwazi's is too large and in the end, she swaps it onto her thumb.

There are so few of them present that they all fit in the Captain's modest office. They are toasted in Portuguese and French and English. The madeira is good and no one seems keen to leave.

Ulwazi marvels at the cut glass and sips the unfamiliar wine suspiciously. She is soon giggling. The captain conjures a passable fruitcake from somewhere. Richard and Ulwazi hold the captain's sword awkwardly as they make the first cut.

When the bottle is empty and only meagre crumbs remain on plates, Richard gets up to go. His head buzzes gently like a contented hive at night. Ulwazi clings to him, face radiant, her joy contagious. Captain da Silva shakes Richard's hand and bows to Ulwazi. Daniel hugs them both. Reverend Dalrymple looks on bemused, as if he has quite forgotten his part in proceedings.

'Thank you, Reverend. You did a fine job.'

The clergyman looks at Richard as if he has never seen him before. 'Fortescue Dalrymple, pleased to meet you,' he barks in a patrician tone.

Richard shakes his hand and tries desperately to think of something to say. 'Richard Davey, sir. May I introduce my wife, Mrs Ulwazi Davey?'

The reverend bows graciously. 'Pleased to make your acquaintance.' They could be in a London coffee house or guests at a garden party.

'No speech?' asks Daniel discreetly when no one else is listening.

'No,' replies Richard emphatically.

That night, Richard lies on the unfurled mattress atop the narrow iron bed, wrapped in his wife's arms. She smells of spice and sweet wine. The springs squeak and groan. Her mouth tastes as she smells, heavenly. The mattress is musty. The touch of her tongue is silky and exciting. When they have exhausted their passion, he refuses to let her go. She does not struggle but nuzzles deeply against his sweating chest, sighing contentedly.

Just days ago, he hurried towards this fort at the prospect of seeing Fanny Bertrand again. He has seen her and been left in no doubt where he stands. She was right, of course. He had never grown up emotionally. How could he? Bereft of parents so young, raised by a chilly maiden aunt. Imprinting on anyone who smiled at him with kindness in their eyes. Arabella.

He hugs Ulwazi even tighter.

Chapter Three

July 1818

Richard stands with Ulwazi on the stone jetty below the fort. The sky is hazy blue, the sea like silvered glass close to shore. He watches Daniel and Reverend Dalrymple climb from the gig and up the ladder to the main deck of the merchantman *Louisiana*. Marshal Bertrand is well enough to travel. Well enough to wonder whether he is abandoning his emperor?

'No one can impugn your service, Marshal,' Richard reassures him before he is helped into the jolly boat. Fanny watches her husband being settled on a bench surrounded by her children. She is holding Arthur. The boy took his first steps just a week ago. 'Richard, I regret I was so harsh with you.'

He smiles awkwardly. Ulwazi watches Fanny closely.

'But I see it had the desired effect!' Her white face is stunning beneath her red locks.

He smiles again as Ulwazi loops her arm around his waist.

'You have chosen a life I cannot imagine but I wish you every happiness. I yearn for superficial pleasures. We are destined for America where we may find a welcome.' She looks down at her husband.

'A good place to raise your children,' Richard suggests earnestly.

She nods and ushers her brood into the boat. 'Goodbye, Mister Davey.' Fanny cannot quite bring herself to address Ulwazi, who stares threateningly until the oarsmen pull away.

The Bertrand family mount the ladder to reach the main deck. Richard sees them gather along the rail to look back at the fort.

'She will not return?' asks Ulwazi as the *Louisiana* hoists her anchor, the chains clanking as the capstan does its work. Richard wonders how many men it takes to raise the flukes clear of the seabed?

'No, we will never see her again,' Richard confirms a little grimly.

'Good,' spits Ulwazi. 'She was a witch for certain. She cast a spell over you.'

Richard does not argue. She is right. He knows it. Sails unfurled, anchor raised, the broad-beamed merchant ship noses towards the open sea, her passengers waving for so long Richard thinks it must be relief that compels them.

At last, he lets Ulwazi lead him away. Away from his last chance to escape what Africa will make of him. He looks at his wife, holding tightly to his hand, hauling him with her slender, powerful arm into the fort. It has already begun.

Each morning Richard braces himself for General Thibault's appearance but day after day he does not call. Nevertheless, they must depart for Bulawayo soon. Richard takes an escort, commanded by the leering lance-corporal, and heads south, leaving Thibault with the six cannon.

He has seen the Frenchman caress their barrels while talking to himself. He sketches and measures when not interrogating the officers and NCOs of the fort.

Marching hard, Richard's party reach the beach where he startled the fishermen and their boys. He orders the soldiers to wait while he heads into the trees. He finds the Fasimba warriors without difficulty. They have cut a clearing and erected rudimentary shelters from broad leaves and slender branches.

Two guards appear from nowhere to challenge him and take him into the camp. He explains to their grizzled leader that they will soon be needed. He tries to describe the cargo. The man's yellow eyes regard him phlegmatically.

His message delivered, Richard hurries back to the Portuguese company. One of the soldiers is a dab hand with hook and line and soon catches enough fish for a fine supper. They sleep on the shore around a driftwood fire. No lions haunt Richard's dreams.

On the journey back, Richard thinks more about General Thibault. He spends a lot of time beyond the walls, Ulwazi reports, talking of wood and iron. She has a knack of knowing everything that is happening. A trick learned in her home village, no doubt.

Captain da Silva's company is civil but casts a pall on Richard's happiness. The man is so resigned, it is exhausting to spend time with him. On one surprisingly chilly evening, two days after returning from his brief trip, Richard accepts an invitation to dinner in the commandant's quarters.

The pair of junior officers are present as are the two NCOs Richard first encountered when his party arrived at the fort. He knows there is a sergeant but he seems to be permanently on duty. General Thibault arrives late and squeezes out a tight-lipped apology.

The dandy manservant waits on table, while the former nursemaid to the Bertrands' youngest appears dressed as a cook. Da Silva is morose and speaks little but drinks steadily. The other ranks match him glass for glass, the NCOs clearly relishing the superior quality of the wine. Just days ago, Fanny sat at the far end of this same table, flanked by her children.

A pot-roasted guinea fowl is the centrepiece of the meal, its meat tender and pleasantly gamey. Richard eats heartily and tries to moderate his intake of the madeira.

With the plates cleared away and the coffee finished, the captain produces a box of Cuban cigars. The faces of his men light up greedily as the wooden box is handed around. The corporals lick their cigars while the officers run them appreciatively beneath their noses. When the half-empty box reaches him, Richard wants to decline but da Silva insists.

Their host uses a taper to light first his cigar and then holds the flame steady for Richard, who reluctantly sucks to ignite the tightly rolled tobacco. Pungent smoke soon fills the dining room. Conversation becomes more relaxed among the soldiers. It is predominantly in Portuguese, with da Silva trying to keep Thibault and Richard involved.

'You have been very busy, General?' Richard suggests during a lull in conversation.

Thibault sips his wine and looks satisfied. 'I have commissioned a wagon to transport the cannon.' He raises his right hand, which holds his cigar, to fend off Richard's objection. 'I know you believe the terrain too rough but I believe the carriage will prove robust.'

Here Thibault turns to Captain da Silva, 'I must thank you for the loan of your carpenter. He has proven a capable wheelwright. His blacksmithing is more than passable too.'

Da Silva looks less solemn. 'I am pleased to assist you.'

Richard is sure money has changed hands.

'If I could have a company of men tomorrow to load the cannon onto the wagon?' Thibault asks.

The captain nods and empties his glass. 'I fled the French with the royal court. Now, I find myself assisting my old enemy. I do not ask where you take these artillery pieces. I do, however, require your word they will leave Portuguese territory?'

Thibault agrees to the condition immediately.

'Good. Your presence has been a welcome distraction.' Da Silva is speaking French while his staff chatter drunkenly in Portuguese. 'I am disgraced. Exiled to this tenuous spot. Surrounded by disreputable men.'

His voice is profoundly sad. 'My sergeant only escaped the noose for desertion during the battle of Badajoz by accepting exile. Both corporals are also military convicts. That one, Lopes, a brawler and the other, Santos, a sodomite.'

Here he pauses to look at the lieutenant in his brown uniform, sitting beside the even younger ensign, in matching colours. The lieutenant is grey haired. Too old for his rank. The ensign has a boyish face but lifeless eyes. 'Even my officers have chequered histories. My lieutenant, Pereira, has been broken to the ranks twice. He is brave but a thief. He has won medals but sold them. The boy is an unwanted younger son who wished to marry beneath him. So, he was shipped far from temptation.'

Richard looks around the table. Are these men become what Africa would make of them? They laugh and talk in an animated fashion, savouring their cigars, and swilling their wine.

As the dinner fizzles out, the NCOs and the ensign make their slurred excuses. The lieutenant produces a deck of cards after ushering the others from the room. Da Silva grimaces but says nothing. General Thibault thanks his host. Richard joins him at the door.

The moon is almost full, shedding a creamy sheen across the fort. Braziers burn on each corner tower, casting light and shadow against the ruddy stonework.

Thibault looks at the sky. 'It is time we returned to the emperor.' His voice is decisive. Richard does not disagree. 'I must thank you for your advice, Monsieur Davey.' Richard looks blankly at the young general. 'You said we needed Portuguese assistance. That I would do well to curb my tongue.'

Richard smiles in the darkness, a wide, relaxed smile. 'You have shown restraint, General,' he replies, eager to put any tension between them in the past.

'The captain has facilitated my efforts. Had I allowed myself to denigrate his nationality, that would not have been so.'

Richard imagines the colour distorting Thibault's face. He blushes easily, especially when needing help or admitting shortcomings.

'Would you like to see the vehicle we have fashioned?'

The air is not too close and Richard wants to clear his head.

'I would be happy to inspect your work.'

Thibault nods. He looks pleased but then pauses. 'I merely commissioned the cart. Perhaps my design guided the work. But there would be no transport without the carpenter and his team.'

Is this Africa at work? General Thibault arrived on the continent scant months ago an arrogant, gauche, insubstantial character, thin skinned and inexperienced. Now, he shows restraint, whatever he really thinks, and gives credit to others where it is due.

Richard shakes his head. For all that, the general remains what he is, an early nineteenth century man of privilege, who cannot see the humanity of people with darker skins.

As they wait for the sentry to open the wicket gate, Thibault drops the stub of his cigar into the dirt and grinds it beneath the tip of his boot. Richard let his own cigar burn out at table and is glad to be away from the heady smoke. His stomach is unsettled and his jaw aches despite the anaesthetic of several glasses of wine.

A cloud shrouds the moon and the ramshackle village beyond the walls is lost in darkness. A dog barks as the door hinges complain but its voice is uncertain and soon peters out.

They walk along the face of the fort to the south-west corner. A lean-to rests lazily against the sloping flank of the wall, open on the other three sides. Beneath the shelter sits a large wooden construction on wheels. Thibault stands proudly beside his wagon, its rear wheels as tall as his shoulder, those at the front up to his waist.

Richard reaches out a hand to the high side of the wagon.

The boards are neatly finished but he feels tool marks beneath his palm. He runs his hand the length of the vehicle. Six paces. Each board is a single plank, braced regularly with vertical stays. He looks closely at the nearest wheel. The spokes are regular, the circumference a perfect circle banded in iron. The protruding hub centres the wheel on its axle.

'It looks heavy,' Richard observes, quickly adding, 'but strong too.'

The sides rise eighteen inches from the bed of the wagon. The wood is freshly cut, a buttery colour as the moon shrugs off the shroud of cloud. Already loaded are four large boxes of munitions. At the front, a single shaft protrudes. It is very long and at regular intervals are yokes equipped with harnesses.

'Ten on each side,' Thibault confirms before Richard has time to count.

'With six cannon, it will take twenty men to pull the thing!' Richard mutters under his breath. 'Let's hope Zulu warriors don't mind acting as beasts of burden!' he adds aloud.

Thibault grins in reply. 'We use the garrison to test the wagon tomorrow morning.' The young general sounds excited.

The golden-skinned carpenter stands by the block and tackle at the stone jetty where the six metal barrels have waited since being offloaded from the *Louisiana*.

Thibault and five men from the garrison are hauling the wagon around the outside of the fort towards the loading dock. The vehicle might fit through the main gateway, with both doors open, but it is too wide to exit the sally-port on the coastward side of the fort.

Wheels squeal in protest and the carpenter runs forward with a leather bucket of grease. He coats the axles until the sound of creaking wood and grunting men is all that fills the air.

Once the flatbed is aligned, the first gun is carefully manhandled into the waiting sling. The rope goes taut as men heave, pulleys rattle, and the gun takes to the air, one man steadying each end.

The men on the rope haul rapidly and the weight of the gun rises slowly. Up a foot and then another, until the darkened gun-metal tube hangs above the sides of the vehicle and can be pushed sideways, to be lowered onto the wagon bed.

By the time the fourth gun is airborne, the smell of singeing rope is in the still air, friction generating heat. The carpenter's mate stands ready with a bucket of water.

As the sixth cannon settles in the transport, the boy puts down his bucket and the men on the ropes collapse in a panting heap. Ladles of water are passed around, and within minutes every man is puffing on a clay pipe. They lie beside the loaded wagon which sits low on its axles.

'Well, your vehicle has passed the first test. It hasn't collapsed! Six guns at close to a thousand pounds each,' Richard estimates.

Thibault says nothing but calls the men to their feet. He puts twelve men in the traces but they can barely budge the carriage. He sends for reinforcements and with twenty men, the wagon reluctantly starts to move.

Once the wheels are turning, things become easier. Richard knows because he is paired with the general at the front yoke. The ground is level and dry. Soon they are moving at a slow walking pace. By the time the wagon is opposite the front gate, Richard is dripping sweat.

He does not want to alienate Thibault. 'Say a little over two thousand paces to the mile.' He takes out his pocket watch. 'Shall we see how long it takes?'

A well-worn path leads from the village towards patchy fields of corn and vegetables. They set off along the narrow track, wheels creaking across the verges to either side of the rutted route.

Richard calls out every pace, his voice increasingly strained as they approach one thousand. They manhandle the wagon around awkwardly. A wheel trespasses on a row of green-leafed vegetables that look like kale.

He is surprised to see crops ripening in winter and then chuckles to himself. He is drenched in sweat. The sun is warm on his slick body. Why wouldn't crops grow?

With the gun carriage now facing the fort, Richard sneaks a glance at his watch. Maybe half a mile has taken close to thirty minutes. An hour for every mile travelled on the flat. Most of the journey is undulating and there are a dozen rivers to cross.

Ulwazi is waiting beside the main entrance to the fort as they return. Richard's arm muscles are painful knots and he is struggling for breath.

Thibault drops from the yoke to sit very still in the village dirt. He does not speak but stares into the middle distance; his face is pale and the tendons in his neck are taut.

The tawny village dog sidles up to him and sniffs. The general does not react. The dog licks his face and darts away. Thibault remains still. Thin and flea bitten, the dog stalks back, tongue lolling and tentatively grips an ankle between its teeth.

The exhausted Frenchman aims a weak kick with his unencumbered leg. He connects with the side of the dog's head, causing it to whimper. 'I fear you were right all along, Monsieur Davey. I have misjudged the force needed to move such a weight.'

Richard beckons to Ulwazi. 'Nevertheless, this fine wagon will prove useful. It can carry the powder and shot canisters, all our supplies, arms, and any who fall ill on the journey.' Ulwazi looks on with a puzzled expression.

'You do not have to let me down gently, Monsieur Davey. How many men will it take to carry one gun in slings?' His voice trembles with tiredness and embarrassment.

'Four should be sufficient, taking turns. So, we will need at least a dozen men, plus enough for the carriage.'

Thibault nods. 'I will make the arrangements with Captain da Silva. His fondness for the emperor's profile in gold is enough to make me suspect he is a secret Bonapartist!'

Richard laughs, although his lungs are still hungry for air. He has never heard Thibault make a joke before.

'I will arrange for the spare rope and rigging offloaded from the *Louisiana* to be made into slings.' He holds out his hands and Ulwazi pulls him to his feet. He gives her some small coins and asks her to buy enough supplies for the return journey. She trips off happily.

Richard knocks at the commandant's door and is soon in conversation.

'There are considerable ship's supplies held at the fort, for sale to passing vessels and for maintaining Portuguese vessels travelling to and from Goa,' da Silva tells him. He is still wearing the eye patch but has a fresh stain on his waistcoat.

'Rope?' asks Richard.

'Of course. But I thought you secured your own supplies from Captain Guidry?' comes the ingratiating reply.

'I am not certain of its quality,' Richard explains cautiously. 'But I am confident you would not supply faulty goods.' He receives an accommodating smile and is ushered towards the fort's storerooms.

'When do you leave?' da Silva asks conversationally.

'As soon as we can fashion slings with which to move the guns.'

'But the general spent so much time and no little money on his big cart! Perhaps our wheelwright should accompany you, along with some native soldiers?' There is a glint in the captain's eye and his gold tooth catches the sunlight.

Two days later, all is ready. It is a little after dawn and still cool. There is enough light to see a clear sky with a yellow, pock-marked moon still floating above.

The wagon is loaded with supplies and, as a compromise, two of the guns. The wheelwright's tools for working wood and iron are stowed. Spare slings are also on board. The other four guns sit in the dust beside the carpenter's lean-to.

Between the fort and the village, a company of twenty troops stand at ease. They are kept almost in order by the young ensign. He reminds Richard of a newly appointed school prefect. Corporal Lopes is also there, but he is more interested in peering, with his bright blue eyes, at what is loaded in the wagon.

Ulwazi wears her cloth wrap, at Richard's insistence, even though it restricts her movement. Thibault appears with Captain da Silva. The pair are chatting in apparent good humour. They greet Richard, who is putting his musket in the wagon.

Thibault inspects the slings and nods appreciatively. Each barrel sits in a heavy-duty net, with a shoulder rig at each corner, crudely reinforced with leather.

Drilling with them the previous afternoon, the soldiers soon managed to distribute the weight, and get into a decent rhythm, keeping the barrel a foot clear of the ground.

The captain talks quietly with his young officer and then barks some orders at the much older corporal, who is now standing smartly to attention. For all the preparations, Richard thinks it will be a long trip. He wonders how many guns will reach Bulawayo?

Richard shakes da Silva's sweaty hand. General Thibault accepts the acting commandant's salute. The ensign, whose name is Tiago Carvalho, gives the order to march.

With two guns on the wagon, they require sixteen men shouldering the weight of the other four guns. The soldiers stow their muskets safely in the cart. The remaining four troopers, along with Richard and Thibault, lean against the yokes of the wagon. The wheelwright, although a civilian, reluctantly lends his weight.

At first, the wagon remains stubbornly stationary but when

the ensign and the corporal join them, the wheels begin to turn. As they achieve a slow walking pace, things become easier. Richard is again partnering Thibault. He glances over his shoulder to check on the others labouring either side of the shaft.

Ulwazi has taken up station at an empty yoke and is leaning forward with a determined look on her captivating face. Richard shoots her an appreciative grin but she is lost in the task.

Richard counts paces and checks his watch periodically. They are moving faster with the reduced load, but still less than two miles an hour.

It took two weeks to travel from Shaka's capital to the fort, a distance between three hundred and fifty and four hundred miles, as far as Richard can estimate. About twenty-five miles a day. At this pace, they will only manage half that total without rendering the soldiers incapable.

In the early afternoon they reach the first river. They have to track the bank for ten minutes to find a shallow stretch. The wagon's large wheels keep the superstructure clear of the murky water, but half-way across, they dig into the soft bottom.

The men on the slings cross before wading back to add their weight to the yokes. The vehicle remains stubbornly marooned in midstream.

Ensign Carvalho orders ten men to the rear of the carriage, insisting the others move around their yokes to face the front of the wagon. He has his squad rock the carriage back and forth until its wheels fight free of the mud.

With the men at the front facing forward again and the men behind shouldering the rear boards, they extricate the wagon. Gasping for air, the soldiers collapse on the churned-up riverbank.

Some dip their heads into the water, while others drink from cupped hands. Richard is reminded of Emile's friends, drinking from the river during the battle of Gqokli hill. Satiated, the men lie on their backs, chests gradually subsiding into normal breathing.

They manage one more river crossing the first day. It is little more than a stream, but its flow has cut into the delta mud so that the channel is two feet below the surrounding ground.

The wheels of the wagon are large enough to cope, despite the absence of suspension. There is a lot of shouting and creaking, groaning and squealing, as if the wood and iron are as alive as the men propelling it.

Long-necked, black-and-white waders with elongated, spatulate bills, flap away protesting at the noisy intrusion.

The men on the cannon have already become self-reliant teams. One pair slips carefully into the knee-deep water, while the landward pair braces. Then the second pair joins their fellows in the stream, and they wade across.

The waterway is no more than four strides wide but exiting is a problem. The first team manages to cradle the metal barrel up the bank and slide it to safety. The following teams copy their method.

They camp just beyond the stream, on a dry island of sandy soil left proud by erosion. Standing on the crown of the half-egg prominence, Richard scans the forest to the south with his spyglass. There is no sign of the Zulu *iviyo*. He is not worried. He looked into their officer's eyes. He will be there.

'You worry the savages have abandoned us?' General Thibault asks.

Richard scowls, 'Why do you call them savages?' His irritation is obvious.

'What else should I call them? Heathens?' Thibault sounds honestly puzzled.

Ensign Carvalho is with them, listening intently. 'The civilized nations of Europe have a duty to transform these lands and their inhabitants.' He sounds pompous and naïve.

'Your people have claimed sovereignty over this coast for three hundred years,' Richard snipes back, earning him a raised eyebrow from Thibault.

Ignoring the Frenchman's gesture, and his own better judgement telling him he needs this green officer, Richard continues his critique. 'I see little evidence of civilization at Lourenco Marques. It took until the 1790s for you to build your fort in stone, and still, you allow slavery. Those who escape that fate are pressed into service in your army or as servants. You send the dregs of your society from Lisbon or Rio to lord it over the locals.'

Richard subsides when Ulwazi pulls at his cuff, a worried look masking her pretty features. His face has coloured and he is sweating heavily, his voice raised to an unnatural pitch. He looks guiltily at the ensign who stands uncomfortably, his uniform still smart, despite wet trousers.

Tiago Carvalho surprises Richard with a smile and a shrug. 'There is truth in what you say, Englishman,' he admits in passable French. 'We have an uneasy relationship with the indigenous peoples of our territory. Our priests make little headway. We extract a paltry tribute from inland rulers. The trade in ivory is managed by Arab middlemen. We parcel up swathes of land to be ruled by *prazo senhors*. I sometimes think the only people who really understand this place are like you.'

Here the ensign pauses and looks pointedly at Ulwazi. 'Those who marry locals and produce offspring sharing the attributes of both parents.'

General Thibault looks aghast. 'You see intermarriage as the answer?' As the words escape the young general's lips, he glances at the half-caste wheelwright he has so praised. He flushes and stops talking.

It is almost noon before they reach the fringe of trees behind the mud flats. There are no fishermen, but Richard does see fresh footprints on the shore, yet to be eradicated by the next tide.

He asks Ensign Carvalho to rest his men, while he pushes through the opulent vegetation into the shade. He reaches the Fasimba camp within twenty minutes. He is trailed by two escorts on picket duty. The veteran in command greets him civilly and Richard explains the composition of the party.

He struggles to explain the wagon, and in the end, it is agreed that the whole Zulu company will follow Richard to where the Portuguese force are waiting.

As they emerge from the trees, some of the black soldiers rush for their muskets in the wagon.

'Ensign! Call off your soldiers! These men are friendly.

They escorted us here and have waited patiently for our return,' Richard shouts.

Reluctantly, Ensign Carvalho orders his men away from their guns. They huddle together, chattering nervously, casting wide-eyed glances at the Fasimba. The Portuguese levies look overdressed in their white jackets and red-edged pantaloons. The near-naked young Zulu warriors point and smirk, until a sharp bark from their commander silences them.

The ageing Corporal Lopes talks with his agitated men and then reports to the ensign. Richard is too far away to hear, so he crosses to the young junior officer who explains.

'The men say they recognise these warriors. They look like the men of Dingiswayo. They used to trade ivory, ornaments, and cattle from the south. The trade suddenly stopped. The rumour is that the Mthethwa kingdom disintegrated on his death. All is chaos now.'

Richard wonders how much he should say, but seeing Thibault is about to speak, he replies, 'There is a new leader exerting control. His name is Shaka.' He leaves it there.

To continue with the wagon, they skirt the forest, heading inland until trees give way to grassland. The large wheels roll easily over the open ground and it is now the cannon in slings that slow them down.

The young Zulu warriors willingly take turns, vying with each other for the longest stints pushing the wagon or sharing the weight of a cannon.

On the second day Richard sees smoke on the horizon. Looking through his telescope, he spots a trail of dust heading west. Driven cattle? A burnt *kraal*? With the defeat of the Ndwandwe army, armed bands have scattered across the plains, marauding for food, tribute, and territory. He agrees with Thibault and the Portuguese ensign that they should investigate.

The next day they reach a burned-out village. Charred rings in the dirt are all that remain of the huts. The cattle pen lies empty. Two grain stores still perch above the ground but not a single kernel remains in either bin. There are only a few bodies. The men have been disembowelled and feasted on by scavengers. Three old women, thin and bony, lie sprawled with their heads crushed in.

Richard is shocked by how unmoved he is at the sight. Africa is hardening him, he thinks, until he finds the heap of babies and young children. He looks away from tiny features frozen in pain.

'Too young to keep up,' grunts the Fasimba *iviyo*'s leader. 'They take the women and any men willing to join them.'

Richard wipes his mouth and stares at the horizon. Is that dust again?

'Likely deserters from Zwide's army, with any cattle they plundered,' suggests the Zulu.

Richard's bad tooth flares pain along his jaw. He screws up his face. Ulwazi appears at his side.

'This is a cruel place,' he says.

She looks puzzled. He steers her away from the heap of slaughtered innocents.

'This village would be intact if not for Shaka's battles,' Richard claims.

She does not deny it but seems to consider his words

carefully. 'Who is really to blame? Zwide? He killed Dingiswayo. He threatened Zulu territory. Was Shaka not defending his people? Is it right to blame him for everything that flows from his actions?' Her sharp mind no longer surprises him. She makes a good point but he cannot stop himself muttering.

'I feel lost in the heart of darkness.' Richard thinks of Conrad's description of a man losing his mind in the centre of Africa. 'I should have stayed in my own place, my own time,' he says in English, his words meaningless in Zulu. He massages the side of his face.

Ulwazi pulls his hand away and makes him bend down. She peers between his lips and inserts her right forefinger, probing from tooth to tooth along his lower jaw, from incisor to canine, premolar to molar.

As she prods the second molar, he yelps and bites down involuntarily. Ulwazi pries her finger free and massages it accusingly.

He murmurs an apology but his thoughts are elsewhere. In 2018 he would be in a dentist's chair, numbed by Lidocaine, only a few minutes' discomfort away from relief.

Chastened by the sight of the obliterated village, no one has much appetite for resuming their march. They make camp.

The Portuguese conscripts sing in a language Richard does not recognise. Their voices rising and falling sonorously. Their words need no translation. A profound sadness pours from their lips.

'A lament for the dead,' Carvalho observes.

'They knew the people here?'

The ensign shakes his head. 'They sing for everyone. We all die.' He sounds compassionate.

'I thought you regarded them as savages. Children of a lesser God?'

Carvalho shakes his head. 'You find me at a crossroads, *senhor*. I am conflicted. My upbringing clashes with my experience. I am trying to find my way.'

An odd sensation rocks Richard. He has not experienced it since he stopped working with children. Awash with a particular form of compassion; the drive to support and encourage. The will to see others discover themselves. For a moment he cannot feel his toothache at all. 'You see that truth lies beneath the skin?' Richard ventures.

The ensign pokes at the fire with a stick. 'I was taught birth defines everything. To be born anything but the eldest son is to feel the truth of that,' he spits bitterly.

Ulwazi sits by the fire working intently. She produces a small hide pouch which contains various herbs and roots. She grinds a combination between two rocks and chews the blend experimentally. She grins and wipes a trickle of saliva from her chin, before offering Richard a damp wad of partly chewed material.

Ensign Carvalho looks relieved at the interruption and excuses himself. Richard is about to refuse Ulwazi's medicine when another flare of pain changes his mind. This isn't 2018. There is no dentist's chair within hundreds of miles. He takes the moist compress and tucks it towards the back of his mouth.

Immediately, numbness spreads. He clamps his teeth together and the effect grows more pronounced. Within five minutes the side of his face is insensible and he is wiping at saliva leaking from his mouth. He marvels the Zulus have access to such an effective anaesthetic.

Ulwazi approaches with a small knife. His eyes widen and he raises his hands but she bats them away. She jabs experimentally at the outside of his cheek. He feels nothing. Her finger extends and then withdraws with blood on it.

She gestures for him to unclench his jaws, and as she kneels in front of him, he reluctantly complies.

His imagination fills in the blanks his senses cannot provide. She slips her finger and thumb towards the back of his mouth until she grips that second molar firmly. He watches her wrist move from side to side and experiences a dull response deep in his jaw. He sees the tendons in her wrist tighten as she increases the rocking motion.

There is a short stab of pain, and his wife removes her hand. She is grinning as she shows him the rotten tooth. He wants to look away but the pride on Ulwazi's face makes him study the odd, yellowish form held between her fingers.

The crown is ridged and worn but not obviously cracked. The roots are a different matter. One is largely intact but the other is a mere stub.

Despite the anaesthetic, he senses he is dribbling again and wipes gingerly at his mouth. His hand comes away wet with bloody saliva. He turns and spits away from the firelight. Fumbling for his canteen, he sips water and swills gently. Feeling returns in a dull ache where the tooth used to be. He does not mind. His jaw feels so much better.

He sleeps well, his wife cradled inside the curve of his body. When he wakes, he does not immediately think of his lost tooth. He risks a smile. No one can see.

He chews his portion of dried antelope tentatively, clumsily. His tongue lingers in the gap left by Ulwazi's extraction, like a dog beside his master's grave.

Back in the traces beside General Thibault, he cannot help smiling.

'You seem cheerful,' observes the Frenchman.

'I had a toothache. My wife has cured it. I feel marvellous,' he admits.

'It takes so little, does it not? The absence of pain is sufficient.'

'Sometimes,' Richard agrees. 'I am no philosopher but I suspect we need pain, from time to time, in order to appreciate the rest.'

Thibault gives him an appreciative look. 'You sound like one of my instructors at military school.'

'No pain; no gain.' Richard cannot help himself.

The young general laughs aloud. 'What a phrase! I will remember that.'

The wheels of the wagon roll onwards, creaking and groaning. The vehicle rattles too. But the undulating grassland presents no problems they cannot steer around, until they reach the next river.

The watercourse has cut a gorge through the millennia, a slot canyon of reddish rock some fifty yards wide, slicing the landscape from north-west to south-east.

The Fasimba officer, who Richard discovers is called Insumpa, the Zulu for warthog, jogs to the wagon scowling.

'We must turn that way,' he indicates south with his short spear, 'otherwise, we reach rough country.'

Richard and Thibault, along with Ensign Carvalho and the corporal, edge to the very lip of the chasm. Corporal Lopes kicks a loose stone over the edge and they watch it tumble. They do not hear any noise as it reaches the river.

After a break for water, they turn their oddly assorted company southwards, shadowing the sunken riverbed. Twice they hear the noise of rapids or waterfalls hidden from view.

By the time they are setting up camp in the gloaming, the walls above the river have shrunk to half their former height. Richard asks Insumpa how long before they reach a crossing.

'For men, half a day. For that,' he points at the wagon, broad spear tip itching to impale the alien technology, 'twice that.'

So, another day spent for no distance gained. Why did the experienced Zulu lead them so far north? Richard considers the question. The wagon forced them to skirt the trees. The sight of smoke drew them further north. He is not to blame.

Chapter Four

July 1818

Another morning dawns. Richard looks across the mist-filled gorge. He is not the only one. The whole Portuguese company stand along the rim, some pointing, others speaking very fast, hands waving. Corporal Lopes breaks away to rouse his officer.

Richard squints through the opaque air and feels for his telescope. He is about to raise it when Thibault appears from beneath the wagon. 'What is it?' he asks sleepily.

Richard focuses the brass instrument and sweeps it back and forth. 'A body of men. Moving parallel with our line of march.' He offers the spyglass to Thibault who accepts it gratefully.

'I count thirty men, maybe more.' The French general does not sound alarmed. 'They cannot harm us,' he concludes, gesturing towards the gorge.

'What if we are looking for the same ford?' Richard asks. 'They will cross first. They move swiftly.' He thinks of the burned village. The discarded corpses.

'Then we must choose our ground and prepare for battle!' Thibault replies excitedly.

Insumpa, the Fasimba officer, holds Richard's spyglass like a poisonous snake. Richard takes the man's rough hand and forces it towards his eye. A frown distorts the veteran's stern features. He moves the brass instrument away and then back again.

Richard tries to help him focus. At first, there is no reaction, but then Insumpa stumbles backwards. His neck shoots forward and he screws up his eyes, defying the brightening light, trying to locate the party of warriors.

Again, he risks placing the eyepiece to his face. This time, although his body tenses, he does not retreat. 'Khumalo,' he says finally, 'this is their land. Allied to the Ndwandwe.'

'We outnumber them,' Richard points out, 'will they leave us alone?' He is trying to convince himself.

'Dingiswayo is dead. Zwide defeated. There is turmoil everywhere. They did not burn their own *kraals*. They will fear our presence.' Insumpa's tone is matter of fact.

'Then we need not worry?' Richard enquires hopefully.

'We should prepare. They will attack.' Insumpa betrays no concern.

'But why, if they are afraid?' Richard asks plaintively.

'It is what a frightened dog does,' comes the reply. Lowering the telescope, Insumpa rubs his eye as if it hurts.

Not far east of the river gorge lies a line of modest hills. They thread through them along a flat-bottomed valley. They encounter no problems for the wagon or the men carrying the guns.

Even with the naked eye, Richard can see the hills are coated in scrub trees. Two hilltops poke above the vegetation, rocky prominences, pale against the sky. One presents a bluff face while the other is a crumpled hat. The slopes of both are too steep for the wagon.

'We put the hills at our back?' asks Thibault, spotting the direction of Richard's gaze.

'Stow the guns beneath the wagon and form up the Portuguese company around it,' Richard suggests.

Thibault and Ensign Carvalho nod agreement. Richard explains their idea to Insumpa.

'We will face them,' is the gruff reply.

Richard shakes his head. 'There is no need. One volley from the muskets should disperse them.'

Insumpa spits in the dirt and scowls again. 'We do not need your witchcraft! We are Shaka's warriors. Our feet are bare and our spearheads broad.'

There is no point arguing. Ensign Carvalho gives the order and his men hurry for the hills. Richard walks with the young officer but senses General Thibault is not in step with them.

Looking back, he sees him staring at the Zulu company as Insumpa issues orders. Richard trots back. 'Is there a problem, General?'

Thibault smiles awkwardly and draws his sword. It glistens in the sun. 'I have never drawn my weapon in anger. I wear this fine uniform. I follow the greatest general of our age. But I am a lackey. I fetch and carry. I organise events. I procure things. I feel a fraud. Those spearmen yonder may not be Wellington's finest but they are coming for us. It is time I lived up to the traditions of the French army.'

Richard wants to dissuade Thibault. Insumpa will want nothing to do with a foreign soldier yearning for his first battle. He is about to speak when he is forestalled.

'No pain; no gain!' bellows Thibault, breaking into a run

towards the Fasimba.

Richard turns away reluctantly and lopes after the train of cannon-carrying soldiers and their heavy cart. After a few minutes, the Zulu company jog alongside. Insumpa seeks out Richard, who is helping propel the wagon. 'We shall fight with the hills at our back, yes?'

Richard grins in agreement.

'A good plan. Their horns cannot encircle us.' The veteran officer refers to Shaka's tried and tested tactic. 'If their spears are long, they are doomed.' Insumpa grins, the yellow stumps of his teeth living up to his name. 'If their shafts are short, we shall see who is more skilled!' He moves off to join his men, already lost in the red dust rising behind their bare heels.

Richard wonders why the Zulu officer has not objected to Thibault's presence in his ranks?

By early afternoon, the wagon is pulled up parallel to the lowest slopes. The black Portuguese company are being fed and watered. Richard is nervous. He fiddles with his loaded musket. He is no longer haunted by dead men in the woods of Waterloo. Other blank eyes accuse him now, set in darker faces, rictus grins exposing finer teeth.

Carvalho gives an order and the men stir listlessly. Corporal Lopes repeats it and they jump up to queue in front of the wagon. The experienced NCO doles out muskets and cartridge boxes fixed to shoulder straps.

The men snatch them eagerly and shrug the leather loops over their heads. They start loading their muskets and neither the corporal nor the ensign intervenes. When they have all cocked their weapons, they are called to order, and form up in two convex ranks, ahead of the wagon.

Carvalho takes up a place on the bed of the vehicle. Richard joins him, having hidden Ulwazi beneath, with the cannon and the terrified carpenter. The NCO stands to the left of the front rank.

The Fasimba form a single, defiant line on the left flank, fifty yards closer to the invisible gorge. General Thibault has insinuated himself into the middle of the line. He has no shield but his sword is drawn. He looks like a peacock surrounded by peahens. The warriors seem to accept his presence.

The sight makes Richard think of his friend, Emile Béraud, a Chasseur à Cheval and bodyguard to the emperor, now become a Zulu warrior. Will this be Thibault's fate? He does not know what to think. He is in no position to judge how others accommodate themselves to this place.

A single, wide-eyed antelope tacks towards the hills. Its pear-shaped body narrows at the shoulder, while heavy haunches power slender legs. As it bolts between the Fasimba and the Portuguese, Richard sees how small it is, barely reaching his knees.

'Not long now.' Carvalho sounds certain but the tremble in his voice finds its way to his right hand. His knuckles whiten on the hilt of his still-sheathed sword. The scabbard rattles against his hip and he jerks his hand free, as if electrocuted, shooting a guilty look at Richard.

'Will you fire as they advance, to thin them out before they engage the Zulus?' Richard asks. 'It is awkward; having no unified command,' he adds, sympathetically.

'No. We shall allow things to play out, preserving our

ammunition. Should they break through, we will mow them down. If those stubby spears account for a third of the attackers, we will be fine.'

It is a fair assessment but makes Richard uncomfortable. A concentrated volley might halve the assault, making the job of the Fasimba much easier. He has no authority. Just the hint of goodness in the young officer beside him, revealed over a campfire as he nursed his toothache. Should he remind the ensign of the universal nature of humanity?

Corporal Lopes calls out, 'Enemy sighted!' Carvalho translates.

The Zulu company jeer and shout, drumming spears against their fine hide shields.

Richard studies the flat plain between the hills and the river. The Khumalos advance at a trot in close order, shouting their own insults, faces stretched into masks of war, conjured from fear and adrenalin.

He scans from face to face, until his circular field of vision frames a tall, oddly proportioned figure, whose small head tops a long neck, split by a mouthful of teeth.

The man moves on thin legs and as Richard studies him, he leaves the front rank, advancing on the defiant line of Zulus. His feet are surprisingly small even in his clumsy sandals. He holds a long spear with two more clasped behind his shield.

He stops thirty yards from Insumpa. His men halt ten strides behind, spears cocked. The man turns side-on to pace across the front of his men, displaying his bravery to both sides.

Richard would be impressed if he wasn't so distracted by the man's improbably bulbous buttocks. The rear of his animal skin kilt jutting out, as if on a shelf.

'He is a chief. He wears leopard,' Richard informs the ensign.

The ungainly leader stamps his foot and bangs his shield. 'I am Mzilikazi, chief of the Khumalos. You trespass on our territory!'

Richard's hand tightens on his musket as sweat pricks his skin. The man's words are shrill but uncompromising, in the language the Zulus use. Richard understands.

'Mzilikazi!' he blurts out.

Carvalho looks puzzled. 'You have heard of him?'

Richard nods before he can stop himself. 'A man of destiny. One day his name will be known even a thousand miles to the north,' Richard curses inwardly and adds, 'or so he believes. He is fuelled by hate.'

The ensign draws his sword. Richard is impressed at how steady the bright steel looks against the green backdrop of the hill.

When no move is made by the forces opposing him, Mzilikazi leers menacingly. 'You have no cattle for me to plunder. Unless you offer tribute or join my forces, your lives are forfeit! What is your answer?' Richard gabbles a simultaneous translation.

'If your Zulus change sides, we are done for!' spits Carvalho in a troubled voice.

'Watch!' Richard replies. Everything is very quiet. Richard hears the rush of blood around his body and the tense breathing of the ensign. A man in the second Portuguese rank sneezes and another coughs.

Insumpa steps forward, one, two, three steps, until he is

easily within range of a throwing spear. 'We travel under the protection of mighty Shaka, father of our nation, the great lion, unbeatable majesty of the heavens! If you stand against us, you will pay the price.'

Mzilikazi's eyes bulge and distended veins spring up from his neck and across his head. 'You dare threaten me on my territory? This Shaka's deeds reach my ears. Perhaps, when I have slit your bellies, I will go to him and see if he truly deserves his reputation!'

Richard is growing hoarse but it seems the talking is now finished. Insumpa turns his back and waits.

Mzilikazi raises his long spear to his shoulder, tip pointing between the *induna*'s shoulders. His lips peel back, exposing large, white teeth clamped together. With an obvious effort, Mzilikazi lowers the spear and returns to his men.

Ensign Carvalho lets out a ragged breath.

'Mzilikazi has twenty-eight men,' Richard informs him. 'We have a dozen more.' He gets no further before the first spears are hurled by Khumalo warriors.

The young Zulu company stand firm, deflecting the spear points with their shields. They jeer. More spears thud against hide.

On the left flank, the Fasimba point man is driven to his knees by a throw from Mzilikazi himself. The spear deflects, cutting the upper arm of the next man in line. He looks in astonishment at the trickle of blood, shrugs, and tucks his injured arm behind his tall shield.

The point man regains his feet, scoops up the bloodied spear and hurls it back. It slithers to a stop at Mzilikazi's feet.

'First blood!' cries the Khumalo chief. 'It will not be the last!' He gives a signal and his men throw a volley. 'See how these invaders cower behind their shields! They are nothing without their mighty Shaka!' crows Mzilikazi. 'They offer no reply. Let us leave them to wallow in their fear. We will capture whatever these others guard so jealously. Then we will finish these Zulus.'

Richard cannot believe it. Mzilikazi could offer no greater insult to Insumpa and his men. He leads his troops around the Fasimba line, his men taunting as they go. Arrogance drips from curled lips and disdainful eyes. They line up in two ranks facing the Portuguese company.

At Carvalho's command, Corporal Lopes orders the front rank to take aim. The watching ensign raises his sword. His fist clenches on the guard as he prepares to give the signal to fire.

Richard watches from the corner of his eye but keeps his gaze ahead. 'The Zulus!' he blurts out.

Carvalho hesitates.

'*Si-gi-di*!' roar the twenty Fasimba as they hurtle on silent feet into the rear of the Khumalos. The rear rank turns awkwardly to meet them, catching shield with shield, fumbling their long spears.

It is too late. The force of the charge knocks several surprised Khumalos off their feet. They are despatched with a rapid stab to the neck. Those who turn in time have their shields hooked aside, short spears punching deep into exposed flesh.

'*Ngadla*! *Ngadla*!' becomes a refrain, punctuating the grunts of men, rising above the cries of the wounded.

The second rank of Khumalos compose themselves. They step back from their struggling fellows, consigning them to their fate. They assemble a firm line, spears held underarm like lances, heavy tips wavering at the end of long shafts.

General Thibault is in the thick of it, conspicuous in blue and gold, sword arcing among thrusting spears. His head is bare and Richard sees he is grinning.

The front rank of Mzilikazi's men breaks. Most lie dead on crushed grass, blood mingling with rusty dust. There is red on Thibault's blade as he forms up with the Fasimba to confront the second rank.

'Devastating,' admits the ensign. 'Alas, I can offer no help. To fire would risk hitting our allies.'

Richard can see this is true. The Portuguese company begin muttering to each other. Lopes barks at them and they fall silent. The corporal trots across to the wagon and reports. 'The men fear the Zulus will not stop when they have finished off the savages.' He sounds like he agrees.

Carvalho looks uncertain, so Richard intervenes. 'You are not at risk. Their commander is wary of all foreigners, but he is a loyal officer. His orders are to protect my party.' The ensign looks relieved but Lopes' expression suggests he is not convinced.

As the two forces face off again, Richard does a quick head count. There are eighteen Khumalos standing with their leader but several bleed profusely. The Zulu ranks remain intact.

Now both sides are aligned in a single row, perhaps three throwing spears apart.

Again, Mzilikazi steps forward. His eyes are wide and flash

with anger. A fallen man moans pitiably until despatched by one of his own. Small, sandalled feet shuffle back and forth as if starting a dance. Arms hold aloft his shield and spears, exaggerating his height.

'I am Mzilikazi of the Khumalos,' he announces shrilly, 'I call out your champion. Let us settle this fight in the manner of our forefathers!'

Insumpa does not move. 'We have tasted blood! Why should we revert to the old ways? Our new spears bite you. Spears given to us by our father, the mighty Shaka!'

Mzilikazi shakes his small head, his paunch wobbling comically before he lowers his shield. 'None of your men dare face me?' he scoffs.

Insumpa says nothing. His men jeer and pound their shields. Richard is wondering what will spark the next phase of the engagement, when General Thibault steps forward, pointing the tip of his sword at the Khumalo leader. 'I challenge you!' shouts the Frenchman in his own language. His voice is manic with bloodlust, gore coating his blade.

Richard makes to jump down from the wagon but Carvalho restrains him. 'Leave him be! You cannot stop this now.'

Richard reluctantly relents.

Mzilikazi eyes Thibault warily, looking him up and down from his bare head to his black boots. 'What are you?' demands the Khumalo leader.

'He is asking Thibault who he is,' Richard explains to Carvalho.

General Thibault seems to understand the intent behind the words. 'I am a general in the service of his imperial majesty, Emperor Napoleon Bonaparte!' His voice is level and full of pride. 'My name is Lucien Hypolite Thibault.' It is the first time Richard has heard the Frenchman's middle name.

Mzilikazi mimics Thibault's words, trying to capture the rhythms of French. His men laugh nervously. This is not the straightforward patrol they expected.

Insumpa steps forward as if he wants to separate the two men. He looks annoyed his plans are being usurped by this outsider. Richard sees his weight shift as he prepares for a second step. But instead, he rocks back shaking his head. It is too late. He orders his men back five paces. Mzilikazi gives a similar order.

Now the two men have plenty of room. Mzilikazi raises the spear in his throwing hand to his shoulder. Thibault bounces on the balls of his feet, shuffling forward and back, skipping side to side. His eyes never leave Mzilikazi.

With little back lift, Mzilikazi launches his missile in a flat trajectory. Thibault dances aside and the spear passes harmlessly by to scuff the dirt behind him.

The French general bounds forward in a skipping gait, while Mzilikazi frees another spear from behind his shield. Mzilikazi sees him coming, realises he will not clear his weapon in time, and braces with both feet. Thibault closes and the Khumalo chief remains still.

As the Frenchman's sword tip extends in a fluid lunge, Mzilikazi rams the top of his shield upwards. The sword deflects away from his head but Thibault's momentum throws him into his opponent, who continues the upward trajectory of his shield, uppercutting the Frenchman.

Richard watches the moment of impact, his view clear over the heads of the Fasimba. The young general's head jerks back viciously. His knees buckle and he collapses in a heap at Mzilikazi's feet.

With a roar of triumph, the Khumalo leader frees the second spear, gripping it midway along the shaft. He stands astride Thibault and kicks away his sword with a sandal. The blade slithers across the grass.

Without thinking, Richard jumps from the cart. He runs to the closest Portuguese soldier and wrenches his musket from his hands. He uses the front wheel to climb back onto the flatbed. Pulling back on the hammer, he moves the weapon to full-cock, and brings the butt to his right shoulder.

He tries to control his breathing as he sights along the barrel. Ensign Carvalho says something but he is not listening. The muzzle is trained on Mzilikazi's centre mass. The chief is stooped over Thibault, buttocks bulging, shield cast aside, spear grasped in both hands.

'These Zulus let this pale peacock do their fighting for them! If he is the best they can offer, I shall think twice before allying myself to their king!'

The musket discharges, the recoil forcing Richard back a step. The ensign's hands brace him. Again, the Portuguese officer speaks but Richard's ears are ringing. He cannot see Mzilikazi or Thibault as the gun smoke obscures them.

Ears echoing, eyes stinging, Richard frowns. He hears other reports and the smell of ignited powder is acrid in his nostrils. He looks to his side and sees the first rank of the Portuguese company step back through their line and begin to reload. Corporal Lopes bellows at the second rank. They hold their fire.

From beyond billowing smoke come the cries and clashes of conflict. For a moment, a flutter of wind pulls back the veil, providing Richard a glimpse of Insumpa.

Muscular arms deploy shield and spear as he hooks and stabs. His stout body acting the warrior while his face tells a different story. He looks deeply offended, and reluctant, as he despatches another Khumalo with a jab beneath his armpit.

Smoke snatches the scene away and Richard searches helplessly for any sign of General Thibault. A breeze rolls down the slope behind them, ruffling Richard's long hair, driving away the powder fog.

Richard spots Thibault lying motionless. Insumpa stands ahead of the blue and gold body, jeering as the surviving Khumalos flee, led by the gangling Mzilikazi who favours his left arm.

Richard again jumps from the wagon. Ulwazi joins him from beneath the cart. 'You will receive no thanks from Insumpa.' Her voice is stony as if she shares the *induna*'s outrage.

Richard has no answer, so he runs to the fallen general and rolls him over. Running his hands over the uniformed torso, he finds no wound. Legs and arms are similarly intact. Richard lifts the heavy head on its slack neck, turning it to one side and then the other. He can find no mark but as he settles Thibault's head on the trampled grass, his hand comes away sticky with blood. Tilting the general's chin, he finds an arcing cut beneath the lower jaw.

'Shield,' Ulwazi says with certainty.

Richard nods. Insumpa is supervising his warriors as they

quarter the field, slitting the bellies of the fallen, regardless of tribe.

Richard tries to ignore the spectacle but Ulwazi notices his reaction. 'It is proper.'

He knows the Zulus believe no warrior killed in battle can rest until his spirit is released. He just does not want to watch.

Returning his attention to Thibault, he detects a shallow movement of his chest, but cannot feel a pulse. He is about to check for breath when the motionless body emits a weak groan. Richard tightens his grip on the Frenchman's wrist. A louder moan follows. Releasing his hold, Richard slaps the drained face until he sees some colour.

'Lucien?' It is the first time he has used the man's Christian name. 'Can you hear me?' Still studying the general, Richard sees his eyelids tremble.

He hears Insumpa calling his men to order. Thibault moves his head gingerly and his eyes open. The Fasimba warriors fall in. Thibault tries to sit but soon gives up. The Zulu *iviyo* chant as they take up their dog trot and move away.

Richard looks up to see them trailing dust as they head towards the gorge, before turning parallel to it, apparently on the trail of the retreating Khumalo survivors.

'No pain; no gain,' whispers a hoarse French voice.

Richard smiles down at the young general's smooth face. His sideboards are full but neatly trimmed. For the first time, Richard realises the man has grey eyes.

'Pain certainly, but for what gain?' Richard asks indulgently.

Thibault feels around in the dirt without moving his head. Richard realizes what he wants and releases Thibault's neck.

The Frenchman is able to support his head now. Richard moves in a widening circle until he spots what he is looking for.

Stooping, he grips the hilt of the man's sword and pulls the blade from beneath a fallen Khumalo warrior. As he returns, Thibault is watching from the corner of his eye. He manages a weak smile as Richard places the sword in his hand. Thibault raises the weapon weakly, its tip wavering, to stare at the blade. It is dull with dried blood.

There is no youthful triumph on his face. Instead, he continues to gaze thoughtfully until the weight becomes too much and he lowers it to the ground.

They spend the night beneath the shallow slopes of the hill. Richard lies beneath the wagon curved around Ulwazi's warm shape. He cannot sleep. Rustling in the bushes. Snoring soldiers mutter in their dreams. A night bird cries mournfully. He tries to match his wife's relaxed breathing. Instead, he tunes into the sound of his heart circulating blood. He has never liked imagining the delicate structures beneath his skin. But he cannot stop.

A porcine snort sounds close by, providing a welcome distraction. He imagines Insumpa's namesakes snuffling across the flanks of the hill. But the *induna* and his men have abandoned them. Richard recalls the accusing look Ensign Carvalho shot him as the Zulu company wheeled away south-west.

What sort of greeting will await them when they eventually reach Bulawayo? If Ulwazi's response is anything to go by, he will have a lot of explaining to do.

Chapter Five

August 1818

Approaching from the north, Bulawayo dominates the landscape, its perimeter walls stark and well maintained. Standing where the ground falls away into the fold of the river valley, Richard is struck by the increased density of huts. Only the cattle pens and the central area remain clear.

Ulwazi trips ahead and then runs back, looking impatient. Richard is reluctant to enter the gateway, standing open to the early afternoon. Overhead, the sky is clear and blue.

The slightest breeze drifts towards them, laden with the smells of the capital. Woodsmoke from cooking fires. The heady spice of hard-working bodies. The humid aroma of maize porridge cooking. He detects these smells beneath the pungent stink of latrines.

Richard sighs and walks briskly down the slope. He hears cattle lowing contentedly but he cannot see them. Perhaps they are screened by the trees along the river?

A shout sounds from the lookout post beside the gateway. Voices trade questions and answers as Richard's party haul their burdens up the slope to Bulawayo's walls.

The Portuguese troopers move slowly, unsteady on their feet after a month hauling cannon and wagon. To Richard's surprise, Thibault's heavy cart has held together with only minor repairs.

Corporal Lopes barks at his men to straighten their backs as he retrieves his musket from the wagon. Thibault walks in the traces with the men, lending his weight, even though he is far from fully recovered. His jaw is swollen and he cannot open it without pain. He is forced to mumble and mutter behind clenched teeth. Considering his discomfort, he is surprisingly cheerful.

As they approach the gate, Ulwazi finally cracks and runs off. Richard smiles happily after her disappearing form.

Inside the stout walls, he is not surprised to find Shaka installed beneath the council tree with his advisers. Richard bows deeply. Pampata is by Shaka's right side and Nandi to his left.

Nqoboka sits sternly at Shaka's feet, proud head topping his improbably long neck. Like his companions, he wears a brass arm-ring, known as an *ingxotha*, above his right wrist. It is a mark of seniority. His scarred face gives nothing away but his eyes rove over the procession, before coming to rest on the wagon.

Ngomane sits beside him, face composed. Mdlaka is there looking thoughtful beside Mgobozi whose face is split by a toothy grin. On the fringe of the group, beyond the shade, lurks English Bill. He looks relieved to see Richard and ventures a quick wave.

Richard scans the assembled group a second time. Where is Napoleon? He needs his artillery expertise to convince the council his actions were justified.

Richard sees Nqoboka smirk as Insumpa appears from the Fasimba huts. The blocky *induna* stops before he reaches the tree.

Another shout sounds from the lookout. '*Umlungu* approaches with the musket company.'

Richard relaxes as Bonaparte strides into Bulawayo. The men with him carry three large antelope slung on poles. Richard thinks they are kudu with their spiralling horns and reddish hides striped with white.

Bonaparte's quick eyes take in the scene. He grins and runs to Richard, hugging him awkwardly, a musket still gripped in his right hand. 'It is good to see you, my English friend.' His voice is genuine. He nods appreciatively to General Thibault who stands by the wagon. 'It is also very good to see your cargo.'

Richard can tell he has questions, but he pulls himself up short and bows deeply to Shaka. 'Forgive the interruption, mighty Shaka. Your musket company bring meat. It is timely, no?'

Shaka inclines his head and allows himself an appreciative smile before returning his attention to Richard's party.

Shaka stands, 'News has reached us of your journey.' The brief smile is forgotten.

Richard glances at Insumpa who stares defiantly, lip curled with disdain. Looking away, Richard studies Nqoboka who struggles to conceal his pleasure.

'You denied my young warriors their full quota of victims!' accuses the Zulu chief.

Richard has had days to choose his words, helping the injured Thibault across rough country, while keeping the six cannon safe. 'Lord king, forgive me. I do not blame the Fasimba for abandoning their posts. Our precious cargo was safe under the protection of these soldiers from the Portuguese fort.'

Nqoboka spits over his crossed legs. Insumpa shuffles from one foot to the other as if ready for combat. Nandi and Pampata whisper together. Mgobozi frowns before elbowing Mdlaka and gesturing towards the Portuguese company, the wagon and the four visible gun barrels.

'What do you bring me that could outweigh the offence given to my men?' Shaka booms threateningly.

Bonaparte steps forward. 'Mighty Shaka, do not blame my English friend. He was doing my bidding. He has brought the greatest weapon of the white man to strengthen your forces. A weapon powerful enough to stand against the English!'

Richard winces at Napoleon's boasting. Does he really think he could defend Zululand against an English invasion with half a dozen six-pounders?

Shaka's brows lower over his penetrating eyes. 'You must prove this claim! If I am convinced, all will be well, and I shall have both English and French members of my council. But if your words prove hollow like a drum, I shall make an example of you both.'

Shaka scrutinises the Portuguese contingent standing awkwardly inside the gates. 'These a*belungu* from the north are not welcome. They must leave their weapons and depart!'

Ensign Carvalho looks on innocently, while Corporal Lopes scans the scene warily. Richard feels sickness spread in his belly. He is the reason matters are spinning out of control. He shot Mzilikazi.

He wishes Ulwazi was with him. But he steps forward alone, until he is a few paces from the assembled council. He looks Shaka in the face. 'Great chief, do not punish these others for my actions. It is true, I fired a musket at the Khumalo leader, to stop him stabbing General Thibault. Who, among your officers, would not act to save the life of a compatriot? I beg you, do not send these innocent soldiers away without the means to defend themselves!'

Pampata leans forward and speaks urgently to Shaka. He listens patiently and nods. 'Very well, they may carry away half their weapons but I want them camped beyond the river by nightfall.' Richard's head swims with relief. 'You are a curious man,' Shaka says, 'you are no soldier and yet at Gqokli hill and again in Khumalo territory, you manage to be at the centre of the action.'

Richard wants to object but thinks better of it. He drops his gaze and waits.

'You will demonstrate this new weapon tomorrow.' There is no room for objection.

Richard turns helplessly to Bonaparte who simply shrugs and then grins. 'No sleep for us tonight, I fear!' he quips cheerfully.

As the residents of Bulawayo settle down for their evening meal, Richard takes the opportunity of one more conversation with Tiago Carvalho. The ensign's once lifeless eyes are bright in his boyish face. He did not resist, when Shaka's order was explained, handing over half his company's muskets and ammunition.

'I am ashamed,' the young Portuguese officer says in his passable French. 'These are a mighty people. I once thought black men little more than beasts. But now I see the truth. We are a sorry outpost of the Portuguese empire, barely clinging to the coastline. Chased off by the Dutch scant years ago. Ordered about by the British whenever their ships weigh anchor.

'Our demands for tribute are often ignored by the tribes of the interior. Evidence I refused to see. But this,' he sweeps an arm around Bulawayo as it sinks into the dusk, 'is more damning! We must hope your Zulus become embroiled with the English. For, if they march north, our settlement will fall.' His voice is thick with emotion. Shame battling with honesty.

Richard claps him on the shoulder and is glad to shake his hand. He does so firmly and only reluctantly lets go when he sees tears welling up in the ensign's eyes.

Bonaparte loiters in the background. 'Ensign, might I have a word?' Richard decides to stay and listen. 'I have need of your men tonight,' the former emperor reveals. Richard is puzzled but does not speak. 'We must mount a six-pounder so that it can be fired tomorrow,' Napoleon explains.

Richard looks at the two ranks of black soldiers waiting to depart. They look eager to be moving. 'We have a wheelwright with us,' Richard comments.

'Splendid,' Napoleon agrees, 'we will make short work of converting your wagon!'

The next morning comes quickly, illuminating a disassembled wagon, the two larger wheels lying on their hubs beside discarded lengths of planking and ironwork.

Defiant on its newly fashioned carriage sits a six-pounder cannon. The smaller wheels are fixed to a shortened axle, supporting the barrel on a bracket trail; two baulks of timber with connecting struts. The length and angle of this timber construction counterbalance the projecting barrel. A wooden wedge beneath the rear of the barrel enables elevation of the piece.

General Thibault yawns. He looks pale but insisted on rising the moment he woke, despite Ulwazi's objections. He regards the remains of his wagon sadly before turning to study Napoleon's project. 'It looks just like a gun carriage!' he admits in a reedy voice that cannot hide his admiration.

Bonaparte stands proudly, eager to point out the finer details. 'Our Portuguese friends worked hard,' he concedes grudgingly.

Richard looks across the river. He can make out a smear against the horizon, as Tiago Carvalho takes his men, and his new-found knowledge, back to Portuguese territory.

'Look how the smith bent these iron sections to shackle the protruding trunnions to the bracket trail.' Napoleon is become that artillery officer from the siege of Toulon, a man on the verge of making his reputation.

Herd boys lead a reluctant cow down the hill. She tugs at the halter, tipping her wet nose to the sky. Her white flanks are flecked with a rash of black spots, like flicked ink across blotting paper. The eldest boy tethers her to the largest tree in a straggling thicket.

Richard knows what is coming. He feels sick. He wants to ask Napoleon if there is another way. But what is the point? He remembers the emperor sacrificing his Old Guard at Waterloo. He sees him raising his long musket to shoot Captain Simpson in the back, compelling Richard to intervene. More recently, he shot an *isangoma*, Shaka's senior witch-doctor, as a show of his magic. Only watching the Old

Guard march to their doom, did he show any emotion.

Napoleon Bonaparte is ruthless, arrogant and until Waterloo, convinced of his destiny. Even now, playing courtier to an African version of himself, his swagger and certainty are unabashed. He has thrown off the fug that was asphyxiating him on St Helena.

The sun is almost overhead by the time Shaka appears. He sits on a throne of rolled mats in exactly the spot he occupied when viewing Bonaparte's musket display. Again, the former French emperor is at the heart of things.

Richard tries to block out the cries from the cow, thrashing her head from side to side. He can be of no use, so he stands with Ulwazi. He detects a frown of disapproval from Nqoboka who has aligned himself with Insumpa. Bridling, Richard curls his arm around his wife's square shoulders.

Shaka does not react to Ulwazi's presence. His eyes are fixed on the scene at the bottom of the slope. There is no sign of the women of the royal court but Mdlaka and Mgobozi chatter together, pointing at the unfamiliar wheeled object. Ngomane's long neck stretches forward as he studies Bonaparte's preparations.

English Bill sits beside the viewing party, his expression unreadable, although Richard thinks he is familiar with artillery. General Thibault loiters, one hand on the hilt of his sword, a hurt look on his face.

Napoleon Bonaparte stands bareheaded and alone beside his makeshift gun. To Richard's surprise, he calls out in a strong voice, speaking English.

'Great king, this weapon can make you as strong as the British! In my army, we worked these guns in teams, but today, I shall demonstrate alone.'

Shaka frowns and summons English Bill. Richard watches him question the translator and nod at the response. 'Continue!' booms Shaka's deep voice, also speaking English. He throws a brief grin at Richard who inclines his head.

Napoleon swabs the barrel with a wet sponge on a stick, explaining this ensures the barrel is clear. He loads the powder-cartridge followed by the six-pound shot, comparing the arrangement to the firing mechanism on a musket.

For a moment Richard remembers the musket demonstration but as the sequence plays out, he is back on the ridge of Mont St Jean, corralled by ropes, with pretty Arabella leaning against him. He recalls her start as the first cannon roared, even though it was a drill devoid of shot.

Ulwazi whimpers and wriggles. Richard loosens his grip and whispers an apology. The onlookers are silent, heads following the artilleryman's every move. English Bill tries his best to explain the more technical vocabulary when Shaka shoots him an impatient question.

Bonaparte uses the reversed sponge-stick to ram the charge home. He pricks the cartridge through the vent with an iron spike forged from a musket ramrod. He inserts a quill of powder into the vent and produces a clay pot of smouldering embers. He lights an improvised slow-match manufactured from the hem of a cotton shirt coated in animal fat and tied around the remains of the ramrod.

A gusty breeze threatens to frustrate Bonaparte. Dust fills the air as he struggles to ignite the charge in the vent.

English Bill wrings his hands, unable to render portfire into Zulu. Richard removes his arm from Ulwazi's shoulders and steps closer to Shaka's group. 'It is a slow-burning taper in a holder; he is trying to light the charge.'

The gun barrel inclines a little above the horizontal, pointing its muzzle at the river. Bonaparte drives a wooden wedge beneath the rear of the barrel to elevate the muzzle. There are several clumps of trees but only one emits pained lowing, mournful as a fog horn.

There is a hiss and a puff of smoke and then a deafening explosion as the main charge is set off. Everyone, except the experienced artilleryman, jumps.

The gun jerks back on its jury-rigged carriage, almost catching Napoleon who skips nimbly away. The force of the recoil cracks the struts holding the bracket trail together. The two baulks peel apart and the barrel drops into the dirt.

Nqoboka begins to laugh but Shaka barks and he falls silent. The Zulu king is on his feet. His retinue part as he walks quickly down the slope towards the gun. No one else moves.

Smoke from the firing is tugged away like a tattered flag by the breeze. Shaka strides past Napoleon and his gun, towards the river, the last remnants of smoke trailing behind.

Napoleon follows, looking small but dazzling, in his Chasseurs uniform of dark green, red and white, with gold buttons and epaulettes.

Richard finds himself trailing after. He is joined by Mgobozi in the vanguard of the councillors, who move, some eagerly, and others more reluctantly, past the broken carriage.

Nqoboka kicks out contemptuously and yelps in pain as his toes crumple against unyielding metal. Mgobozi laughs at him but Insumpa hurries across only to be shrugged off.

Shaka stops and Napoleon draws alongside. In a stand of umbrella-shaped acacia trees hangs the dismembered cow, bloody, and tattered. The tree trunk is shattered. The cow's head and neck are entirely severed from her broad shoulders, which in turn are no longer connected to legs. One shank is visible, as is the shattered ribcage, partially covered in hide. Much of the hindquarters look flensed. The fallen crown of the tree lies on one haunch.

Shaka prods the horned head thoughtfully with his little spear as Richard approaches. The cow's blank eyes stare at him. He is surprised that his stomach remains calm. He has counted his paces from the cannon. Almost a thousand yards.

Shaka fingers the remainder of the tree trunk thoughtfully. 'You are forgiven, both of you,' he admits with a hungry look in his eyes.

Nqoboka makes a sound in his throat and Shaka swings around. The force of his presence compels the stern, muscular adviser to wave his large hands and squeak in apology. Mgobozi pokes him in the ribs and gestures at the deconstructed carcass. Nqoboka studies the destruction warily and makes a sign warding off evil.

That evening, Richard and Napoleon are invited to eat inside the royal enclosure. Pampata plays hostess but Nandi is there too, a regal dowager watching everything, deferred to by everyone.

All Shaka's senior advisers are present. They wear their regalia of best hides and furs, feathers, necklaces and arm rings. No one carries a weapon, not even Bonaparte. Shaka beams around his large hut and his good mood is infectious.

Even Nqoboka manages to smile.

The roasted beef is delicious. Richard fears it is the unhappy cow used as a target. All are favoured with the choicest cuts: sweetmeats and glistening slices of fat. Pampata hands around the platters herself. Every man present tries not to look at her and fails.

The diners smack their lips and quaff beakers of milky sorghum beer. When everyone has eaten their fill and the remains of the meal are cleared away, Shaka gestures for Richard and Napoleon to step forward.

He turns them to face the select group and places a powerful hand on each man's shoulder. 'I want everyone to bear witness. These a*belungu* are now Zulus! Let no one speak of their pale skin or doubt them for being born beyond these lands. We are forging a new nation from many parts.'

There are murmurs around the gloomy room. The fire casts monstrous shadows. Richard shivers. Shaka lifts his right hand from Napoleon's shoulder and points to one guest after another. 'Mdlaka of the Gazini clan. Nqoboka of the Sokhulu. Mgobozi of the Msane tribe. My peerless mother, a princess of the Mhlongo. Ngomane of the Mthethwa.'

Richard notices Insumpa has not been invited. He glances at Bonaparte, who stands proudly in his uniform, sporting his bicorn hat complete with cockade.

Shaka has spoken in Zulu. Basking in the king's favour, Richard risks a whisper to the Frenchman. 'Do you understand?'

Bonaparte smiles. 'He is pleased. We are to join his council.'

Richard nods. 'More than that. We are Zulus now!'

A calculating look flickers across Napoleon's face. He turns and drops onto one knee, lowering his lips to kiss Shaka's left foot.

Richard's mouth drops open. He tries to remember seeing the former emperor humble himself before. He cannot.

Shaka beams and pulls the Frenchman into a bear hug. There is nothing for it. As Bonaparte is released, Richard drops to the tamped floor and kisses Shaka's right foot.

'See! My newest councillors accept their posts. Who can doubt their sincerity?'

Nqoboka drifts to the rear, his features hidden in shadow. The flames from the hearth leap as Pampata prods the glowing logs. Nqoboka's outline is cast in caricature against the rear wall. The whites of his eyes flash before he turns and slips from the building.

By the time Richard gets back to his hut, Ulwazi is asleep. He wants to wake her and tell her what has happened but hesitates.

Why does he keep thinking of Arabella? He met her once, three years ago. She is surely married by now.

He looks at his wife's relaxed face. Her lashes are long and luxurious. The whorls of her small ears sit flush with her skull. He sees the strong planes of her face. Her long, slender legs are tucked into her concave belly, accentuating the curve of her buttocks.

Her hair, tight at the temples, is gathered on her crown in a modest topknot, the sign of a married woman. Richard sees her teasing it out every day, as if sheer willpower can make it grow faster.

He smiles as he reaches out and shakes her gently by the shoulder. She murmurs and rolls onto her back before her eyelids shoot up. For a second, worry creases her forehead but her eyes focus and she smiles. Her teeth are regular and bright in the faint light from the smouldering cakes of dried dung in the hearth. Richard smiles back. He feels as if he is letting go of something he has carried all his life. Never satisfied but refusing to take a risk.

In the end, he did risk travelling through time searching for Napoleon. He found him too! But what did that do for his wellbeing?

'What is wrong?' Ulwazi asks, the frown back on her face.

'Nothing. I was just thinking of the journey that brought me here.'

'I walked it with you,' his wife replies gently, worry still tingeing her words.

'I mean the journey that brought me from my old life to this one.'

Her worry evaporates. She sits up and nestles her back against his chest. 'From England?' she murmurs.

What to tell her? England is alien enough. 'Yes. Three years ago, I was a teacher. I gave it up to witness one of the greatest battles in history. I met Bonaparte and followed him into exile. We escaped by ship. It brought us here.'

Ulwazi does not speak. Bulawayo is quiet, he cannot even hear the cattle in their great pens. There is a buzzing in his ears. He could tell her more. He bites his lip until he tastes blood. She wriggles in his arms and he tries to relax. 'Africa is very different. Until today, I did not belong,' he confides.

She turns to kneel in front of him, taking his head in her

hands. Her honey-gold eyes bore into him. There is such intelligence there; he tries to look away. Her strong hands do not let him. Her lips part. 'You belong with me. We said the words of your ceremony.'

He nods awkwardly, his cheeks squashed between her palms. 'That is not the same. But now it is different. Shaka made me a Zulu!' His voice quavers. Tears mist his sight and he is sobbing, his chest heaving.

Ulwazi drops her hands from his face and scrambles into his lap, wrapping her arms around his shaking form. Her small breasts press firmly against him. His face is in her neck. The smell of her fills his nostrils and he subsides.

'Why do you cry? I have never seen a man cry before. Surely it is a good thing to be honoured in this way?' Ulwazi sounds perplexed.

He is in control now. He wipes his face with the back of his hand. Her outline merges with the shadows of the interior. He moves her aside and tosses more dung cakes on the fire. At first nothing happens. 'I have never really felt I belonged anywhere. My parents died when I was young.'

There is a crackle from the hearth. 'I was raised by my aunt. She did her duty but I was a burden.' A flicker of flame. 'Even as a teacher, I never felt my pupils needed me.' The cakes are glowing from beneath now.

There is compassion in his wife's touch as she strokes his arm. 'But you changed all that. You found Bonaparte. You found this land. You found me. Now mighty Shaka has declared you a Zulu. You live in heaven, for that is what *iZulu* means!' Ulwazi's lips stretch into a tentative smile.

Richard leans forward and kisses her hard. She responds by

opening her mouth and moaning. Flames leap in the hearth and a hint of ammonia teases his nostrils. He does not register the chlorine tang. Ulwazi's fingers are fumbling with the buttons of his shirt. Her hands are on his flesh. He shivers with pleasure and pulls her down on top of him.

Later, their two bodies entwined, Richard whispers in her ear. 'I shall be a Zulu!'

Richard is not listening. The air is hot, even beneath the shading branches of the council tree. He thinks it is January 1819. *Induna* after *induna* reports on the state of his regiment, recounting recent engagements and the number of cattle plundered.

The Qwabes have fallen to Shaka's regiments, joining almost thirty other clans swelling Shaka's territory and population.

'But Zwide is not dead!' Shaka's voice bursts out across the reports like thunder.

Richard's head snaps up to see a petulant look distorting the ruler's face. 'My enemy plots my downfall. He will seek revenge for the death of his five sons, killed at the battle of Gqokli hill!'

Bonaparte coughs discreetly. 'Might this be an opportune moment to demonstrate the power of your new weapon, sire?' he asks eagerly. English Bill translates carefully.

Shaka looks thoughtful, rubbing his chin. He has allowed Napoleon to train a dozen warriors in the art of artillery. He has granted access to his blacksmiths for the forging of brackets and tools. All six guns now sit atop sturdy carriages with iron-bound wheels.

Richard studies Nqoboka. He has kept a low profile since the two *abelungu* were elevated to the council. Might this be the day he renews his opposition? He looks on the verge of speaking but misses his moment.

'This is not the time for a major war. My kingdom has swollen. There is much work to do. I must learn patience. Zwide will keep. I declare a great *umkhosi*, to be held at the next full moon.'

English Bill translates for Napoleon, explaining the various elements of an *umkhosi*. 'It is a harvest festival but much more. A full dress review of the whole army, new laws will be announced. Every adult male will attend, along with many wives and all marriageable girls!'

Bill licks his lips and leers even though he already has seven wives. 'There will be dancing and singing and new songs will be composed. Finally, the king submits to questioning by his warriors. They may ask anything without fear of reprisal and Shaka must answer!'

This sounds like the largest civic event since Shaka took power. Richard considers why he announces it now, when he is so clearly eager to eradicate the threat of Zwide?

He did not listen as the military captains made their reports but he knows what they said. More land captured, more men for the army, more women to work and marry, more cattle as tribute.

The council meeting breaks up and Richard joins Napoleon and English Bill. The three of them wander through the open gates of Bulawayo and stroll lazily down the slope towards the river.

Bill is chewing a wad of tobacco and Bonaparte surprises

him by producing a traditional snuff spoon from his pocket. He comes to a stop as he removes a small, hollowed-horn container from a necklace. 'A gift from Shaka,' Bonaparte mumbles, as he scoops fine powder with the long-handled spoon.

Napoleon awkwardly lifts the spoon to his left nostril, sniffs and pinches his nose quickly. Richard watches as his eyes water, his pupils dilate and his body tenses. When it comes, his sneeze is modest, but followed by aftershocks. His handkerchief appears in his hand as if by magic. It is improbably white.

When he is finished, Napoleon walks on with a beatific look on his face. 'He is a wise ruler. He curbs his emotions when necessary. He yearns to eliminate this Zwide and yet he calls for a festival. Why? Because he must weld his disparate people into a nation!' Bonaparte's admiration is obvious.

Richard imagines him reflecting on his own years as a ruler. Starting out as a tool of the revolution, co-opting its symbols, only to force the pope to crown him emperor! Would he do things differently if he had his time over again?

Richard wonders where General Thibault has got to? Unlike Richard's friend, Emile, he does not seem determined to attach himself to a regiment, despite fighting alongside the Fasimba against the Khumalo patrol. Perhaps his first taste of battle was sufficient?

'It will be interesting to see how a tyrant deals with open criticism,' Richard suggests. He is teasing, even though he is unsure how Napoleon will react. Since he resolved to live as a Zulu, it is as if his old reticence has dissolved.

Bonaparte reaches the green fringe bordering the river. He

stops to admire an anthill almost four feet high, a miniature Matterhorn of red dirt. He taps it with his foot. 'Solid as rock!' he exclaims. 'As will be Shaka's resolve in the face of his people!'

Richard inclines his head.

'But I think you were asking about me, rather than Shaka, yes?'

Richard repeats his gesture. His pulse quickens, colour flushes his cheeks. He feels alive.

'I did not set out to build the empire,' the former emperor begins. 'I thought there was a middle way. Promote talent wherever it was found but rule with a firm hand. Alas, I became too certain of my own abilities!' Napoleon fingers his snuff spoon but he does not take another pinch.

English Bill watches them closely. He spits voluminously to one side and chuckles. 'It is a hard thing.'

Both Richard and Bonaparte turn to regard the stooped figure, his wrinkles and paunch belying the strength of his limbs.

'To see a way to improbable riches and know you will never achieve them.' Bill's voice is low and he rubs his bald pate before smoothing his thin, yellowish hair.

'What are you talking about, Bill?' asks Richard.

'The British would make me rich if I returned their captive to them.'

Bonaparte stiffens and his right hand reaches for the hilt of his sword. Bill's honey eyes follow the motion and he hurries on. 'But I am a wanted man on British territory. They would execute me whatever news I might have!' He cackles and sputters. Richard thinks it is laughter.

'We had an understanding. You have been well paid.' Napoleon's tone is threatening. The top inch of his sword blade is free of his scabbard.

Bill nods emphatically. 'Yes, yes! My wives wish to see the festival. One, Two, Three, Four and Five will join us. When that is over, we shall all return home. I will take my payment in gold and go. I am no longer needed. You speak each speak the other's language. Mister Davey's Zulu is very good now. Even Shaka has some English.' Bill bobs and wrings his hands as he scuttles off.

'Will you pay him?' Richard asks.

Napoleon watches the retreating figure, fleet and sure for all his years. 'Can I afford not to?' Richard stays silent. 'I do not think him trustworthy but nor do I believe he would risk his neck with the British. I will pay him and let him go. Perhaps Shaka can be persuaded to keep an eye on him?' Bonaparte muses.

As they walk back towards Bulawayo, Richard sees a figure appear in the gateway. He hears a peal of laughter like a glass bell ringing and quickens his pace.

Bonaparte skips forward to keep up. 'Love changes everything, does it not?' There is deep loss in the fallen emperor's words.

Richard's gaze is fixed on Ulwazi as she laughs with her friends. She turns to answer a question, putting her in profile. The bulge of her belly is barely visible but Richard stumbles and Bonaparte reaches out a hand to steady him.

Chapter Six

January 1819

Bulawayo is bursting at the seams and family groups continue to arrive. Richard looks around the town. Every hut is full. Makeshift shelters sprout everywhere, even against the fences of the cattle pens. Only the central parade ground remains unoccupied.

Walking through the gates, he finds twice as many people encamped as he counted the day before. Many have brought materials to construct shelters while others plunder the thickets scattered across the grassland ringing the capital.

He sees one party and then another climbing back from the river with felled branches and leafy boughs.

'They will denude the area entirely,' observes a familiar voice in the accents of southern France.

Richard turns rapidly and grins. 'Emile! It is good to see you.' The Frenchman steps forward and Richard pulls him into a hug. 'I have missed you.'

'The regiment has been busy extending Zulu territory. But now it is time to celebrate!' The Frenchman, once a lieutenant in Bonaparte's bodyguard, is dressed as a Zulu warrior of the Ama-Wombe regiment. His shield is mottled brown and stretches from his ankles to his shoulder. He carries it casually. Richard glimpses the back of the shield and smiles to see his friend's cavalry sabre safe in a makeshift scabbard fastened to the shield stick that keeps the hide rigid.

Emile's good mood matches his own. 'You have heard my news?' Richard asks with a smile.

'You are married, I hear?' Emile replies with a laugh.

'And you?' asks Richard trying to strike a balance between lightness and concern.

'I too have a wife.' Deep affection coats these five words. 'Thabisa, truly she deserves her name, for she brings me joy!'

Richard remembers tracking the girl to her home village, when his friend was unable to leave barracks.

He is very happy for the former lieutenant. 'We have much to talk about. Are you free from duties tonight?'

Emile nods cheerfully. 'It will be good to catch up and compare notes!' He makes a lewd face and Richard blushes hotly.

'Is Thabisa not with you?' Richard enquires.

'She was summoned by the Queen Mother, Nandi. They have not met since Thabisa was a little girl. She was very nervous when the messenger arrived.'

So, Emile's wife is being cross-examined in the royal enclosure. 'I can only imagine what she will ask,' Richard teases. It is Emile's turn to colour but he forces an unconvincing smile onto his handsome face. 'When she is released, bring her to my hut. The four of us can eat together,' Richard suggests.

'How will I find your home?' asks Emile.

'Ask anyone,' Richard replies nonchalantly, 'I am a member of the royal council!' He walks off, imagining the look on Emile's face. He makes for his hut to warn Ulwazi of their impending guests.

On the way, he passes fires heating large earthenware vats, each tended by two women. Richard pauses to watch an older woman fetch a container emitting a sour odour. She saves a portion of the contents into a smaller pot and adds the rest to the large vat. He thinks they are preparing *utshwala*, the Zulus' beer.

Moving on, he spies a similar scene outside another hut. Here, the vat is being removed from the heat. He wanders closer and peers into the large receptacle. The contents are covered in a crusty sediment. He wonders if he will be able to drink the finished product having seen its preparation?

When Emile and Thabisa arrive, dusk is settling lightly on the capital. There is a buzz of noise, like a vast hive of bees, as the swollen town prepares food and readies itself for the festival.

Ulwazi dips her head, smiles, and says, '*Sawubona*!'

Thabisa reciprocates but the two women eye each other with interest.

'I see you!' Richard adds in Zulu, then English.

Emile echoes him, adding a French version for good measure. Such a beautiful piece of etiquette, Richard thinks. Not mere politeness but a recognition of the dignity of each person.

Richard looks from his wife to Emile and Thabisa. The three of them really are beautiful. They move with grace and sit with poise. He feels an utter fraud in their company, with his thinning hair, sloping shoulders, and clumsy self-doubt. No, he is past that now, he is a Zulu!

Emile has donned the *isicoco* of a married man. It suits him, with his full hair hanging below the head ring. Richard

124

studies the fibre circle sewn into Emile's hair, coated in gum, and polished with beeswax.

Emile notices Richard's attention and grins. 'Thabisa did it for me. Now I look a proper Zulu husband!'

Ulwazi laughs at that before joking, 'You look like one other Zulu in Bulawayo!' She slaps Richard's trousered leg.

Emile laughs lightly, 'But at least I dress like a Zulu not an *umlungu*!' he quips back.

Richard looks at his stained and patched clothes and then at his friend's bare torso and kilt of fur tails.

Settled around the hearth, with a low fire warming an aromatic porridge, the four talk over the past months.

Emile recounts life in the barracks town of Belebele and offers a few glimpses into the life of a warrior in Shaka's service.

Richard tells the story of the journey north to Lourenco Marques before Ulwazi has them in stitches recounting details of their marriage ceremony from her perspective.

Richard picks up the story of their trip home although he glosses over his part in the engagement with the Khumalos.

Thabisa smiles and nods, her face open and her eyes interested. But she says almost nothing. Without realising, Richard, Emile and Ulwazi turn to her at the same moment. She looks uncomfortable and smooths her skirt over and over again.

Emile leans close and whispers in her ear. She nods and manages a weak smile. 'I met Nandi, the Queen Mother today.' Her voice is modest but clear. She keeps her head low. 'She is a distant relative. She asked me whether I was happy married to Emile.' She pronounces the Frenchman's name perfectly.

Richard leans forward for her answer, as do the others. 'I told her it is hard being a wife.' Ulwazi nods sympathetically, while the two men scowl comically. 'She asked me why. I told her.' Just as her voice is warming up, Thabisa stops. She looks up and her face splits into a beaming grin. 'I told her men are of little use. They are away so much of the time. There is so much work for a wife to do.'

Emile looks with genuine concern to Richard.

'She agreed but asked if there were no compensations.' Ulwazi's peeling laugh fills the hut. Richard feels oddly giddy. 'I told her I enjoy the nights when Emile shares my mat,' Thabisa says without embarrassment.

Emile is about to speak when the background buzz of Bulawayo becomes a cacophony. Emile is first to the doorway. He listens briefly before springing into the deepening dark. He calls a question to a passing warrior who shouts something as he hurries on.

'The Khumalos are coming!' he reports as Thabisa fills the doorway.

Richard jumps up and Ulwazi follows. All four of them crowd out of the hut into chaos. Messengers run back and forth while a contingent of the Fasimba garrison turns out, fully armed.

The gates to Bulawayo are closed and barred; torches flame, dancing orange against the velvet dark. High above hangs the silver sliver of a new moon.

Shouts jump from one guard post to the next. The herds of cattle, confined in their pens, add their slow, sad voices to the discord. More and more torches bloom along the town perimeter, chasing the night from the walls.

The pre-party atmosphere of muted excitement and intense preparations is forgotten in a surge of apprehension.

The entrance to the royal enclosure opens and Shaka emerges, flanked by servants bearing lit brands. His councillors converge on his reassuring presence.

Napoleon is there quickly, in bare feet, breeches and a thin linen shirt. Richard thinks how rare it is to see the man out of uniform. Tall, stiff-backed Ngomane appears from the right, while Nqoboka trots over from the main gateway. Mgobozi, not grinning for once, walks swiftly beside trusty Mdlaka who towers above him. Richard squeezes Ulwazi's hand and crosses the central square to join them.

As Shaka's presence is felt through the town, the noise abates. He calls out to the sentries. 'You sent a message. Who disrupts my evening?' His bass filling the space relinquished by a hundred worried words. Richard sees the gathering relax.

'A messenger at the gates, mighty Shaka. From the Khumalo chief. His people are nearby. He begs an audience.' The sentry's voice is shrill and strained.

'What is this chief's name?' Shaka asks, his feigned ignorance a calculated slight. The sentry shouts over the wall.

'Mzilikazi!' comes the reply, loud enough to need no relay to Shaka's ears.

'Ha! Zwide's grandson. He rules at my enemy's pleasure. This will be an interesting encounter. Tell this messenger, Mzilikazi may approach my walls but he must come alone!'

Within a quarter of an hour, the sentries see Mzilikazi in the flamelight of their torches and announce him.

Shaka is installed beneath the council tree, his advisers

around him. Richard and Bonaparte are to the chief's right. Nqoboka is on the left, deep in conversation with Mdlaka. The others sit at Shaka's feet.

Two companies of Fasimba flank the space between the entrance and the dignitaries.

'Open the gates!' orders Shaka. As the wood and brush doors are dragged aside, a tall figure strides confidently forward. The interior of Bulawayo is well illuminated, flames casting the visitor in parody. His shape, exaggerated against the walls, looks like a monstrous shadow puppet.

His small head is almost round, as are his oversized buttocks. His long spider-like legs top petite feet. He carries a small paunch at his waist. His face is lost in shadow but his eyes spark as he studies the scene. He carries no shield or spear.

Shaka does not rise. The gates are closed. Mzilikazi drops to his knees, bowing his face into the dirt. He remains a picture of perfect obeisance until Shaka grows impatient. 'Rise, chief of the Khumalos, and tell me why you come to my door in the dead of night?'

Mzilikazi raises his shaven head on his long neck, visible now in the ring of light surrounding the parade ground. His face is coated in fine, sandy earth. He does not wipe it away.

'Forgive my untimely arrival, mighty Shaka. I come to beg protection for my people. I am Mzilikazi, grandson of Zwide, your mortal enemy. I renounce my affiliation to the viper! That bitter old man killed my father and then my cousin. He has laid waste to my lands. It is no longer safe for my people to remain. We throw ourselves on your mercy!' His voice is high and grating but he does not whine nor is there shame in his tone.

Shaka does not reply immediately but studies the man before him. Sniggers and whispers undulate through the crowd as they point at Mzilikazi's physical eccentricities.

'I suspected no rift between you and Zwide. Did he not grant you the throne upon your father's death?'

Richard can hear caution thrumming through Shaka's words.

Mzilikazi stands awkwardly, only to bow again. 'Yes, lord king. I took the throne of my murdered father. But I held my hate tight. When my cousin, Donda, warned you of Zwide's ambitions, retribution was swift. He killed my cousin and ransacked Khumalo lands, driving off many cattle. What remains of my people and my herds, I bring to you.'

Mzilikazi subsides, drawing a deep breath. Hearing the lowing of the royal herd, his eyes seek out the corral beyond the spectators. A brief smile lights up his face.

'What would you have me do with this gift?' Shaka asks, projecting his most regal tone.

'Accept us. Take us in. Allow us to become Zulus. Let us be part of this new nation you are building.'

Richard squirms. Mzilikazi's words are calculated to win Shaka over. The Khumalo glances first right then left. His expression is neutral until he spies Napoleon's paler face. His head juts forward and he screws up his eyes as he peers at the Frenchman. A scowl sweeps over his face before he regains control. But then he sees Richard. His mouth drops open and he raises an accusatory finger.

Shaka shoots a glance towards Richard and Bonaparte and frowns. 'Why do you point at my Englishman?' he asks in an annoyed voice.

'I have seen this man before. He was part of a force that invaded my territory! I am surprised to find him occupying a place of honour in mighty Shaka's court.'

Mzilikazi's eyes flash dangerously and his fingers bunch into fists. 'It was the strangest force I have encountered. White men in uniform commanding a force of black soldiers dressed in white, wielding spears that spat. I took them for a Portuguese raiding party until I spied other warriors, disciplined men with shields like these your honour guard carry.' He indicates the Fasimba lining the route from the gateway, proud behind their white shields.

Shaka turns to Richard and asks quietly, 'This is the man you shot?'

Richard nods apologetically.

'The upstart who mocked my warriors and threatened to invade my territory?' Shaka's voice rises. 'To see if I deserve my reputation?'

Richard spreads his hands and nods again. Shaka grins at him before turning to the supplicant Khumalo chief. 'It seems you have changed your tune. You kneel in the dirt at my feet, begging to be accepted as a Zulu, when you so recently spouted disrespect?'

For a second Richard thinks Mzilikazi will deny it. His angry eyes spark dangerously and he clenches his teeth so tightly the sinews in his neck vibrate. But he drops his gaze and lowers his forehead back into the loose dirt. When he rises, again coated in dust, his face is pleading.

'I spoke in anger. Forgive me, I beg you! I come to save my people. To make them yours. Do not punish them for the careless words of their chief, spat out on the eve of battle.

Take what cattle we have left. Welcome my warriors into your regiments. Let my women and children swell your ranks.' Mzilikazi's voice is tense and shrill but Richard does not doubt his sincerity.

The Khumalo chief squats on his heels and rubs his thin beard with his left hand. 'As for me. Do with me as you will. I ask only this. Let me die in your service and with a spear in my hand.'

Shaka's stern face creases and then cracks into a grin. He lets out his bull-bellow laugh and claps Nqoboka on the back so hard his long neck slams his chin against his chest. When he raises his proud head, complete with puckered scar running from nose to ear, he manages a sickly grin, but his eyes bore into Mzilikazi. Richard can see the loathing. Nqoboka whispers to his monarch, gesturing aggressively with his large hands towards Mzilikazi. His brass arm band flashes in the firelight. Shaka nods thoughtfully.

'I accept the offer of your cattle. I accept the service of your warriors. I welcome your women and children.'

Richard sees the tension leave Mzilikazi's body. His jaw relaxes, his teeth part, and his shoulders dip a fraction.

'So, I am left with only you to consider. What use are you to me? You carry the long spears I have made obsolete. You turned your back on my fighters in your arrogance and paid the price! What need have I of a chief driven from his lands? What need have I of a commander whose judgement is suspect?'

No one moves. No one speaks. Even the cattle stop lowing. Mzilikazi sucks in a lungful of air and lifts his huge buttocks from the backs of his legs. He opens his arms wide, palms facing Shaka. 'Enlist me with my men. I ask no great rank, just the chance to prove myself. Send me on the most hopeless mission. I will not baulk! But first, hear the news I bring of Zwide's intentions.'

Shaka leans forward, his muscular frame bronzed in the torchlight. Richard knows he has enjoyed belittling Mzilikazi, blood relative of his sworn enemy. But all that falls away in an instant. Now the same man offers him that which he values most.

Shaka stands and gestures towards the royal enclosure. 'Come! I will hear you.' His councillors are dismissed. Richard and Emile walk back to find Ulwazi and Thabisa deep in conversation.

Richard wakes to find Ulwazi has already disentangled herself from his sleeping grip. He is alone in the hut. Emile and Thabisa are sleeping in one of the shelters set aside for the Ama-Wombe.

He stretches lazily and opens his eyes. He listens intently to the sounds outside. The ground shakes as the vast herds are escorted to pasture, complaining as they go, the fluting imprecations of the herd boys pitched high above the beasts' deep-chested, mournful bellowing. The smell of cattle and dung and dust drift into the hut.

Richard sits up. As the sounds of the cattle recede, he can hear excited chatter shuttling from hut to hut. He is not used to so many high-pitched voices. Bulawayo is a predominantly male place. But today it is full of women's calls and the happy cries of children.

Soon the smell of dung is replaced by the mouth-watering

tang of roasting meat. Clambering to his feet, Richard sees the hearth is cold, the grey-white soot unswept. Ulwazi's breakfast bowl is unwashed.

He smiles. His wife is fastidious. She must be inordinately excited. Guilty at how easily he takes her for granted, Richard clears the hearth and sets a small fire to warm some grain porridge. Most Zulus eat it cold but Richard prefers it warm. He eyes the remains of his wife's breakfast in a hollowed-out gourd. The chief staple of the Zulus is milk curds they call *amazi*, it is too sour for his palate and he shudders.

While he waits for the dung cakes to catch, Richard peers outside. The sky is a pale blue and the air pleasantly warm. Judging from the sun's position close to the horizon, he reckons it is not long after six in the morning. He pulls his watch from his shabby waistcoat and is pleased to see his estimate is accurate.

Once his porridge is warm, Richard adds a spoon of honey, takes his bowl with him and sits outside, against the domed frame of his hut. He spoons mouthful after mouthful without paying his meal much attention. The texture is like crumbly mashed potato but the taste is clear and fresh, overlaid by the floral syrup of the honey.

He finds himself watching two women working outside their hut. This is more of the beer making he watched the day before. The women tend large clay pots of liquid left to cool overnight. They pour liquid from one container into a larger vat, before adding the wort he saw set aside yesterday. Handfuls of sorghum and maize malt are added.

The brew is stirred with a long wooden spoon. Both women peer into the container and nod contentedly. One ducks into the hut and reappears carrying a fur blanket which she drapes over the large vessel. Richard imagines rapid fermentation will produce beer by the time the sun sets, although he knows the process usually stretches over several days. This beer will be young and less potent. Ideal for a long festival.

Richard dips back into his hut to wipe his and his wife's bowls clean. The unusual noises of the overcrowded capital drop away and he peers outside. Shouts ring out in the hush before he hears one word relayed from mouth to mouth. 'Khumalos!'

Mzilikazi appears from the royal enclosure alone. He is beaming and nods enthusiastically to anyone looking in his direction. He strides forward, his small head bobbing on his long neck, thin legs swallowing the yards, powered by his exaggerated haunches.

A mass of faces appears through the open gateway. At first, the guards block the way, but Mzilikazi rushes over on his petite feet, berating them. 'What are you doing? Did you not hear Shaka decree my people to be Zulus?' His voice is high and grating but oozes confidence. 'Let them through! They come to enjoy the *umkhozi.*'

Richard senses someone join him, although his eyes are locked on Mzilikazi. The man is dangerous. Already he is issuing orders.

'I forget what Bill told me. What will happen at this *umkhozi*?' Bonaparte's Zulu accent is improving.

'It is their first-fruits ceremony. Ulwazi explained it to me. Shaka will bless the land, and receive medicines to strengthen him, as will his army. There will be a full dress review. New laws will be announced. Warriors will question Shaka without fear of punishment and he must reply. Then there will be singing and dancing, drinking and eating.'

Napoleon grunts in thanks but Richard can tell his attention is elsewhere. He too is studying Mzilikazi.

'What are you thinking?' Richard asks.

'Which of my marshals this man will prove to be. Will he be Davout, the best of them? Perhaps not a skilled administrator like Berthier? Tenacious Massena? Is he a MacDonald sprung from foreign blood? Or Grouchy who did not come to my aid at the very end? Murat who loved me until it was inexpedient? Brave Lannes or treacherous Marmont?' Napoleon looks towards the Khumalos spilling into the central square and Richard follows his gaze.

'Where will they put them all?' Richard wonders aloud as a gaggle of Shaka's advisers bustle through the milling bodies and shout for calm.

Soon orders are being barked, messengers despatched, and Mzilikazi's ego smoothed by statesmanlike Ngomane.

Poles are slid aside, opening the empty cattle pens. Richard watches with interest. Surely Mzilikazi will take it as an insult if his people are herded into cowpat-spattered corrals?

Sniggers of laughter escape a few watching warriors, young men of the Fasimba regiment, their muscular bodies oiled for the festivities.

Ngomane swivels his head on his long neck. His eyes unerringly lock onto the soldiers, even as they wipe any hint of amusement from their faces. His rich, firm voice carries easily. 'Gather your regiment! Vacate your huts! You will camp in the cattle pens while our guests, these newly anointed Zulus, take shelter around your hearths.'

There is a brief murmur of discontent but the coordinated stares of Ngomane, Mdlaka and Mgobozi soon quash any objection. 'You!' shouts Ngomane, pointing to one of the sniggerers. 'Run to the herd boys. Tell them they must move the Bulawayo cattle to nearby homesteads until the festival is over. They are to leave only those beasts set aside for the feasting!' The warrior jumps away, settling into a dog trot before he reaches the gateway.

Looking around, Richard spots Nqoboka hanging back among the onlookers. The scowl on his face is one of undisguised loathing.

Richard tries to count the Khumalos as they wait awkwardly at the centre of the capital. The residents of Bulawayo drift away. They are still in a party mood. Last minute preparations must be completed. Bodies need oiling, hair dressing, food cooking, songs and dances rehearsing.

His tally is rough but there can be no more than two hundred Khumalos. Shaka's regiments may gain a few dozen soldiers and a handful of apprentices, but that is all. He shakes his head. None of the other clans or tribes that have drifted in over the past months is large. But they add up.

Shaka has not been seen since welcoming Mzilikazi. Ulwazi tells Richard he is in seclusion, attended by doctors administering medicines, beneficent spells, and conducting the ceremonies to cleanse and strengthen him.

Ulwazi's skin is glowing. Her eyes are extraordinarily bright. Her hair is piled regally atop her head. Her temples are shaved. Richard cannot help but reach out a hand. He thrills at the unfamiliar feel beneath his fingertips. Her white teeth flash. He wonders what techniques she and Thabisa use to achieve so devastating an effect? He wants to ask but knows she will not give up such secrets to a man.

The sun climbs in the sky and Richard dozes on his mat in the relative cool of his hut. Ulwazi comes and goes, chattering with excitement then falling quiet. She does not want a meal at midday so Richard does not eat either. It is a little after three in the afternoon, according to his scrupulously wound watch, when Richard ventures back outside.

He can see the Khumalos have moved into the Fasimba quarters and are doing their best to adorn themselves for the festival. Richard wonders where Mzilikazi's promised cattle are? Shaka loves his herds. It is resentment over captured cattle that will lead Mzilikazi to defy Shaka, Richard recalls from his days at university. When will that be? Two years, perhaps?

As the sun dips towards the horizon, Richard watches from his doorway as messengers fan out from the royal enclosure. 'Assemble, assemble!' they chorus.

Quickly, every adult in Bulawayo shuffles into ranks, ringing the central space. Thousands wait in almost total silence. Anticipation is thick in the air, deadening sound. Minutes tick by. Richard stands with Ulwazi and Thabisa. Emile is lost in the crowd with his regiment.

Bonaparte strolls over nonchalantly with General Thibault in tow, as if unaffected by the atmosphere of expectation. Richard is not fooled. The Frenchman wears his immaculate

Chasseurs uniform with boots that glisten. He lifts his ubiquitous bicorn hat and bows to the women, as if no one else is present. His dreamy, dark-blue eyes twinkle.

Thibault parrots his master, looking a little threadbare in his uniform, although his boots are buffed to perfection.

As the entrance to the royal enclosure opens, the quiet becomes a hush. Shaka strides out, bedecked in leopard skins and crowned with red feathers.

'*Bayete*!' shouts the assembled population.

'*Bayete*!' This time even Richard gives the salute.

'*Bayete*!' Even Napoleon and reluctant Thibault join in.

Shaka points his tiny ceremonial spear at the setting sun and spits a jet of blood-coloured medicine.

His warriors cry out, 'He stabs with the red tail!' The whole thing is repeated and, miraculously, Shaka is able to spout red liquid again.

The ceremony is brief. Shaka turns on his heel and returns to the royal enclosure. As soon as he is lost from sight, beer and food start to circulate.

Ulwazi laughs and hugs Richard, before dragging him to the fire of a neighbour where beer is being handed around. He accepts a beaker and sips experimentally, trying to distract his nose with the scent of roasting beef, a rare treat in the largely vegetarian Zulu diet.

Napoleon and Thibault have followed and accept drinks, grateful for something that makes them part of the festivities, Richard suspects. The beer is opaque, almost creamy. The texture is thick and gritty with a yeasty tang. Richard braves a second sip and waits. He knows this is the trick.

The flavour sits heavy and sour on his tongue but he does

not find it unpleasant, unlike the cloying milk curds. He tips the beaker and quaffs more enthusiastically, drawing nods of approval from around the fire.

Bonaparte tosses back a gulp and manages a weak smile. Thibault sniffs his cup suspiciously and wrinkles his nose, extracting guffaws from the older men.

With his fingers still greasy from choice cuts of meat, Richard finds himself pulled from the fire into a seething mass of dancing bodies. He has downed three portions of beer without much effect. He usually needs to be drunk to risk venturing onto a dancefloor but Ulwazi won't let go.

She gyrates to the rhythm of the drums and raises her voice to join hundreds in a joyous melody. He tries to keep his hands on her hips. She feels so alive. Beneath his hands, her skin is slick with perfumed oil.

His feet begin to move, he sways his hips, rotates his neck and tries to mouth a semblance of the song. The night shrouds his embarrassment, despite the flickering fires, and his wife beams her approval.

He does not blush nor does he stop. Instead, he pulls Ulwazi close and shouts into her delicate ear, 'I am Zulu!'

Her laughter blends with the music. There is no mockery in it, only pleasure. By the time they stop dancing there is no sign of Napoleon or Thibault.

Most of the fires have been allowed to die down. A few younger men stagger about smelling sourer than the beer they have drunk. They are teased and prodded by their elders as they pass and ordered to bed.

It is time to turn in. As they head for their hut, Richard

thinks he sees Emile being led away by Thabisa. He hopes so.

Richard wakes with a clear head to the sound of singing. Again, Ulwazi is already up. She stands in the doorway lifting her voice to join with the giant choir outside. Her crystal alto dances over the deeper tones of the assembled army.

Richard springs up and joins his wife, looking over her shoulder. A faint haze is visible in the dawn light, but it is rapidly dissipating, as the whole Zulu army crowds towards the royal enclosure.

He sees the colours of every regiment: the white of the Fasimba; the brown of the Ama-Wombe and the rest of the Belebele brigade; the cream and black shared by the regiments of the Izim-Pohlo brigade.

He rests a hand on Ulwazi's shoulder and she leans against him with her hip. The front ranks shake the vertical posts of the royal enclosure. The singing peters out and a single voice, deep and tempered by time, calls out.

'*Woza ke, woza lapa*!' The refrain is taken up by those close to Shaka's residence, rippling out from the point of origin until every warrior's voice repeats the words, '*Woza ke, woza lapa*!' Come out, come hither! The chant repeats for a minute and then another.

A group of women's voices join in from the far side of the wall.

'The royal women!' Ulwazi announces as the gate is pulled open from inside and Shaka finally appears.

Richard is surprised by his appearance. In place of his red lourie bird feathers, he is festooned with ears of corn, a camouflage of leaves, along with string after string of beads.

His forearms are decorated with a profusion of bangles.

Shaka acknowledges the royal women with a respectful bow and acclaims his warriors with open arms. He strides through the massed ranks to the cattle pens. They look forlorn, devoid of the burgeoning herd so beloved of Shaka, the symbol of his wealth and how far he has risen, Richard thinks.

Just thirty prime animals stand docilely before their owner. The first rays of the sun breach the horizon as the king of the Zulus again squirts a jet of red liquid between his teeth. Richard imagines crimson spattering the flanks of the cows, dripping down their legs into the hoof prints that pattern the earth.

All is quiet now around the capital, quiet enough for Richard to hear the breaking of pottery.

'Shaka breaks the *uselwa* gourd.'

Richard does not know the word. Ulwazi senses his uncertainty. 'It is the dried shell of a fruit, decorated with beadwork. The flesh has medicinal properties.'

A trickle of grey smoke rises above the heads of the assembled Zulus. A whiff of breeze nudges the haze across the town until its odour reaches Richard.

It smells a little like sage. He inhales deeply, reminded of stiff Sunday dinners with his Aunt Patricia. For a moment he imagines returning to her Victorian villa in his threadbare clothes to tell her he has become a Zulu.

'*U! U! U!*' chant the urgent voices of the men.

'They are exorcising all evil and disease from the land.' Ulwazi's voice is reverent, as if she is in church. More and more smoke billows skyward. 'Shaka adds medicine to the fire. He burns wormwood.'

It is the hallucinogenic in absinthe, Richard recalls. He cannot stop himself drawing in a gulp of the aromatic smoke. He detects another aroma, not smelled since his university days: it is cannabis. Ulwazi breathes deeply too, and grins at him, before dissolving into giggles. Richard smiles broadly and finds he cannot stop. His cheeks soon ache. Laughter fills the air from hundreds of mouths.

Shaka barks a command and a murmur of approval swells to a roar.

'He is ordering the slaughter of the cattle. Half are a sacrifice to our ancestral spirits, the rest in praise of the king. Listen!'

Richard concentrates on the recitation taken up by almost every voice. They are naming Shaka's deeds and those of his ancestors. By the time it is finished, all the cattle are dead and the men assigned to butcher them are already at work.

Richard can hear blades slicing into flesh and the sound of joints being dislocated. Firepits are kindled to cook the glut of meat.

Chapter Seven

January 1819

Richard tries to spot Napoleon in the milling throng without luck. He scans the melee for Thibault but there is no sign. He seeks a glimpse of Emile but cannot identify the French Zulu warrior. At last, he catches sight of a familiar face. English Bill, stooped but wiry, flanked by his two youngest wives, dancing an improvised jig as the other five clap a rhythm, beaming broadly.

Richard smiles at the old reprobate and hugs Ulwazi. 'I am glad we are married,' he whispers in her ear.

She pinches him playfully on the arm. 'That is proper,' she replies, 'I am glad too.' When he looks up again, breaking their kiss, English Bill and his wives have vanished as a hint of order creeps into the kaleidoscope of bodies thronging the central square.

The sun is overhead. Noon is near. The gates of the royal enclosure open and Shaka appears. Gone are the symbols of harvest, replaced with full battle dress. As they see their ruler, the warriors form up in regiments, and the unmarried women do likewise.

Ulwazi nestles against him. '*Vutwamini,* the maidens' regiment,' she tells him. He cannot fathom her mood. Instead, he studies the three lines of young women, each close to a thousand strong.

To European eyes they are almost naked, wearing only a fringed apron some four inches long; although bracelets adorn wrists and many wear bead necklaces.

A clay mound ten feet high has been constructed at the royal end of town, overlooking the parade ground. Shaka escorts his mother up the ramp to sit on a roll of rush mats. He seats another haughty female figure to her right, before guiding a less confident woman to his mother's left.

'Nomcoba, his sister and Nomzintlanga, his half-sister,' Ulwazi explains. Richard has never seen them before, so secure is the royal household. Finally, Shaka draws Pampata forward, and indicates she is to sit at Nandi's feet.

Shaka takes up his position below his mother but elevated sufficiently to look out over the sea of his people. The regiments of his army, each a thousand strong now, are arrayed to his right, while the three thousand unmarried women are aligned to the left.

Richard notices men and women searching for a particular face. Every few moments, there is a smile of recognition.

The gap between the men and women is about two hundred yards. Without any apparent signal, both groups move slowly inwards, feet dancing and voices lifted in a lilting call and response.

The atmosphere is thick with yearning. Childhood sweethearts sing to each other. Eligible women eye prospective husbands hungrily. Frustrated men, some young, but others close to their middle years, ogle forbidden fruit.

Despite their fluid, expressive movements, the lines maintain an almost perfect straightness. Each block of warriors raises and lowers shields of a uniform colour, white, black and white, dun and cream, their ostrich plumes waving as they sway and stamp. Spearhead after spearhead glints in the sunlight.

Richard feels the earth tremble as choreographed feet beat a rhythm underpinning their seductive song. As the front rows draw within a few paces, they recoil like a wave before rolling together again. They draw close and recede a second and a third time, before halting some distance apart. Shaka steps down from his viewpoint to stride between them.

Shaka lifts his head, inhales deeply, and parts his lips. His fine voice is as deep as a canyon, as rich as spring growth, and as powerful as a lion's roar. He sings with his whole body. Chest heaving, arms gesturing, he walks between the men and women of his nation.

He reaches the coda, and song leaders sing out the opening line for the massed ranks to repeat. Richard marvels at how faultlessly they pick up the new composition.

'The leaders of the song have practised for a week!' Ulwazi reveals with a smile. It seems his thoughts are an open book to her. When the song is finished, another is begun. This one has a quicker tempo, more suited to women's voices, and they naturally take the lead, with the men joining in on the chorus.

Richard drifts away on a beautiful wall of sound, falling into the story of a warrior seeking to prove himself, while his mother worries at home. More songs follow, all seemingly familiar to the massed choir; some sound sad and others gallop along, accompanied by swaying and stamping.

Finally, the assembled voices fall quiet and the ranks shuffle into a packed semicircle in front of the mud platform.

Shaka takes centre stage. Richard thinks he is going to sing again but instead he begins a shuffling step. A hidden drum begins a beat and Shaka's feet match the rhythm. His leopard-skin cloak sways with his body, his miniature shield and spear held aloft in one pose after another.

His red-feathered head rolls left and right. Richard can only see the whites of his eyes, as if he is in a trance. His great muscles writhe rhythmically beneath glossy skin.

The tempo increases, doubling the drumbeats. Now Shaka is leaping, spinning while airborne, in a display more akin to gymnastics than any dance Richard has seen before.

The performance reaches a dramatic conclusion as Shaka leaps higher still, landing on both feet as the final reverberation of the drum fades. His people whoop and cheer and he beams with pleasure before raising his arms for calm.

'Why is it, if a coward is a contemptible creature, that a double coward is held in high esteem?' he riddles, barely out of breath. His people lean forward to catch the answer. 'Because it is *i-gwala-gwala*!'

Richard is pleased he catches the witticism as thousands of voices roar in laughter and approval. The Zulu for coward is *i-gwala* but double this to *i-gwala-gwala* and it becomes the red lourie, whose flight feathers are an award for outstanding bravery.

Ulwazi squeezes his arm and smiles. He feels like a schoolboy praised by his favourite teacher. He hears Aunt Patricia scoffing and returns his attention to the festival as a new bout of dancing breaks out, with warriors and maidens matched in large groups.

The warriors without dance partners ring the parade area, keeping the beat with their short spears against the taut hide of their shields. These include the resident Fasimbas, who are still being punished for their lack of courtesy to Mzilikazi.

Every dancer is bathed in sweat. Some stumble and are replaced by fresh feet. After almost an hour, Richard sees groups entirely composed of men, dancing enthusiastically in front of their peers without embarrassment.

As a particularly slow dance comes to an end, the two halves of each group peel away to form companies that advance towards the mound, acclaiming Shaka and his mother, Nandi, Queen Mother, first lady of the Zulu nation.

'*Ndlovukazi*!' The Great She Elephant! They cry in her honour. Shaka stands behind his seated mother in breach of all etiquette, promoting her with a satisfied smile on his face.

Richard imagines the Zulu king is remembering the slights and struggles he and Nandi endured before his rise. He catches a glimpse of Napoleon surveying the scene. The former emperor is closer to the royal party. Is he also remembering earlier times or reflecting on the strange journey that brought him to the Zulu court?

When all have saluted, the formal proceedings break up. Ulwazi tells Richard there will be more eating and drinking. It will be a noisy night. He wonders why she looks so pleased, until she drags him into their hut and pushes him down on the sleeping mat.

Richard is tired. Ulwazi's passion raged from late afternoon until dawn. He has never seen her like this. Standing by the door frame, watching for the first lightening of the sky along the horizon, he wonders at the urgency she showed, aggressive yet vulnerable, insatiable, as if only their physical intimacy kept her alive.

He turns to look at her spent body, lying awkwardly on the mat, one arm thrown above her head, one leg bent at the knee towards the hearth. She looks like she has fallen from the sky. He feels a lurch in his stomach, peering through the gloom of the hut until he sees her ribcage rising and falling.

Outside is quiet now. Even the most resolute party-goers have crawled to their bed rolls. The air is saturated, although it is not raining. He looks at his watch. Dawn should be spilling over the horizon but a wet fog is settling over Bulawayo, muffling the light and sounds of morning.

Richard watches figures stoop beneath their hut entrances to stand stiffly, studying the unseasonable weather. He sees English Bill and his wives file from their hut. Each wife has a bundle balanced on the *inkatha* atop her head. English Bill carries a satchel of leather slung over one shoulder. He grips the strap tightly. Richard has no doubt it contains the gold coins from Bonaparte.

He watches as they walk towards the city gates, until a distinctive figure appears out of the opaque air, stealing his attention. Long, spindly legs step stealthily, while a small head swivels this way and that, as if expecting an attack.

Richard follows Mzilikazi's route as he skirts the far side of the central square, shying away from the waking figures in front of their huts. He is not close enough to read his expression but hairs stir on the back of Richard's neck.

He shivers theatrically, certain it is not the damp chill of the air. He shot this man. He has no doubt the Khumalo chief wants his revenge. He can see it in his eyes whenever he is near. Where has he been? Where is he going? He emerged from the direction of the cattle pens, where the Fasimba camp in makeshift shelters.

He is heading towards the royal enclosure. For a second, Richard considers heading him off or running to warn the guards. He shakes his head and relaxes. Let the guards do their duty. They will not let Mzilikazi enter before their ruler has risen for the day!

Richard is ducking into his hut to wake Ulwazi in the gentlest way, when a muffled voice pulls him back outside.

'My English friend! I am glad you are up.' Napoleon's compelling voice is usually soft, and in the fog, it is muted. Richard smiles and raises a hand in greeting. They walk off together. He will let Ulwazi sleep.

'Yesterday was quite something,' he offers.

Bonaparte nods. 'But today will be fascinating! Shaka submits to the scrutiny of his army.'

The regiments march past Shaka, who stands alone as he reviews his men. As each cohort passes their king, they wheel to form up in close order. When they are all assembled, a single figure steps out from the ranks of each regiment to stand before Shaka.

There are eleven regiments on parade, so quickly has the Zulu army grown, thanks to the influx of Mthethwas and Qwabes, along with fragments of numerous other clans.

Richard recognises Emile's Ama-Wombe, standing proudly with their brown shields. These are the oldest men in the Zulu *impi*. Retained in service when it was time for them to retire, they form the bedrock upon which Shaka has built his military might.

Beside them stand the white shields of the Fasimba. The youngest men in military service, men who remember no other commander. These are the men Shaka intends to make entirely his own, a personal guard of fanatical loyalty. Richard thinks of Bonaparte's Old Guard, his trusted veterans, who combined both functions.

The Fasimba look subdued to Richard, still smarting from their dressing down before the festivities began. They do not retaliate when their elders tease them, keeping their eyes fixed on Shaka.

Flanking the Fasimba, closer to Richard, are the other regiments of the Belebele division: the U-Kangela and the recently formed Izin-Tenjana, made up of men born at the end of the last century. They bear dark-tan and light-tan shields respectively.

The regiments of the Bachelors' brigade are further away from Richard but he knows their names. They are the Jubingqwanga, the U-Dlambedlu and four more recent regiments that form a sub-division: the Um-Gumanqa, Isi-Pezi, U-Mbonambi and U-Nteke. Their shields are all variations of cream and black in differing proportions and patterns. Richard cannot tell them apart, just as he can often not distinguish between cows in the royal herds, something every six-year-old herd boy does easily.

Facing Richard is the final regiment, the Izi-cwe, sometimes known as Ngomane's own, as he brought the regiment over to Shaka wholesale upon the death of Dingiswayo and the collapse of the Mthethwa state. Their shields are a reddish hue.

Bonaparte joins Richard, who senses his enervated mood. Thibault hovers in the background. 'Magnificent! Look how Shaka's army has grown! How many men could he call upon when we were first escorted to Bulawayo?' asks Napoleon breathlessly.

'Less than four hundred,' Richard replies, 'and now he has close to ten thousand!'

Shaka claps his hands and nods his head. The spokesman for the senior men of the Ama-Wombe steps forward. He has grey hair and his body is striped with scars but his bearing is stately. He bows respectfully to Shaka then looks him directly in the eyes. Without flinching, he calls out his question in a sing-song tenor that reaches the rearmost ranks.

Richard translates for Napoleon. 'Why do you promote outsiders over the heads of your own people?' There are murmurs of agreement from the Fasimba, and for once they are in tune with their elders on either side.

'This goes straight to the heart of the matter!' enthuses Bonaparte. Shaka has addressed this matter in council and in front of his *impi* but he betrays no annoyance.

'Any man who joins my army becomes a Zulu. Promotion is a matter of merit.' Napoleon murmurs in agreement. A roar of approval greets the reply, loudest, Richard notes, from the ranks of the newly constituted regiments, where most men have only recently shifted allegiance.

The second questioner takes a pace forward. He speaks for the Jubingqwanga who are all over thirty years of age. His voice is deep and echoes around the vast *kraal*. 'Why were the E-Langeni and the Qwabes treated so lightly while we slaughtered the Butelezis and Ndwandwes when they stood against us?' Richard repeats the question in French while Shaka nods and paces before the rapt audience.

'Brother does not eat brother, and three brothers are better than one.' Richard can tell which regiments contain E-Langeni and Qwabe soldiers, as they raise their shields and shout their approval.

The questioner hesitates, as if he is not satisfied. Shaka's lips tighten but after a pause, he nods again. 'The E-Langeni, the clan of my mother, yielded, accepting my overlordship without bloodshed. The Qwabes, the clan most closely associated with our own, gave offence and balance was restored. Their chief died. Our southern borders are secured. So, they became one with us again.'

Here, Shaka pauses for effect, eyes roving over the questioner's regiment. 'The Butelezis are a different story, are they not? Their chief, Pungashe, he called me a barking pup and threatened to beat me with a stick to silence me. How I barked! My *impi* was a great stick with which I beat the Butelezi.'

Cheers from the Fasimba regiment at the memory of their overwhelming victory. Shaka acknowledges his youngest regiment while Richard winces, recalling the indiscriminate killing of women and children.

'Speaking of the Ndwandwes, no one should have to ask why they must be dealt with severely. They are the greatest threat to our way of life. We have beaten them but they are not broken. We have killed his sons, but Zwide still lives. He plots against us and tries to turn our neighbours into enemies.' Every warrior in the capital beats his spear against his shield in agreement.

It takes a long time for calm to descend but when it does, the third questioner steps proudly before Shaka. 'Why do we not strike against the Ndwandwes before they grow too strong?' he asks on behalf of the U-Kangela in a whistling baritone.

Shaka beams his approval at the question. 'This is fine. I am pleased my soldiers think as I do. The time is coming, be assured of that.' Richard sees Napoleon nodding with a satisfied look on his face.

'He wishes to break his arch-rival forever. My cannon will give him this victory!' Richard can only just hear the shouting Frenchman over the roars of the pumped-up regiments.

The next question comes from the U-Dlambedlu regiment, nicknamed the wild men. Their representative is tall with staring eyes and hair teased into tufts. 'Why does the king not marry and father heirs to inherit his kingdom?' This time Shaka scowls and the questioner takes an involuntary step back, glancing over his shoulder, accusing his fellow wild men with a panicked expression.

Shaka steps up to him and grasps him by the shoulder. His face is calm again and he smiles, his face kindly. 'Do not worry. You ask the question on my own mother's lips. I cannot chastise you for that! Listen, this is my answer. A bull has a peaceful life until the young bulls he sires dispute his supremacy. Thereafter, all is friction and conflict.' Bulawayo is silent as ten thousand soldiers ponder Shaka's words. A bird of prey calls overhead, a piercing two-tone cry.

It is the turn of the second Izi-cwe, the regiment of Ngomane but founded by Shaka when he was Dingiswayo's protégé. Their spokesman is very handsome. He is only an inch shorter than Shaka as he steps close. His broad shoulders and highly defined musculature do nothing to detract from his bright eyes, strong nose and firm chin. Richard imagines how many of the maidens dancing opposite him had hoped to catch his eye.

'Tell us, mighty Shaka, when will the warriors be allowed to marry?' Strong murmurs of interest, particularly from the regiments made up of older age groups.

'Young warriors should not marry. Their all-consuming duty is to protect us from our enemies. If they have family ties, they will not do this so effectively. When they grow older, and have proven themselves, then I am prepared to consider individual cases, regiments too, if they have achieved something remarkable. But until our borders are safe, the ban on marriage will be strictly enforced, save in exceptional cases.' Richard is peering at the ranks of the Ama-Wombe. He sees heads turn towards a soldier he cannot see. He suspects it is Emile.

The questioner does not yield his ground but speaks again. 'Must all the most beautiful young women live lives of frustration, denied the pleasures of motherhood?'

Shaka glances at his mother and then to Pampata. 'A mature woman is a better mother. Fewer, well-spaced children fare better than too many.'

Before there can be any reaction from the gathered troops, the Izi-cwe spokesman presses on. 'Must they be wasted then, on the few old men who survive the wars through caution, whilst the bravest go to their graves never knowing the tenderness of wife and children?' The handsome speaker's voice trembles with conviction.

'He makes a strong point,' Bonaparte admits. 'Look at him, what fine children he would sire, what strength his blood would add to the Zulu race!' Richard remembers years of celibacy before his passionate dalliance with Fanny, before his marriage to Ulwazi. He thinks of the little bump just beginning to show. Shaka is the ultimate dictator: to seek control over reproduction.

The Zulu chief wipes sweat from his brow. Before he lowers his hand, his fingers run around the head ring he wears. 'Consider Mgobozi. He is a fine, mature bull. He will sire great fighting stock, far better than a dozen untried youths. All of you who are my age or younger, look at me! I am the king, I have the power, and yet I have not taken a wife. I do not ask you to step where I do not step. Remember the thorns scattered across this very ground! Did I not stamp on them just as I asked you to do?'

Spears sound against shields, voices rise in acclamation and the Izi-cwe representative returns to his fellows looking crestfallen.

'*Bayete*!' call ten thousand voices as ten thousand feet stamp the ground. '*Bayete*! *Bayete*!' Richard wonders how long such devotion can be sustained as the regiments fall out.

Bonaparte and Thibault drift away in conversation. Richard catches a brief glimpse of Mzilikazi, grinning broadly, chanting wildly with everyone else, before the press of bodies obscures him from view.

Bulawayo seems unnaturally quiet after the throng of the harvest festival. Richard's notebook suggests January has become February. Summer still clings to the land with febrile fingers.

He is walking towards the river, noticing how few trees or bushes survived the influx of people needing material for shelters.

He is reminded of his lectures at university on the sustainability of the Shakan military model. Tying up almost the entire male capacity of a nation in barracks towns places an almost intolerable burden on both women and land. To feed his army of already more than ten thousand, will become more and more of a problem.

Napoleon appears from further along the river, walking back towards Bulawayo. He has a musket slung over his left shoulder and is carrying a brace of guinea fowl by their rubbery necks. He looks pleased with himself as he holds his prize aloft. In place of his bicorn hat, he has repurposed a white-silk cravat as a head scarf, transforming from general to pirate captain!

'I see you, my fellow Zulu!' he jokes. Richard scowls. He has decided to live this life. He does not need a reminder from another world ridiculing it.

'Why so serious?' asks the former emperor, all frivolity forgotten.

Richard shakes his head. 'Take no notice of me. I was pondering the future.'

Bonaparte nods. 'War is coming,' he says eagerly.

'Yes, and when will it stop? Can it stop? All the strongest men serve. The army grows. The barracks towns expand. The demand for food increases.' Richard is a teacher once again. 'Seizing cattle and grain is the solution but it also feeds the problem.' He sits by the river at a spot where the bank is low and has been cleared of bushes.

Napoleon sits beside him, laying the guinea fowl down with exaggerated care. 'With more conquests come more recruits but also more mouths to feed.' Bonaparte sees straight to the heart of the matter. 'No number of victories can pull free of the cycle,' he adds.

Richard sighs and watches the somnolent surface of the river. Summer is a rainy season but the ground is dry and the river low. The crops that ripen are stunted and sparse. Drought plagues the lands to the north; is it coming here?

'I think this is a problem for another day. I cannot look so far ahead.' There is something confessional in Napoleon's tone and Richard turns to study his companion. Looking closely, the outward good humour cannot disguise the hollow look to the Frenchman's eyes. His skin has a yellow tinge despite his tan and his lips, when resting, draw a thin line.

As Richard studies him, Bonaparte grimaces and doubles over, a mournful groan escaping his wracked body.

Richard reaches out an arm and enfolds Napoleon's shoulders, hugging him as they sit side by side. 'The pain is getting worse?' he asks and receives a nod of affirmation.

'It was bad on St Helena. As I shed weight and grew fitter, it receded but over the last year, it has gnawed at me more and more. This morning I felt fine. I went hunting. My hands were steady and my aim was good!' His bravado is half-hearted. 'But then I sit with my English friend and teeth chew at my intestines from within.' There is a depth of tiredness in his words that reminds Richard of the lethargic general letting his chances slip away at Waterloo.

'When did it start?' Richard asks, loathing the academic excitement that insists on knowing.

'Escaping from Elba was an attempt to convince myself all was well. By the time I stood on the field of Mont St Jean, I knew there was something seriously wrong, sapping my strength and clouding my thoughts.' Napoleon breaks off and grasps a fistful of powdery earth. Slowly, he lets it slip through his hand. 'It was this internal enemy that defeated me, you know, not your Wellington!'

Richard is used to Bonaparte's bluster, this ability to reframe the past to his own narrative, but on this occasion, he suspects he is hearing the unvarnished truth.

Napoleon's body goes slack and Richard feels his full weight against his side. He uses his free hand to lift the Frenchman's drooping chin. Bonaparte has fainted.

Richard eases him back until he is lying on the riverbank. He lifts an eyelid but can see nothing but the whites of his eyes. He tries slapping the slack face but gets no response. For a moment, he fights panic. He stands and turns towards the gates of Bulawayo up on the hill, only to turn back.

He kneels down and feels beneath Napoleon's collar for the necklace he always wears. Following the beads like a rosary, he encounters the snuff horn. He does not search for the snuff spoon Bonaparte has become so adept at using. Instead, he removes the stopper and takes hold of a large pinch, which he thrusts awkwardly into Napoleon's nostrils.

At first, nothing happens and he turns again towards the Zulu capital. But then, Napoleon's head jerks as he releases an enormous sneeze, followed by another. He splutters and Richard rolls him onto his side, barely noticing the dusty, orange soil coating the immaculate blue uniform of a general of the Foot Grenadiers of the Imperial Guard.

A weak moan follows and Napoleon's hands twitch. He lifts his head from the dirt to peer up at Richard. 'Tell no one!' he hisses.

Richard nods in reply as Napoleon gets his hands flat against the ground and starts to lever himself up. Richard helps him sit and supports his back as he begins to brush himself down. Loose dirt comes away in clouds until the uniform is once again recognisably blue.

It is almost an hour before Napoleon is able to get to his feet and walk, like a man crossing a desert without water, painfully up the hill. Richard walks beside him, solicitous but careful to do nothing that might draw attention to his companion's distress. They reach Napoleon's hut without being intercepted. Once inside, Richard settles Bonaparte.

'I will fetch General Thibault,' he announces, despite his earlier promise. He thinks Napoleon will object, but he nods weakly.

Richard finds the young general with the artillery beneath a makeshift roof resembling the market at Lourenco Marques. He is checking the boxes of munitions.

'Lucien,' Richard calls, 'the emperor needs you.' The young aide replaces the lid of the box he is auditing and hurries off, squeezing out his thanks as he goes.

Richard returns to his own hut and is relieved to find Ulwazi inside. He recounts Napoleon's turn before explaining what he thinks ails him. He cannot use the word cancer as it does not exist in the Zulu vocabulary. Instead, he describes the symptoms of poor appetite, weight loss, abdominal pain, and nausea.

Ulwazi looks serious. 'How long has he suffered?' she asks.

'Several years,' Richard replies, hopelessly.

'There is one person, an *inyanga*, a doctor, who can help him, but I do not know if he will treat an *umlungu*.'

A tiny green shoot pushes through the barren soil of Richard's hopelessness. 'We must try!' he insists. The shoot sprouts tiny leaves.

'We will have to travel into the mountains,' Ulwazi reveals, 'is he well enough to make the journey?'

Richard nods although he is unsure. Four leaves now adorn the little plant. A fresh idea strikes him. 'We are Zulus, he and I, and members of the council. I will ask Shaka. Surely, he can make this doctor treat Napoleon?'

Ulwazi is nodding but she does not look convinced.

Shaka listens attentively as Richard explains. Bonaparte was reluctant to involve the Zulu leader, fearing any sign of weakness would put him at a disadvantage. Richard pointed out death was a greater disadvantage! At first, Shaka nods, then, as Richard continues, he frowns and when Richard finishes, he is scowling deeply.

'You ask a big thing of me. To put myself in the debt of one who deals in magic.'

Richard keeps his face neutral. From what he has gathered from Ulwazi, the man is a herbalist, not a witch-finder, rain-maker or diviner. It seems Shaka draws no such distinction. He understands the fraud at the heart of the witch-finders' profession and he has taken steps to weaken that cabal. But that does not mean he is free from superstition. Richard checks himself. He is a Zulu now. This is what they believe.

'Mighty Shaka. It is a very big thing I ask. To save the life of your councillor. The man who formed and supplied your musket company and has now gifted you an even greater prize, your artillery.'

Shaka nods his agreement but his face remains intensely serious. 'What you say is true. But I have these things now.'

It is a brutal logic, Richard acknowledges, but then he recalls his conversation with Daniel, the Guernsey fisherman, before he left Bulawayo. 'Yet, you have no way of replenishing your ammunition without Bonaparte.' Shaka is quiet for a long time. There is no fire in the hearth, so hot is the day. Richard's eyes flick from Shaka to look behind him. Sure enough, Pampata is there, sitting on her heels, listening intently.

'There is truth to what you say. I could attack the Portuguese to the north. They are not strong like your British. Would that not solve my problem?'

Richard tries to keep calm. The conversation is getting out of control. He does not want to discuss regional strategy today. He will not get what he wants if he tries to beat Shaka in debate. Richard looks at the floor.

'Indeed, mighty king. I ask you to do this thing, in recognition of Napoleon Bonaparte's service to you. I ask you to do this thing, because he is my friend and I too have been of service to you.' He looks up, unsure whether his words will have had any impact. Pampata is beside Shaka, whispering in his ear.

The summer rainstorm is heavy. Richard is drenched. He huddles beneath the brim of his hat, watching the water bead on Ulwazi's perfect skin. The droplets coalesce until they grow heavy and slip down her arms and back in rivulets. Nothing about her gait suggests she has even noticed the change in the weather. The cow she is leading plods on, its four feet somehow in step with her graceful stride.

General Thibault mutters under his breath. His boots squelch through the instant mud conjured from the dry ground by the downpour. They are climbing steadily now, leaving the rolling grassland for the foothills of the Drakensberg mountains. The slopes are green with ferns where the ground is marshy. The trees have peeling bark like paper and grow in widespread groups. They have narrow, yellowish-green leaves, forming a spreading canopy on angled branches that diverge from modest trunks. They remind Richard of aged olive trees. Irises, orchids and red-hot pokers are scattered everywhere, thrusting through the green grass.

Ulwazi halts beside an outcrop of reddish rock, sculpted by wind and rain into an anvil. She signals for them to join her. In the lee of the rock lies an adolescent youth, eyes closed, narrow chest rising and falling gently. Ulwazi stoops down and shakes his shoulder.

The boy's eyes pop open and he lets out a yelp. He struggles up, pressing his back against the rock, open-mouthed at the first white men he can ever have seen.

'You were sent by the *inyanga* to guide us?' Ulwazi asks in a kindly voice. The boy nods. His eyes are like saucers and his thin limbs tremble as he picks up his stick and points deeper into the hills.

As they climb, the boy shoots nervous glances at Richard, Thibault and Bonaparte but will not look at them directly, as if he fears they may hypnotise him. He walks close to Ulwazi and the brown-and-white milk cow, keeping them between him and the three ghostly figures. At least, this is what Richard imagines is in the boy's head.

They enter a gorge which twists and turns, splitting and doubling back, a sunken maze cut by wind, rain and a long-lost river. Twice they have to skirt sinkholes that echo with running water. The rock walls of the gorge close in and recede, orange sandstone capped by harder rock.

General Thibault leaves the trail to tap at samples with the hilt of his sword. He returns nodding. 'Basalt cap. Where the sandstone is exposed, it erodes like this gorge. Where the basalt protects, you get upstanding features like the rock where we met the boy.'

Richard is surprised by the young aide's knowledge. It must be obvious from his face because Thibault explains, 'My father was a road builder. He knew everything about landscapes.' Richard is happy to hear pride in the man's voice as he talks of his father.

'An honourable profession,' Bonaparte comments. 'The empire built more than thirty thousand kilometres of imperial roads. Not to mention the canals.' He is at his boastful best.

'My father oversaw the construction of a road across the Alps, through the Simplon Pass,' Thibault reveals enthusiastically.

Napoleon smiles and pats him on the back. 'One of the

great achievements of the empire. It is regrettable that my military genius has overshadowed my civil works. They will be my lasting legacy.'

The cow begins to tear at the grass, grinding it with a sideways motion of her jaw. The sound echoes along the canyon.

When they reach a widening of the gorge, an underground river bubbles up to the surface, forming a clear pool. They startle a pair of slender antelope which bound off, graceful necks stiff with panic. Here, the boy turns and begins to climb an improbable staircase of rock steps that zig-zag precariously up the western cliff of the gorge. His small, bare feet adhere to the smooth rock, toes gripping at fissures and edges.

Richard is soon breathing heavily, as he follows the swaying rump of the cow, whose hooves look poorly designed for climbing. Ulwazi maintains a sing-song chatter in its ear, larger than Richard's hand, and lined with the finest hairs.

As the base of the gorge drops away, the air feels weightless and the light grows brighter. At last, they step over the lip onto a highland plateau of knee-high grass, punctuated with red, orange and yellow gladioli, like floral flames. Richard has never seen them outside a formal garden.

The cow pulls up mouthfuls of sweet grass as she sways across the gently undulating high land, trampling any flowers interrupting her route. Her stomachs grumble and she emits a long burst of flatulence.

Richard steps quickly to one side and hurries forward to Ulwazi. Soon they are all walking abreast, enjoying the open vistas after the confines of the gorge. They are heading for a flat-topped outcrop of sandy rock. A meandering path has been worn through the grass and the boy follows it assiduously without ever looking at his feet.

'Fine country,' Napoleon comments cheerfully but Richard can see the pain in his eyes. He walks with an exaggerated gait and is always leaning forward. He tries hard to keep his hands away from his belly, gripping a long musket in one hand and resting the other on the cow's spine.

Closer to the rocky protuberance, they see it is pock-marked with caves. A few goats roam about, keeping the immediate vicinity cropped bare. Outside the largest opening sits a figure. He appears to be asleep. The boy calls in his piping voice and a head lifts, a hand is raised and very slowly, the cave-dweller eases to his feet.

Ulwazi hands the tether to the boy and he pulls the cow the last few steps, before holding the rope out proudly. Richard studies the man as he accepts the cow and ties the animal, with deft fingers, to a nearby section of fencing. Richard imagines the fence is to keep the goats corralled. Not one of the animals is inside.

The man is in his later years. His hair is grey and his chin bristles with a predominantly white beard, cut short. His eyes are small but sharp, set in an open face with a wide nose, and slender lips. He is of average height but stoops, as if his head is too heavy for his shoulders.

With some effort, he looks from the cow to the boy and on to Ulwazi. He nods to her and she smiles as she speaks.

'I see you, esteemed *inyanga*.'

'I see you, girl,' his voice is warm and kind. 'You bring not one but three *abelungu*. And the promise of another life.'

Ulwazi smiles and cups the base of her belly. 'Mighty Shaka thanks you for agreeing to treat his *umlungu* councillor,' Ulwazi says respectfully, her eyes downcast. The cow lows and stamps her feet.

'This is the one,' the ageing doctor says. There is no hint of a question as he indicates Bonaparte.

Ulwazi nods in agreement. Richard smiles, sure the wily herbalist has seen the discomfort in Napoleon's gait.

'I will examine him inside. It will take time, the rest of you should make yourselves comfortable.' He indicates a low burning fire, 'If you wish food, you may use my hearth.'

The air in the highlands is cooler but there is no need for a fire. Richard spots several containers set to one side, one of which is still steaming. It seems their host was preparing his potions as they arrived.

The *inyanga* leads Napoleon into his cave. Ulwazi pulls some *biltong*, salt-cured kudu meat, from her bundle. She cuts off strips and hands one to Richard and another to General Thibault. Catching their gangly guide's expression, she offers him a portion which he snatches eagerly before gabbling his thanks.

The dried meat takes a long time to chew but it is finished and they have fetched water from a nearby stream before Napoleon reappears. He has a grim expression on his face.

'Is everything alright, sire?' asks Thibault in a worried voice.

'My Zulu is still shaky and this one's dialect unfamiliar. Nevertheless, I understood his diagnosis.'

The reclusive doctor looks on impassively. Ulwazi crosses to him and offers him some *biltong*. He grins at her with pink gums, causing her to apologise. Richard hears her ask what he has learned of Napoleon's condition. He begins to explain in a matter-of-fact tone.

'I have seen this before. Many times. The outcome is always the same. More pain, swelling, blood and death.' The man's dialect is thick.

So, it is cancer, Richard thinks, feeling sick and much sadder than he expected. He looks at Bonaparte who stands stoically beside Thibault. A soldier facing death as he has asked so many others to do.

'I take it from your expression, that his prognosis is dire?' Napoleon asks. 'I know he expects me to die, I take it the manner of my death will not be pleasant?' There is nothing Richard can do but confirm what he has heard.

'Even in my time, survival rates for stomach cancer were never better than seventy per cent, and that depended on an early diagnosis and treatment that will not be invented until the 1940s.' He wants to tell Napoleon how sorry he is but his throat tightens.

The former emperor nods to the doctor and walks off to stand on a low prominence looking out over the flower-flecked plateau. Here and there, rocks thrust up like the bones of long-dead dragons.

Richard thinks about joining him but decides against it. He looks at Thibault who is also giving his master some privacy. They stand together, watching Bonaparte. One hand finds its way into the other, behind his back, kneading at his palm. He wears his green Chasseurs uniform and his bicorn hat.

He looks so out of place and yet his presence thrills

Richard. Napoleon Bonaparte, escaped from St Helena, become councillor to Shaka Zulu. If history keeps to its course, he has a little over two years to live.

Ulwazi finishes speaking with the doctor and joins Richard. 'Bonaparte needs to hear this,' she says without further explanation. Richard can tell by her voice it is important. Reluctantly, he walks over to the forlorn figure contemplating his mortality.

They are all seated around the fire. The old doctor has produced a spicy distillation that burns the mouth. It is the strongest alcohol Richard has ever tasted and he sips cautiously. The herbalist swigs from his beaker. He is already grinning.

'Why do you all look so glum?' he asks with concern.

'Because you said there was no hope,' replies Richard. Ulwazi leans forward and reaches out a hand to his sleeve, as if to restrain him.

'Is that what I said? Well, perhaps it was, but I refer to those who do not accept my treatment!' He is grinning even more broadly.

'Why would anyone refuse treatment?' Richard presses incredulously.

'Because they do not believe. Because they will not pay.' There is contempt in the *inyanga's* voice. 'Many fear I am a wizard and will not come near.'

Richard relays what is being said to Napoleon, whose chin lifts to stare at the ageing physician.

'Tell him, I will pay any price, undergo any procedure, I will do anything to go on living.' Every syllable drips with determination.

This is a man whose appetite for life is still strong. For some reason, this frightens Richard at the same time as it makes him glad.

The *inyanga* looks pleased. 'I can tell you will be a good patient. You must remain here. Send your friends away.'

Napoleon frowns and Richard translates. 'He says we must leave you here.'

Bonaparte nods decisively. 'Then I shall remain. Explain things to Shaka. Do not let Nqoboka sabotage my efforts,' he instructs Richard.

Next, he turns to General Thibault. 'I entrust you with the artillery. You must ensure it is used to good effect in the upcoming war with the Ndwandwes, if I do not return in time.' Lucien Hypolite Thibault grins nervously, pride and fear at war on his face.

Finally, Napoleon looks to Ulwazi. 'You are good for my English friend. Do your best to keep him safe until I return.' There is a depth of affection in these words that forces Richard to look away.

As they start walking towards the path to the gorge, Ulwazi slips her hand into Richard's. He is glad. He feels unaccountably lonely as they leave Napoleon Bonaparte to the ministrations of the reclusive medic. It is as if he is leaving something of himself behind. As if he is not truly whole, separated from the man who drew him across the centuries.

He has no idea what treatments the *inyanga* will use, but there must be some risk. After all, chemotherapy is his era's solution, a double-edged sword if ever there was one. He wonders if he will see Napoleon again?

Chapter Eight

June 1819

R ichard eyes Mzilikazi suspiciously. Shaka has granted him command of an *iviyo* of his own Khumalo fighters in the new U-Mbonambi regiment. Bonaparte appears from his hut, stooping as he exits, before straightening his back. He stands in his green and red Chasseurs uniform, surveying Bulawayo. By the time Richard looks back, Mzilikazi has disappeared.

Richard waits for Napoleon to skirt the parade ground filled with Fasimba companies practising with their long shields and short spears. Watching the Frenchman approach, Richard is surprised. He looks taller, as if he is able to stand fully upright for the first time since Richard first saw him.

'Why do you frown, my English friend, my Zulu brother?' asks Napoleon in a jovial tone. 'Are you not pleased to see me so much less afflicted by my belly?'

Richard nods and smiles. 'Of course. It seems there is much to be learned from the herbal medicines used in this country.'

Bonaparte slips a hand inside his waistcoat, rocking back and forth on his heels. 'I have not felt so well in years. It seems Africa has saved my life. Had I faced Wellington in such form, he never would have bested me.'

Richard looks away. It is four years since the battle near Waterloo.

'Things might also have turned out differently had I listened to your advice, no?' The defeated emperor's modesty manages to sound defiant.

'I prefer to think of the present and look to the future.'

Bonaparte claps Richard on the back. 'It is good to be alive. The future, yes, that is certainly intriguing. I hope General Bertrand is in the Americas by now. Will he be able to secure more muskets and artillery along with sufficient munitions? I have been thinking how useful a battery of mortars would be, given Shaka's tactics. Mortars certainly battered the poor 6th division, squandered by my brother on the slopes to Hougoumont. Men dead for no purpose, sacrificed to his arrogance... you did warn me.'

Bonaparte falls silent, his eyes focused beyond Bulawayo, perhaps on the battlefield of Waterloo, replaying moments that might have gone differently. In the months after the battle, Richard often did the same thing. But now, he hardly ever gives it any thought. He is an adviser to the Zulu king, an honorary member of the tribe. He is married.

He experiences a pang. Ulwazi? He looks towards their hut. She is there, sitting by the entrance, hands clasped beneath her improbably huge belly. She sees him and waves without shedding the contented look she has worn every day since the *inyanga* confirmed their suspicions. Even plagued by morning sickness or tortured by back pain, she smiled and sang. Every day she sings. The stories of her people she sings. Hope for the future she sings.

'It will not be long now,' Napoleon observes gently, 'your child will be beautiful... just like my Josephine.' He sounds wistful. 'Perhaps it is time I found a woman?' he muses.

Richard keeps his eyes on his pregnant wife. 'I did not seek this,' he says, 'but my life is better for it. I am better for it.'

'So, you agree?' presses Napoleon.

'At first, I resisted. I did not want to misuse her. She was Shaka's to dispose of as he wished. If I had been stronger, I would have refused her company. But she is kind and clever and beautiful. She is prepared to share her life with me. She will never see the world as I do. But she is wise and patient and funny.' Richard takes a breath as Bonaparte holds up his hand.

'You do not have to convince me.'

Richard shakes his head. 'What I am trying to say is, proceed with caution, with a conscience... I am not making myself clear.'

'Love. You are talking about love. You think this man who abdicated twice cannot be trusted. That he will impose himself for physical gratification?' Napoleon talks as if such suspicions are reasonable.

Richard says nothing. He has made his point. He was dreaming of Fanny only months ago. He is not that much of a hypocrite.

'I promise you this, Richard. I will wait until someone shows interest in me.' He is standing straight as he speaks, resplendent in his uniform, still an iconic figure to Richard's eyes. How does he appear to the women of Shaka's *isigodlo*? Unfamiliar, strange even? But he has presence. He is a member of the inner council. He conjures new weapons to strengthen the Zulu army.

Bonaparte inclines his head towards an approaching messenger. Richard looks longingly at Ulwazi, who is stroking her belly as she sings to their unborn child. Reluctantly, he turns towards the youth.

'Mighty Shaka requests your presence. He assembles his council.' The boy is breathless as he points to the tree at the centre of the town and rushes off to find other councillors.

Attendants pile rolled mats together to form Shaka's temporary throne, unrolling others for his council to sit on. Richard spots Mzilikazi. He is loitering, watching the preparations with a hungry look.

By the time Shaka emerges from the royal enclosure, all the council members are assembled. Mzilikazi still watches intently from just beyond the shade of the tree. He hops from one small foot to the other as if the dirt is baking hot even though a winter sun shines down on Bulawayo. His odd proportions no longer exact comment. None of the councillors pay him any attention, not even Ngomane, who defended Khumalo dignity and punished the Fasimba for their insults.

Shaka processes in his full leopard-skin regalia. He walks with deliberate steps, head held high but eyes roving around his capital. When he glimpses Mzilikazi, he ushers him forward.

'Sit at my feet with my council. We are assembled to hear you.'

There are murmurs from the assembled dignitaries at this unexpected promotion.

'I see,' says Napoleon thoughtfully, 'he is like me. Although he has lost his throne and most of his people, he still hungers, he still dreams, he watches and he schemes.'

Richard is surprised the fallen emperor admits so much. It is not a flattering comparison. Mzilikazi may found the great Matebele empire, but he betrays Shaka's trust and plunders across hundreds of miles, leaving death behind him in the smoking ruins of villages.

Richard notices how little ornamentation Mzilikazi wears. He bows humbly as he sits on his heels at the edge of the outermost mat.

Shaka smiles down at him. 'I summoned my council because there is news of Zwide,' he announces in his booming voice. 'Our new recruit, Mzilikazi, has received intelligence from those living under Ndwandwe occupation.' Shaka offers the floor to Mzilikazi with a wave of his miniature spear.

With apparent reluctance, Mzilikazi stands and shuffles a few paces closer to Shaka atop his throne. He turns to face the seated council, his shoulders level with Shaka's knees.

'My spies report Zwide is rebuilding his army. He drills his troops day and night. They have short, broad spears now, like those mighty Shaka designed. They practise manoeuvres and close combat with spear and shield.'

Mgobozi scowls and scuffs at the ground with the back of his hand, as if dismissing the very idea. Shaka notices and with one look halts his demonstration. 'We must hear this news and accept it, but there is more.'

'King Shaka is right. Zwide will not wait for you to act. He intends an invasion very soon. Soshangane will command. He is no fool.' Mzilikazi's respectful recitation receives worried expressions but no one contradicts him.

Tugging at his left ear, fingering the little drum of snuff in his pierced lobe, Ngomane signifies his wish to speak. Shaka nods.

'Tell us, Mzilikazi, how many men will Zwide send?'

'Twenty thousand will cross the fords. They will travel light and look to feed from the land.'

A thrill runs down Richard's spine. He leans forward. Shaka rises gracefully on his muscular legs and spreads his arms.

'Let them come! I want messengers sent to every *kraal* within forty miles of our border. This is what they must say: the harvest is gathered in; here are bags for your grain; carry them into the Nkandla forest and hide in the caves there.'

Richard sees Napoleon nodding beside him. 'Scorched earth. A logical extension of his tactics at Gqokli hill when he had his men drive off all game. It is a bitter strategy to confront, as my *Grande Armée* discovered in Russia.' There is admiration in Bonaparte's voice.

Mzilikazi raises his hand and Shaka waves him back to his feet. 'I have three men close to Zwide. He believes they are loyal. When I send a coded message, they will advise him he has an opportunity to catch the Zulus asleep. But when the Ndwandwes cross the border, there will be no animal or person within forty miles.' He sits down.

Richard marvels at the synergy between Shaka's thinking and Mzilikazi's plan. Shaka is smiling broadly.

'I think soon we will see an end to the Ndwandwe threat. Mzilikazi, we will find a role for you in the fighting.'

Mzilikazi bows until his face is in the dirt.

Napoleon Bonaparte chews at a jagged nail. His blue eyes are unnaturally bright as Ndwandwe regiments pour across the fords of the Umfolozi river. He is standing on the flat top of

Gqokli hill, where Zulu tactics and weapons, coupled with the musket company he trained, inflicted a major defeat on Zwide.

Richard stands to the left of the Frenchman while Lucien Thibault is to his right. Scattered across the floodplain are white bones. Even Thibault seems untroubled by the sight.

Through his telescope, Richard peers more closely at the remnants of warriors killed a little over a year ago. Not a scrap of flesh or cartilage remains. Every single skeleton has been dislocated. Ribcages lie forlorn, shorn of arms or legs. Skulls grin emptily, eye sockets vacant, far from vertebrae, scapulae or clavicles.

This time, there are no Zulu regiments hidden on the plateau. Just a few ragged formations at the foot of the hill. As the Ndwandwes emerge from the river in ever greater numbers, these under-strength companies turn tail and run.

The jeers of the invading horde chase the running Zulus on a playful breeze.

'And so, Soshangane is deceived,' declares Napoleon in satisfaction. 'Mzilikazi's agents have convinced his master the Zulus are unprepared. Now his general sees the proof. No regiments guard the border. He expects to plunder his way to Bulawayo.'

The last of the enemy regiments are crossing the river. They make quick time. The sluggish waters are shallow after a dry spell.

'See! There is no baggage train. No companies hauling supplies. This army travels light. Just a gaggle of youths carrying food for three days, no more,' scoffs Napoleon.

'Wait! Look at the very rear: boys driving cattle. Perhaps a hundred head?' Richard points out. 'If they keep them, they will be supplied for much longer.'

Napoleon smirks. 'An army this size will eat that little herd in no time!'

It is as Richard remembers reading about it. Unless something unexpected happens, there will be no need for the artillery Bonaparte has been allowed to position flanking Bulawayo.

Richard sees this bothering the great artilleryman until he is swept along by the mass movement of troops and the unfolding of a carefully planned strategy. He is no longer a man with the smell of sulphur in his nostrils but with ink on his fingers and a telescope to hand.

Richard knows that as the Ndwandwe regiments press forward, they will sight a single Zulu regiment moving south across rocky heights. Soshangane will decide to camp in a bleak stretch of highlands. It is winter and nights at altitude are cold and frosty.

Mgobozi barks an order to his small party.

'We should go,' suggests Napoleon, 'he likes you, but we are so slow, it is tempting to leave us behind!'

Zulu trackers tail the massive Ndwandwe force. They will shadow them until they make camp.

Richard imagines the massed regiments huddled in the cold, shivering through a sleepless night. The thinly vegetated uplands offer no fuel for fires. Zulu companies make rapid forays, raising the alarm, forcing tired men to turn out and stand tensely. War cries echo between hilltops, interspersed with haunting calls, designed to disrupt any hopes of sleep.

The Ndwandwe *impi* marched for three days to the border and now a fourth day is beneath their sandalled feet. Tired and chilled, they eat their millet bread eagerly for breakfast. Already, their supplies are running low, if the account Richard read at university was correct.

Thibault returns from accompanying a scouting party. He is wheezing and red in the face. Slick with sweat, he throws himself carelessly onto the ground in his fine blue uniform.

When he has recovered, he reports to the man he still regards as his emperor. 'We met two companies returning from the high ground where they harried the enemy in the night,' he announces hoarsely. 'The enemy regiments are searching for food as they go but they find nothing.'

'They have their cattle,' Richard points out.

Thibault manages a tired laugh. 'We were passed by a whole Zulu regiment with red and black shields.'

'One of the new regiments of recruits from surrounding tribes,' Bonaparte asserts with confidence. No one questions how he knows this; it is the way his mind works to accumulate such information.

'They were driving a modest herd of cattle. My Zulu is poor but it was clear they had taken the beasts from the enemy. I think the Ndwandwe herd boys left too much distance between the cows and the army.'

Richard looks at the sky. The sun is low now. Soon it will be dark. Mgobozi returns to the makeshift camp, joking with the sentries as he gives the password.

'They camp beside the Umhlatuze. They are almost in our grasp. The Zulu *impi* shelters in the eastern fringes of the

Nkandla forest.' The army's drill-master sounds satisfied and his thumb caresses the edge of his spear.

A messenger calls to the sentries and enters the camp. A central fire spreads friendly light across Mgobozi and his squad. They are sheltered in the lee of a rocky outcrop. This is where the sentries are stationed.

Richard, Thibault and Bonaparte are on the far side of the fire from Mgobozi and his men, but they are close enough to hear.

'Mighty Shaka worries the Ndwandwe *impi* will withdraw. He orders us to tempt them deeper into our territory,' Mgobozi summarises. 'We are to drive a large herd within two miles of the enemy. We will spatter them with ox-blood to make them bellow at the smell.'

'This should be worth watching,' Napoleon enthuses before returning his attention to a strip of *biltong*.

Richard and the Frenchmen jog beside a small contingent, the rearguard of Mgobozi's mobile column. Napoleon is running easily, a musket clasped in one hand above the trigger-guard, his sword swinging easily on his hip. General Thibault has a pistol in his waistband but has drawn his sword. Richard is carrying his telescope, there is a knife at his belt and a pistol too.

As the light fades, Mgobozi takes personal charge of the subterfuge. By the time Richard arrives, a cow lies in the dirt, throat cut. Bowls of blood sit beside the carcass, shockingly red against dun pottery.

A dozen *udibi* stand nervously around the herd, keeping the agitated animals from bolting. They are assisted by

Mgobozi's men, while their commander walks among the restless beasts, flicking blood with a wildebeest tail.

Red gore decorates the animals' flanks. Every few paces, the buck-toothed drill-master tips the bowl he is carrying, spilling blood on rocks and bushes, anywhere it will remain visible. By the time he finishes, the sky is darkening as is the blood.

The cattle roll their big eyes, raising their heads to voice their displeasure in a chorus of manic groans. The herd boys stake the lead animal firmly and hobble others to prevent the herd from dissipating.

Mgobozi orders everyone behind the nearest hill, stationing lookouts on the brow. Soon, the sentries are relaying reports of Ndwandwe scouts appearing out of the darkness. The gibbous moon's sickly yellow illuminates the ghostly movements of man and beast.

At a signal from Mgobozi, three warriors, together with most of the herd boys, move around the hill. As they confront the Ndwandwe scouts, they feign panic and turn tail, shouting that they must fly to the nearby Zulu army to warn them their herds are at risk.

Richard pieces this together from the pantomime shouts and wonders whether the Ndwandwe scouts will be convinced. From his hiding place, he sees three Ndwandwe warriors slip away to be lost from sight in a fold of the land.

Richard dozes beside Thibault and Bonaparte. He is cold. Before dawn, they are roused and sneak away with the cattle. As daylight slips across the land, they are on the ridge of Sungulweni hill, immediately east of the Nkandla forest where the Zulu *impi* hides.

By the time it is light, the Ndwandwe vanguard is pouring over the horizon. Minute by minute the dark mass of humanity swells, surging closer to the answer to their supply problems.

'If he waits much longer, we will be overrun,' Thibault squawks. As if he has heard, Mgobozi sweeps his right arm in an arc. The boys whip the cattle into motion and they lumber away, leaving billowing dust in the early morning air.

It is a crisp, fragrant day but the pursuing mass of soldiers do not notice. They are hungry as they chase the herd through dust and droppings.

Several times, Mgobozi halts the retreat, letting the animals graze, before urging them on again. As a ribbon of trees appears, the lead units of the Ndwandwes are less than half a mile away.

'The Tugela river!' shouts Richard over the noise of the cattle. Mgobozi's little company drive the tiring beasts hard now, until they are knee-deep, fording the river on a broad front. A few lose their footing and bellow in panic. Necks stiff and eyes wild, their heavy bodies are cumbersome and their slender legs ineffectual. But the current is weak and most manage to haul themselves back onto their hooves.

The herd boys keep them moving while Mgobozi's warriors are reinforced by two companies carrying the shields of the Ama-Wombe. Richard notices they are men close to retirement.

The Ndwandwe's lead regiment throws itself across the river as Mgobozi orders his team away. Richard turns willingly but has to haul Napoleon after him, so reluctant is he to miss the action. Glancing over his shoulder as they jog-trot away, Richard sees a Zulu company fall back in the hope of luring their enemy deeper into unfriendly territory.

As Mgobozi pauses to survey what is happening behind, the Ndwandwe close on the Ama-Wombe. Soshangane appears with his retinue of commanders on the riverbank. He shouts furiously and despatches runners after his vanguard. They run furiously, knees high, feet flying despite heavy sandals. Unencumbered by shield or spear, they soon catch the *induna* leading the pursuers.

Within seconds, the Ndwandwe halt and turn, withdrawing to the far side of the Tugela river.

The Ama-Wombe companies rejoin Mgobozi. They watch Soshangane carefully. Richard scans the scene with his telescope, as do the two Frenchmen. The Ndwandwe commander is a big man, but he is not out of breath. His large head is topped by a heavy ring, his hair short beneath it. His beard is cropped, emphasising the natural smile of his lips. His face is broad and his nose proud. He has a high forehead and a thoughtful expression as he talks with his lieutenants.

'He is going to pull his men back,' observes Bonaparte confidently. 'Shaka will not be pleased,' he adds unnecessarily.

As the Ndwandwe army wheels about, heading for the dark forest of Nkandla on the horizon, Mgobozi calls his men to order, directing them to Shaka's headquarters on the Nkandla heights.

Richard is hungry. They have not stopped for food all day. It is mid-afternoon as they approach the trees and high ground of the forest.

Shaka is surveying the Ndwandwe withdrawal with Mdlaka, his number two and, to Richard's surprise, Mzilikazi. Mdlaka looks pleased rather than concerned at the latest development. 'A crocodile in the water is dangerous but lure him onto dry land and he is easy prey!' he crows.

Mzilikazi points meaningfully towards the eastern extremity of the forest, jutting defiantly into the surrounding grassland. 'Soshangane sends regiments and scouts hither and thither but they are mere distraction. He is pulling his forces into those trees where he hopes to find game before emerging to surprise us.'

Shaka smiles, affection sparkling in his eyes. Richard gnaws at the inside of his mouth until he tastes blood. He edges away from Shaka and his military advisers into the gloom of the forest.

He has not gone two dozen paces when he stumbles to a halt. There are men everywhere, four to a tree, sitting with their backs to the bark. The air is close, musty, redolent of mushrooms. The whites of men's eyes and the flash of ivory teeth shine out beneath the canopy, an interlocked tapestry of branches.

'Fine trees,' says a familiar voice to Richard's left. He turns, scanning the seated men, noticing the brown shields of those nearest him. 'I said, they are fine trees.' This time the voice speaks French not Zulu.

'Emile!' Richard exclaims, still searching for his friend's form in the murk. A figure stands, closer than he expects, an arm raised, straight hair to the shoulders.

'It is good to see you, my friend,' Richard gushes as Emile pulls him into an embrace.

'It is good to see you too! But tell me, you have been beyond these trees, while we have skulked here for days. What is happening?'

Richard sits with his friend and fills him in. He speaks in Zulu and soon attracts a large crowd who tilt heads to catch the news.

He has just finished when messengers arrive from Shaka, ordering the Ama-Wombe to be ready for action as soon as night falls. Richard feels a surge of excitement. Emile is going into battle.

Richard is also an honorary Zulu, and although he is no warrior, he wants to share the battlefield with his friend once again! He hurries back to Shaka's command post, only to find Napoleon in conversation with the Zulu king.

'If this Mzilikazi, who so recently joined your number, is allowed to take part, then you cannot deny me the chance to draw blood!' General Thibault nods agreement although his face looks pale.

Shaka glances at Richard as he approaches and scowls. 'Here comes my other white adviser. Look at his face, he too wishes to risk his life to no purpose. Mzilikazi needs to prove himself. You have demonstrated your value, and it is not as fighters in the night!'

Shaka turns to Mdlaka, cutting off any possibility of a rejoinder from either Richard or the frustrated fifty-year-old former emperor. Mgobozi slips away to join up with the Ama-Wombe force preparing for an attack on the Ndwandwe.

Without thinking, Richard tugs at Napoleon's sleeve, drawing him into the trees that edge the escarpment from which Shaka commands. As if linked by invisible thread, Lucien Thibault moves with them.

Once hidden from the Zulu king's sight, Richard whispers urgently. 'We are both resolved to live in this place and not simply observe. Let's slip away and join the Ama-Wombe. Lieutenant Béraud will find a way for us to tag along.'

There is no hesitation. Bonaparte grins and pulls him into a hug that crushes the air from his body. When he is released, Richard inhales sharply, his chest still feeling the embrace.

They find Emile testing the edge of his cavalry sword. His giant friend, who refused Shaka's offer of a head ring, stands beside him, hefting his war club nonchalantly.

'We are coming with you!' Richard blurts out. Emile looks astonished and shakes his head.

Napoleon steps closer, piercing blue irises like coal in the white halo of his eyes. 'Lieutenant! I am proud of you. You have made yourself a decorated Zulu warrior against all the odds. Do not deny us the same opportunity!'

'You have Shaka's permission?' asks Emile, sounding conflicted.

'I do not require his permission!' snaps Napoleon irritably. 'But I do require your cooperation. Have I come to mean so little to you that you baulk at my request?'

Richard has heard Bonaparte like this before, when railing against his youngest brother.

'Forgive me, sire. I remain true, despite my new allegiance. Njikiza here, and I, will vouch for you. Our company commander is pleased with us since we saved Mgobozi. They are both Msane. They were *udibi* boys together.'

There is no going back now. Richard's heart is racing as he keeps up with the Ama-Wombe warriors. He carries a knobkerrie, a Zulu war club, awkwardly, persuaded by Emile it requires less proficiency than a spear.

The forest is a silent, dark backdrop against which they move. He is beside Emile, who moves as stealthily on bare feet as the others selected from his regiment. In contrast, Richard's boots scuff and catch, stomp and snap, forcing him to cringe every few steps. He takes comfort from the fact that Napoleon is just as noisy, while Thibault is worse.

He rehearses the plan as they move. It is a simple one. Five hundred warriors sneaking through the forest to reach the Ndwandwe encampment from the far side. They will pose as returning foragers. In the darkness it will be impossible for sentries to distinguish Zulu dress from their own. Both tribes speak the same language, so the Zulus will call out they bring meat, hopefully forestalling any challenge.

They will approach from many directions, numerous parties guided by the fires of the enemy. Once inside the camp, they will sow as much confusion as possible. Kill and cause chaos, bamboozling the enemy into fighting amongst themselves.

One historian, writing in the early 1960s, referred to this as the first commando raid, Richard recalls as his boot cracks a twig. He winces, remembering Shaka's stern briefing, as he loitered with Napoleon and Lucien Thibault, behind a dense thicket.

A steady voice calls out, 'Ndwandwe!'

'*Qobolwayo*!' comes the rapid reply.

'*Qobolwayo*!' confirms the first speaker. This is Shaka's plan in action. Any man encountering a possible enemy is to call out. If he does not receive the correct reply, 'I am truly one', he will strike.

The Zulu king's last words echo in Richard's head. 'Creep like snakes among them; strike them as they lie!'

An owl hoots but receives no reply. The eerie query echoes away. The assault force halts in a clearing and is divided. Richard is assigned to a party of a dozen. Napoleon and Thibault are allocated to other groups, to spread out the liabilities, he thinks.

As they head for the edge of the clearing, there is a disagreement between the NCO heading Richard's group and Mzilikazi. Richard is at the centre of the line and cannot make out what is said. However, it is Mzilikazi who leads their party back into the trees.

Richard shivers as the hairs on the back of his neck stir. No longer convinced he wants to be a part of this, his wavering nerve is shored up by a very French, '*Courage, mon ami!*'

It is Emile, slipping into the line immediately behind him. In English he whispers, 'I could not leave you to fend for yourself when I saw Mzilikazi take over.'

It is a shock when their line pierces the forest fringe. The land is bathed in moonlight, forcing Richard to squint until his eyes adjust. They follow the boundary until they spy a Ndwandwe outpost and the flicker of fires in the trees.

Mzilikazi leads them back into the woods, winding between trunks, evading the outpost and a second before they are challenged.

'Returning foraging party!' the Khumalo calls, inflecting his words in the Ndwandwe way. He receives a grunt of acknowledgement and they press on.

Richard has to force himself to breathe. He cannot believe he is walking through the enemy camp of close to twenty thousand warriors.

'Who is there?' calls a sentry.

'Returning patrol,' Mzilikazi replies calmly, gesturing to the two closest Zulus who slip away. Emile places a reassuring hand on Richard's shoulder. His anxiety must be obvious, even in the intermittent firelight.

'Where from?' snaps the sentry. Seconds draw out and the silence grows oppressive.

'The forest edge,' Mzilikazi offers reluctantly.

'But all patrols from…' The sentry never finishes. There is a muffled gasp and the tell-tale noise of a spear thrusting into flesh and pulling free. *Iklwa* indeed, the short stabbing spear's name is as good an onomatopoeia as Richard has encountered.

Richard steps with exaggerated care between sleeping forms curled beneath shields around fading fires. As he rounds one group, a man rolls over, his shield slipping into Richard's path. With one foot raised, Richard manages to pivot, avoiding a fall as Emile steadies him. Nodding his thanks, Richard continues forward.

Men snore and mutter, dreaming of the fight to come or those they left behind when they marched to war. Richard peers over his shoulder. The ghostly scene stretches all around. Fire after fire, burning low, surrounded by sleeping forms, like beetles beneath hide carapaces.

Every sightline is broken by the straight trunks of trees.

Mzilikazi signals a halt. Richard's heartbeat is rapid and adrenalin floods his system. There are twelve of them and many thousands of the enemy.

Richard thinks of Ulwazi and the unborn child impatiently waiting to enter the world. Will he arrive to find his father is dead, killed scant days before his birth? Why is he here? Why did he encourage Napoleon to join him?

A muffled cry is followed by a shout of panic far to their right. A yell and a curse sound to their left. The men at Richard's feet begin to stir. Mzilikazi stabs his spear, striking like a snake at the throat of the nearest Ndwandwe.

Eleven warriors fan out, stabbing with their spears, moving urgently from one prone man to the next. Richard stands helplessly, watching the slaughter. Each Zulu has despatched three of the enemy and none have made a sound. Those disturbed by the shout of alarm, roll over, mumbling in their sleep, settling their hips against the ground.

Richard can smell the spicy aroma of so many men, hunkered close by, the odour of four days' marching on their skin. He looks at the club in his hands. It is not like the heavy clubs of Shaka's executioners or the mighty weapon Njikiza Ngcolosi used to win his praise name as Watcher of the Ford. The hardwood handle is no thicker than a snooker cue, while the spherical head fits in his palm like a cricket ball.

Close to hysterical, Richard bites his lip to keep from laughing. He stands amidst twenty thousand Ndwandwe warriors, attached to a commando party of just twelve men. He is deep in the Nkandla forest, an adopted Zulu, watching men deftly butcher their enemies in exaggerated silence. But he is thinking about snooker and cricket. The former is not be invented for decades, while the latter will not be played internationally for twenty years.

He shifts the weapon into his left hand. He raises the reassuring weight above his shoulder, peering down at a sleeping Ndwandwe.

He is not meant to be here. He is no soldier. He is afraid. It is a relief to admit it as he lowers the club. At that moment, the man directly behind him throws off his shield and starts to rise. Richard spins. The man is on all fours, head raised.

The club arcs through the air, its glossy finish glowing in the light of the dying fire. Richard swings it from his hip, bringing it across his body to strike the startled figure's temple. A look of astonishment collapses from the man's face, as the dense wooden orb snaps his neck to the side.

To Richard, it happens painfully slowly. The air is too thick, his swing ponderous, the club clumsy. Nevertheless, he hears the crack of wood on bone and watches the stricken man fall back on his shield.

The Ndandwe's spear, a fair facsimile of Shaka's design, is still in his hand. Without conscious thought, Richard prizes it free from resistant fingers but as he does so, the felled fighter moans.

Startled, Richard attempts to use the spear. His blow is so weak that the tip only grazes the skin and glances off. Richard staggers forward at the lack of resistance, drops the weapon, and falls on the reviving warrior. He manages to roll off, kicking urgently to get onto his feet, swinging the club wildly from side to side.

Dazed and bleeding, the Ndwandwe sits up, reclaims his spear and thrusts with it. Richard grasps the shaft but his hand is sweaty and slides up to the broad blade. The shoulders of iron are sharp and his tensed flesh parts from little finger to wrist.

Shock and pain make him let go of the spear. He has the clubhead down at his side, so he swings an uppercut that takes the man beneath the chin, driving lower jaw against upper, shattering teeth with a sickening, brittle impact.

The battered fighter drops limply to the forest floor, eyes rolled back in his skull. But Richard is taking no chances, he brings the head of the club down again, closing his eyes so he does not see the damage he inflicts.

He turns away to see Emile slashing his sword through a man's neck, right to left, whilst withdrawing his spear from the belly of another assailant. All around is noise and confusion but until this second, Richard has heard nothing. He hears other members of his party call out.

Many fires have been kicked over, deliberately or in the struggle. A feeble light from the heavy moon filters through, allowing glimpses of the action.

'Ndwandwe,' shouts an urgent voice.

'Ndwandwe,' comes the reply. Richard cannot hear the sound of the spear stabbing but knows it is inevitable. Another shout is meant for him.

'Ndwandwe!'

'*Qobolwayo*!' he yells desperately, hearing his reply echoed nearby. Glancing in that direction, he again sees Emile, back against a tree, grappling with a wiry fellow with dancing feet. They look evenly matched as the smaller man skips beyond the reach of Emile's sabre while catching the thrust of his spear on his shield.

Motionless bodies scatter the ground between Richard and the struggling pair. Stooping to claim a discarded spear, he dodges an intervening tree trunk with a slight spiral to its yellowish girth. The tree thrusts willow-like foliage into the meshing canopy, unaffected by the struggles at its base.

Richard pulls his gaze from the tree and breaks into a run. Five strides are all it takes. The broad spear blade drives between the agile Ndwandwe's shoulders.

The force of Richard's blow drives the warrior forward, his shield slipping aside, onto the curved tip of the Frenchman's sword. Pressed against the man's back, Richard hears the hiss as the blade punctures a lung.

'Thank you, my friend. He was a handful.'

Richard barely hears Emile nor can he register the confusion of noise bouncing between the trees. He stares at the man he has just helped kill.

'I stabbed him… in the back,' he manages, horrified.

'You saved me!' comforts Emile as he turns to deflect the thrust of a spear before driving forward with his long shield to unbalance his attacker.

Richard manages to raise both club and spear, giving the impression of a formidable opponent as he tries to gather himself. A squat, burly Ndwandwe advances on him, eyes wide with terror.

'*Udeveli omhlophe*! *Umoya omubi*!' his voice is squeaky with superstition as he calls Richard a white devil ghost. But he keeps coming, one tentative step at a time.

'Run away, you fool,' Richard shouts, waving his knobkerrie, 'I am more than a ghost, I am an echo of the future! Get away from me, you were never meant to die at my hands!' Richard dances a manic jig and without thinking, begins to sing his favourite hymn, inspired perhaps by the memory of poor Reverend Dalrymple.

'Guide me O thou great Jehovah
Pilgrim through this barren land
I am weak but thou art mighty
Hold me with your powerful hand.'

By the time he reaches the chorus the blocky Ndwandwe has lurched away, seeking an enemy he understands.

'Bread of heaven, bread of heaven

Feed me...' He doesn't have time to finish the chorus before an insistent hand grabs his elbow and hauls him towards the edge of the forest. It is Emile, who is laughing loudly. They break into a run, the survivors of their party around them. Richard counts eight including himself. He can still hear scattered sounds of fighting.

'They killed as many of their own as we did!' shouts a tall Zulu gleefully as he overtakes them.

'It will take hours to restore order in their camp,' Emile yells as they burst from the fringe of the forest into the open. Immediately, the Zulus adopt their jog-trot, an infernal pace they can maintain for hours. Richard feels as if he is sprinting to keep up, but with every step, he is closer to safety, closer to Ulwazi, closer to the child he has yet to meet.

Chapter Nine

June 1819

Richard wants to tell Shaka this is a mistake. Mzilikazi is not to be trusted. He will take advantage of his elevation to grow in wealth and power until the time is right to reject Shaka's overlordship. History tells Richard this is true. But it is not what Shaka wants to hear.

Mzilikazi is being fêted as a hero. No one can deny the bravery he showed against the Ndwandwes. Richard only saw the beginning. Much more followed. The praise songs are already written.

Never again will young Zulu warriors mock the former Khumalo chief. His unorthodox profile is become part of his legend. Head too small for his shoulders. Engorged buttocks and a slack paunch at his waist. All carried on improbably spindly legs and the feet of a child. None of this matters. For Mzilikazi has expressed himself in the language of the new Zulu state. He has written his achievements in the blood of Shaka's direst enemies.

Shaka claps Mzilikazi on the back, forcing a spurt of beer from his pursed lips as he drops his bowl. The Zulu king bursts out laughing and offers the new favourite his own beer.

The dry winter air is mild as they sit beneath the council tree. Shaka is surrounded by his advisers and *indunas*, along with the senior ladies of his court. Everyone chatters happily, drinking beer and chewing dried nuts.

Nqoboka clenches and unclenches his fists unconsciously, his teeth gritted as he forces a smile onto his face. He loathes Richard's influence but at least they agree about Mzilikazi.

Throughout Bulawayo, gathered in their regiments, the surviving warriors sit while in the densely packed huts the seriously wounded fight for their lives.

Shaka calls for quiet. Even the cries of the badly wounded drop away. 'Mzilikazi, you asked for a chance to prove yourself. Truly, you have succeeded! This is a country where the able rise. I am minded to reward you.'

Shaka pauses to reclaim his dish of beer and swallows a long draught. He smacks his lips theatrically. Richard has never seen him so happy. The ebullient king continues, 'We have defeated my greatest enemy and the old fox has slunk off. We shall never be troubled by him again. You, Mzilikazi, have played your part in that!'

Shaka settles on his rolled-mat throne draped in the skins of lions and leopards. 'Tell us the story one more time. I have heard reports. I have listened to the songs already sung to the very borders of my kingdom. Now, before I decide on your reward, I would hear the story from your lips.'

Mzilikazi smiles and bows from his place close to Shaka's feet. His heavy buttocks lift from the backs of his legs, he bends his neck but his face never comes close to the ground. This is not the same supplicant who buried his face in the dirt.

'As you command, mighty Shaka! My part was but small compared to the bravery of your *impi*. Even so, I am happy to relate it and be counted among your warriors.' Richard refills his bowl from an earthenware jar. Bonaparte is not drinking but his azure gaze is fixed jealously on Mzilikazi.

Shaka has forgiven them their disobedience, the Ndwandwes they killed earning them a reprieve. More than that, Shaka treats Richard more fondly, as if the blood he spilled enhances his standing. Richard grimaces as he turns his attention back to Mzilikazi's story.

'I led my party into the forest. We killed and sowed confusion, as did others, masquerading as returning hunters. Your tactics were masterful! I saw my men to safety, but returned, hidden in the dark among the milling Ndwandwe army. I took up an enemy shield, cast off my fine spear and replaced it with a clumsy copy. Nothing distinguished me from the nervous fellows around me talking of ghosts and devils.

'I lay down with them as they rekindled their fires. The men around me could not sleep. They chattered fearfully, and stoked their fires, certain they would be attacked again. I lay beneath that enemy shield, so happy, knowing I would be your instrument!'

Richard looks around the audience of rapt faces. Even dignified old Nandi, usually aloof from matters of battle, leans forward, a frown on her face as she struggles to catch every word.

'As their fuel ran low, they sent men to gather wood. Few returned. Cries sounded as your bands continued to intercept any Ndwandwe separated from the army. I was tempted to act but I bided my time.

'I was close enough to hear Soshangane discussing the situation with his commanders. They argued the attacks were supernatural. Men used to open grassland often fear the forest. But Soshangane is no fool. He understood what we had done and feared there were Zulus within the camp.

'I do not claim I was the only Zulu in that camp, but I was one!' Mzilikazi's well-chosen words delight Shaka, Richard sees, as the king again drains his bowl of beer and calls for more.

'The moon shed little light beneath the trees and fuel was too scarce to bank up their fires to ferret out interlopers. Soshangane decided to wait for morning. I did nothing to draw attention to myself. As I waited, I wondered how I would get out alive, but then it struck me. If I died, it was for a worthy cause. To further mighty Shaka's plans and re-establish my name!

'But a night is long; another thought came, a hopeful thought. These men around me were terrified, they believed the forest was haunted. I resolved to use their fear against them!'

Mzilikazi pauses dramatically, drawing out the tension. He is a fine storyteller, Richard admits.

'When I judged the night at its darkest, I sat up and struck at the man beside me. My spear pierced his chest. He screamed and gurgled. I called out I was stabbed by a sorcerer riding a hyena. All around me was confusion. Men jumped up, lunging in panic with their spears, killing their own brethren. As the camp consumed itself, I slipped away.'

Shaka stands as Mzilikazi finishes. 'Truly, you have proved yourself a brave and resourceful warrior. I shall give you command of an *isigaba*, a division, made up of your own people.'

Mzilikazi inclines his head, a small, satisfied smile on his face but his eyes dart towards Richard and Napoleon brimming with hate.

'Now, I will take up the story of our great victory,' Shaka announces, signalling for more beer to be distributed. The mood is joyful, and growing raucous, as the survivors revel in their delight at being alive. 'Our enemy had lost men and was fearful. They were tired and hungry. I decided to strike immediately.'

Richard listens carefully as does a frustrated Napoleon, who had hoped to use his artillery in the conflict with the Ndwandwes.

'I led the pursuit myself. We caught them east of Sungulweni hill. They were like hungry locusts covering the land. I bloodied the Izin-Tenjana and U-Kangela of the Belebele division, deploying them in columns, five men wide. They pulled left and right. As I intended, Soshangane widened his front to prevent us flanking him. He detached two regiments to deal with our columns. That is when we pressed our advantage!'

Shaka looks around, his eyes resting on Mgobozi and Mdlaka who had been with him. They nod in confirmation of his account.

'The detached Ndwandwe regiments were easy prey for my mobile columns.' Shaka pauses. He has a far-away look and rubs at his eyes vigorously. 'They fought stubbornly and we lost many men before they were crushed and forced to retreat. Another day passed. We harried them. Hunger gnawed at them. Their discipline broke when we attacked at the Umhlatuze ford.'

Mgobozi jumps up, unable to contain himself as Shaka pauses for breath.

'Mighty Shaka gave the order. Up! Children of Zulu, your day has come. Up! Destroy them all! Thousands who had been sitting on their shields sprang to their feet, shouting *bayete*!'

Shaka nods magnanimously at his old friend's interruption but one look suggests he wishes to resume. Mgobozi sits quickly, picks up his bowl and drains it.

'*Bayete*! *Bayete*! *Si-gi-di*! Our war cry thundered across the valley. Every regiment advanced with precision, feet stamping in time. *Si-gi-di*! We charged. We killed beside the river until it was clogged with bodies. Our Jubingqwanga regiment hammered their rearguard.

'The enemy fought desperately as we tried to cross the river. Not even my trusted Ama-Wombe could establish a foothold on the far bank.

'But I was not satiated. I sent the Fasimba downstream and the Izi-cwe upstream. By the time Soshangane realised we were behind him, it was too late! The Ndwandwe *impi* fractured and scattered, only thinking of escape.

'Still, I was not finished. We drove many east, away from the safety of their own lands. I sent fresh regiments, the Monambi and the Isi-Pezi straight to Zwide's royal *kraal*. It is my one regret that Zwide had fled.'

Stately Ngomane interjects, 'Mighty Shaka, it is of no matter that the weasel bolted, for you have united the Nguni speaking world. From the Tugela river in the south to the Pongola in the north, from the Buffalo river in the west to the sea!'

Richard thinks Shaka will call an end to the gathering but the chief surprises him by pointing to the depleted ranks of his *impi*. 'See how many eat the earth, that we might survive! We must not forget their keening mothers. The reward their sons would have earned, shall be theirs. Let it be a double measure!'

Murmurs of surprise turn to shouts of approbation as Shaka's declaration is relayed to the farthest confines of the capital.

Napoleon Bonaparte is drunk. It is the first time Richard has seen him in such a state. His compact body has shed any sign of fat. His muscles move confidently beneath his skin as he paces urgently across the flat hill overlooking Bulawayo. The stench of the crowded town reaches them despite the distance.

An empty brandy bottle lies discarded in the grass. The Zulu capital is a dense agglomeration of huts, its pens unable to contain all the cattle. Additional pens house the overflow west of Bulawayo's walls. Huts proliferate beyond the perimeter, housing newly arrived vassals eager to share the security of Shaka's domain.

'Remind me, my English friend, how long it is, that we have lived in this land?' The alcohol makes him sound petulant, Richard notices.

'It has been more than three years, sire,' Richard replies.

'And in that time, have I not contributed much in strengthening Shaka's army?'

'Muskets and artillery, sire,' Richard agrees.

'And yet, I am still on the fringes. My beautiful cannon see no action. This newcomer Mzilikazi is praised and promoted but I see what he is. He would have all that Shaka has!' Napoleon raises his right hand and stares at it in surprise, as if he thought the brandy bottle was still in his grasp. He looks around for a moment and sees the glass glinting on the ground.

'Sire, are you so very different?' Richard asks tentatively, bracing for an onslaught. Instead, Bonaparte nods in agreement, a rueful expression replacing his sneer.

'I permit you to speak the truth to me. Every wise ruler must have someone unafraid to advise them.' A thoughtful grimace stretches Napoleon's features. 'Did you ever imagine you would be a soldier?'

It is not a question Richard ever expected to be asked. He is a teacher. An historian. Even a time traveller. But he is no warrior. He shivers. The sniper in the woods, the pirates on the *Arniston*, the charging bodyguard at Gqokli hill, the Ndwandwe clubbed to death in the forest. How many men must he kill before he can think himself a soldier? He has his answer as he forces himself to look Napoleon in the face.

'This continent changes us, I think?' Napoleon observes wryly.

Richard nods numbly.

'You have a wife and a son!' Bonaparte prompts with affection. Richard smiles as the image of his little family chases away the ghosts.

'Me? Certainly. But you? How are you different, sire?'

Richard does not get his answer because Napoleon sinks to his knees in the grass, tears leaking down both cheeks.

It is six months since the Ndwandwe invasion was repelled and Shaka assumed overlordship of his extended kingdom. Richard sits beside the tearful Frenchman he crossed time to meet.

He thinks of his son, born before the celebrations of victory had petered out. He has certainly changed. He must live in the company of the men he has killed, but he does so with a wife at his side and a son who looks up at him with unquestioning devotion in his surprising blue eyes.

He thinks he understands Napoleon. He lost everything, including hope. Richard has seen him regain that hope and escape his fate, first by fleeing St Helena, and again, at the hands of the inscrutable *inyanga* whose ministrations purged his body of cancer.

Gifted a healthy body in a new land, Napoleon hungers for influence. He is not a man to follow others. He must feel he is exerting an influence. Can six small cannon satisfy him? Richard thinks not.

New Year 1820. It is summer again; damp and humid. Richard watches the face of his pocket watch, its mechanism still functioning smoothly. He follows the sweep of the second hand, as it closes on XII. It passes and the minute-hand follows. Midnight!

No fireworks, no happy exchanges amidst raucous crowds, no singing garbled Scots. No best friend to carouse with. Emile is back in barracks miles away. He has tried to explain the significance of New Year's Eve to Ulwazi. She seems to understand but he is putting out conflicting signals. He tells her it is a celebration but he is melancholy, even as he nestles his baby in the crook of his arm.

The boy is heavy and he braces his elbow with his knee as he sits against the exterior wall. Richard gazes at his sleeping face, just visible in the firelight from the hut. His eyes, shut tight, are darker now like the depths of the sea. What colour will they become, he wonders, struggling for breath.

Hearing a faint noise, Richard looks up to see a distinctive figure slipping between the packed huts of the resident Fasimba regiment.

What is he doing there? His company is billeted further from the gates and closer to the cattle pens. Sure enough, that is the direction Mzilikazi takes. He swings his arms, head stiff, as if he has almost forgotten how to walk.

In a flash, Richard realizes what looks odd. It is not the man's bloated buttocks or spidery legs. Nor is it his small head. He is a bad actor trying too hard to look nonchalant.

Richard presses down a rising panic. His family are safe behind him. Napoleon can look after himself. Nevertheless, he is sure Mzilikazi has done something dire, in the dark, on the cusp of the old year and the new.

He should act but will learn nothing following Mzilikazi back to his quarters. He stands carefully and dips his head to enter the hut. Ulwazi looks up and smiles.

'I do not understand why your festival makes you frown!' she jokes.

Richard smiles weakly and hands over their son. The boy is a Zulu and he has a Zulu name. He is Zwelakhe. It means, this is his land.

'It's Mzilikazi. I think he has done something bad, tonight.' He looks apologetic as he backs out. He heads towards the

Fasimba huts, cutting across the open ground in front of the council tree. The town's stink is particularly bad but he barely notices.

He is scarcely half-way when shouts of alarm sound. The cries come from the Fasimba section of town. Distinct voices emerge from the noise.

'Murder!'

'Help, come quick!'

'Blood everywhere.'

'His throat has been cut!'

Before Richard reaches the hut at the centre of the commotion, sentries have checked the gates are barred and sent for Ngomane and Nqoboka.

Ngomane is first to arrive and in his commanding presence the hubbub stills. He is every inch a statesman as he questions the crowd.

Richard hears a name. Insumpa. The Fasimba company commander who escorted him to Lourenco Marques. Stalwart, brave and traditional, he is an ally of Nqoboka in resisting outside influence. His men humbled Mzilikazi's raiding party.

Nqoboka arrives in time to hear who has been killed. He ducks into the hut but is back outside quickly.

'There can be no doubt. His throat has been cut. It is murder!' he declaims in a steady voice. 'Who can have done this thing? He was loved by his men!'

Richard opens his mouth. He has information. Mzilikazi acting suspiciously. Taking his revenge? Richard brushes the hair on his neck. He could easily have been the target.

He shuts his mouth without uttering a word. What can he

say? I saw Mzilikazi walking through Bulawayo just before the alarm was sounded. He was walking oddly.

He has nothing to connect Mzilikazi to the killing. Doubtless, the former Khumalo has an explanation ready. He is in Shaka's favour. He has a full division under his command. Richard shot him to save Lucien Thibault. People will think he is the one with a grudge!

This man is poison. He will betray Shaka and the Zulus. But he is wily and popular. No one laughs at him. He is the coming man. Bonaparte is right to worry. If they are not careful, their standing will fall as that of Mzilikazi rises. If he gets the chance, he will see all his rivals discredited or killed. It has already begun.

Bonaparte appears, rubbing his face. He buttons his waistcoat but carries no coat. His feet are bare. Spotting Richard, he hurries over with a puzzled look.

'What is all this disturbance?' he asks sleepily.

'A Fasimba officer, the one I travelled with to Portuguese territory, has been murdered.'

Napoleon registers no surprise but he is immediately awake. His brow creases, shifting his kiss curl. He studies Richard for a moment.

'I see we are thinking along the same lines,' he whispers, 'Mzilikazi?'

Richard nods reluctantly. 'I saw him just before the body was found. He was walking back from these very huts looking too innocent!' He expects Bonaparte to mock him but instead the Frenchman nods thoughtfully.

Richard is tired. He tossed and turned all night. He feels

205

sweaty and irritable. The air is close even when he leaves the hut to visit the foetid latrines. He decides to stetch his legs and is only a hundred yards beyond the gates when he sees General Thibault walking up the slope from the river. His hair is wet.

'Good morning, Richard,' he calls, waving above a friendly smile, 'I have learned to enjoy bathing in the wilderness!'

The young man's enthusiasm is a balm to Richard's sour mood. He wonders if he has heard the news?

'I was sorry to hear about the warthog,' Thibault confides, using the Zulu officer's nickname, 'he was grumpy and resented me but he saved my life!'

There is nothing else to say, but without thinking, Richard falls in step with Thibault as he heads back to Bulawayo.

'The town is grown too crowded,' the Frenchman observes, wrinkling his nose.

'Indeed,' Richard replies, 'there is certainly one man too many inside those walls, and I mean to do something about it.' Thibault looks confused but Richard does not explain.

Richard waits beside the great cattle pen occupying half the length of the northern palisade. Its sturdy fences thrust out, almost to the edge of the parade ground.

A dazzlingly white cow, flanks marred by a single black blot, noses his arm hopefully. Richard strokes her muzzle without taking his eyes from the erstwhile Khumalos' huts.

It is not hot yet, although the ground steams. The cows stomp impatiently, waiting for the herd boys to release them, eager to reach the green grazing that awaits beyond the dun-and-ochre town.

The cow butts him gently, her nose wet on his wrist. He spares her a glance and when he looks back, Mzilikazi is heading towards the enclosure. His eyes are fixed on the cows and he is smiling. He loves cattle and visits the pens every day, doubtless dreaming his own herds might match those of his master.

Richard takes a deep breath and forces the words out, 'I see you, Mzilikazi.'

Startled from his reverie, the Khumalo automatically replies, 'I see you... *umlungu*.' But there is no doubt, from his use of that word, that he has neither forgotten nor forgiven.

'I have been waiting for you,' Richard says in the sternest tone he can muster.

Mzilikazi looks him up and down with disdain, 'Why do you trouble me? Was shooting me not enough?'

Richard forces a smile and keeps his eyes locked on Mzilikazi. 'I know what you did. You think yourself free to act with impunity, sheltered by Shaka's approval.'

The Khumalo gives nothing away. 'What is it you think I have done?' he asks, sounding uninterested. Perhaps he is a better actor than Richard thought?

'You murdered Insumpa in his bed.' Richard is pleased he sounds calm.

'You cannot prove it. No one will believe you. You may be tolerated in Shaka's council but you have enemies there. Would you add me to that list?'

He has denied nothing, Richard notices, going on the offensive instead.

'You think to ally with Nqoboka when even his closest friend Mgobozi disagrees with him. Nqoboka hates all outsiders, you will never be a Zulu to him,' Richard insists.

A flicker distorts Mzilikazi's composure. A tick troubles his left eye and his feet fidget in the dirt.

Richard presses his advantage. 'Gather up your supporters and flee! Shaka will not pursue you if you go far enough north.'

Mgobozi studies the cows, pressing together, crowding the exit from their pens as the herd boys call to them.

'I will not run. I came here to regain what Zwide took from me. He is defeated. I will regain my lands.' There is no doubt in his voice.

Richard smiles. 'I would be glad to see you gone with your titles restored. Shaka promoted you but you have asked for no reward since your bravery in the forest. Ask for the chieftainship; I promise I will support you. So too will Bonaparte. It is likely to suit Nqoboka too. You will have the numbers.'

Mzilikazi watches the cattle ambling past, chivvied by the slap of the herd boys' sticks. He runs his hand along the flank of a dun cow as she draws level. He smiles wistfully and nods his head. It is a decisive action.

'Very well, I agree. If, before this season next year, I am restored as chief of the Khumalo lands, I will depart and trouble you no more.'

Richard does not trust this wily, ruthless man. But he does believe him. He wants this more than further revenge.

'I will speak with Bonaparte today. If I die, he will oppose you. If he is harmed, I will reveal your treachery. But, if we are unmolested, I will argue this thing for you.'

Mzilikazi nods brusquely, turns on his heel, and lopes

towards his hut. Richard watches him go, wondering whether he has made a mistake.

The Tembu and their allies gave stiff resistance but have migrated south. Mzilikazi is restoring order in his reclaimed lands. Shaka's herds grow again. There is not room for them at Bulawayo. The captured women and children crowd around the capital, sleeping beyond the walls like refugees. Men from the routed army drift in, offering their services, eager to be reunited with their loved ones.

Richard stands outside his hut with his one-year-old son, Zwelakhe. The boy grips Richard's thumb in his fist, steadying himself as he stands proudly beside his father. He looks up as Richard looks down. His eyes are no longer blue. He will not be another Napoleon. They are burnished brown flecked with gold. He is his parents' son.

Richard remembers being impressed by the Zulu capital, when it was still unfinished. Scant years later, it looks inadequate and smells intolerable. What was an ideal base at the heart of the tiny Zulu state is now an overcrowded mess, awkwardly far from Shaka's recent acquisitions.

Ulwazi joins them, resting her hand gently on her boy's close-cropped crown. The child gurgles contentedly.

'He is right to move the capital,' Richard confides to his wife.

She does not answer immediately. Richard senses her sharp mind at work. 'It is not so very far,' she finally concedes. 'But it is hard. This is not Esiweni, where I grew up. But it is where I became a wife and mother. It will always be that, no matter how much better this new place may prove.'

Richard thinks of the Victorian villa where he was brought up. Aunt Patricia comes to mind, a wry expression on her haughty face. Her sapphire eyes fix him coldly. Only the warmth of the morning sun on his shoulders and the tug of his son on his thumb pull him back.

'This is the place where I have been happiest,' he confesses. 'But we have our lives ahead of us. I want Zwelakhe to grow and prosper. The new capital will be the place for that.'

Ulwazi leans against him from behind. He can tell she accepts it.

Mobilizing the resources of his vastly extended empire, Shaka has taken less than three months to erect his new capital, Richard realizes. He looks out across the lower Umhlatuze valley to the completed town.

Today, the royal household transfers from the old Bulawayo to the new one. Below, he traces the stately progress of the royal women and their attendants. They walk proudly, guarded by detachments of the Fasimba regiment, singing as they go. Their lyrical voices easily reach him on his outcrop.

Ulwazi and Napoleon are playing with Zwelakhe, who has taken a strong liking to the spectacularly uniformed Frenchman. He giggles as he brushes his cheek against the fringes of his epaulettes and jingles his medals with chubby, playful fingers.

Thibault stands nearby watching the approach of the royal party, a conflicted expression on his face. Napoleon's aide sighs and turns to Richard. 'A fine sight, in its way. I acknowledge Shaka's achievements. His influence grows rapidly. But I am not like you. I cannot accommodate myself to this Africa. It will forever be alien to me.'

Richard can see the young man has more to say and tries to look encouraging.

'I saw my voyage with General Bertrand as an adventure. I was happy to serve the emperor whose uniform I was proud to wear.' Here, he pauses to look at his threadbare jacket and stained breeches.

He grimaces. The blue material is tinged green and his white leggings are grey despite assiduous washing. The shine he maintains on his boots shows the pride he still feels, Richard knows.

'When the general departed for America, I could have gone with him. But he was ill and unable to complete his mission. I saw it as my duty to do that for him. So here I am.' He looks over to where Napoleon Bonaparte, former Emperor of the French, is playing horse, with Richard's grinning son riding on his back.

'I fear I met the emperor too late. He is not what I expected.'

There is so much truth in Thibault's words that Richard has to look away to the valley floor. He studies the raw wood of the new palisade. 'It is time, Lucien, for you to seek a life you can live rather than one you believe you owe.' Richard is surprised at himself. 'As you say, I have made this land my home. The emperor too, in his way, accepts his circumstances, although he ever works to improve them!'

General Thibault, once so gauche and awkward, wipes a tear from his eye and thanks Richard in a voice choked with emotion. 'Doubtless, the emperor will have some final use for me,' he manages, 'some message I can deliver, perhaps?'

Richard pats him discreetly on his forearm and returns to his family. As he bends down to relieve Napoleon of his son, he is struck by a thought that fills his body with well-being. He is content.

Napoleon studies him with interest while still on all fours. 'What is it, Richard?' he asks.

To have the former emperor use his Christian name still affects him. It also convinces him he is right.

'Napoleon,' he says. It is the very first time he has spoken directly to the man using his given name, 'I would like you to be my son's godfather.'

Bonaparte stands and brushes himself down. He does not, at first, lift his head, as if he is buying time before replying. Richard's euphoria is replaced by burgeoning disquiet. Has he asked something inappropriate? Has the Frenchman taken offence?

The famous bicorn hat is in the dust, Richard sees. He takes a step towards it but gets no further before he is restrained by Napoleon, who pulls him into a bearhug.

Chapter Ten

April 1821

Richard strolls with Ulwazi and their son around the new capital. The cattle have returned and are noisily chewing the cud in their vast pens. Zwelakhe watches them closely.

'*Okumhlophe*,' he says, pointing to a snowy cow; '*nsundu*,' he declares, indicating a dun animal. Richard beams with pleasure.

Ulwazi leans down and whispers in her son's tiny ear. The boy nods earnestly and peers up at his father.

'White,' he indicates, followed by 'brown,' as he extends his forefinger again. Richard laughs and sweeps his son into his arms, burying his head in his sweet-smelling neck to hide his tears.

Recovered, he hugs his wife and kisses her despite the stares of passers-by. 'Nothing can spoil this,' he gushes.

Shaka's new capital is a fine place. The valley in which it sits is a broad expanse of grassland, punctuated with the thorny profile of acacia trees. It offers fine grazing for the Zulu herds. The river provides a reliable water supply. There are no signs of drought.

The site itself is on the gentle valley slope. The area within the palisade is a mile wide and tilts enough to shed heavy rain but not so much as to make building difficult.

Just uphill from the central area of the town are the fences of the cattle pens, flanked by a concentric interior wall that separates the huts from the open space inside. The huts are arranged in six rings between the palisade and the internal fence. Richard knows how many there are, because he has counted them meticulously. There are fifteen hundred and eleven.

The segment immediately north of the cattle pens is defined by another palisade. Here are the royal quarters divided into sections: for servants; the women of the *isigodlo*, to be disposed of as Shaka wills; those chosen as Shaka's hareem, the *umdlunkulu*; Shaka's family members; his own residence; and the large council hut.

From the surrounding hills the town looks like a massive keyhole or a giant's life preserver.

Richard and Ulwazi have almost completed a circle of the town. He misses the council tree at the old capital. Their son nestles in his mother's comfortable grip, suckling noisily. Richard marvels at how easily she carries Zwelakhe, now that he is nearing twenty months old.

There is a commotion at the gate into the centre of town. A panting pair of herd boys, almost old enough to serve their elders in the regiments, are being quizzed by the guards. Whatever the news, it is attracting a lot of interest.

Richard leads his little family towards the growing scrum of listeners. He is not surprised when Napoleon appears, heading in the same direction. They arrive just after Mbopa, who runs the royal household. He is short and pudgy but his pinprick eyes are everywhere.

'*Abelungu*,' someone whispers in the official's ear. He nods grimly and summons a servant whom he instructs pedantically before sending him running towards the royal enclosure.

Listening at the edge of the crowd, Richard pieces together snatches of information, relayed from the herd boys. Ulwazi gives their son to Richard, and moves into the crowd. Richard clasps the boy protectively to his chest.

Ulwazi returns within five minutes. Zwelakhe is beginning to grizzle but stops as soon as he sees his mother. 'They say there is a party of *abelungu* heading this way. They have set up a camp on the coast.' She pauses and frowns. 'They say a giant white-winged bird sits on the water there.' She sounds uncertain, as if her own language has become suspect.

'It will be a ship like the one you saw at Lourenco Marques,' Richard replies, a quaver of concern audible as he speaks.

Ulwazi's face relaxes. 'Then we need not worry,' she concludes happily.

Richard is not so sure. His wife's encounters with Europeans have given her no cause to fear, but history suggests she should be wary. Who can it be? The first white men to make sustained contact with the Zulus arrive in 1824, three years from now.

He does not have to wait long to find out. It is less than an hour between the youths arriving with their news and the unexpected visitors' arrival. But in that short interval much is done to prepare Bulawayo.

Attendants flick brooms across the dusty earth of the town centre. The Fasimba form up as an honour guard flanking the narrow funnel that leads from the town gates into the heart of the town. More of them parade in a semicircle facing the entrance.

Shaka sits atop a throne of rolled mats strewn with leopard hides, flanked by Nandi and Pampata, while his councillors sit in their feathered finery at his feet. Richard stays with his wife at the edge of the gathering. A relay of calls announces the imminent arrival of these unknown travellers. The king signals everyone to silence.

With the cows grazing the slopes of the valley, there is nothing to disturb the hush. It is so quiet, Richard can hear the approach of men on horses, bridles jangling, the animals breathing heavily in protesting snorts.

A coal-black crow flies low over the vast *kraal*. Heads look away, refusing to acknowledge the omen. But Richard watches it settle on the palisade beyond the royal enclosure, a hunched presence, tainting the stillness with a mocking voice.

A collective gasp makes Richard turn back to the entrance. Men on horseback, dusty but dignified, ride sedately from the mouth of the guarded channel. Thousands of Zulus stare at the horses and then up to the men balancing on them.

The man leading the party looks to be in his mid-thirties. He wears a cocked hat and a uniform with epaulettes that looks suspiciously home-made. Behind him is a young man in civilian dress, his shirt open at the collar, a lightweight jacket and cotton trousers over dark boots. His face is shaded beneath a broad-brimmed straw hat with a black band.

'Brown zebras, I have never seen such a thing,' Ulwazi whispers. 'They are bigger than our striped beasts.'

More men follow. They are armed with swords, muskets or rifles, although their weapons remain in holsters and waistbands, hanging from hip or saddle.

Many of the men are heavily bearded beneath slouch hats. Their knee-length coats are blue or grey, with wide lapels and beneath them, unexpectedly, most have colourful waistcoats under short jackets. Every man has a powder horn hanging from his belt.

The last ten men look different, uncomfortable on their horses and dressed like artisans or tradesmen.

Richard's mind races as the very last man appears, trailing a little behind the others. There is something familiar about him. He is a tall, thin man, gripping his reins with bony hands. His calculating green eyes look watery but rove everywhere above his proud, straight nose. White hair protrudes beneath the rim of his straw hat.

'Now that is an unpleasant surprise,' quips a French voice behind him. Glancing over his shoulder, Richard finds Bonaparte looking serious. 'You should have let me shoot him!' he continues sternly. 'This will mean trouble for us, I have no doubt.'

Napoleon's accusation takes Richard back to his first moments on an African shore, sand beneath his feet, watching Captain Simpson of the East India Company being rowed away towards his damaged ship, the *Arniston*. What was it he had said?

'You have made an enemy of me today and I do not die easily. It is my fervent hope we meet again. Perhaps I will get the jump on you?' Those words have stayed with Richard, although he has not thought about them for a long time.

'I think you should make yourself scarce, there is no sense revealing your presence unnecessarily,' Richard cautions.

Bonaparte says nothing but takes several steps back so that

his bright uniform is shielded from view. Richard is glad he is not wearing his bicorn hat today.

Dressed in cotton and canvas in white and buff, the man on the final horse looks nothing like a ship's captain. On the other hand, his calculating eyes warn against underestimating him.

Richard is glad he is standing to one side as the former merchant captain's eyes slide across him to focus on the magnificent form of Shaka Zulu standing to welcome his uninvited guests.

The leading pair halt their horses at a respectful distance and dismount. Their party lines up in three ranks behind them, before slipping from their makeshift-looking saddles to stand, less confident now, soothing their mounts.

An eerie quiet holds Bulawayo in its thrall. Even the crow has flapped away without further comment.

Shaka looks momentarily troubled, scanning the array of his advisers and clearly not finding what he wants. Guiltily, Richard shuffles closer to the king draped in his leopard skins, a red-and-white headdress accentuating his physical presence.

Seeing Richard, the king beckons impatiently but does not speak to him. Instead, he holds his arms wide, the ceremonial, miniature spear in one hand and a tiny shield in the other.

Several of the assembled Europeans laugh nervously before their commander barks at them to show more respect. Shaka pretends not to notice.

'Welcome to Bulawayo, capital of the Zulu empire!' he booms proudly in his rich bass. 'I am Shaka and I rule here.'

The look of astonishment on the face of every visitor is

precisely what Shaka intends. He grins widely, delighted at their surprise.

'You are English, then?' he insists.

The man in the ramshackle uniform steps forward a single pace. The Fasimba warriors tense but do nothing. The clean-shaven figure bows elegantly, removing his straw hat to reveal a full head of dark-brown hair, parted on his right.

As he lifts his head, Richard is struck by his strong nose with flaring nostrils. He has a cleft in his chin that many might hide beneath whiskers. His mouth rests naturally in a smile.

'I and some of my party are English,' he speaks confidently, hiding his surprise now, 'the others are Boers but they answer to me.' He indicates the blue-and-grey-clad men in short jackets.

Shaka is not in a hurry to interrupt, so the man continues. 'I am Lieutenant Farewell, formerly of the Royal Navy, I travel under warrant from the governor of the Cape Colony to establish trading relations with your kingdom.'

Richard should be more surprised. This meeting is happening three years early. He eyes Captain Simpson, doubtless the catalyst. The Boer contingent stare at the massed Fasimba warily, while the Englishmen Richard thinks tradesmen, huddle together, whispering uncertainly.

'Tell me, Fearwall, what it is you wish and what you offer in return.' There is a hungry look in Shaka's eyes but Richard barely notices. For a moment, he is a teacher again, drawing satisfaction from the mastery of a pupil. Shaka's English is much improved.

The lieutenant does not correct the pronunciation of his

name. 'I seek ivory. We have many wonders from our civilization to brighten your lives!' he declares, conjuring a string of multicoloured beads from his coat pocket.

Shaka looks unimpressed but Nandi and Pampata lean towards him, each whispering in an ear. The chief nods and smiles.

'We will examine your goods shortly. I invite you and your chief councillors to join me in the royal enclosure.'

Farewell looks at his casually attired companion and is about to introduce him when Shaka holds up a hand.

'Introductions later. First, I would see more of these animals you arrived upon. I have seen the beasts of burden used by my French friends but they carried equipment not men.'

Mention of Frenchmen causes Farewell to start. Deliberately, Napoleon Bonaparte steps forward into his line of sight.

'No, don't!' Richard cries impotently.

Gone is the piratical headscarf Bonaparte often sports, replaced by his ubiquitous hat. He looks every inch the Emperor of the French restored to his prime. He smiles and slips his right hand between the open buttons of his waistcoat.

Farewell turns to Captain Simpson, whose expression is eloquent. Smug satisfaction wars with a greedy look Richard first saw in his trading office on St Helena.

Shaka does not notice their reaction: he is consulting his council.

It takes a few minutes for Shaka to decide precisely what he wishes to see. The bulk of the party are escorted back through the defile that cuts through the huts between inner and outer palisades. When they are all safely outside, the gates are closed, despite their protests.

Farewell calls for them to remain calm and do nothing that might be interpreted as an act of aggression. The men outside quieten. Farewell and Simpson remain with the unnamed third man.

'Show me how you do this thing!' Shaka commands.

Farewell springs into his saddle while Simpson levers himself up, relying heavily on his stirrup. The third character, by far the youngest, vaults carelessly onto his mount.

Farewell gestures forward with his right arm and the trio heel their horses into a trot around the central area of the town. Their animals look in good condition and pick up their hooves willingly.

When they have circled three times, Farewell calls for them to halt. Simpson's mare backs up a few paces before he brings her fully under control. He slides from the saddle with a look of relief on his face. 'That is enough for me,' he mutters just loudly enough for Richard to hear. The other two laugh at him but they mean no insult.

Shaka looks dissatisfied. 'Is this all?' he asks before tapping Mgobozi on the shoulder and instructing him rapidly in Zulu. Mgobozi runs off and returns in less than a minute with two Fasimba warriors. They hand him their shields and spears.

'I wish to see which is faster, you on these animals or my men on their bare feet,' Shaka explains.

A look of concern tugs at Farewell's brows. 'Lord Shaka, it is not my intention to humiliate your fine soldiers. They have but two legs and our horses four. There has never been born a man who can outrun a horse.' Farewell's precise voice is warm and considerate.

Shaka fixes him with his sternest expression. 'Have you encountered a Zulu warrior before?' he demands.

'I have not, King Shaka… but I am sure they are swift and strong.'

Shaka looks mollified but does not concede. 'Do you wager in your country?' he asks.

'At times,' Farewell replies.

'Very well, if you win, I will gift you a dozen pairs of elephant tusks. But if my warriors are victorious, I claim all the goods you have brought with you!' The Zulu king looks to his mother, who smiles her approval. Pampata too is beaming.

The massed onlookers press back against the inner palisade and Shaka's throne is moved against the fences of his cattle corral. He and his advisers settle down to watch the competition. Richard sits on a mat, no longer awkward without a chair. Napoleon joins him, smiling as if nothing has happened.

'You may very well have doomed Shaka's empire to a war they cannot win, a war not meant to be fought for half a century!' Richard hisses, utterly exasperated. Bonaparte accepts his outburst calmly.

'He will have to make use of my artillery now, will he not?'

Farewell and the youngster heave on their reins, the tension around the vast *kraal* making their horses skittish. The two lithe Zulu warriors stretch nonchalantly, joking with each

222

other, naked bar a partial kilt of fur tails. They are dwarfed by the horses; the riders loom above them. It looks a hopeless mismatch.

Mdlaka stands on the far side of the starting line. He raises his hands, palms skyward. He brings them together forcefully. The single clap is improbably loud.

The Fasimba pair react first, launching themselves forward, running close to the deep crowd ringing the makeshift racecourse. The mounted men gather their horses and urge them on. Within a dozen strides they overhaul the Zulu athletes.

'They think it is a sprint,' Napoleon says, 'but that is not what Shaka intends.'

The horses' hooves thunder beneath their jockeys, kicking up dust until the air is gritty and the onlookers are forced to squint. Farewell sits his horse confidently. His gelding is a muscular chestnut of some fifteen hands with a long, even stride. He is in the lead as he crosses the start-finish line after one lap.

Close behind comes his young companion on a roan with a black mane and tail, smaller-boned and shorter in the leg. The rider leans forwards against the mare's straining neck.

The two Fasimba run abreast through the dust tailing the cantering horses. Richard cannot imagine how they can see but they do not stumble as they cross the line.

'They are a quarter of a lap behind already,' Richard laments. He is surprised how much he wants the Zulus to win even though it seems impossible.

'Patience,' Bonaparte counsels, 'I may have been an artilleryman but I know a thing or two about horses.' A far-away look steals over his face. He is no longer watching the race. 'I miss Marengo, my fine Arab stallion,' he shares, 'but perhaps it was better he was lost in battle.'

Napoleon returns his attention to the race and Richard does not tell him of his horse's fate. Marengo was caught and claimed by the Eleventh Baron Petre who later sold him to a lieutenant-colonel of the Grenadier Guards. He lived to be thirty-eight and his skeleton was eventually displayed at the National Army Museum in Chelsea.

Two more circuits and the horsemen are a clear lap in the lead. Richard studies the Fasimba who continue unperturbed, still side by side, bare feet flying. They breathe easily, he notices, while the roan, now coated in dust like her young rider, foams at the bit, chest heaving.

'That is not a horse to ride on the limit,' Bonaparte suggests as the animal falters. Her rider recovers skilfully but they are now a good half a lap behind Farewell who whoops at every pass of the line.

The air is warm and gritty: even Bonaparte's Chasseurs uniform is sandy and dull. A lap passes and another, the two Zulus' pace is unaltered, although they are sheened in sweat. The smaller horse stumbles again and cannot maintain a canter, dropping to an ungainly trot before her rider turns her head, pulling the mare from the race.

All around, the shrieking crowd celebrates. What must the men beyond the walls think, Richard wonders? He half expects them to storm the palisade, guns drawn.

Bonaparte nudges him. 'This Farewell rides well but he is reckless. Look how his horse strains to please him. He is riding that loyalty too carelessly.'

Richard watches another passage. The runners are holding pace with the gelding now. The chestnut horse is lathered and his stride shortening. After a further lap, it is clear the Fasimba pair, still shoulder to shoulder, are unravelling Farewell's lead.

Three more laps and they are close on his heels, while his horse's breathing is louder than the thunder of his hooves. The Zulus split for the first time, moving around the faltering horse on either side. Once past, and back on the same lap as the riding man, they resume formation.

Farewell kicks his mount's flanks, slapping his rump and shouting in his flattened ears but nothing can energise the flagging beast. As he approaches the next turn, the gelding's right foreleg crumples and the animal concertinas to earth, flinging Farewell over a dipped shoulder into the dirt.

The two Fasimba warriors complete another lap and then halt in front of Shaka. They are blowing hard, chests heaving, fine dust coating their slick bodies. All around Bulawayo echo cheers of praise for their victory.

Farewell rejoins his companions, panting heavily and walking gingerly as he leads his blown horse.

'Did you see that, Fynn? Incredible! Those unshod fellows ran me down,' he gushes, eyes wide and bright with excitement. 'What a place this is, look at the scale of it!'

The man Farewell named as Fynn lets his mount nose the trembling gelding, while Captain Simpson stares implacably at Napoleon Bonaparte. Richard can imagine what he is thinking. Here is the man who bested him. The deposed enemy of the British empire, escaped from exile, and ripe for recapture. Simpson will be pondering the acclaim that will be his if he returns with this prize.

Mbopa approaches Richard, 'Shaka requires his full council to meet with these *abelungu* visitors.' Here the subtle administrator pauses, looking uncomfortable. 'Mdlaka and I do not know what should be done with the men outside.' It is clearly uncomfortable for him to admit uncertainty, doubly difficult to seek advice from Richard, but he has done so.

'Send that one,' he points to Simpson, 'the tall one, with a message from their leader that all is well. Send him with food and water for their horses.' He can see relief in Mbopa's eyes as he nods and turns away. Richard is glad to be rid of Captain Simpson, even for a short time. He must speak privately with Shaka Zulu.

Reluctantly he hurries after Mbopa and waits for him to finish issuing instructions. The man's pudgy face almost hides his eyes but Richard senses the cruelty in this man.

'It is vital I speak with mighty Shaka, I have knowledge of these visitors he needs before he receives them in the council hut.'

Richard watches Mbopa's wily mind weigh the consequences of agreeing and refusing. He decides to press his point. 'It would be unfortunate should he find he was denied vital information that meant he was outmanoeuvred by the *abelungu*.'

Mbopa glances over to Nqoboka who is talking intently with his old friend Mgobozi as they walk towards the royal enclosure.

'Tell me what you know and I will ensure my king receives it,' he suggests in oily tones.

'So that you can take credit?' counters Richard firmly. 'That cannot work. What I know, only I could know and Shaka would see you for what you are!'

Mbopa scowls and his eyes dart between Farewell and the receding figure of his master, surrounded by attendants.

'Follow me!' he barks reluctantly, hurrying after the royal entourage. Richard falls in step immediately behind the scuttling figure.

They overtake Ngomane who is escorting Farewell and Fynn. Drawing alongside Nqoboka and Mgobozi, they receive contrasting looks. Mgobozi grins while Nqoboka turns his head away haughtily, looking offended.

Richard shadows Mbopa as he skirts the royal party to whisper in his sovereign's ear. Shaka comes to an abrupt halt, his followers barely avoiding a collision with him.

'Provide our guests with refreshment,' Shaka commands, 'while I prepare to receive them in the council hut.' Turning his handsome face to Richard, he adds, 'You will accompany me, and explain yourself!' He does not sound pleased.

Richard bows and then scans ahead for a sight of Bonaparte. He cannot see him. Biting his lip, he reluctantly follows the Zulu monarch.

The new council hut is twice the size of the one at old Bulawayo, but in every other respect it is the same. He still has to duck through the entrance. The floor is tamped and polished dirt. The rafters arc gracefully and the thatch is immaculate. The hearth flickers with flame and smoke palls above Richard's head, gradually escaping through the close-packed reed roof.

Fragrant wood burns slowly. Shaka seats himself on his throne of bundled mats, overlain with leopard and lion pelts. Richard approaches and bows deeply before sitting back on his knees at a respectful distance. No one else is present.

'Speak!' Shaka's voice fills the domed building, reverberating through the rafters.

'This Farewell is an adventurer. He genuinely wishes trade. The young one, I heard him called Fynn, he is the same. But the third one, who did not race his horse, he is different. I have met him before.'

Shaka's eyes widen and a calculating look claims his features. He senses an advantage. 'Tell me!'

Richard gives an edited version of his dealings with Captain Simpson, finishing with a warning, 'This man will not stop until he has ensnared Bonaparte and delivered him to his enemies. If he is not dealt with carefully, more like him will follow.' Richard stops, worried he has fired the shot he prevented on that beach three years ago.

Shaka leans forward, chin jutting belligerently. 'This whole party of *abelungu*, they are vulnerable. They have no more guns than my musket company. Should I let my French adviser dispose of them? He would like that, I think?'

This is what Richard wants to prevent. He risks looking straight into Shaka's penetrating eyes.

'Mighty Shaka, you could, no doubt, kill them all. But when none return, others will come. There will be more of them and they will be heavily armed. Only one of them presents a danger.'

'So, I kill the tall one and agree trade terms with the rest?' Richard can tell Shaka finds the solution appealing, but his mind is a steel trap, he calculates every angle.

'Grant Farewell and the others the right to remain on the coast, to establish a trading post. Send a trusted man to live among them as your representative.'

Shaka is quiet as he considers Richard's suggestion. His big hands rest lightly on his knees. 'I agree. Mbikwane has been with me since the beginning. He has tact and everyone likes him. He shall be my ambassador.' Here Shaka uses the English word with a flourish. He grins at Richard who relaxes.

'I would be happy to accompany your man for as long as he needs a translator familiar with *abelungu* customs. I only ask you allow me to take my family.' Shaka stands and descends, holding out a hand. Richard takes it and feels the man's power as he is hauled upright.

'Agreed. I may not need an English teacher any more, but it seems I still have uses for my English adviser! I shall also despatch Mhlope to watch and listen. He is my best spy. He will infiltrate this trading post and report to Mbikwane.'

Richard realizes his hand is still clasped in Shaka's strong grip. A shiver runs down his spine, engendered by pleasure rather than fear.

Farewell and Fynn look pale and scruffy before the royal council. They bow and sit without complaint. Shaka studies them for several minutes.

'It is good you have come,' he confides finally, 'I am happy to grant you the right to trade.' Shaka's English is clear but he deliberately switches to Zulu, emphasizing they are the strangers here. 'You may establish yourselves on the spot you currently occupy. I shall send an embassy to live among you.'

Richard translates, adding, 'I shall join that delegation.' He risks a smile.

'In exchange, I require an ambassador from among your party. I should like the tall one.' Shaka has reverted to English. 'Captain Samson?' he adds for clarity.

Farewell looks to Fynn and then across at Richard who is sitting discreetly in the shadows beyond the modest firelight. His expression is troubled, as if he is being asked for something beyond his power.

'I am not sure Captain Simpson will wish to remain,' Farewell offers apologetically.

Shaka waves his words away with a dismissive gesture. 'Samson remains or you depart my lands immediately! My trusted Fasimba will escort you to the coast and ensure you depart the way you came.'

Chapter Eleven

May 1821

A sorry cluster of makeshift shelters, stacked crates and canvas awnings spill across the flat beach into the dunes. Ulwazi hugs Zwelakhe, despite the presence of two hundred Fasimba warriors driving a small herd of cattle.

Mbikwane strides confidently beside them, his amiable, open face betraying no anxiety. Richard has been teaching him a few words of English as they travel and he is a quick learner.

It is three weeks since the trading party made their appearance at Bulawayo. Farewell and his companions remained for a restrained feast and departed the next day, leaving a surly Captain Simpson behind with the promise he would be relieved within three months. Richard wonders if he is still alive?

As they pass the last tree in the dune forest, Richard notices a cluster of indigenous-style huts on the fringes of the shoddy settlement. He sees a few older men but mainly women and children. Richard is sure Mhlope, Shaka's spy, will already be among the locals attracted by European medicine and trade goods.

Within minutes of their arrival, the Fasimba fighters are gathering building materials from the dune forest to construct the Zulu embassy.

Mbikwane is greeted with smiles and deference by Farewell and Fynn. The former, now wearing sailor's trousers and a ragged shirt worn open at the chest, adds, 'We apologise for the state of our poor settlement. We lost most of our supplies in a storm. Our ship is badly damaged and will require months of work before it can sail. So, we make do with what we have!' He sounds inordinately cheerful for a man who has sunk his savings into a venture that has, so far, achieved nothing, Richard thinks. He does, however, translate faithfully.

Mbikwane's reply is friendly but unambiguous. 'Mighty Shaka grants you permission to establish a *kraal* on this shore. You may hunt to feed your people. But if you wish ivory, you must trade with Shaka's representatives. He will set the price. To start, he wishes to trade for horses.' Mbikwane refers to the animals as big zebras.

'Why does he need horses if his warriors are superior to a mounted man?' asks Fynn with a touch of irritation.

Farewell elbows him firmly in the ribs and continues to smile ingratiatingly. 'We will be happy to oblige but at present we have no means of transporting livestock from the Cape. Once the *Julia* is repaired, things will be different.'

Mbikwane is unperturbed at this news and turns to watch his soldiers returning. The Fasimba troops stack their materials and pace out the dimensions of the huts they intend to build. They have chosen a site close to the dunes, equidistant between the Europeans' shelters and those of the locals.

Richard expects Farewell to express some view on this development, but he simply nods his approval. Among the lean-to shelters, the eyes of his party study the activity of the Fasimba. Several of the watchers surreptitiously grasp their firearms for comfort.

Boer members of the expedition talk in an animated way with each other. One heavily bearded fellow, with a grizzled appearance and a particularly floppy hat, scowls and spits in the sand. A younger companion is talking fast, tugging his sleeve and pointing at Mbikwane.

Reluctantly, the older man joins Farewell and Fynn in front of statesmanlike Mbikwane. Richard studies the man more closely and receives a cursory appraisal in return.

'Lieutenant Farewell, my men are uncomfortable with so many armed warriors in camp,' he growls in thickly accented English. 'The experience of living on the frontier does not encourage trust. Cattle raids, ambushes, broken promises, servants disappearing in the night. You cannot trust these men.' There is a certainty to his declaration that irks Richard but he holds his tongue having relayed the man's meaning to Mbikwane.

'What did your men expect to find this far beyond the borders of the Cape, Jan?' Richard can hear the effort required by Farewell to keep his question civil.

'Opportunity,' the Boer leader replies, 'land, hunting,' he adds, 'and freedom,' he finishes with feeling.

'I understand,' Farewell admits, in seemingly genuine tones, 'but when you signed on with me, there was no ambiguity. No one will offer violence to the indigenous peoples while you remain under my command.'

Richard watches the Boers trying to follow what is being said from a distance. There are about twenty of them, twice the number of Englishmen present.

'You should listen, Lieutenant. My people have lived on this continent for over one hundred and fifty years. You arrived last year, your empire only seized the Cape in 1806,' Jan insists in his intractable voice.

Farewell looks unhappy, glancing apologetically at Mbikwane who has kept his own counsel as Richard translates. 'Are you questioning my authority?' the former naval officer demands brusquely.

Jan gazes out to sea, his eyes coming to rest on the sloop wallowing in the bay. The *Julia* sits low in the water, de-masted and devoid of canvas. He shakes his head, mumbles in his own language and wanders back to his followers who gather around, firing questions at him.

'You must forgive Jan Malan,' Farewell says to Mbikwane, 'his people are not happy under English rule. They seek a place of their own.'

The Zulu diplomat looks sharply at the lieutenant. 'Not here,' he says, his words devoid of their usual niceties, 'they should go far away or incur Shaka's displeasure!'

Richard relays Mbikwane's meaning but Farewell has already grasped it. 'I shall keep them in hand. We will respect Shaka's dominion but it would help if he would grant us a larger area within which we can move freely.'

Mbikwane does not reply at first, his attention fixed on the work of his soldiers. Farewell and Fynn wait patiently.

'I will relay your request, but for now the beach is yours, while you may hunt for food inland. But go no further than necessary, for if you do, Shaka shall hear of it.'

Richard thinks of Mhlope, lurking among the local

tribesmen, his eyes ever active. There is no way for any of Farewell's group to move beyond the sands without it being noticed.

Darkness descends quickly. Richard sits with Mbikwane on the sand. Ulwazi and their son are being hosted in one of the local's huts. On the other side of the fire are Fynn, Farewell and Malan. They are eating venison, carving chunks from the bone with sturdy knives. The remainder of the antelope crackles and spits fat into the fire, suspended on a pole resting on forked supports.

Malan gets up and turns the spit a quarter revolution, raking the coals to spread them out, ensuring the meat cooks evenly. He then calls over his shoulder.

Two youths, dressed in the grey cloth and leather of their elders, appear and begin carving the remainder of the roasting animal, placing the cuts on the lid of a tea chest. They make short work of the task and disappear, their trencher piled with meat. Soon the sounds of hungry men eating quickly can be heard all around.

The meat runs with fat but tastes delicious; it is moist, bloody at the centre and mildly gamey. Richard eats enthusiastically, as does Mbikwane, who smacks his lips in appreciation. Richard mimics him, as this is Zulu etiquette. Soon the Europeans are copying him, competing to outdo each other in volume.

Farewell peers through the flames, catching Richard's eye. He tilts his head before rising and leaving the ring of firelight. Richard makes his excuses and does the same. The two men meet on the seaward edge of the camp, just above the reach of the surf.

The beach and the sounds of the sea remind Richard of his very first night sleeping on the African shore.

'How do you come to be here, Mister Davey?' Farewell asks without further preamble.

It is a question Richard has been expecting from the moment Bonaparte chose to reveal himself. He has considered a number of stories but rejected them as unconvincing.

'What has Captain Simpson told you?' he counters.

'That you hoodwinked him, sir, into smuggling Boney from under the noses of the British garrison on St Helena.' There is something close to admiration in his words. 'I tell you, I teased him mercilessly for his imagination, until that moment in Shaka's capital, when Napoleon Bonaparte appeared in full dress uniform!'

'You believe that man is really Napoleon?' Richard asks levelly.

'You cannot expect me to believe he is an impostor? Do you deny you booked passage with Simpson on the *Arniston*, accompanied by a friend and a maid?'

Richard watches the fizzing surf retreat down the gentle slope of the sand. He cannot construct a credible denial. Captain Simpson's revenge may be in hand.

'It is he,' Richard admits, 'I have been with him since Waterloo.'

'But you are English, dammit!' exclaims the former naval officer incredulously. 'Encountering Napoleon in the wilds of Africa is not so surprising as finding an Englishman his ally... you do not carry Irish or Scots blood, do you?'

Richard does not answer directly but tells a version of his story close to the one he wove for Lieutenant Béraud on the eve of Waterloo, although he sees no point in claiming American citizenship.

'You are a traitor, sir!' Farewell declares as Richard finishes.

'I am a Zulu now. My wife and son are of this land. My motivations are my own. I do not choose to share them with you. But let me ask you, what do you make of Shaka's kingdom? You have travelled a fair portion of it, you must have formed some impression?'

It is the adventurer's turn to watch the sea, the breakers white in the night, defining sea from sky where they foam against the reef.

'I confess to being astonished. Law and order prevail. The land is rich and well populated. Bulawayo,' his tongue clumsily shapes the name, 'the scale of the place…' he grows thoughtful again and the sounds of men turning in for the night fill the silence.

'How long will you stay?' Richard enquires gently.

'Until I have made my fortune,' Farewell replies confidently.

Richard tenses. There are many ways to make a fortune but few so easy as returning to Cape Town with a captive Napoleon Bonaparte.

'And how do you intend to achieve that?' Richard hears the concern in his voice with annoyance.

'Gold or ivory, those are my best bets, I think.' Francis Farewell pauses and rests a hand on Richard's shoulder. It is a surprising gesture from a practical stranger and Richard cannot help tensing. Farewell withdraws his hand.

'Forgive me, I was unforgivably rude. A man must find his way in this life. That is what I left the navy to do, that is what Malan seeks, it is the same for you. I may not approve of your chosen allegiance but we all face difficult choices. These Boers I travel with, they are not my people. Indeed, they hate all I stand for.'

Richard feels a rush of warmth towards Farewell. Few would try to see things from his point of view, even fewer could approach understanding an Englishman siding with the ogre and tyrant used to scare children across the British empire!

'But surely you feel compelled to report what you have discovered to the authorities in the Cape?' he asks.

Again, Farewell is thoughtful and does not rush to reply. When he does speak, his words are deliberate. 'Let us make a bargain, you and I. Francis Farewell will make no mention of Bonaparte's presence in Zululand to anyone. In exchange, Richard Davey will use his considerable influence to secure extensive trading rights for my endeavour.'

Richard nods enthusiastically and shakes hands. Farewell's grip is firm and dry.

'Agreed. But I must warn you. The words you spoke with Malan in front of Mbikwane. I translated them all. He will hold you responsible for the actions of all your party.'

They walk along the beach. Richard looks back to the camp. He can see the fires as bright pinpricks against the night. The smell of the sea is in his nostrils, the soft sand is beneath his feet. His blood courses to the rhythm of the coastal night.

Francis Farewell grips his elbow briefly and this time

Richard neither tenses nor pulls away. 'It might suit you, some misdemeanour resulting in Captain Simpson's life being forfeit?' It is not an accusation. 'While he has put some funds into my company, I see him for what he is, a man whose actions are purely predicated on profit.'

Richard notes the contempt oozing from Farewell's assessment.

'You would ally yourself with a traitor against a member of your own party?' Richard asks, genuinely surprised.

'When you put it that way, it does not sound pretty. Nevertheless, there you have it,' Farewell admits.

Richard looks at his face, hidden in the dark but split by two rows of whiteish, even teeth. Is it a face he can trust? He thinks it is.

'I have too much blood on my hands already,' he confesses. 'I do not relish adding to the tally. Captain Simpson is no friend of mine. He seeks Napoleon's capture and would happily see him dead.'

The lieutenant does not demur.

'So, I cannot deny his elimination would suit me, but I shall not actively pursue that end.' The ambiguity makes him cringe, and sure enough, Farewell seizes on it.

'I believe we understand each other, Richard. I trust I may call you Richard?'

'Yes, and shall I call you Francis?'

Days at the camp pass easily. Richard watches the Fasimba construct Mbikwane's embassy. It is complete in three days and puts to shame the hodgepodge of materials that passes as a settlement for the traders.

An outer palisade with a reinforced gate surrounds a miniature Bulawayo, with council hut, a pen for several dozen cattle, a barracks block, and a hut for Richard's family. Mbikwane's hut is furthest from the gate.

Farewell and Fynn are studying the construction, deep in conversation. Richard crosses the beach with Ulwazi on his right and Zwelakhe toddling through the sand on his left, clutching his thumb.

Passing the section of the scruffy camp occupied by the Boer contingent, he hears tuts of disapproval. An exchange in their own language sounds equally critical but he ignores it. Ulwazi is relaxed. He is glad she has no sense of these men's views but she will find out soon enough.

By the time they are approaching the pair of adventurers, the lieutenant has spotted them. He bows to Ulwazi and Fynn copies him awkwardly.

'Perhaps your motivation is not so secret as you might pretend?' jokes Farewell in a friendly manner.

.Richard smiles in reply and changes the subject. 'What do you make of Zulu building methods?'

Fynn bristles, 'Primitive at best. Wouldn't stand up to British weather.'

'Nor does it need to,' points out Farewell, as ever, eager to keep the peace. 'Still, they put our slovenly settlement to shame. We have been here weeks. Look what they achieved in a handful of days. It is time we took ourselves in hand.'

Fynn does not disagree with the lieutenant, indeed, he seems pleased at the idea and hurries off to allocate tasks.

'He is a good-hearted lad,' Farewell confides to Richard, 'and I hope Africa will be the making of him.' There is a paternal feel to his comment that Richard understands.

'I have seen men broken here and others find themselves,' he says carefully, his eyes seeking out his son among the huts.

Richard and Ulwazi leave their hut together. Mbikwane departed the previous day with half his contingent of soldiers to visit nearby *kraals*. Zwelakhe is playing in the compound, chasing his pet kid bleating between the huts of the embassy. The baby goat's mother watches suspiciously, full of milk, from her tether close to the gate.

The Fasimba sentries open the gate as Ulwazi and Richard approach, agreeing to keep an eye on the boy while they take a morning stroll on the beach.

The tide is out and the sand stretches far out towards the horizon. The air is clear, the temperature mild, the sky a hazy blue. The sand is blindingly white and fine between Richard's toes. Within an hour, he will be forced to don his boots or hop manically from foot to foot.

Richard takes in the changes wrought in the past fortnight. Gone are the makeshift lean-tos and tarpaulin shelters, scattered tea chests and larger containers. In their place are two rows of huts defining a central street. Lieutenant Farewell has dubbed the hamlet Port Natal.

Closest to the dunes and set off the main axis of the settlement is a larger building, reminiscent of a barn. This is the main warehouse containing the stores and surplus equipment. Nearest the high tide line, but safely above it, is a large roof of sail canvas on poles, with a rudimentary refectory table and chairs knocked up from driftwood, packing cases and a couple of condemned ship's timbers.

Richard waves casually to Farewell who is hunched over a map spread out on the long table. As always, Fynn is at his shoulder, while Malan looks on with a non-committal expression. The lieutenant does not see him but Fynn raises a hand in acknowledgement before returning his attention to the map.

'How long will we stay here?' Ulwazi asks as she looks away from Malan's disapproving sneer.

'I have an understanding with Farewell. I believe I can trust him. Bonaparte and Shaka are not threatened by his presence. But I am less sure of this Jan Malan. The sooner he heads off in search of lands to settle, the better.'

Richard looks out to sea, his eyes coming to rest on the sloop. Several men are working on the vessel despite the hour. Soon they will have to beach her to complete their repairs.

Drawing close to a rocky headland that thrusts out from reddish cliffs to bisect the curve of the beach, they turn around.

'The man we must worry about remains a guest at Bulawayo. I think we should return to the capital once Mbikwane is back from the surrounding villages.'

Ulwazi smiles at the news and leans against him. They are still pressed close as they walk past the open-sided meeting space. Ulwazi sticks her tongue out at Malan who is staring at them with coal-dark eyes that ignite at her defiance.

The Boer turns and mutters something to Fynn who looks up briefly but is soon drawn back into Farewell's orbit.

Later that day, the bulk of the inhabitants of Port Natal mount up and ride a well-worn track through the dunes, winding into the patchy forest to be lost from sight.

Richard watches the last of them go and turns back to admire the drawing his son has completed in the sand. Two stick figures separated by a smaller figure, all holding hands. He feels a pressure in his chest and cups the boy's tiny crown in the palm of his hand as he chatters in a mishmash of Zulu and English.

'Where are they going?' Ulwazi asks from the threshold of their hut. The embassy gate is open and the departing party jingle and rattle as their horses scuff through the sandy ground.

Richard is surprised his wife is interested: she rarely comments on the activities of the adventurers, of whom she remains suspicious.

'I have not seen so many leave camp together since we arrived,' she adds.

It is true. Usual hunting parties consist of no more than ten men. Twice this number have just trotted inland.

'I am not certain,' he admits, crossing to the gate which he hauls open to reveal the almost deserted village. He is in time to see a furtive figure trot in pursuit of the riders. 'But Mhlope will find out,' he concludes as he returns to their hut.

Mbikwane calls out as he enters the compound, flanked by his escort. Richard and Ulwazi duck out of their hut to greet him. He is smiling as always but wastes no time.

'Why are there so few *abelungu*? Where have they gone and why?' Richard has no answer but assures him Shaka's spy is on the case.

It is three days before a dusty and weary Mhlope reports to the Zulu ambassador. Richard sees him arrive, looking more footsore than any Zulu he has ever seen. Mbikwane calls for a gourd of water and waits patiently while the man slakes his thirst. Richard enters the council hut with Mbikwane and Mhlope.

Their first exchanges are very fast but Richard's command of Zulu is up to the task.

'I see you, Mhlope, what news of the *abelungu* who travelled inland?' Mbikwane enquires.

'I see you, my lord,' Mhlope replies, 'they rode far but the land is cut with rivers and I was able to keep them in sight. They sighted a herd of elephants close to a mud wallow. Mothers and calves mostly. Their leaders called a halt and argued for a long time but then they rode on.'

Mbikwane nods and Richard can see his relief. Shaka has forbidden the Europeans from hunting elephants.

Mhlope looks uncomfortable and resumes his account. 'The next day they spooked a bachelor group who stampeded into a wood. This time the *abelungu* did not ride on. Several of the men had very big guns, much bigger than those of our musket company. They were longer, heavier and thicker.'

He pauses to drink again from the gourd, his face apologetic. 'They entered the trees trying to be stealthy. There were several loud bangs. I heard bellows and big bodies crashing through the undergrowth. Two animals fell.'

Richard frowns. Why has Farewell condoned this hunt? Had Malan or even Fynn gone off on their own initiative, Richard would not have been surprised. But Farewell appeared to appreciate the balance of power. Yes, his men have guns. Yes, they could kill many warriors. But they would be overwhelmed.

Mbikwane's face transforms. His smile melts from his face as his lips set in a stern line. His eyes spark with anger and he slaps his thigh in disgust. He faces Richard with a quizzical expression. 'I thought our terms were clear?' he asks, steely and menacing.

'They were clear,' Richard admits.

'Then why have these men defied mighty Shaka? He told them of his willingness to trade ivory for horses and other goods.' Richard shifts uncomfortably on his mat.

'They have no spare horses and no way of sourcing them at present. Their ship is damaged.' He does not want to be an apologist for these men. 'But there is no excuse. They could wait or offer other trade goods for the ivory.'

'Mhlope, remain here. Maintain your cover. Only desert your post if it is essential to bring intelligence to Bulawayo. I must report to King Shaka.'

Richard is torn. Should he evacuate his family and travel back with the Zulu diplomat? That is, no doubt, what Ulwazi will want. He feels sick as he thinks of his little boy caught up in a violent dispute between Farewell's men and the Fasimba stationed at the embassy.

On the other hand, is it not better someone with standing remains to receive the hunting party? Might he engineer a sufficient apology from Farewell to stay Shaka's hand?

Mbikwane calls for his attendant to prepare for departure. Richard remains motionless on the floor wrestling with himself. He doesn't owe these reckless freebooters anything. They pose a threat to Shaka and Napoleon and by extension to his family. A part of him would be glad to see them gone, one way or another.

It has been a long time since Aunt Patricia put in an appearance while he is awake. She has reverted to her silent self but her expression is eloquent, as she taps the frame of her glasses with a perfectly manicured nail.

Richard cannot prevent himself imagining what she is thinking. How can you even contemplate leaving these men to their doom? You are here and have an opportunity to intervene. A sin of omission is a sin still.

Maybe she would steer clear of religion. Nevertheless, she is the manifestation of his conscience, and he knows what he must do.

'Mbikwane, I will remain, I only ask that you take my wife and son, to keep them safe, whatever happens.'

The usually cheerful Zulu stands, his imposing presence forcing Richard to get up in a hurry.

'I will see them safely to Bulawayo. Do what you must but do not expect to save these foolish fellows who defy Shaka in his own kingdom!'

It is with relief that Richard watches Mbikwane's retinue tramp away from the embassy, the muscular Fasimba warriors in two files, with the diplomat, Ulwazi and Zwelakhe between them. His son insists on walking.

Dawn is slowly yielding to day as they disappear into the scattered trees thrusting from the furthest dunes. He sees Zwelakhe stumble, only to be swept up by Ulwazi.

He recalls Ulwazi's reaction when he told her of his decision to stay. Two emotions battled for control of her beautiful face. Her eyes flashed defiance while her brow furrowed and her eyes filled with tears. Her nose started to run, her lips set but then parted with a sigh.

'I know you would rather I came but I must see what can be done here. You do not like living among these people and this is the end of it for you. I will not be long, I promise.'

But then he imagines Ulwazi unprotected in Bulawayo. 'Stay close to Bonaparte. He will keep you safe. I have trusted him with my life and now I do the same with yours.'

They kissed before she left. She was still angry and bit him spitefully before melting into his arms, her strong limbs like a liana strangling its host. He feels the welt on his lower lip with his tongue and smiles.

It is after dark when the hunting party returns. They move slowly as six of their horses shoulder plundered tusks, compelling near half the party to walk. The tusks' elegant curves almost brush the ground.

Judging against the height of the horses, Richard estimates the largest pair is eight feet long. He can see axe marks on the roots, where the men hacked each tusk free of the skull.

He cannot tear his eyes from the ragged butts of the tusks. Farewell waves brazenly, as does Fynn, while Malan slaps the nearest tusk possessively. Richard turns and vomits into the sand, preferring to watch it coagulate, rather than look these men in the face.

He has never felt so marooned from his previous life. Many animals face extinction in the twenty-first century, and wealth still seeks ivory, tiger and bear, but at least most of his peers would be as horrified as he by this sight.

But this is the nineteenth century. Whaling, seal clubbing, ivory hunting, slaughter of the buffalo, beaver trapping, big game hunting, none of these activities raise an eyebrow at afternoon tea in the kind of middle-class villa he grew up in. There is nothing he can say to Malan or Fynn or even Farewell to convince them their actions are reprehensible in any way.

But what he can do is explain the likely consequences of taking ivory without permission within Shaka's kingdom. He spits the sourness from his mouth and strides towards the dusty travellers as they dismount and start unloading the ivory.

Men and horses are stained with salty residue. Richard walks slowly, fighting his anger and rehearsing what to say. Before he can speak, Lieutenant Farewell places an arm around his shoulder and steers him beneath the canopy of the meeting place.

'I know what you are going to say, and you have every right to do so. We have defied Shaka and there shall be consequences,' Farewell admits in a conciliatory tone, 'although, I am not sure you will mourn should Captain Simpson's life prove the price exacted for our hastiness.'

Richard opens his mouth to object, but Farewell raises a hand. He takes a long swig from his water canister and ploughs on conspiratorially. 'No doubt you are astounded by our actions. I am a reluctant participant myself. But had I not allowed this hunt, I would have lost more than half of the men.'

Is this the same man who showed such understanding? Who made no judgement on his choices?

Chapter Twelve

June 1821

Port Natal is behind Richard and he is glad. The atmosphere was unpleasant after the unsanctioned elephant hunt. With Mbikwane gone and Mhlope maintaining his assumed identity, hiding among the huts, Richard was quite alone.

Reminded of his years as a lonely bachelor, unfulfilled and friendless, he slipped into a gloomy mood he could not shake.

Quarrelling with Farewell and Fynn became a daily occurrence but that was better than his confrontations with Jan Malan, whose intractable contempt for everything but his own men was suffocating.

Richard withdrew behind the walls of the embassy, only venturing out in the early morning and at dusk. He bought rough spirit from a Boer tradesman. He missed his wife and son. He could not like these men trying to establish a trading post beyond the edge of their understanding.

Richard struggled internally. He felt a hypocrite. He drank. He has always railed against the new orthodoxy pulling down statues and renaming buildings, returning plunder and issuing apologies for slavery or empire.

Judge people in their context, he used to insist, although he kept his words to himself. Slavery is evil and many evil things were done in the name of empire. But these things happened at a time when they shocked no one. Which of us, brought up to believe in our own superiority, would have the strength of character to shake off that conditioning?

When the harsh liquor ran out, he was left with a sore head and a little clarity. He does like Farewell, although he laments the slaughtered elephants. He understands the lieutenant and Fynn.

Their men are not monsters. They are desperate and this makes them brave. With few prospects, they risk everything in the hopes of making enough to set themselves up for life.

Even Jan Malan, who embodies much about his people that makes Richard uncomfortable, is simply seeking a place of his own, where he may live as he wishes. That is something Richard does understand.

He recalls his final meeting with the triumvirate under the patched sail, flapping in an onshore breeze, the tang of the sea in his nostrils. They sit on one side of the trestle table and he on the other.

'I must return to Bulawayo,' he reveals. 'I miss my family and there is nothing left for me to do here.'

Malan smiles beneath his beard. Fynn is barely listening. Farewell nods in understanding.

'You are lucky to have something that anchors you,' the lieutenant says kindly.

'I leave you with this plea. Cease your ivory hunting. Send the tusks to Shaka with a generous gift of horses and an unconditional apology. Beg his forgiveness.'

Jan Malan mumbles something guttural and spits over his shoulder. Fynn shakes his head. Farewell eyes the men of his trading base sawing and hammering around the beached hull of their sloop.

'I do not doubt your sincerity. Nor do I doubt the logic of your advice. Nevertheless, we are here to profit from our endeavours. I can find no gold in the streams. But white wealth parades across the plains projecting from the head of every bull elephant. Demand is great. My men impatient.'

Farewell pauses to watch a seagull hanging beak into the breeze. 'The *Julia* is almost seaworthy. We can bring in more men, along with the horses and other goods that will placate Shaka. All will be well. You will see.'

Richard tries one more time. 'Are you really prepared to sacrifice Simpson?' He knows it is his own guilt speaking. He was the one who suggested Simpson as hostage to Shaka.

'Fortunes of war, don't you know?' Farewell replies, sounding for once, every inch a naval officer.

So, Richard rides away, sitting awkwardly on a borrowed horse, his head in turmoil. He is the architect of this mess. The Farewell and Fynn expedition should not have left Cape Town until March 1824. That is almost three years in the future.

Richard's dealings with Captain Simpson resulted in the former East India captain limping into Table Bay in a badly damaged ship, all hopes of a successful voyage wrecked. Along with his surviving crew, the captain brought knowledge of Bonaparte's escape and a desire for revenge.

Simpson meets Farewell and accelerates the ambitious former lieutenant's plans. His modest funds tipping the balance in favour of an earlier departure for the interior.

If Napoleon Bonaparte was still captive on St Helena and Richard still teaching at St Anne's, then Farewell would be a modest trader, Fynn a directionless teenager and Jan Malan a resentful burgher.

Instead, Farewell has forged an odd alliance of adventurers, landed on the Natal coast, established a beach-head, made treaty with Shaka Zulu and broken his oath in an attempt to maintain his authority.

As his placid horse climbs the hills beyond the coastal plain, Richard's eyes are drawn to the castellated mountains. Above them, spiral elongated shapes, moving almost imperceptibly. He knows immediately that something has died. The shapes are the outspread wings of vultures riding thermals with a grace Richard cannot achieve, sliding on his makeshift saddle.

But he too is caught in invisible forces, drawing him towards what he is almost certain will be a corpse. He knows the face that body will display. He knows what death looks like. He knows the man. Dead because of Richard's actions.

He feels madness and despair clawing with inky fingers and ragged nails, sharp and remorseless. His horse stumbles as the reins go slack and he grasps the mare's dark mane awkwardly.

There is a fissure inside him through which darkness spills. It is like time travel in reverse, he thinks. He tries to seal it with willpower but fails. A cackling laugh mocks him, reminiscent of the witch-hunter Nobela.

Richard thinks of Zwelakhe. What new achievements will his little boy show him when he returns? He imagines Ulwazi waiting for him. She is smiling as she holds their son's hand.

The boy waves. His heart constricts and the dark rift seals.

Richard sighs and halts his horse. He dismounts and leads her down the bank into the broad river, letting her drink as the gentle current tops his boots.

Richard's back aches from nights sleeping on hard ground. He has got lost twice but righted himself by sighting the coast and resuming a north-easterly course. He should reach Bulawayo today.

Breaking through a fringe of forest, he blinks in the brightness illuminating the rolling grassland. As his eyes adjust, he gapes at what he sees. Penned in a large corral, an agitated herd of zebras stand stark against a green backdrop. Their striped flanks are not meant for his eyes but lions which see in monochrome, rendering the hooved animals as shadow and shade, perfectly camouflaged in long grass and scattered woods.

Beyond the wooden rails, parties of Zulu warriors struggle with haltered zebras bearing rudimentary saddles. He watches two men try to calm an animal, as a third vaults onto its back.

There are shouts and braying, whinnies and curses. To one side of the corral, Richard sees stacks of spears and brown shields. He urges his mount forward. It does not take long to spot Emile, among the Ama-Wombe.

His friend's flowing locks and aquiline nose set him apart, as does his skin, although it is almost mahogany. He is trying to calm a rearing stallion, hooves dancing in the air.

Richard dismounts, watching Emile's quick feet get him out of trouble as he shortens the lead rope, never breaking eye contact. The whinnying beast's lips draw back in complaint. Emile talks in the patois of his homeland, reassuring words born of the empathy his blood has for wild horses.

'Does that zebra speak *Camarguais*?' Richard jokes, his loud voice competing with the braying stallion.

'No, he bloody doesn't!' spits Emile. 'The wildest horses in the Camargue were compliant compared to this devilish offshoot of the equine world.' The cavalryman's frustration is palpable as he tussles with the recalcitrant animal.

Looking around, Richard sees even the smallest mare giving a good account of herself, until the Watcher of the Ford deals her a roundhouse punch that causes her to stumble sideways, collapsing to her knees. While the small beast is still recovering, the giant lifts a leg across her back.

Stunned but aware something is wrong, the mare bucks, collecting Njikiza, before landing four-square. His weight on her back causes her eyes to roll back in her head. She brays desperately and rolls unexpectedly onto her side, dislodging Njikiza and crushing the air from him like a striped rolling-pin. Before he can haul himself upright, her back legs punch like pistons.

Her well-aimed shot lands both hooves on the giant's chest, expelling the air he has just drawn in. Gasping, he topples into the trampled grass, gesturing weakly with his enormous paws. The mare kicks up her heels and gallops away, two Zulus in hot pursuit.

Emile pauses in his face-off with the stallion to smirk at his big friend's antics. Richard is crying with laughter and drops his reins. It does not matter as his mare is pointedly ignoring the dazzle of zebras.

'What made you try this?' Richard asks when both of them have wiped their eyes. Emile hands off the angry stallion to another warrior, who takes the lead rein reluctantly.

'The emperor was talking with Shaka,' the former French lieutenant confides.

Richard cannot help but smile. 'And he suggested this?' he asks.

'He was describing the use of cavalry in conjunction with disciplined musket fire and artillery.' Emile surveys the chaos, spotting one warrior failing to extract his arm from a zebra's clenched jaws. 'It was Shaka who suggested these zebras might make a good substitute, at least until he procures horses from Farewell.'

Eyeing the stallion Emile has relinquished, Richard estimates its height at thirteen and a half hands making it no more than a pony. Some of the mares, like the one that battered Njikiza Ngcolosi, are considerably shorter at the shoulder.

'We stampeded the herd into a screen trap, it took but a moment to realise most are too small. They are also excessively aggressive and jumpy. Even the larger animals have weak backs. These are the most promising!'

Richard shakes his head. 'Good luck, my friend. I must reach Bulawayo. Things are not going well with our European guests.'

Emile nods. 'Mbikwane returned with Ulwazi and your boy. They are safe but Captain Simpson is not.'

Richard hauls himself into the saddle, wishing he had proper stirrups, wincing at the wood frame hard between his legs.

'I will see you again soon,' he promises Emile as he urges his mount forward with his knees.

Somehow, Bonaparte is waiting for him at the gates of the new capital. He waves, an enigmatic smile on his clean-shaven face.

'It is good to have you back, my English friend,' Napoleon says as he takes Richard's horse by the bridle. Richard slips gratefully from the saddle.

'Tell me what has transpired,' he asks. His eyes rove around Bulawayo. All looks as he left it. He singles out his own hut and the turmoil tormenting him is crowded out by the sight of his son toddling unsteadily towards him. Ulwazi is grinning in pursuit.

'I see you, Richard,' she says, 'it does my heart good.'

'I see you, Ulwazi, mother of our son,' Richard replies more seriously than he intends.

Ulwazi frowns for a moment, but Zwelakhe stumbles and she sweeps him into the safety of her arms. Bonaparte waits patiently for the family reunion to be completed. Richard explains to Ulwazi he has urgent business with Shaka. She moves off towards the gates to play with their son by the river.

'Mbikwane has painted a damning picture of Farewell's behaviour, it seems the English remain poor at honouring the treaties they make!'

Richard does not rise to the bait, simply nodding in distracted agreement. 'What of Captain Simpson, he is still alive?'

'For the moment, but Shaka has decreed his life forfeit, he awaits an auspicious day for the execution. He broke the power of the witch-finders but he is still in thrall to superstition.' Napoleon sounds more sympathetic than critical.

'Then there is a chance,' Richard suggests.

'A chance for what?' quizzes Bonaparte. 'Surely, the captain's demise serves our purposes? It keeps my presence from the authorities in the Cape, at least for a little longer. That favours Shaka too, allowing his army to develop before he faces the firepower of the British!'

Richard has had these same thoughts as he journeyed from Port Natal. But there is a difference. Bonaparte sees Simpson's death as a boon while for Richard it is another ghost to haunt him, another man sacrificed because he, Richard Davey, is where he should not be.

He hears high-pitched squeals from outside the palisade, where Ulwazi is chasing her son through the trampled grass. Perhaps Captain Simpson's death is the price for Richard remaining precisely where he belongs?

Richard points out the problems facing Farewell in controlling his men. He stresses Captain Simpson's innocence in their transgressions. He admits a personal antipathy between him and the former East India man and still pleads for his life.

Shaka smiles down at him, shaking his head indulgently. 'Still trying to be the man you used to be, Richard,' he chides, his voice friendly, 'you are a Zulu now, bloodied in battle. All of your insights cannot make this less so. You regret you chose this man as a hostage; you feel your hand on the executioner's club?'

Shaka has seen to the heart of what troubles Richard. He understands him. But the Zulu king is not going to change his mind, although he glances at Pampata, sitting in the shadows of the council hut.

Richard hopes she will intervene but she does not. Captain Simpson is nothing to her. Richard recalls Napoleon's assessment. The former emperor is right, all Zululand is better off with this man dead. As a Zulu, he should be glad.

At dusk, Emile rides proudly through the gates astride a zebra stallion. He has to saw on the primitive reins as the defiant animal fights for his head, but he compels his mount to step forward in an orderly fashion.

A crowd quickly gathers. Richard cannot decide if Emile looks magnificent or comical, with his feet little more than a foot from the hard-packed earth. His friend's triumphant grin is infectious as he turns the zebra to complete a circuit. The animal's eyes bulge at the sight of so many people and Emile dismounts, calling for two warriors to lead the zebra away.

Richard notices Shaka watching from the royal enclosure, clapping his hands with pleasure. Mgobozi is with the king, dancing a little jig of excitement at this latest gift from the white Zulus of his master's court.

Beside the capering drill-master stands his old friend, Nqoboka, a look of utter disdain on his stern face. When Mgobozi slaps him on his back, the long-necked figure simply walks away, to be intercepted by Mbopa, walking from the royal quarters. Richard sees the pair put their heads together before they disappear.

The following day is grey, the air saturated. Richard slept well in his wife's arms. Stretching, he audits the aches and strains plaguing his trim body. He hopes he will not have to repeat such a lengthy ride on so rudimentary a saddle.

Ulwazi enters and Richard smiles. He looks for his son but cannot see him.

'He is playing with the *udibi* boys,' she announces breezily.

Richard knows he is frowning, worried they will be too rough with the toddler.

'Do not worry, they will be careful, he is the son of a councillor, one of Shaka's inner circle,' she reassures him. He cannot tell if she is teasing. She sits by the hearth, idly stirring the ashes to see if any heat remains, before adding two dried cakes of cow dung.

'There is to be a festival tonight,' she announces gleefully, 'with dancing!' she adds, swaying a little as if she can already hear the music.

'What is the occasion?' Richard enquires, trying to sound enthusiastic.

'It is Nandi's birthday,' Ulwazi explains before hesitating.

'What else?' Richard prompts gently.

'The *umlungu*, Simpson, he will be put to death as a gift for the Great She Elephant, to show the consequences of disobeying Shaka.'

Richard spends the day wandering aimlessly around Bulawayo, trying to think of some way to preserve the avaricious captain's life. As the hours pass, he becomes increasingly bad-tempered.

Watching the herd boys return with the royal cattle from a

day of grazing in the rolling downlands, he admits defeat. Simpson's death will be one further weight bearing down on the balance of his conscience: all he can do is set some positives in the other scale.

Ulwazi and Zwelakhe peer from their hut. The boy is scrubbed and glowing with health, while his mother wears her most prized garment, the butterfly silk bought in Portuguese territory. The dress she wore at their wedding. Richard sighs as the scales realign.

Light fades. Richard changes his shirt and polishes his boots with dyed beeswax. Most of the regiments billeted nearby have arrived, joined by a welter of women and children from outlying *kraals*. He is pulling on his boots when there is a knock against the threshold.

'May I come in?' asks a French voice.

'Emile!' Richard exclaims, 'I see you!'

'I am not alone,' the zebra-riding former lieutenant admits.

'Is Bonaparte with you?' Richard asks, tugging at his second boot.

'I see you, Richard,' greets a mellifluous but timid voice.

'Thabisa! I see you,' Richard says enthusiastically. 'I am so glad you are both here. Ulwazi will be delighted.'

Thabisa bows her head but she is smiling and her eyes sparkle. 'I will go to find her while you catch up,' she announces and withdraws into the deepening night, where brands of dried reeds flare.

Richard watches the ritual slaughter of cows without wincing. Throats cut, necks twisted, blood collected in bowls to add power to the spells calling for long life upon the queen mother.

Drums sound, the beat almost deafening until they stop abruptly, leaving a silence that assaults ringing ears. Shaka and his entourage appear with Nandi leading the procession. The whole of Bulawayo cheers at the sight.

Richard notices a slight falter in her step. He tries to study her as she nods to the assembled masses. She holds herself regally, although noticeably thin. She dies in October 1827, if history holds its course. Six more years stretch before her.

Shaka beams with pleasure and signals that the music should begin. Drums and horns sound and voices lift in song all around the vast capital, filling the night air, already heavy with the scent of roasting meat.

Zwelakhe is staying with distant relatives of Ulwazi, who live in a *kraal* nearby. Richard suspects they are part of Nandi's extended family but does not ask. As his wife begins to gyrate, Richard is drawn into the dance, step by step, move by move, beat by beat. Sweet incense fills the air and he inhales deeply, his head swimming.

Ulwazi sings with the massed choir, her crystal voice high yet rich. Music, Richard thinks to himself, is a universal constant. He mouths the words and after a couple of repetitions, he risks sound.

His wife grins at him, before spinning around and around as the drums reach a crescendo. Just too soon, the beat falters, screams and shouts replacing the song as the lit rushes go out.

Confusion and consternation swallow the population, wrenched from their celebration.

'What is it?' Richard asks.

Ulwazi points, her sharp eyes piercing the gloom with the help of one guttering brand held by an attendant whose face is a parody of horror in the shadows. She indicates the royal party and instinctively she steps closer. Richard follows. Soon everyone is pressing forward.

Murmured questions and speculation start as drops of rain before their frequency builds, volume increasing until a panicky storm roils around the giant *kraal*.

Richard sees Nandi, wringing her hands, leaning towards her son who lies on the ground. Pampata crouches over the Zulu ruler, her delicate hands fluttering against his left side. A ring of attendants close around him, blocking Richard's view.

Without thinking, he covers the remaining distance, pushing past the press of bodies. A scream echoes above the hubbub, and then another.

'The king is killed!' cries a female voice, one of Shaka's *umdlunkulu*.

'Murder! There is an enemy among us!' A commanding, male voice. Richard thinks it is Mdlaka.

'Blood, so much blood. It comes from his side,' announces a tearful female. Richard is sure this is Pampata.

Richard claws at the shoulders of the inner ring surrounding the fallen king. 'Let me through!' he barks, not recognising his own voice. To his surprise, the blocking bodies move aside. Ulwazi slips in with him.

Richard sees Shaka, flat on his back, eyes closed. Two attendants have lit fresh brands and others are nervously preparing to move Shaka. The king's chest rises and falls as if he is asleep.

'Wait!' Again, it is as if someone else is speaking. Again, his command is respected and the attendants step back. Richard kneels beside Pampata and tries to give a smile of reassurance. She cannot see through her tears, he realises.

Reluctant to touch the king's favourite, Richard turns to Nandi, who is now beside her son. 'Queen Mother, will you take Pampata away? I will check the wound and have mighty Shaka transferred to the council hut.'

Nandi does not scowl or demur, instead she nods in relief that someone is taking charge. Richard watches her lead the sobbing Pampata away and looks around the assembled faces. Most are familiar. Upright Ngomane, calm Mdlaka and raging Mgobozi look to him. Disdainful Nqoboka eyes him suspiciously and moves to prevent him touching Shaka, only to be restrained by Mbikwane, who murmurs diplomatic words.

None of the men who have known Shaka for most of his adult life dare approach their fallen leader. Richard is reminded of Stalin's discovery in the Kremlin having suffered a stroke. No one acted, no doctor would examine him, no one would essay any care, for fear of being blamed for his death.

Richard calls for light above his shoulder. It reveals a puncture wound in the left arm that has sliced right through. Gingerly he lifts the arm to find an incision beneath the left pectoral. Shaka moans but does not open his eyes.

The arm is bleeding freely and Richard applies pressure to both sides of the cut. Before he can call for a bandage, he hears a tearing sound and Ulwazi passes him a strip of cloth. Butterflies dance gold against a sky-blue background, as he wraps Shaka's muscular bicep tightly.

The wound to the ribs is not deep, the force taken by

Shaka's powerful arm, but it is seeping blood. Richard decides it can wait and signals for the attendants.

They hesitate but Mgobozi clouts one of them across the back of the head and four leap forward, gently gripping the king by his shoulders and hips. A passage opens through the throng, a corridor to the entrance of the royal quarters.

Inside the giant-beehive council chamber, Richard calls for more lights. Soon the walls are ringed by attendants with torches. He hears the hearth being stoked.

'Boil water!' he orders, his voice curiously steady and confident.

Napoleon appears, looking worried, his sapphire eyes sweeping the scene.

'We need the healer from the hills,' he declares, in passable Zulu. 'If he could cure me, a mere stab wound should be child's play.'

'He is not here, but we are,' Richard counters, annoyance fraying his concentration. 'Send for him, by all means, but it will be days before he arrives. By then, we will know.' Richard stops.

'If he will live or die?' asks Bonaparte in French.

Richard nods and turns back to the wound, probing between Shaka's ribs with steady fingers, although his stomach is bilious. There is a drone in his ears and his vision blurs.

'Where is the royal physician, his *inyanga*?' Richard asks.

Shaka groans, his lids flicker and penetrating eyes lock onto Richard's face. The injured ruler tries a smile but it trembles on pale lips before evaporating. His eyes roll back in a dead faint. The watching attendants sigh while Shaka's inner circle murmur nervously.

Nandi stands at her son's feet with Pampata clinging to her side. 'He has been summoned. He will arrive shortly. But do not wait!'

Richard tries to look confident as he accepts a bowl of steaming water. Looking around, he cannot see what he needs, so he strips off his clean shirt. He uses part of the material to bathe the wound to the ribs and the remainder as a second bandage.

'What about poison?' asks Nqoboka, his eyes furtive and his intonation sly. Richard has no idea how to reply. He remembers Irish surgeon, Barry O'Meara, Napoleon's doctor on St Helena, discussing the possibility the imprisoned emperor was being poisoned with cyanide.

Much to Richard's relief, the doctor arrives, clutching his drawstring bag of medicaments, his thin chest heaving as he kneels beside Shaka. He is a small man, hair grey around a bald pate. His nose is wide, his eyes pale and his skin wrinkled. But his hands are steady.

Delicate fingers loosen the bandage on Shaka's arm. He studies the beautiful cloth, soaked with blood, and sniffs it. Apparently satisfied, he hands it to Richard. His narrow fingers slip into his master's cut muscle and withdraw bloody. He sucks his forefinger and waits expectantly. He calls for water and washes out his mouth, spitting discreetly away from the body.

Opening the drawstring bag, he rummages inside, withdrawing several packets wrapped in vine leaves. A cup is provided and he mixes a blend that he holds over the fire with a pair of wooden tongs. When he is satisfied the decoction is ready, he smears it on the entry and exit wounds, while muttering an incantation.

The king rolls his head but his eyes remain closed as the physician unwraps his ribs. He repeats the inspection and treatment. Once the salve is applied, no blood exits the injuries. The *inyanga* then binds up both wounds, reusing the hem of Ulwazi's dress and Richard's shirt.

The doctor adds more boiling water to the reduced unguent, along with a powder, and holds up Shaka's head. He is struggling to open Shaka's mouth, keep his head tilted, and administer the tonic. Richard intervenes, supporting the king. He shivers part in fear, part in pleasure, as he cradles Shaka Zulu's head. The medic prises Shaka's mouth open and dribbles in the medicine, stroking his throat until he swallows.

Beyond the palisade of the royal enclosure, Richard hears a racket of disconnected shouts and cries, as Bulawayo absorbs the news. Shaka Zulu, founder of their nation, has been stabbed in the heart of his capital.

Rumbles echo in Shaka's chest followed by a poignant moan. He rolls onto his side and tries to lift his head. His eyes partially open as he heaves and sighs until a flood of vomit spouts from his mouth.

Cries of concern run through the council hut but the royal physician smiles and nods. Richard immediately understands: he is purging the king to expel any poison he could not detect.

Richard leaves the council hut bleary-eyed and with a pounding headache. Shaka has vomited several times and awoken once, bemoaning his fate, convinced he will die. He is now sleeping, his breathing shallow.

Bulawayo is transformed into Hades. Richard sees bodies scattered across what had been a dance floor. Guards patrol, and wherever they tread, the people claw at their faces, weeping copiously or run away because their tears are spent.

Ulwazi clings to Richard. 'It is a good thing our son is not here,' she whispers fearfully. As he looks at her, she pokes a forefinger into each eye, apparently unconcerned as to the damage this might cause.

A patrol of armed warriors stalks past, peering suspiciously at them. Satisfied Ulwazi is demonstrating sufficient grief, they turn on Richard menacingly, until a distant voice calls them away.

'This is madness,' he confides, threading through the milling people towards the gates, only to find them barred. Mgobozi stands at the exit, his face grim. Seeing a man who loves his people and his king, Richard hurries over.

'Can you not stop the killing?' he enquires. 'People cannot cry indefinitely. Who ordered this?'

Mgobozi looks solemn, his eyes swimming. 'If I intervene, I will be seen to show too little compassion for Shaka. The best I can do is track down the men who did this thing. I have sealed the town. We have found six men stabbed, inside and outside Bulawayo. The bodies establish a trail. I have sent a company of Fasimba in pursuit.' Mgobozi is preternaturally calm, the antithesis of his usual demeanour.

'Who do you suspect?' asks Richard.

'They came from Ndwandwe territory,' Mgobozi reveals icily.

There is nothing Richard can do about that. But he does want to leave Bulawayo and take Ulwazi with him.

Will you allow us passage?' he asks uncertainly.

'For what purpose?' enquires the nation's drill-master, not unkindly.

'My wife wishes to join our son who is staying with her relatives nearby and I must summon the *umlungu* Farewell, for he may have medicines to ensure Shaka survives.

Mgobozi is immediately interested. 'But I heard Shaka admit he is fatally wounded! How can I hope he will survive?' Mgobozi is not lamenting the demise of his sovereign but the loss of his oldest friend.

'Feed your hope by doing what you can!' Richard advises gently. 'Let me go. I promise you, Shaka will not die.'

As Mgobozi orders the gates opened, Richard runs to saddle his horse, shouting to Ulwazi to join their son at her relatives' *kraal*.

Riding out from Bulawayo, he looks over his shoulder to watch Ulwazi trekking in the opposite direction. Richard feels hollow. What if he is wrong? What if history has lurched off on a new path, one he and Bonaparte have built?

He remembers there was an attempt on Shaka's life in 1821. It was thought to be part of a cleansing ceremony overseen by Zwide's son. But what if Zwide is not dead in this new timeline? What if the spear is poisoned in this timeline? What if Shaka dies in this timeline?

He tried to convince Napoleon to accompany him but the Frenchman could not be persuaded, insisting he is needed to help counter the hysteria. Emile too felt his duty was to remain.

So, Richard rides alone, sick with worry for his family and his friends. But he has done what he can and is doing what he feels he must. At least, he has made Ulwazi promise she will remain with her relatives until he returns.

Chapter Thirteen

September 1821

Lieutenant Francis Farewell, formerly of the Royal Navy, looks inordinately smug. Captain Simpson sits quietly to one side, but his eyes are everywhere. Shaka proudly displays his scars, face split by a huge grin. His white teeth gleam and he looks in perfect health. He has rescinded Simpson's execution, in exchange for Farewell's medicine, which is little more than applications of camomile lotion!

But, on Richard's advice, and with Bonaparte's fervent support, the former merchant captain remains a hostage. The king wears his full headdress, a head ring bound in leopard skin, topped by red lourie feathers. He is rarely seen now without it.

Richard knows why. Although Shaka no longer needs English lessons, they meet weekly for conversation. While recovering, the Zulu king became garrulous, sharing his innermost thoughts with Richard.

That he dreads an heir Richard already knows. That he fears death comes as a surprise. An imperious warrior whose reputation was forged in the teeth of his enemies; he is the last man Richard expected to obsess about his demise.

'We all die, mighty Shaka,' he offers by way of comfort.

'But my death will be a tragedy for my people!' It is an honest kind of arrogance and founded on a truth. The state

Shaka has forged is built on the force of his personality. He has melded a ragtag of tribes and clans into a powerful unit, cohesive because he is at the centre. Even so, he has suffered defections like that of Mzilikazi, fled with many cows. Richard played his part in that but it would have happened anyway.

Can Shaka's empire survive him? Without an heir? Richard knows what history tells him. But history has changed thanks to him. And now, he watches as Farewell makes more promises than he can keep while Shaka argues with him about civilization.

'You claim your empire is superior? Have you seen a more orderly state than mine? More obedient people? You tell me of King George's greatness and the size of his capital. Yet he has few cattle. On the matter of wives, at least, he is wise to have just one, but I am wiser, having none!' Shaka is enjoying himself. His eyes are bright and he grins as he finishes.

Captain Simpson looks on angrily while Fynn seems distracted by the design of the council hut. Farewell's forehead furrows as if contemplating a chess move.

'Yours is a well-ordered kingdom, I freely admit. But our laws are administered by professional judges, who fit sentence to crime.' There is needle in the ambitious man's voice and Richard wonders how Shaka will react.

'You imprison criminals rather than granting the swift release of execution. To the Zulu people, there is nothing worse than confinement.'

Richard finds himself on Shaka's side. He knows enough about the penal code of the 1820s to refute Farewell's claims of superiority. The Bloody Code, as it became known, refers to some two hundred and twenty capital crimes. Only in 1823 will the death penalty be made discretionary for crimes bar treason and murder.

So, in this present day, the one Richard finds himself living, there is not so much difference. Hanging or clubbing to death, just a matter of method.

His curiosity apparently satisfied about King George's kingdom, conversation shifts. 'How old is your sovereign?'

'Over sixty years old,' replies Farewell proudly.

Shaka fears ageing and is sensitive about the thinning of his locks, while angrily plucking any grey hairs.

'I know of a great secret, mighty Shaka,' Farewell reveals theatrically. 'It is a concoction that can turn grey hair black.'

Shaka's eyes light up, he jumps from his throne and glances at his grey-headed mother.

'It is called Rowland's Macassar oil, and many of my countrymen swear by it,' Farewell elaborates, almost smirking.

'Your people know the secret to extending human life?' Shaka demands suspiciously.

Farewell pauses. Richard can see him considering how to respond. His eyes are wide and he licks his lips surreptitiously. 'We can prevent hair from greying and reverse it in even the oldest subjects.'

Shaka fingers his head ring and leans towards his mother. He whispers with her and then nods decisively. 'You will supply me with enough of this elixir to keep all my warriors young. With it, I will not have to disband regiments once an *ibutho*, an age cohort, reaches forty. They can serve longer and still retire to father children.'

Richard realizes he is fidgeting. Shaka is only hearing what he wants. But Farewell makes no move to correct his error. He must step in; he cannot allow Shaka to be deceived like this.

'Mighty Shaka, while Lieutenant Farewell may be right about the properties of this oil, I promise you, it merely dyes the hair. It can do nothing for wrinkles or baldness, stiff joints or blurred vision.' Richard is surprised at how angry he sounds.

'What do you say, Farewell? Have you tried to hoodwink me in my royal enclosure?' Shaka snaps.

'I assure you, great king, the Rowland's oil is widely used. In no way did I intend deceit.' The adventurer holds out his hands, a slight tremor in his voice.

'So, it is true, you can supply the elixir of life to my people?' Shaka insists.

Captain Simpson coughs discreetly. Farewell looks furtively at Richard. Fynn appears unaware of what is unfolding, but Shaka's councillors lean forward hungrily. Meanwhile, Bonaparte seems content to let Richard handle the situation.

'In time, I will be able to supply it for you. My ship is almost repaired. First, I must return to Cape Town and report our agreement, that you have leased the land around Port Natal to the Farewell Trading Company. I must transport more men to the port and bring other goods, including horses, as you requested.'

Shaka frowns at news of such a delay. But then Pampata appears at his side and talks rapidly *sotto voce*.

A grin blooms on Shaka's leonine head. 'Very well, I see an

opportunity here. We will send ambassadors with you to Cape Town. From there, they will voyage across the great seas to your King George, with gifts of ivory and cattle.'

Here Shaka pauses and rubs his chin. 'We will confirm our trade relations. Also, I must seek his permission to wage war to the south-west. I have no wish to clash with your forces but I must bring the Tembu into my empire. They speak the same language. It is inevitable they should become Zulu.'

Napoleon nods and leans towards Richard. 'He is right, it is the natural order for those of the same language to be united. My empire was an example of that.'

Richard thinks of the polyglot French empire of client states, its subjects speaking most of the languages of Europe. Equally, Bonaparte sold French-speaking Louisiana to the Americans and never controlled Francophone Quebec. He clenches a fist behind his back, digging his nails into his palm, but he does not let himself be drawn into an argument. He must ensure Farewell is kept in check.

'Great king, I will be happy to transport your ambassadors,' Farewell confirms cheerfully. 'I am sure King George will be delighted to receive them.'

Richard has his doubts. George III never really accepted the loss of his American colonies. His grandson was only crowned George IV in 1820 after many years as a dilettante Prince Regent.

Richard does not envy whoever is tasked with representing the Zulus to this man. George can be charming and is a sophisticated patron of the arts but he is also a degenerate boor, a spendthrift and naturally lazy. Richard has always viewed him as one of the least savoury of British monarchs.

He is startled out of his musings as Shaka announces, 'I shall send my most trusted Mbikwane along with Mister Richard Davey of my inner council!'

Ulwazi is crying, hugging her wailing son to her chest, rocking back and forth on her heels as she squats beside their hearth.

'I don't have a choice,' Richard pleads, 'would you have me defy Shaka?'

His wife subsides but Zwelakhe, nose pressed against his unhappy mother, continues to cry. Richard takes the boy so that Ulwazi can wipe her face. When she is finished, she watches the pot simmering over the low fire.

'We could come with you? I remember you speaking of wonders beyond the wide waters. All those books you miss so much. Why teach me to read if I shall never even see a book not written by your hand?' The challenge in her voice is obvious.

Richard tries to imagine presenting his Zulu wife to London society. He winces. While the British empire banned the slave trade in 1807, it will be more than a decade before it abolishes the practice in most of its colonies.

In London, black faces remain rare and almost always confined below stairs. Richard will be presented at court; to appear with a dark-skinned wife and half-caste baby would scandalise the very people he should be impressing.

'It would not work. The job I must help Mbikwane carry out is daunting already. London is not ready for us,' he admits, feeling ashamed.

'Why?' demands Ulwazi as her son finally settles in her

husband's arms.

This is a conversation Richard would rather spare his wife. He sighs. 'The white men regard themselves as superior. You see how Farewell and Simpson behave, let alone Malan. London is the heart of that white world. It may be more tolerant than the *abelungu* in the colonies, but… it remains the source of their attitudes.' Richard sees Ulwazi is far from persuaded.

'I do not understand.' She is accusing him of a failure to communicate.

'Most white people believe themselves destined to dominate the world. They claim a mission to spread Christianity, but really, they hunger for power and wealth.' He is avoiding the point.

'But why should this stop me travelling with my husband?' Ulwazi insists.

'Because they would not see you. They would see difference. A lesser intelligence,' he rushes on, blushing, his tongue awkward as he forces out the unpalatable truth, 'inadmissible to their society along with any *umlungu* married to you. Your presence would make my mission impossible.'

Ulwazi is silent for a long time. Zwelakhe is asleep now, snuffling gently despite his father's discomfort. Eventually, she moves from the hearth to his side and leans against him. Her face is wet with tears.

'In this land, any may become Zulu,' she whispers, looking at him meaningfully, 'yet, where you travel, tribe is a fixed thing?'

He nods sadly, the gesture shallow to keep from disturbing

their sleeping son whose lengthening body makes him awkward to hold.

'But if you go on this journey, it will be many seasons before we see you again… if you come back.' Vulnerable, her tears fall again, choking him as he watches them.

'You doubt I will return?' he asks gently.

'It is the world you come from, why would you not wish to remain?' she replies sadly. 'Besides, that witch will be there, looking to ensnare you!'

Richard understands she is talking of Fanny Bertrand. He looks at her lovingly and rubs his cheek against her wet face. 'I love you, woman, never doubt it. I hold the proof in my arms.' He looks down at the little boy they made together. 'I will come back to you. I will come back to my son.' He has never been so sure of himself.

Ulwazi sighs. It is a profoundly sad sound but it is also resigned. Richard feels guilty: a part of him is excited, even though every word he told his wife is true.

Port Natal looks bigger and better ordered than the last time he saw it, looking over his shoulder, as he rode away to Bulawayo. Farewell's brig, the *Julia*, rides high in the water, sails furled tidily. Beside her, to his surprise, is moored a second vessel. Richard peers through the humid sea fret to make out the name, *Ann*, painted close to her bow in letters edged with gold.

Mbikwane, who refuses to ride, stands beside Richard astride his mare. Behind them are a company of the Ama-Wombe, Emile among them. They carry three magnificent pairs of elephant tusks and lead a perfectly white brace of cattle from Shaka's personal herd.

'So, these are not giant egrets that fly from distant lands?' Mbikwane asks affably.

Richard cannot tell whether the diplomat is joking, so he replies seriously. 'No, they float on the water and tame the wind to drive them where they wish to go.'

Mbikwane nods, apparently satisfied, and steps from the crest of the dune, towards the welcoming party of hats, his feathers swaying as his strides swallow the sand.

Farewell waves as they approach. Young Fynn is at his side and beside him lurks Malan's implacable presence. Fynn is deeply tanned now, his hair bleached, his eyes watery. Farewell remains a wiry, coiled mass of energy.

The warriors stack the tusks close to the canvas-roofed meeting place. The two fine cows are tethered to a supporting pole. Richard wonders if this is wise but the animals stand placidly, even though there is nothing to eat. Soon they are chewing the cud, stomachs rumbling like a processing plant.

'I see you have been reinforced?' Richard asks Farewell.

'Supplies and horses,' Farewell replies, indicating a sturdy corral in the shade of the dune forest, containing close to twenty mounts. Their ribs protrude, hips stark beneath dull coats.

'The voyage has not been good for them. We are feeding them up before presenting them to Shaka,' Farewell explains, eyeing the elephant tusks hungrily.

The following day is misty as the brig *Ann* is loaded with her cargo. The vessel is hauled into the shallows by every able-bodied man, the Ama-Wombe warriors gleefully joining in, singing as they haul on the ropes, seeking to outperform their white counterparts.

With the ship gently grounded on shelving sand, the ivory is easily man-handled on board. The two cows present a greater challenge. A block and tackle is rigged on the brig with a cradle suspended from a rope. Richard is reminded of the cannon being unloaded from the *Louisiana* in Delgoa Bay.

The cradle consists of two leather slings with holes for a cow's legs. The first beast is led, complaining, across the wet sand. The tide is out but she is soon knee-deep in water and lowing mournfully. The second cow calls back just as plaintively.

Quick hands grapple with one leg at a time, lifting a hoof and threading it through the tough leather, until the animal wears the contraption around her belly.

'Quick, boys!' calls Farewell. Richard watches Fynn as he gives the order to start hauling. He does not look convinced as the cow's hooves clear the shallow salt water, dangling comically.

The animal struggles, kicking and rolling her horned head, threatening to throw the whole manoeuvre off-balance. Panicky bellows echo along the beach, only ceasing when she senses something solid under her hooves.

Table Mountain grows ever larger against the horizon, its flat top draped in cloud. Richard stands by the starboard rail, as close to the prow as he can get without obstructing the crew. The brig has made good time in benign weather.

Cape Town is smeared at the base of the imposing

mountain. The *Ann* digs her prow into a wave as she comes about to enter the harbour. The sails on her twin masts fill, driving her forward, slicing through the lively waters.

Richard can make out sea walls and fortifications. White buildings stretch from the shore to the lower slopes behind the town. Steep hills spill from the flank of Table Mountain, enclosing the harbour in a hug. A dozen substantial vessels swing lazily on their moorings as the *Ann* noses into the sheltered anchorage.

With wind against his cheek and salt on his lips, Richard enjoys his last moments on board. His hair is ruffled by the wind. He feels good, although a ball of guilt lurks in his belly. Ulwazi and Zwelakhe are back in Bulawayo. He will not see them for many months.

Farewell and Fynn lean over the side to carry on a shouted conversation with a port official in his rowboat. They are assigned a spot and drop anchor.

Richard thinks of Captain Simpson as he studies the nearest East Indiaman, very similar to the *Arniston*, the ship he captained for the Company. Richard remembers Simpson's avarice, his frustration he could not afford a marine chronometer, his sense of bad luck as pirates and then weather wrecked his vessel.

Richard wonders what will happen to the former captain, still hostage at Bulawayo? Will he yet play a part in Napoleon's fate? Or will he fall to the executioner's club, sacrificed as others manoeuvre?

Richard imagines Simpson surveying the harbour, holding his straw hat on his head with one hand, while the other runs down his buff cotton lapel before falling away, disappointed he no longer wears the Company uniform.

Ashore, Farewell is known to everyone. The port officials treat him with respect, the harbourmaster oversees their landing personally and chats jovially. A servant is despatched and within minutes a carriage arrives to convey them to lodgings.

Mbikwane's appearance in feathers and pelts causes a stir as he walks with Richard to the vehicle. He smiles at everyone and this seems to work. Men doff hats and ladies nod appreciatively. The port city is a jumble of raw timber structures, new brick buildings and defiantly whitewashed houses with rounded gables, dormer windows and green-painted shutters reflecting a century and a half of Dutch influence.

The streets are busy but it is not far to the wooden warehouse of the Farewell Trading Company. An office occupies one end of the building with rooms above. While the Europeans take it in turns to shave at a single basin, pouring cool water from a glazed white pitcher, the Zulu diplomat stands looking out across the town.

'This is a big place,' he admits.

'Compared to our capital, London, it is insignificant,' boasts Farewell.

Richard is enjoying the sharp precision of the cutthroat razor, but he pauses mid-stroke.

'But it will continue to grow,' he adds, before completing his shave. Rubbing his chin, he smiles appreciatively.

Farewell watches as Fynn insists on taking his turn with the blade, although his downy fuzz is barely visible. Once he is finished, Farewell sends him to the market. By the time he returns with bread and cheese, their trunks have arrived.

Each man selects his most respectable clothes and dresses deliberately. They are to be received by the governor this very afternoon and first impressions matter. None can match Mbikwane's magnificence, even though Farewell chooses his lieutenant's uniform.

Richard wishes he could wear his fine red suit, granted him by Napoleon, but he is not here as part of the French court. He represents Shaka Zulu, another man who has welcomed him into his innermost circle. More than that, he is here as a Zulu, despite his shirt and breeches.

Lord Charles Somerset, the governor, is back in England with his ailing daughter. Sir Rufane Shaw Donkin is acting governor. He greets them on the steps of the residence with all due courtesy, showing no surprise at Mbikwane's appearance or Richard's lack of coat or cravat.

They follow their host into an elegant study with marvellous views over the bay. Richard studies him closely as Farewell makes his report. A few phrases intrude as he paints a picture of vast potential and boasts unashamedly of his achievements.

Donkin nods attentively, but there is an unresolved pain behind his eyes. He wears the uniform of a lieutenant-general, red above and off-white below. He is middle-aged, perhaps fifty, with clean features and a receding hairline. He sits at the governor's desk confidently and yet it is obvious he does not want the job. He is doing his duty.

'You've done admirably, Farewell. You are to be congratulated. We must formalise this treaty you speak of and the land grant. The settlers Somerset lobbied for arrive in ever greater numbers. We must secure all the land we can.' Donkin's voice is decisive but his fingers caress a watercolour on his desk.

Richard makes out a pyramid on a hill close to a coastline with a lighthouse nearby. The acting governor notices Richard's interest. He holds up the unframed painting.

'Algoa Bay,' he comments, 'I had this memorial built to commemorate my late wife, Elizabeth.' His voice trails away and his eyes fill with tears. Composing himself, he continues, 'She died too young. I am determined to rename the spot Port Elizabeth in her honour.'

Mbikwane remains standing, although he was offered a chair. He eyed the seat suspiciously and shook his head. Now, sensing the governor's vulnerability, he steps forward and executes an immaculate bow. Richard hides a smile. It is he who taught the Zulu ambassador British etiquette.

'I am pleased to be received by this warrior. I can tell he has lived through much. Please tell him, I understand both service and loss.'

Richard is not surprised by the Zulu's perception. It is his stock in trade. He translates quickly, and Governor Donkin nods appreciatively. He wipes his face and summons his secretary who sits at a modest desk, paper and pen to hand.

As they trail down the steps at the end of their audience, Mbikwane is still smiling. Richard glances at Farewell, who is muttering with Fynn. He can tell how annoyed the adventurer is with the way matters unfolded. Richard reviews the rest of the meeting.

Farewell claims Shaka granted his trading company a vast hinterland to administer. Mbikwane firmly refutes this, clarifying Shaka's intentions and stressing the need for permission before ivory may be taken. No mention is made of Captain Simpson's precarious position nor is Bonaparte's presence revealed. It is a truce of sorts.

It takes several hours before the secretary has drafted a treaty to be signed by the governor and Mbikwane on behalf of King Shaka and King George IV. Richard reads it carefully. It is deliberately ambiguous. He knows such documents cannot be relied upon.

'Do not sign,' he advises the Zulu representative.

Donkin looks astonished at his intervention.

'Forgive me, Governor. I should have made it clear. I am part of the Zulu delegation sent by King Shaka to represent him at the court of St James. We call here first as a courtesy.'

The experienced army officer retains his composure but insists some preliminary agreement needs to be completed before he can approve the proposed embassy.

'Might I borrow the draft? I could amend it as a starting point for further discussions,' Richard asks. He is surprised when Donkin agrees without demur.

The following day, Richard and Mbikwane sit in the governor's study. Mbikwane looks stiff, as he refuses to lean against the chair back. Richard explains to Donkin that Zulus do not use furniture.

'Do not let that deceive you,' he adds, 'they are formidable warriors and their society is highly organised.' He must make a success of this meeting; his son is growing quickly and he is missing it.

The acting governor does not dismiss the Zulu state out of hand. 'I have served across the world. The West Indies, Ostend, Portugal, India and now here. I do not underestimate my enemies. I fought at Talavera with some distinction.' He is not boasting.

Mbikwane sits stoically, trusting Richard to brief him. Donkin pulls a much-annotated document across his desk.

'I have read your reframing of the preliminary treaty,' he reports levelly, indicating it on his blotter. 'I can see you are familiar with the game.'

Richard inclines his head, accepting what he takes to be a compliment. But he keeps quiet, sensing Donkin has more to say.

'Governor Somerset may be back in England, but the settlers keep coming. Our Dutch inhabitants, Boers they call themselves, are not happy with us. There are rumours they may take themselves off into the interior. Either way, men will move east in increasing numbers. There has been much friction between natives and settlers already.'

The acting governor sounds weary, as if the squabbles of children confined to the nursery have spilled downstairs.

'King Shaka wants no more than to assert his right to bring the tribes on his border under control. He wishes us,' Richard looks at Mbikwane meaningfully, 'to seek approval from King George. In return, he offers trading opportunities, gifts and a guarantee he will not extend his kingdom beyond the land of those who speak his language.'

Richard translates for Mbikwane. The cheerful but observant Zulu listens and reflects before responding.

'This man lacks the necessary authority, is that not true?' he asks Richard calmly.

'In truth, yes,' Richard agrees.

'And yet, he insists we reach an agreement with him before we may proceed to visit his king?' Mbikwane sounds amused.

'Indeed,' Richard confirms, unsure where Mbikwane is going with his questions.

'Then we must do what he wishes. Make your marks and I will approve them.' He sounds unperturbed by the prospect of signing something he cannot read.

'What would you have me say in this treaty?' Richard asks. 'The British look for any advantage and will exploit it ruthlessly.'

'It does not matter,' Mbikwane reassures a surprised Richard, 'for mighty Shaka is not bound by your writing. He will only acknowledge the words that come from the mouth of this king across the waters.'

Richard looks to Donkin, who sits patiently as they confer.

'I will sign your version, Mister Davey,' Donkin concedes. 'For, I sense I will extract no concessions by trickery here!' The plain speaking of a soldier is a relief to Richard and seems to have the same effect on Donkin.

'Thank you, Governor.'

'It is of little import; I shall soon be gone. Lord Somerset returns and I am resolved to return to England. I shall write and perhaps stand for Parliament.' Donkin sits more lightly behind the desk, daring to imagine an existence beyond his sorrow.

'I wish you the best of fortune, Governor,' Richard offers. A minute later, it is done: the scruffiest treaty ever seen receives Donkin's flowing signature and three scratches and an ink blot from Ambassador Mbikwane. As an afterthought, Richard presses the Zulu's thumb into the ink spill.

The first vessel sailing to England is calling at St Helena. Richard makes his excuses and wanders further along the harbour, until he spots a Portuguese three-master riding at anchor not far from the East Indiaman he spotted on arrival from Port Natal.

At first, he is told there is no room for ivory or livestock, although he and his companion can be accommodated. The captain is a tailored dandy but the scars on his hands and face suggest he has seen plenty of action.

Richard eases open his purse. At the flash of gold in the bright sunlight of a spring afternoon, the captain hesitates and strokes his chin.

'London is not my destination. I call at Benguela and then Lisbon.'

Richard opens the neck of the purse a little further and smiles encouragingly.

'I suppose I could rearrange matters below deck to accommodate your cargo. It is not so far from Lisbon to London. You will find many ships plying that route.'

Farewell stands in front of his warehouse doors while Fynn looks on from the rickety stairs that climb to their rooms above.

'You have frustrated my plans, why should I release your property?' Farewell demands tersely.

'Perhaps you and your black friend should meet with an

accident?' Fynn calls down threateningly.

Richard fixes him with a stare. 'Shaka is no fool. Should we not return, your Port Natal will be burned to the ground and every inhabitant slaughtered.' He has not bothered checking with Mbikwane before speaking but relays what he has said. He receives a grin and a slap on the back.

'What if I reveal the presence of Bonaparte in Zulu territory?' Farewell counters.

'At the first sign of the British moving against the Zulus, Port Natal burns and Captain Simpson is executed.' Mbikwane nods his support even though Richard has not translated.

'Take your bloody ivory and cows,' Farewell concedes petulantly. 'It seems we must cooperate. I shall shower Shaka with horses and hair oil upon my return. Perhaps I will have replaced you in his favour by the time you return?'

Richard appraises the scheming adventurer once again. He is dangerous. A club hovering over Captain Simpson's head is not enough to control him. But he has ambitious plans and Port Natal is at the heart of them.

'We may want different things, but we need to work together. I will get your land grant and permission to take ivory. In return, Bonaparte remains a secret. Are we agreed?' Fynn curses and kicks a wooden railing so hard it splinters. But Farewell turns and hauls open the doors to the warehouse.

Chapter Fourteen

December 1821

A lmost twelve weeks at sea to Lisbon. Now another deck rocks beneath Richard's feet. Richard eyes the coast hungrily. White cliffs shoulder the grey sky while a slate sea batters their feet. Mbikwane stands unperturbed, his leopard-skin cloak offering some protection against the damp. On the long journey from Cape Town, Mbikwane mastered English so well, he rivals Emile for fluency.

Richard misses his friend but draws comfort from Mbikwane's stoic presence. They are close to the prow as the cargo ship makes the crossing from the Portuguese coast to England. The vessel is broad of beam, designed to maximise carrying capacity. She is half the tonnage of the ship that endured a tortuous journey from Cape Town.

In her hold sit barrel after barrel of port, crossing the gunmetal seas separating sunny Portugal from overcast England.

'The taste of a happier climate,' the captain observes proudly as he joins the pair. 'We have exported wines to England since the twelfth century!'

Richard knows the addition of brandy to wine was as much an English invention as Portuguese, an attempt to make vintages travel better. He keeps this to himself and smiles.

As the English coast looms through the murk, Richard

reviews the long weeks that have brought him to this point. At first, the voyage was smooth, harnessing strong south-easterly trade winds. But north of Ascension Island they endured the doldrums off west Africa, before having to beat upwind against the north-east trades.

The Portuguese crew knew what to expect, proving efficient and resilient. But they look haggard now. Richard can only imagine what state landlubber Emile would be in had he made the journey!

The docks are a hive of activity. Stevedores hurry back and forth, harbour officials bark orders, sailors joke and spit, hurrying towards the pubs that crowd close.

Everybody is staring at Mbikwane, representative of the Zulu nation, as he studies them in return. He smiles at men and women alike, seemingly unaffected by their frowns, pointing fingers and gasps of disapproval. His stately bearing and fatherly features hidden by the spectators' prejudices.

He refuses to adopt European dress, suffering the cold in bare feet, letting drizzle bead on his head, gathering around his head ring to drip relentlessly onto his leopard cape. His kilt of animal tails hangs limply.

Waiting for a coach, sheltering beneath a canvas awning, Mbikwane slips his snuff spoon from a pierced ear lobe. A passing porter runs his cart into a stack of crates, as he stares at the Zulu snorting snuff.

Richard feels the two tickets in the pocket of his overcoat as the coach pulls up in front of the depot. Several passengers move forward, only to freeze in mid-step when they see Mbikwane fingering the carriage door with interest.

'I say, my good man, tell your servant he has to ride up top!' brays a tall-hatted man of middle years with a bulbous nose and watery eyes. Richard sighs, he has been expecting this.

'He is not my servant. He is an ambassador from the Zulu nation of southern Africa, He has travelled thousands of miles to be presented at court. I trust you wish no offence to His Majesty?' Richard is pleased with himself. He presents two tickets to the driver and shows Mbikwane how to open the door.

The Zulu caresses the padded-leather bench with interest while they wait for their luggage to be stowed. When no other passengers join them, Richard lowers the sash-window and sticks his head out into the drizzle-filled air. There is no one waiting at the depot. The prospective passengers have melted away. Richard shrugs as the driver calls to the horses and the carriage begins to move. In nine hours, they will be in London.

Richard gazes out of the full-length sash-window of his set in the Albany, his fingers gripping the edge of an opulent curtain. The drizzle of yesterday has turned to snow, coating the grimy, crowded city in a pristine coat that glows as dusk falls and lamps cast golden pools of light.

This morning he presented his letter of introduction from Acting Governor Sir Rufane Shaw Donkin. A royal equerry treated him with a mixture of suspicion, amusement and contempt as he studied the document. Only when he reached the section suggesting lucrative trade did he grow civil. For all that, he merely noted the address for Richard's set of rented rooms just north of Piccadilly and told him he should await a summons.

'And when might that be?' Richard asked, reining in his frustration. Ulwazi was not happy about his mission. He wants it over with as soon as possible. He wants to be back with her and his son.

'Whenever His Majesty chooses,' the irritated lackey snapped back.

Snow settles, accentuating the railings opposite as infrequent carriages etch their passage. In less than ten minutes tracks are obscured as the snowfall grows heavier.

'King George is the fourth of his family to rule this land?' Mbikwane asks, reclining on a plush, gold-trimmed *chaise longue*.

'His family have ruled here for over a century,' Richard replies, adding without thinking, 'they are not from this land but…'

'They conquered your people?' Mbikwane finishes his sentence.

'Not exactly.' Richard puzzles at how to explain the Act of Settlement. 'George the First was seen as the right person at the time.'

Rather than pressing further, Mbikwane nods sagely before speaking. 'It is like Shaka. Many accept his rule without conquest.'

Richard decides to change the subject. 'We may have to wait some time before we are summoned to court. Even in the capital, you are an unusual presence. Will you remain in these rooms for your safety?' Richard hates making such a request.

'I saw the shock on people's faces. No one would ride with us. I know about the effect of skin colour on your people.' Mbikwane pauses and rises fluidly before crossing to the window. He pulls another curtain back and takes in the view.

'I will do as you ask. It will not serve Shaka's purpose for me to cause trouble before we meet King George.'

Richard thinks Mbikwane has finished and he is warmed by his understanding. 'You are a wise man and a fine diplomat. But do not expect too much from this king. He spent many years indulging himself before his father died. I am told he can charm when he chooses but he can be petulant and difficult.'

The Zulu ambassador looks at Richard and shakes his head. 'Do not worry. It is not for us to question the ways of kings. But I will tell you one thing I have learned already. This British empire of yours, it is doomed. How can it not be, when it sees only one colour? That is but one step from blindness.'

Richard continues to study the snow, transformed to gold in the lamplight. What can he say?

Mbikwane sighs. 'I sense you agree. Look at you, your friend Emile and Bonaparte. See how Shaka spotted your talents and honoured you. Surely, there can be no doubt, the Zulu empire will endure long after yours is gone!'

Richard wanders in wonder around the streets of the city. There is no Big Ben, no Tower Bridge or Admiralty Arch. Trafalgar Square is a building site but at least the Tower of London and St Paul's are familiar.

It will soon be Christmas. The snow has stopped but it

remains cold. Today, the sky is an unbroken blue and the winter sun glitters powerlessly. Richard is walking by the river, his route often interrupted by wharfs and warehouses. He is melancholy. The city's festive mood makes him think of his little family, so far away.

He stops to watch as a river barge is unloaded. Behind him, he hears raised voices. Turning, he sees a couple arguing in front of a classically styled building covered in cream stucco. The man is slender, imperious and dismissive of his companion. She is tall for the time, close to Richard's height. She juts her chin as the man grasps her roughly by the arm, propelling her towards a waiting carriage.

The girl, for that is what she seems to Richard, resists and her bonnet is dislodged, revealing dark ringlets. Her neck is long and her skin shockingly pale. Her round face is distorted by discomfort and Richard takes a step towards her.

She turns an imploring gaze towards him. Richard stumbles to a stop in the middle of the granite-cobbled road. She gasps before being bundled into the carriage which is rapidly whipped into motion.

He just has time to make out the coat of arms painted brightly on the door. He sees a bear in chains, and white stars within a red chevron on a blue background.

'Arabella!' he mouths as he watches the carriage turn left away from the river.

Spying a group of well-dressed young men exiting the building, Richard finishes crossing the road and accosts them. 'Forgive me, gentlemen. Do you happen to know whose coach I just saw leaving?'

All four men tower over him in their tall hats. Their blue

overcoats are buttoned tightly to the waist. They wear grey trousers above delicate black-glossed shoes. Their cravats and waistcoats are ivory. It is as if they are wearing a uniform.

The portliest looks him up and down with surprise, as if trying to understand his appearance. Richard shuffles his feet. He purchased several changes of clothes on his first day in London. He feels awkward but they resemble these men's outfits, although his trousers are buff and his coat a mid-brown.

'I do not know you, sir. Why should I furnish you with the information you seek?' the plump fellow enquires in a high-pitched voice.

'Richard Davey, man of letters, at your disposal,' Richard replies, offering a modest bow. The shortest of the group titters into his sleeve but says nothing.

'Now, now, you fellows, be more accommodating. If Mister Davey craves the gentleman's company, who are we to deny him?' This voice comes from a handsome face, dominated by grey eyes.

'Quite right, Reynolds,' agrees a thin man with red sideburns.

'I believe Lord Everard Dalrymple left in his carriage a few moments ago. This is his club. He is always here on a Thursday,' explains the kind, grey-eyed man, holding his cane nonchalantly across his shoulder.

Richard can hardly breathe. Could this brutish aristocrat be related to the hapless missionary he knew at Bulawayo? He gathers himself.

'Thank you for your kindness,' Richard gushes, 'can you tell me his London address?'

'Mayfair, of course. Well away from the stink of the river! Grosvenor Square, number eight.' Here the thin redhead pauses and smirks. 'The family haven't recovered from having John Adams as a neighbour, when he was American ambassador. They gave a party when he was elected President because it meant he would move out!' Laughter from all four men.

Richard barely squeezes out his thanks before his feet are stepping out to find a hackney carriage.

Grosvenor Square stands proudly, an oasis of gentility in the city. Every façade is immaculate, rusticated stone below and brick between pilasters above, topped by a host of chimneys attesting to the warmth and comfort within.

Number eight stands resplendent in a row of grand houses of five and seven bays, forming one perfect whole. Pillars and porticos, sash-windows and entablatures conform to Palladian patterns.

Dusk cloaks the scene and as Richard watches, lights bloom behind windows all along the imposing terrace. A warm yellow spills outwards, reaching towards the finely manicured green at the heart of the hundred-year-old development.

Richard stands on the pavement, with his back to the railings which surround a large, tree-edged lawn. Looking across the wide street, he catches a glimpse of a drawing room before the curtains are closed by a maid.

'What am I doing?' he asks himself as mist tugs at his ankles. He looks at the confident lines of the house. Arabella is in there. There was something about the way that man took hold of her. Like she was a disobedient child or a mere possession.

Lamplight leaks around the edges of the curtains and he imagines Arabella in the room. Is she crying, begging or pleading? Or is everything fine? Perhaps he saw no more than a momentary disagreement, he tells himself as he turns away.

He decides to walk back to the Albany, where Mbikwane waits, even his patient good humour wearing thin after days of confinement.

Richard opens the door to the sounds of laughter. The Zulu diplomat's deep, rolling mirth beneath a tenor chuckle and a canary chirp.

Entering the sitting room, Richard is not surprised to find Mbikwane kneeling on the floor. Although he loves the *chaise longue*, he remains suspicious of furniture, sleeping on the Axminster rug in his bedroom.

What does surprise Richard is the sight of a chambermaid and a footman on their heels either side of the Zulu. The young maid has a scrubbed face and sparkling cornflower eyes. A wisp of blonde hair escapes her cap as she bends to move a piece on the chequered board. She jumps her white counter over first one and then another black one, scooping up her trophies deftly.

Mbikwane looks up at Richard with a grin. 'This is a fine game,' he enthuses. 'Miss Gladys is teaching me to play.'

The footman claps Mbikwane on the back, a friendly and familiar gesture. Gladys's pink cheeks deepen as she crowns her counter. Richard marvels at the diplomat's good humour and the relaxed mood in the room. Where is the rigid hierarchy, the subservience of servants, the suspicion of a man with different skin?

As if sensing Richard's unspoken questions, the footman rises and is immediately transformed. He bows deferentially. 'Forgive us, sir. We were just helping your companion pass the time. We are off duty, so no harm done. The name is Simms if you need anything, sir?' His tone is ingratiating, almost pleading. His accent from the fringes of the city but burnished by service.

Richard smiles kindly even though he keeps his lips together, hiding his uneven yellow teeth.

As Mbikwane lowers his gaze to the board, his big hands caress the fine rug. 'I like this floor covering. It is good to sleep on. We must secure one for Shaka. Perhaps it might depict his victories?' he suggests.

Richard nods, although he hopes they will not be in London long enough to commission such a work. He looks again at the footman and chews his lip. 'Simms, tell me. Do you find nothing strange playing draughts with this exotic visitor?' He tries to pitch his voice so that Mbikwane does not hear. From his continued fixation with the game, it seems he has succeeded.

'Forgive me, sir. I'm not sure I take your meaning?' comes the reply.

'This man is black. He wears animal skins. Hardly usual London apparel, let alone for someone staying in such distinguished lodgings.' Richard feels awkward, as if he is a racist for asking.

'Plenty of coloured fellows around the docks. Good stories and hard fists most of them. Come from all over. My sister got in the family way with a darkie. Mam cried for days but it's all fine now they're married proper.'

Richard smiles weakly, nods his thanks and looks back to the game in time to see Gladys sweep Mbikwane's final pieces from the board.

'I win again!' she celebrates in the lilting accents of the Welsh valleys. Mbikwane claps with delight before turning a more serious face to Richard.

'I would see where these good people live. They tell me it is very different to this cliff carved into the cells of a beehive. Among the Zulus, all live in the same manner. My hut is no different to that of any family head even though I am a chief.'

The implied criticism is not lost on Richard but he is imagining the reaction to Mbikwane's appearance in a working-class London street.

London is the biggest city in the world and growing fast, its port the hub for global trade. Richard knows the city swells with cheap housing for those flooding the city in hope of a better life.

'I'm not sure that's such a good idea,' Richard counters, speaking in Zulu.

'Why not? Can you doubt my welcome when you see how these fine people treat me?' Mbikwane's reply is, just as deliberately, in English.

Exasperated, Richard snaps, 'Where do you live, Gladys?'

'St Giles, sir. Although I spend most nights here at the Albany. Tommy Simms there, he lives but a few doors down. Was him who got me a job here.' As more words flow from her lips, Richard realizes her accent is not pure Welsh but overlaid with the strains of the city.

Shaking his head, Richard tries to explain to Mbikwane.

'This place where they live. It is a dense warren of crowded alleys. All kinds of depravity thrive there. Prostitutes. Criminals.' He wants to explain about gin shops but cannot capture the destructive nature of that cheap spirit in Zulu nor find words the Zulu will understand in English.

'I am Shaka's ambassador. I am sent to meet with the king. He is ignoring my presence. It is time I understood more of this London, this England, this empire. To understand a king, you have only to speak with his people, is that not so?' Mbikwane's fierce resolve is irresistible.

'At least dress to fit in,' Richard begs as he concedes.

That very evening, a message is delivered by a royal footman. They are summoned to appear at court on Saturday. As it is a formal event, they will be received at St James's Palace, despite the fire a decade earlier that destroyed the monarch's apartments. The king now lives in the comfort of Buckingham Palace, only venturing to St James's for official business.

'All the more reason to expedite my outing,' Mbikwane insists.

The streets around the Albany are clean. The passage of hundreds of horses means there are always boys sweeping manure into carts and carrying it away. On the street corners, optimistic hawkers cry until they are chased away by parish constables.

Richard watches a scuffle as one determined pie-seller clings to the railings, as the constable tries to remove her. In the struggle, her pies tumble from her tray onto the damp pavement. She drops to her knees, scrabbling to save her precious inventory. Clumsily, the constable treads on her goods and drags her off screaming and cursing. It will be eight years before the first Peelers start professionalising policing in the capital, Richard muses.

Their hackney carriage passes rows of classical architecture, interspersed with both brick and black-and-white survivors of earlier centuries. Street cries touting wares echo from most corners. Sing-song or bass, they are lyrical advertisements for handmade goods, trinkets, lucky heather, fruits and nuts, meat pies, sprats and shellfish, kindling, pottery and much more.

Reluctantly, Richard has paid the manager of the Albany over the odds to release Gladys and Tommy for the day. The pair chatter excitedly. Richard studies them surreptitiously. They are both wearing their Sunday best although it is a Friday. They look smart if a little threadbare and both smell as if they have washed.

The hackney coach is a cumbersome vehicle in dingy yellow, pulled by two puffing horses, whose breath precedes them in the crisp December air. The coach is a brougham, much like the carriages once used by nobility, able to convey four passengers in relative comfort. It is almost ten o'clock when the driver pulls up.

'Can't go no further, gov'nor. Streets is too narrow,' he calls down from his seat up top. 'Want me to wait? Can't imagine you'll want to be in there for long,' he adds disparagingly.

As they step down from the carriage, Richard looks around nervously, peering down the nearest alley, which is barely wide enough for two people to pass without rubbing shoulders. Tenements rise on either side, upper floors jutting out to maximise space. These overhangs cut off light, rendering the warren of narrow ways a dark, foreboding maze.

Richard shivers despite his overcoat. Mbikwane's face is a picture of interest as Gladys describes the purpose of each building.

'That one's rooms for rent, that's a grog shop, over there, that's a butcher's below, they live above the shop and let rooms, my cousin Alf has one and porters for them.'

The carriage-driver is still waiting, Richard realizes. He hesitates, seeing the vehicle as an escape route he may need. He hands up a coin and receives a knowing grin in return.

Tommy shouts towards the mouth of the alley, seeing someone he knows. 'Here, Bobby, where's that pal of yours, the one from Jamaica?' he asks in his strident tenor.

The sound of horses' hooves, the cries of costermongers, the hubbub of a crowded neighbourhood settling to work. None of it matches the cacophony of traffic-clogged, siren-swamped London two hundred years from now.

'He's sleeping off a good night, wot you want 'im for?' asks bearded Bobby good-naturedly, despite being obviously the worse for wear himself.

Tommy Simms indicates Mbikwane, Mthethwa chief and ambassador from the Zulu empire. 'Got someone who'd like to meet him,' Tommy replies, managing to avoid dropping his aitch.

Bobby eyes Mbikwane with interest, taking in his head ring, his imposing physique crammed into a Georgian outfit, and finally, his bare feet. He looks down at his own scuffed ankle boots, one bound with twine to keep the sole in place.

'Reckon they'll know each other 'cause they're both touched by the tar brush?' he jokes without malice.

'Don't be daft!' Simms shoots back. 'Just figure it'd make him feel a bit more welcome.'

Two bleary-eyed women, in tight but unbuttoned bodices, saunter over, eyeing the Zulu with undisguised appreciation.

'Now that's a fine figure of a man!' the taller brunette purrs.

'Give me a black'n any day, Em', they know how to do the blanket hornpipe!' jokes her shorter, red-headed companion.

'Piss off, Em' and take Mary with you. It's too early for you doxies to be on the prowl!' orders Bobby, slapping first one and then the other on the rear with calloused hands.

The pair giggle, pout, cast a final longing look at Mbikwane and sway back down the alley where they are soon lost in the gloom.

They sit in Glady's family home, a single room on the first floor of a crowded, noisy and smelly tenement opposite a gin shop. They are drinking tea from the best china, a little chipped but most of it matching. The walls are peeling in places and the floorboards creak but there is not a speck of dust in the place.

'Well, I never did. Fancy you getting a day off apart from Sunday,' gushes Mrs Jones. Tommy is on the floor with Mbikwane, while Richard and Gladys sit with her mother at the table.

Richard looks around the shabby but well-kept room. A bed occupies one wall with a truckle beneath. 'Is your husband working, Mrs Jones?' Richard asks, searching for a safe topic of conversation. She does not answer him but glances at her daughter with a far-away look in her eyes.

'Pa's a seaman. Took ship for the Indies more'n two years ago. We haven't seen him since. His ship came back alright six months back but he weren't on it. I tried asking round the docks. No one would tell me anything.' The resignation in Gladys's voice tells Richard all he needs to know.

'I'm sorry,' he says. 'I lost my parents when I was five. An accident.' He receives a smile of sympathy and solidarity from Mrs Jones before she refills his cup.

Shouting sounds through the thin walls. A slap and then quiet sobbing. A door slams. Outside, curses are exchanged. A hawker calls his wares, primarily cat meat.

'Tell me, do you like your king?' asks Mbikwane from the floor, looking more out of place in his borrowed coat and trousers than he would in cape and kilt.

'Beggin' your pardon, sir but it's not the place of the likes of us to be likin' or dislikin' our monarch, is it?' Gladys replies to nods from Tommy and her mother.

For a moment, Mbikwane frowns as if he has not understood but his next words show he has grasped her meaning.

'Indeed. But if I were to ask what the others living in this building think? Those in the next building, anyone in the whole of your vast city?' His voice is kind and encouraging but he cannot disguise his appetite for an answer.

Mrs Jones smiles. She gestures to the teapot and the diplomat offers his cup. He seems to be enjoying the tea and has already polished off two slices of sponge cake.

'Well, I'm not one to gossip, sir. But what it is, there are those who remember all those years he was Prince Regent. London may be large but even the likes of us got to hear about his carrying on over by there.' Mrs Jones subsides with a look of surprise as if she cannot believe what she has said.

'Ma, it must have been hard. Waiting all those years, what with the old king being mad most of the time.' Gladys sounds genuinely sympathetic.

'I don't see why a body should wish his pa dead, no matter the circumstances,' Mrs Jones objects.

Tommy snorts derisively. 'I wished me old man dead from the moment I could walk. He were a spiteful bully and me mam's better off since he drank himself to death!' His voice is a torrent of loathing.

'Mistresses paraded without shame, debts beyond imagining, a drunk and a glutton, rude, spendthrift and addicted to laudanum. Not a great preparation to rule.' Everyone turns to the figure standing in the doorway. None of them heard the door open.

The newcomer is in shirt-sleeves, rolled up above the elbow. He wears a bow tie and a once-white apron smeared with blood.

'Good day. I heard Mrs Jones had visitors so I left my boy in charge. My name's Hoggard, Percy Hoggard. I run the butcher's shop over the way.' The speaker has a generous moustache and a friendly face. He holds himself confidently and his speech is a cut above.

Mrs Jones blushes, gets up and sets another place at the table, giving up her own chair.

'Now, now, Myfanwy, no need for that. This is still your home, no matter what that wretch of a husband has done with himself. You know I'll always look out for you.' Percy holds the chair as she sits back down before pouring him a cup of tea and cutting a generous portion of what she calls Shrowsbury cake.

'Alright, Percy. You are good man and no mistake,' Myfanwy Jones admits.

Mbikwane has listened carefully, Richard can tell. 'I see you, Percy,' he says in greeting. The butcher inclines his head in reply. 'Only a trusted man may prepare a carcass for the fire,' the Zulu adds as a show of respect. 'It seems you are not afraid to speak your mind. Tell me, can I trust the word of your king? If he makes a promise, will he keep it?'

Gladys and Tommy, Richard and Myfanwy all turn towards Percy. He takes a moment to consider.

'I think he would leave his old life behind him but it is hard to shed a reputation.' Percy looks like he might say more but his lips tighten and he sips his tea before cramming cake into his mouth, precluding further comment.

'So, he may grasp a chance to make his mark, to signal he is worthy of his feathers... his crown?'

Most of the party squeezed into the room shrug but Percy nods slowly. 'Perhaps, if the politicians let him,' is all he manages before two more figures crowd the threshold. One is Bobby from the alley and the other, a short, powerful figure leaning heavily against his companion, has the darkest skin Richard has ever seen.

'Found 'im!' Bobby announces unnecessarily. 'Still a bit the worse for wear but I sobered 'im up as best I could.'

Richard can see the man's tight-curled hair is damp. His eyes are red-rimmed and watery and his lids look so heavy he can barely keep them open.

'Meet Jamaica Jim,' Tommy announces. Hearing his name, the hungover figure looks up and studies the crowded room. As he scans from face to face, his expression changes from blankness to recognition and then surprise as his eyes settle on Mbikwane.

'I ain't never seen a dark fellow dressed so fine!' he exclaims in an accent that troubles Richard. He can detect no hint of patois nor random or omitted consonants.

Mbikwane returns the man's gaze with equal interest. 'You do not come from Zulu territory. Where do your people dwell?' he asks politely.

Jamaica Jim's eyes lose focus. He stares at a peeling wall without expression before shaking his head and wiping his face. 'That is no simple question,' he finally replies. 'I was born in Jamaica but sold to a plantation in Georgia. My grandaddy was from west Africa. His people were Kongo. I picked cotton and then tobacco. When I was manumitted, I signed on with a merchant ship. Been a sailor ever since. But somehow, I always end up back here.'

Richard wonders how Mbikwane is processing Jamaica Jim's tale. He can know nothing of Jamaica or Georgia and likely no more of Africa. He wonders if he should try to explain but does not get the chance.

'There are no slaves in my land,' the Zulu insists. 'But tell me, where are your family?' There is real concern in Mbikwane's voice.

Jim shrugs. 'Any still alive will be in Jamaica, I s'pose.' He looks reflective. 'I barely remember their faces. T'was only five when I was sold off the island,' he explains sadly.

'You didn't go back once you were freed?' Richard asks aghast.

'How could I? A freed slave I might be, but to a Jamaican landowner? A black skin is all he sees. A slave is what that means. I wasn't goin' to give up my freedom to visit parents who long ago pushed my memory away.'

The Zulu ambassador stands and crosses the room in three long strides. He relieves Bobby of Jim's bulk and embraces the Jamaican-born sailor.

'If you travel to my homeland, you shall have a family!' Mbikwane offers.

It is almost Christmas and it is snowing again. Carriage wheels turn snow to dirty slush on the roads and pedestrians leave tidy trails along the white-draped wooden pavements.

Richard and Mbikwane wait beneath the Albany's portico for their transport. Richard is dressed in the latest fashion. His silhouette tapers from wide, puffed shoulders to a narrow waist. Refusing a corset, he finds the cut of his double-breasted frock coat rather tight and is glad his trousers are adjustable.

His high collar rubs the back of his neck but his ornate cravat is soft at his throat over a linen shirt. As it is an evening reception, he wears dark breeches and stockings in place of his usual trousers, as this is still expected at court.

Had he not grown used to his red velvet and gold suit, he would feel impossibly ostentatious but instead, he studied his outline in a dressing mirror with satisfaction.

Mbikwane has reverted to his traditional garb and looks magnificent. Richard can see his golden skin raised in an armour of goosebumps but the Zulu ambassador does not shiver.

Richard turns the brim of his tall hat in nervous hands, peering through angling snow for sight of their carriage. His long hair has been curled by a pedantic little Italian barber who lamented the absence of substantial sideburns, even offering to glue a fake pair in place. Richard refused politely.

A heavy cart appears, carrying the gift of ivory Mbikwane is to present to George IV. The matching pair of cows did not survive the journey to Portugal, furnishing the crew with fresh meat at a time when they could never have expected it. He hopes the ivory will impress the king.

Scant moments later, the carriage draws up beneath the portico and a footman opens the door, emblazoned with the royal coat of arms in red, gold and blue. Richard just has time to note lions in three of the four quarters before he is handed up. He hopes they are not an omen, recalling that night on the beach surrounded by the carnivores, as they move off.

It is not a long journey to St James's Palace but the cart carrying the ivory is slow and the coachman lets it set the pace, giving his passengers plenty of time to anticipate their reception at court.

By the time they pull into the wide-open space in front of the palace's red-brick gatehouse, with its twin towers facing Pall Mall, Richard is queasy with nerves. He glances at Mbikwane, who is peering at the view through the carriage window. He looks interested and eager but quite uncowed by his surroundings.

They are ushered through the gatehouse, across a courtyard and along increasingly grand corridors to arrive on the threshold of the Presence Chamber. Richard sent their cards to the Lord Chamberlain's office when they first arrived in London. These are now used by the Master of the Ceremonies to announce them.

The Presence Chamber is oddly plain compared to the spaces they have already passed through, but dominating the far wall is a magnificent red, brocaded canopy over a modest throne in matching material. The king sits upon it with his feet supported by a footstool in the same design.

Along both walls stand groups of men and women, in the highest court fashions, punctuated by ramrod blue or red uniforms. Beneath their feet are sanded floorboards and overhead a ceiling of unadorned cream plaster. The walls are painted panelling, topped by heavy coving, punctuated by tall, shuttered windows.

To Richard's right, a steady fire burns in a simple marble fireplace. The walls are hung with tapestries and gilded sconces outshine the royal coat of arms above King George's head.

At the sound of his name, Richard steps forward, trailing after Mbikwane, who strolls boldly towards the king. All eyes follow him and a murmur washes back and forth as courtiers and guests discuss his appearance. George notices their reaction.

Drawing level with his Zulu companion, Richard executes a lavish bow, while Mbikwane drops to his knees and presses his forehead to the wooden planking, as he would before Shaka.

Richard waits for Mbikwane to rise onto his heels before completing his obeisance. He can now study King George.

Richard sees a dashing, handsome man, an immensely strong man gone to seed. His fine features are blurring into fat. Neither his broad shoulders nor his extravagant clothes can disguise his growing obesity.

Behind them, Richard hears a whispered discussion as the ivory tusks arrive.

'My lord king, you are master of a mighty empire. I have travelled beyond the comprehension of my people to pay you homage on behalf of Shaka Zulu, mighty lion, he who makes the earth tremble, devourer of his enemies. My great king greets you as an equal and wishes me to present this gift.'

Taking his cue from Mbikwane's declamation, Richard gestures to the uncertain, liveried servants to bring the tusks forward. Each curving tooth is supported by two men. They move two abreast and three deep until they are all clearly within the Presence Chamber.

Richard indicates they should set down their burdens at the king's feet. The first two cumbersome tusks are deposited successfully. The third is also clumsily lowered to the floor in front of the monarch who looks on with interest. The lead man of the next pair catches his foot on the king's footstool, forcing a shriek from the monarch as his gout-ravaged foot is jolted.

Gasps fills the room. The stumbling servant regains his balance and sets down his burden, before backing away, bobbing his head, only to collide with the pair immediately behind him.

The footman in front is knocked sideways and drops the truncated point to the floor, yanking the base of the tusk from his partner's grip. The sound as it hits the wooden floor is like an axe against a tree trunk. For a split second, the curved tusk balances on its tangent, before toppling over into Mbikwane's lap.

The Zulu ambassador pushes it aside with his big hands. Richard expects him to apologise but instead, Mbikwane begins to laugh, his broad chest heaving as his bass guffaws fill the shocked silence. It is an infectious sound and Richard finds himself smiling.

He risks a nervous look at King George, who is thin-lipped and pale with pain beneath his make-up. He can see tears in the monarch's eyes as attendants hover around him, offering brandy, food and sympathy.

George refuses everything until a plainly dressed man of middle years appears at his shoulder, proffering a small vial. This, the king seizes, unstoppers and sips from. Almost immediately, a beatific expression relaxes his features and his lips part.

The monarch's laugh is not as deep as he expects, indeed, Richard thinks it more of a titter but he is glad to hear it. Soon George's laugh finds Mbikwane's rhythm and Richard joins in. Within a minute, everyone at court is laughing, although much of it sounds forced.

Finally, the Zulu's mirth subsides and just as quickly, George's trilling ceases. The assembled courtiers fall silent. The last pair lay down their tusk with exaggerated care and scurry away.

'I thank you for your king's kind gift. I have never seen such great tusks. Truly, they are a gift fit for my standing. Now, tell me why you have travelled so far, to endure weather I doubt you ever experienced in your homeland?'

Mbikwane bows again as the ladies and gentleman of court smile at their sovereign's wit. 'My lord Shaka asks, as one king to another, for permission to expand his territories to the south-west. He is troubled by unruly neighbours and wishes to impose order. He has no intention of reaching the borders of your domain.'

King George nods. It is clear he has been briefed. Richard wonders precisely what the acting governor put in his report?

'I am not my father. It was his misfortune to lose our colonies in the Americas. I do not intend to make the same mistakes he did. Nevertheless, I am minded to grant your overlord's request. It seems prudent to remain on good terms with a growing power and ensure stability on our borders.'

Mbikwane shuffles forward on his hands and knees. Richard has seen this happen many times. Even Shaka's most trusted advisers would kiss his feet when he issued a favourable decree.

Richard holds his breath, looking on helplessly as the muscular ambassador draws closer to the king's inflamed foot, wrapped in silk bandages. He sighs with relief as Mbikwane stops short of the stool, shuffles to his right and kisses the monarch's left slipper.

King George IV smiles beneficently and waves the diplomat up. 'Tell me, how did you learn to speak our language so well? In truth, you speak it better than my great-grandfather!'

Mbikwane indicates Richard who stands beside the kneeling Zulu. 'I learned from this man, Richard Davey, who is a member of King Shaka's inner council.'

King George studies Richard. His eyes look small in his

fleshy face but they are penetrating and he feels uncomfortable under their scrutiny.

'Astonishing, a white Christian in service to a barbarian prince!' exclaims the king. 'I suspect that is a tale worth hearing. A pity we do not have the time.' George squints at an ornate clock above the fireplace. An attendant leans forward to whisper in his ear.

The king nods. 'It is as I thought. *Tempus fugit!* Was there anything else?' the king's voice is kind, as if reluctant for this odd interlude to end.

Mbikwane bows again. 'King Shaka would confirm trading relations between our two nations. He offers a regiment of his soldiers so that you can benefit from his innovations.'

Several ageing men in red army uniforms scoff but the king waves them to silence. 'I have no doubt your army is formidable. I have reports of the speed with which Shaka's influence spreads. I will instruct the relevant authorities to draw up a trade agreement between our peoples. As for the offer of a military exchange, I shall give that serious consideration. Please convey my thanks and appreciation to Shaka.'

As they back from the Presence Chamber, Richard wonders at what has just happened. He expected a contemptuous, bored, embittered king who would denigrate their embassy and dismiss them out of hand. Instead, it appears they have successfully completed their mission.

As they step up into the carriage that will return them to their lodgings, Mbikwane chuckles.

'What amuses you?' Richard asks as the door is closed

behind him. The coachman sets his well-matched pair to a steady trot.

'It seems kings are the same all over the world, no matter how big that world may be.'

Richard smiles his agreement as his eyes droop. He only awakens as the carriage is brought to a halt beneath the portico of their apartment building.

'Tomorrow is Sunday and then it's Christmas Eve,' Richard says as they enter the building. Mbikwane looks nonplussed.

'A day of rest and then we need to buy some presents,' Richard offers by way of explanation.

Chapter Fifteen

December 1821

M onday morning dawns crisp and clear. It is bitterly cold and the remaining snow crunches loudly underfoot. Richard is on his way to book passage for Cape Town. His route to the shipping agent's office takes him past Grosvenor Square. Unable to resist, he strolls along the splendid townhouses to stand outside number eight.

He means to keep walking but his feet stop and he turns to the gloss-black front door. He mounts the steps and his hand reaches out, as if it belongs to someone else, grasping the brass door knocker shaped like a dolphin. He raps three times and descends one step.

His heart pounds in his chest. What is he doing? Why is he here? The door opens to reveal an immaculately turned-out footman. Feeling foolish, Richard realises it is not yet nine o'clock.

'How may I be of service, sir?' enquires the compact, composed servant, disguising any surprise at this appearance so early on Christmas Eve. 'Are you expected? Breakfast is not served until ten o'clock. I do not believe the master is expecting anyone,' the footman continues in a puzzled tone.

'Forgive me, I am an acquaintance of Miss Arabella Fortescue.' A deep frown distorts the servant's brow and Richard realises his mistake. 'I misspoke, of course, I know the lady of the house from her time in Brussels.'

His correction does not alter the footman's expression. 'Lady Arabella is not at home to visitors, sir.'

There is something sinister in the way this man talks about Arabella. Richard cannot pin it down but it drives him to insist. 'I know the hour is unconventional but I am soon to leave overseas. This is my only opportunity to pay my respects.'

The frown deepens and colour flushes the cheeks of the obstructive servant. 'Perhaps you would like to leave a calling card?' the footman suggests through gritted teeth.

Automatically, Richard reaches for his inside pocket where he carries some cards in a silver case. The efficient staff at their lodgings arranged for them to be printed as soon as he arrived in London. He proffers a card, feeling defeated.

'Who is it at this hour, Simpkins?' demands a familiar voice in hoarse tones.

'Reverend Dalrymple?' Richard calls out, trying to look around Simpkins' immovable frame. 'It's me, Richard Davey!'

Fortescue Dalrymple replaces the obstructive Simpkins in the doorway. 'Good Lord, Mister Davey... Richard?' The failed missionary is dressed in the fashionable Georgian manner with no sign of a dog-collar. His hands reach out in greeting, friendly, welcoming, no longer clutching his bible.

'It is good to see you looking so well, Reverend,' Richard replies.

Dalrymple frowns for a split second before his smile returns. 'Come in, come in, my dear fellow, it is perishing out, no doubt?'

Richard steps over the threshold. Simpkins takes his hat and coat, transformed from dogged gatekeeper to respectful servant in a moment.

Richard is ushered into a smart room with elegant panelling and restrained plasterwork. A fine chandelier hangs from the ceiling rose. The furniture's gilded frames contain plump, striped silk. He sits cautiously in an armchair, while Dalrymple throws himself nonchalantly onto a *chaise longue*, stretching out lazily while his active eyes study Richard.

'It is truly good to see you, Richard. I was not myself when last we met, although I seem to recall a wedding?' Dalrymple grins and fingers his complicated cream cravat, as if still unused to anything so luxurious at his neck. 'I have taken a step back from my ministry for the moment. I am seeking sufficient patronage that I might re-enter politics.'

Richard is not sure what he should say, so he says nothing. He looks around the room as Dalrymple calls to Simpkins and orders tea.

'I have foresworn strong drink,' he explains as if apologising for his choice of beverage, even though it is so early in the day. 'Now tell me how you come to be on my brother's doorstep on Christmas Eve?'

'I was hoping to speak with the lady of the house,' Richard admits, unsure what reaction the truth may elicit.

'And why might that be?' Dalrymple asks without showing much interest.

'Because I saw her the other day with her husband and realized I know her slightly. I thought it the season to renew our acquaintance.' His voice sounds unconvincing but

Arabella's brother-in-law merely nods and pulls a tasselled cord. A bell rings and Simpkins materializes in an instant.

'Simpkins, kindly inform Lady Dalrymple that she has a visitor. You might also let my brother know we have a guest.' Simpkins bows and is gone.

Richard squirms uncomfortably. 'There's really no need to trouble your brother,' he rushes out, 'I have called shockingly early. I'm sure he has no interest in me.' Richard's hands are shaking and he slips them beneath his thighs.

He thinks Fortescue Dalrymple will disagree but instead he nods. 'Quite right. I spoke merely for form. Simpkins is my brother's man. You can be sure he will go nowhere near my brother's chamber at this hour without his express instruction.'

When Arabella appears, it is without fanfare. She slips into the room as Richard is describing the voyage from Cape Town. Only as he finishes does he look up and spot her canary-yellow silks against the muted panelling.

He gets awkwardly to his feet and executes a bow.

'How chivalrous,' teases Dalrymple.

Arabella snaps her brother-in-law a curious glance. 'Mister Davey, what a delightful surprise. It has been some years since we met. Indeed, I have a bone to pick with you.' Although she is chiding him, her voice is musical, and amused. 'You broke your promise and left me to the ennui of diplomatic parties in Brussels.'

Richard flushes. He remembers promising to look her up after the battle of Waterloo. Instead, he became embroiled in Bonaparte's flight to Paris.

'Forgive me, Lady Dalrymple, I never meant to disappoint you. I felt sure you would attract no end of admirers and immediately forget the correspondent who you so kindly befriended.'

His mouth is dry as he studies her pretty face. She is carefully made up, her skin powdered. Is that a hint of a bruise he can see around her right eye? She clasps her hands around her elbows and winces.

'But as you see, I did not forget,' she says, her eyes holding his. They are hazel and liquid beneath her long lashes. He never forgot her either.

'It is good to see you settled, and mistress of such a fine home,' Richard offers, hoping to extract some sense of her predicament.

Fortescue Dalrymple is watching their exchange with mild interest and coughs before studiously inspecting his manicured nails.

Arabella's composed expression slips for moment and Richard spies a depth of pain behind her cheerful fencing. She wipes away a tear irritably, turning so that her brother-in-law does not see.

He has to do something. But he cannot speak in front of Lord Dalrymple's brother. 'I am entertaining tomorrow. I expect you will be too busy but if you are able to get away, even for a short while, I would be delighted. Any time at all.' Richard glances towards the doorway to the hall. 'Your man has my card.'

At the sound of someone moving about on the floor above, Arabella starts, glances around like a startled deer and mumbles her excuses.

Richard is up in a moment and crossing the room. He takes her delicate hand in his and kisses it lightly. 'Please come,' he whispers.

Her thumb presses hard. 'I'll try,' she replies *sotto voce*.

By the time Christmas Eve is over, Richard has explained the festive season to his Zulu companion. They have spent happy hours scandalising shoppers and shopkeepers, purchasing presents for Gladys and Myfanwy, Tommy and Percy, even something for Bobby and Jamaica Jim.

Richard has despatched messages inviting them all to the Albany before the Christmas Day church service. Gladys and Tommy have helped prepare their set for the party. They assure Richard that everyone will come.

Christmas morning. Church bells peel in untimely competition. A light dusting of snow drifts on a playful breeze. Richard is up early. He opens a sash-window, startling a robin who flutters off, feathers puffed, voicing his displeasure. Richard sees him alight on the railings lining the far side of the road and smiles.

There is no Christmas tree. How can there be when the notion will not be popularised until Victoria marries Albert some twenty years in the future? Nevertheless, he has insisted on holly garlands sporting bright red berries.Gladys and her mother arrive first. They are in their Sunday best with bonnets tied neatly beneath their chins. Myfanwy is obviously overawed as Gladys shows her around the set as if she owns it.

Tommy, Percy and Bobby arrive next, their boots polished

and their threadbare jackets pressed with care. Now it is Tommy's turn to show his friends around.

When they are finished, Richard surveys the group as they sit, a little awkwardly, drinking hot chocolate from fine china and nibbling fruitcake. A Yule log, wrapped in hazel twigs, burns merrily in the grate.

'Where is Jamaica Jim?' Richard asks, although he is really thinking about Arabella.

'He should be here by now,' replies Bobby in a puzzled voice. Richard decides to head downstairs and await his visitor in the lobby, leaving Mbikwane to play host.

When he reaches the foot of the stairs, he hears a commotion at the front door. Crossing the hallway, he finds the doorman manhandling Jim by the collar and one arm.

'What are you doing?' Richard demands.

'My job, sir. This miscreant claims he has business here. As if a resident would have anything to do with the likes of him!'

Richard thinks of his other guests, accompanied by servants who work in the building. They were passed without objection. 'What makes you doubt his word?' Richard snaps, attempting to loosen the doorman's vice-like grip on Jim's arm.

The doorman is tall, young and full of self-importance. He also looks like he resents working on Christmas Day. He sneers as he replies, 'Well, look at 'im, sir. He's no more'n a savage. Scruffy too.'

Richard studies Jamaica Jim. It is obvious he has made an effort with his appearance. His boots are clean, his jacket is shiny but free from creases. His face is shaved and scrubbed.

'Let him go immediately! He is my guest.' Richard frees

Jim's arm as the doorman releases his collar.

Jim's eyes are dark coal, his true thoughts drowned in the depths of his experience. Richard escorts him across the threshold, sparing a final look of indignation for the doorman who stammers an unconvincing apology. As Richard shows Jim into the apartment, they are greeted by a cheer.

Once Jim has a cup of steaming chocolate and a slice of cake, Mbikwane proudly removes a drape from a side table, revealing a small pile of neatly wrapped parcels.

'Presents for all!' Richard announces with a smile. Myfanwy almost drops her cup, Bobby looks furtive, and Tommy colours visibly. Gladys nibbles her lower lip. Only Jamaica Jim eyes the gifts with undisguised interest.

'Mister Davey, you shouldn't of done that,' objects Myfanwy demurely. 'We don't have nothing for you!' she explains further.

Mbikwane laughs as he steps forward with one of the gifts, holding it out to Myfanwy. She sets down her cup and saucer but keeps her hands in her lap. 'In my land, the host distributes gifts to thank his guests for attending,' the diplomat explains, 'it would be an insult should they try to give a present in return, for they have gifted their presence!'

And with that the tension dissipates. Richard and Mbikwane's guests grin sheepishly and in turn accept small parcels from the Zulu diplomat.

'Please, open them!' Richard encourages as the nearest church rings out the hour. He counts the strikes. It is ten o'clock.

Myfanwy cries so much at the sight of the mother-of-pearl

brooch that butcher Percy hugs her around the shoulders and offers her his clean handkerchief. Wiping her face she mumbles, 'I really needed that *cwtch*, Percy.' Gladys explains to the others she means a hug.

Myfanwy has to return the handkerchief when Percy is quite unmanned by the sight of a beautiful carving knife and fork with bone handles.

Gladys gushes as she lifts the lid of her decorated box, carefully preserving the bow. 'Oh my! Well, I never!' She holds the brocade scarf to the nearest window, pale sunlight turning cream to gold. A riot of sunflowers and daisies decorates the edges of the silk square.

Bobby gets a shiny rosewood pipe and a leather wallet of the finest Virginia tobacco. He mimes puffing with a satisfied look on his face.

Tommy is next to open his present. His hands eagerly claw at the ribbon. Inside the rectangular box sits a pair of calfskin gloves. When Richard saw them in Burlington Arcade, he bought them immediately. They remind him of the pair he first saw in Madame Odillet's shop, and then again, abandoned in Bonaparte's carriage during the flight from Waterloo.

Finally, it is Jim's turn. He grins as he opens the gift with surprisingly deft hands. Nestled on a bed of ruched material lies a traditional Zulu snuff box.

Mbikwane shows Jim how to open it. 'This belonged to my grandfather,' he reveals. 'I want you to have something from the continent that spawned you!'

Jamaica Jim lifts the lid and extracts a pinch of the powder. He snorts it up both nostrils, smiles with pleasure and then sneezes a rapid salvo. He gratefully accepts Percy's handkerchief.

Richard and Mbikwane exchange looks. 'Keep the boxes your gifts came in. Each contains a little surprise for you when you get home,' Richard advises. In each box, beneath the interior packaging, is an 1820 gold sovereign, bearing the profile of George III as a Roman emperor and an image of St George killing the dragon on the reverse. Each coin is worth £100 in the time Richard has left behind.

As his guests file out, chattering and smiling, effusive in their thanks, Richard is glad he made the effort. He notices Mbikwane has detained Jamaica Jim as he closes the door behind Percy.

'We are building a great empire in the most beautiful land you will ever see!' Mbikwane confides to Jim. 'There is always a place for newcomers. My king welcomes all who devote themselves to his cause. Look,' the Zulu points to Richard, 'this white man is declared a Zulu for his service and has married a woman of the royal blood!'

Richard is surprised to find himself both blushing and standing a little straighter, proud to hear his new truth spoken aloud.

Jim glances at Richard and then returns his steady gaze to Mbikwane. 'You speak of this land as if I am connected to it. Yet I was born in the West Indies, my ancestors are from west Africa, thousands of miles away from your Zulu kingdom.' There is regret in his tone.

'The people here, they will never treat you with respect. All they see is the colour of our skin,' Mbikwane counters.

'You were received by the king!' Jim objects. 'I have travelled the world. I am no longer young. There are people here, like Bobby and Percy, who treat me right.' He sounds wary and tired.

'We leave before your New Year. If you change your mind, you know where I am,' Mbikwane finishes reluctantly.

'If they let me in!' jokes Jim.

In the street outside, couples and families walk carefully along icy pavements towards the sound of bells. Richard would like to attend a Christmas service but he is not in the right mood. He still hopes Arabella will appear.

He looks over to the Zulu diplomat, who is eating fruitcake. Richard can tell that he too is carrying a disappointment. Something about Jamaica Jim has touched Mbikwane deeply. Richard sits beside him on the long, upholstered bench.

'It was a nice party,' he sighs, 'although we seem in need of some Christmas cheer!' Mbikwane nods sadly. Richard eyes the decanters on a walnut-inlaid side table.

Draining his glass, he reaches for the whisky but Mbikwane beats him to it. The Zulu's big hand pulls the stopper deftly and tilts the cut-glass container until Richard's glass is half full. He then serves himself a similarly sufficient dram.

By the time the church bells sound one o'clock, the pair are well oiled, although their mood remains sombre. They have demolished the cake, which has soaked up some of the alcohol, Richard hopes. He gets up unsteadily and totters to the half-open window.

The same couples and families walk wreathed in smiles as they return from church.

'I need to get outside!' he declares.

Mbikwane eyes him suspiciously. 'Do not do anything foolish, my friend. We are finished here; we should turn our thoughts towards home.' The big man's deep voice tugs at Richard, that final word conjuring his wife and son, so far away.

'Yes, we need to be gone. But first, there is one thing I must do.' He is resolved as he moves towards the door.

Mbikwane nods and stretches out on the richly upholstered sofa. 'Wake me when you return,' he mumbles, his eyes already shut.

Grosvenor Place stands proud in its elegance around lawns dusted with snow. Richard loiters on the garden side of the square looking at number eight.

Although it is only three o'clock in the afternoon, the interior is ablaze with warm light. The sash-windows are open an inch, letting the chatter and laughter of the partygoers drift outside.

He has walked for over an hour, sucking in lungful after lungful of cold air. His head is clearer but he knows his judgement is impaired or he would not be standing here.

He leans against the railings, trying to convince himself to leave. Twice he pushes his back clear and takes a step; and twice he falters and resumes his watchful position.

He begins to feel the cold as he stands transfixed by the bright windows. Figures move back and forth, purposeful in black and gold livery, contrasting with the riotous colour and movement of the guests.

The door opens and a party of five young men crowds the threshold, laughing and calling goodbye. Richard hurries across the road and up the steps, embedding himself in the gaggle of dandies.

As they reclaim their hats and gloves, he sidles across the threshold and as the harassed maid sees them out, he slips to the back of the hall. Struggling out of his overcoat and removing his hat, he searches for a hiding place. He slips them behind an ornate trunk and pushes through the door on his left.

He remembers the room from yesterday, although the furniture is now pushed against the walls and a sideboard is loaded with food and discarded glasses. Richard spies a half-full drink and picks it up, immediately feeling less conspicuous.

He scans the room and soon spots Lord Dalrymple, decidedly red in the face, laughing uproariously at what seems to be his own joke. He is surrounded by similarly aged men who play chorus to his lead.

Richard does not dwell, letting his sight rove until he detects another figure with a cluster of acolytes, albeit decked in flimsier materials.

Colour abounds. Sleeves are puffed, busts underpinned and decorated. Gauze shimmers over silk, swags and floral patterns. Waists are hidden while hair is piled in intricate confections with ringlets at the temples.

His eyes bore to the heart of the crowd. Arabella smiles, head tilted to one side. She asks a question and giggles demurely at the answer. She reaches out a hand, placing it delicately on the speaker's arm. She looks every inch the practised hostess.

It would be easy for Richard to believe nothing is wrong. To leave Arabella and her husband to their Christmas entertaining and slip away. If only she had not let that tear fall, gripped his hand so firmly or tried to hide that bruise on her cheek.

He must get her away from the orbit of her ladies without attracting her husband's attention. Without a semblance of a plan, he sees Lord Dalrymple nod decisively to his cronies and cross the salon to Arabella's side.

Richard edges surreptitiously closer, as if making for the sideboard, in time to hear his host's haughty bray.

'Hold the fort, darling. I'm taking the fellows to the games room for cigars and billiards.' He kisses her carelessly on the cheek and strolls away.

Richard sees Arabella scrub at her face with the heel of one hand. He moves to her elbow, interposing his maleness in the female circle.

'Lady Dalrymple, forgive this intrusion,' he begins. She is immediately looking at him, unable to disguise her surprise, colour suffusing her throat. 'May I borrow your hostess for the briefest moment?' he asks the assembled ladies. He feels them eyeing him with interest and forces his shoulders back to hide his natural slouch.

Nods, titters and one suggestive smile greet his enquiry. Arabella lets him steer her towards a door in the far wall. He opens it swiftly and ushers her through, closing it behind him with relief.

'Richard! What are you doing here?' she demands breathlessly. 'It was kind of you to invite me to your set but as you can see, it is quite impossible.' Her voice is richer than he remembers, but sadder too.

There is no time. He reaches out his left hand and grasps her elbow. She winces. He pushes up her sleeve to reveal a dark bruise and a raw, weeping burn the size of a modern ten pence piece in the soft crook of her elbow.

'Cigar?' he demands. She nods, apparently unable to speak. 'What else?' She shakes her head and looks at her feet. He lifts her chin to find the dam of her tears has burst. She cries silently, as if this is something she has learned by necessity.

In a moment she is leaning against him. She smells of lavender and roses. Her body trembles. After a few seconds she stills and steps back, a determined look on her face. She looks directly at him with wet eyes as she lifts gauze, satin and petticoats in an impatient bundle, revealing slender legs sheathed in opaque stockings tied with blue-ribboned bows.

With one hand holding up the layers of her dress, she uses the other to roll down her left stocking. Richard gasps and reaches out involuntarily. Arabella shakes her head. Her skin is a cat's cradle of raised welts, dark where blood lies close beneath the skin.

'Riding crop,' she admits, no longer maintaining eye contact.

'This is why I am here,' he whispers urgently, 'we must get you away while your brutish husband plays billiards.'

Arabella's mouth gapes but she has no time to speak before the door is thrust open and Reverend Dalrymple appears.

The clergyman stands stock-still, his gaze glued to the sight of Arabella with her dress lifted to the waist. The door is still open to the cheerful party beyond.

Richard edges to one side and pulls the door shut. As the lock clicks, Arabella regains control and lets go of her dress.

'Please, Fortescue, it isn't what you think,' Arabella pleads. Richard takes an involuntary step back.

'I rather fear it is precisely what I think,' replies the younger Dalrymple in a surprisingly tender voice. 'I should have acted sooner. I had suspicions. My brother, my own flesh and blood, he did that to you?'

Arabella nods slowly as if reluctant to admit the truth. She is crying again.

'I'll kill him!' declares the former missionary.

'No, please, don't do anything rash. He has so much influence. He is untouchable.' Arabella sounds utterly hopeless.

'But you are not, as we have seen!' Richard blurts out. 'The law will not save you. But I will. Come with me! I can get you on a ship for America.' The Honourable Fortescue Dalrymple immediately nods agreement.

'What about my reputation?' she murmurs uncertainly.

'Does it matter more than your life?' Richard demands, expecting her brother-in-law to object.

'He's right, my dear. I didn't learn much in Africa but I did come to realise what nonsense I have believed my whole life! There are other ways to live, other places to live. You are young. Grasp this chance!'

Laughter leaks beneath the door, the carefree birdsong of seasonal cheer.

'But how can I get away? The servants have their

instructions. I'm never allowed out alone.'

'Go upstairs. Pack a bag. Take all your jewellery. I'll get some money. I know where Everard keeps his gambling float.' Richard stares at Fortescue Dalrymple as if he has never met him.

'What can I do?' he asks.

'Simpkins, the footman, he's my brother's man through and through. He'll stop us if he can. I rather think we must incapacitate him. Are you game?' Dead men's faces loom but Richard blinks them away and nods. In that moment, he knows he will kill if necessary.

'Stay here, I'll send him to you,' suggests Fortescue.

Richard looks around the room. 'I need a weapon,' he suggests calmly, eyes settling on a pair of candlesticks atop the mantelpiece. He crosses and lifts one experimentally. Although ornate and silver, it has a satisfying heft. 'This should do.'

Arabella leaves with Fortescue. Richard stands beside the door, knuckles white around his makeshift weapon. He tries to control his breathing and listens to the party. Glasses chink, voices rise and fall, laughter punctuates the hubbub.

He is beginning to relax when the door opens to admit a gold-and-black liveried figure. Richard does not hesitate as the man crosses the threshold, peering into the room. He lifts the candlestick, holding it by its capital. The sconce stops it slipping as he brings the base down with force against the back of the servant's skull.

The dark-haired footman crumples forward. Richard kicks his feet clear and shuts the door. Kneeling, he is relieved to see the prone figure breathing. Richard pulls a curtain tie free, tying Simpkins' wrists together as he moans faintly.

Richard wonders whether he should hit him again as he uses a second tie to truss the man's feet. He cannot do it. He unstuffs a cushion and thrusts the cover roughly between the footman's fleshy lips. He ties it in place with the remains of the first cord, forcing Simpkins' bound hands towards his mouth as if in prayer.

He drags the body to the corner of the room to his right, where it is obscured by a settee. He picks up the candlestick and inspects it. The sconce is dented as is the capital. He wipes away a trace of blood with the unsheathed cushion and replaces it above the fireplace. He hides the bloodied cushion beneath the settee and tidies the curtains as best he can.

He has barely finished before Fortescue returns. 'All gone to plan?' he asks.

Richard looks a little guiltily towards Simpkins' trussed form.

'Good man. No time to dawdle, Arabella's waiting at the rear of the house. Take this,' he thrusts a large leather wallet into Richard's hands. It is about an inch thick. Lifting the flap, Richard sees it is stuffed full of white banknotes. The value of the top one is ten pounds. Richard tries to fit the wallet into his pocket but it is too bulky.

He follows Fortescue in a slaloming route through clusters of revellers, some clearly the worse for drink. He nods and smiles while his companion breezily greets one woman after another.

In the hall, Richard reclaims his coat and shrugs it on, pocketing the wallet and gripping his tall hat. He follows his co-conspirator into a corridor. They pass doors on both sides, along with a curtseying maid, before they reach a rear door.

Outside, Richard finds Arabella waiting nervously in a narrow lane hemmed in by buildings. She is holding a decorated silk reticule in one hand and an overstuffed velvet drawstring bag in the other. Without speaking, Fortescue leads Arabella to the right. Richard trails behind. They pass through one wooden gate after another until they reach an alley that disgorges them into the square.

'Go with my blessing, dear girl. Rest assured I shall do all in my power to prevent Everard finding you.'

Fortescue turns to Richard. 'I found this in the butler's pantry.' Richard takes his calling card with a smile of gratitude.

'I would never have thought to…'

Fortescue Dalrymple holds up his hand. 'No time, hide her somewhere a lord will never think to look. Eschew obvious routes. Do not sail from London or the south coast. Liverpool perhaps?' He pushes Richard and Arabella around the corner to Duke Street.

Richard mumbles over his shoulder, 'You are a better man now than you ever were wearing a dog-collar!'

Feathery snowflakes drift out of the darkening sky as they hurry away. They reach the far end of the road before clattering hooves make Arabella jump. She drops her bag in the slush. The carriage creaks past on complaining springs, iron-bound wheels harsh across the cobbles.

Richard retrieves the bag and slings it over his shoulder, slipping his free arm around Arabella's waist. She feels impossibly insubstantial as she shivers in her flimsy dress.

St Giles is less than a mile and a half from Grosvenor Square, but it takes almost an hour. As they reach the working-class suburb, Arabella is shivering uncontrollably, her flimsy slippers sodden and her lips blue.

Gladys answers his knock at the door with a look of astonishment that doubles as she takes in his pale companion.

'Who's callin' so late, Glad?' asks Mrs Jones in her lilting voice.

'It's that nice Mister Davey, and he's brought a friend,' reports a doubtful Gladys less tunefully.

'Well, show them in, it's cold out there,' orders the lady of the house.

Richard is glad to find a fire lit. Myfanwy Jones sets a chair by the grate and he eases Arabella onto it. Within minutes there is steaming tea and sympathy. Richard explains as much as he dares while Arabella recovers.

Gladys is sent to find Percy, who arrives in a bloodied apron with a concerned look on his face. He looks Richard up and down, resting a proprietorial hand on Myfanwy's shoulder.

'You bring trouble where none is invited,' Percy scolds. 'This family has been nothing but kind to you, and how do you reward them?'

Richard looks at Arabella, colour returning to her cheeks as she continues to warm herself, and then down at his soggy feet.

'You are quite right, Mister Hoggard. We will go. This has nothing to do with the good people of St Giles.' He sounds tired and resigned but crosses to Arabella and helps her from her seat.

'Ma?' asks Gladys in a strangled voice.

'I know, dearie, I know. Sit yourself back down, Lady Dalrymple,' Myfanwy insists in a voice full of emotion. 'Percy is just lookin' out for us, isn't it? But as he likes to remind me, this is still my 'ouse.'

Arabella looks almost convincing in Gladys' uniform.

'Try being a bit less... upright,' Richard suggests tentatively.

Arabella rounds her shoulders and Mrs Jones immediately claps her hands in approbation. 'That's it, dearie, now you don't look like you're in fancy dress!'

Gladys, on the other hand, is utterly compelling in Arabella's dried and freshly pressed dress. She strolls back and forth across the small room, swinging her embroidered reticule nonchalantly from her right wrist.

Richard recalls Napoleon dressed as a female servant and poor Marchand impersonating his master, mimicking every mannerism, only to be shot for aiding Bonaparte's escape from St Helena.

'Let's go over your story once again, Gladys,' Richard insists in a worried voice. Myfanwy clears away the evidence of a modest breakfast as if it is a normal day.

Gladys Jones smiles indulgently. 'I was minding my own business walking to work when I was accosted by her ladyship. She gave me this dress, saying she had no more use for it because it reminded her of a very sad time that she was leaving behind her. She said she was taking ship from the south coast for the continent.'

Richard smiles with satisfaction. Gladys beams too. She didn't falter or hesitate, reeling off her story with conviction.

Mbikwane, summoned by Percy Hoggard, shakes his head. 'This is a dangerous thing you do,' he advises, his deep voice filling the room. He looks first at Richard and then to Gladys. 'To take a man's wife, even if he has several, is a great insult unless she is forfeit after a defeat.'

'Are you sure you won't accept my offer?' Richard asks. He has offered the Jones family enough money to relocate in comfort but their lives are in London and they have refused him.

'Don't worry so, I ain't done nothin' wrong. I never stole the dress. None of her ladyship's people have ever seen me. Why should there be trouble for me or Ma?' Gladys smooths the flimsy overlay of muslin with hungry fingers. 'Let me get out where I can be seen. Lord Dalrymple must have missed his wife by now? He'll have men searching.'

Richard holds up his hands in defeat. Gladys opens the door and Mbikwane joins her.

'Miss Gladys, will you show me Jamaica Jim's lodgings?' he asks as they disappear down the stairs.

The mail coach from London to Liverpool departs on time at five in the afternoon from Gloster Warehouse, Oxford Street. Arabella sits behind the driver, with Mbikwane and Jim beside her, both in workmen's clothes. The damp air beads on her bonnet, which is fastened tightly over her head, freshly shorn of ringlets. The peak of Jim's cap steers the gathering rain into his lap, Richard notices, while the Zulu remains bareheaded and apparently oblivious to the weather.

337

Richard shares the interior of the coach with a governess and her charge, a pallid, grizzling six-year-old Richard initially mistakes for a girl despite the pale blue suit. The other passenger is a jovial, garrulous tailor who keeps conversation flowing regardless of the wishes of his fellow passengers.

The guard sits at the back of the coach, also outside, carrying a fearsome-looking blunderbuss and a pair of pistols. He wears the maroon and gold livery of a Post Office employee.

They call first at Snow Hill and then outside the post office in Barnet. The guard hands off and collects the mail from each postmaster, sometimes before the red wheels stop turning. It is properly dark before they reach St Albans. The post office at Dunstable falls behind them after a driver change.

The guard remains a constant: stoic, reassuring and efficient. Fenny Stratford gives way to the Cock on Stony Stratford's straight High Street, followed by the Talbot at Towcester. His cheerful, no-nonsense voice jokes with stable-hands and postmasters, serving girls and landlords. He is personally responsible for the mail and well paid to see it safely to its destinations.

At the Wheat Sheaf in Daventry there is a delay. Fresh horses are not ready. The postmaster is late. The driver disappears into the inn. Richard sticks his head out of the coach, craning his neck for a glimpse of Arabella. Frustrated, he steps out. It is dusk. The rain has stopped.

A dog barks. He hears hurrying feet. Hobnailed boots on cobbles. Lord Dalrymple's men have found them! He feels sick and has to cling to the coach door. There is a shout.

'Hold there!' Two figures appear out of the gloom into a weak puddle of light from the stable lantern. Richard reaches to his waistband but there is no pistol, not even a knife. He hears an intake of breath from Arabella. The carriage creaks as Mbikwane and Jamaica Jim shift in their seats.

Richard can see the pair clearly now. One man is tall but stooped, the other figure a mere boy, weighed down by a heavy-looking sack.

'You're late!' growls the guard, although he doesn't sound annoyed.

'Broke an axle. Shanks's pony for the last mile!' shoots back a phlegmy voice. 'Lucky I had the lad with me or I'd never have made it.'

Richard almost faints with relief. It is the postmaster and his boy.

Richard dozes past Southam to wake at the Bath in Leamington. Daylight makes him blink. After the Castle at Warwick they reach Solihull. They are in the Midlands and Richard begins to relax. They are far beyond the orbit of London now and, he hopes, Earl Dalrymple.

Fresh horses are swapped in at the Swan in Birmingham, along with another change of driver. They make steady time, and on good stretches of road get close to eight miles an hour.

Richard leaves his watch in his pocket. Time is no constant in these days before the railways. Each town sets its own clocks. Walsall and Cannock. Horses are changed. The tailor departs at Stafford, heading straight into the George for lunch. The interior of the coach seems immediately larger.

At the Crown in Stone the governess chivvies her charge outside and reclaims their luggage. A pony and trap waits for them. Richard eats a hunk of bread smothered in beef dripping that Mrs Jones wrapped for him in a threadbare cloth.

The Roe Buck at Newcastle-under-Lyme, Holmes Chapel, the Angel at Knutsford and Warrington are reached in turn. It is dark again. The sun setting less than eight hours after it rose. Only their destination, the port of empire, Liverpool, remains ahead.

They arrive, bone-weary, close to nine-thirty in the evening according to the guard, barely thirty minutes late.

As Richard helps Arabella down in the forecourt of the Saracen's Head, he feels elated. He can hear the sea breaking against wharfs, although a heavy fog has rolled in from the Atlantic, obscuring masts and hulls, docks and warehouses.

It is still foggy the next morning, the thick air dampening sound. Richard walks along George's Dock with the imposing red-brick Goree warehouses to his right. Sailing vessels crowd the wharfs and many more stand off, awaiting their turn to unload before taking on fresh cargo.

Through a tear in the heavy grey cloak, he catches sight of a gothic tower beyond the six-storey cathedrals of commerce. It looms above everything else. A passing stevedore spots him peering through the fog. 'That be St Nick's, the sailors' church,' he offers in an Irish brogue.

Richard has never been to Liverpool before. He thinks of The Beatles and shakes his head, although he cannot help whistling 'Penny Lane' as he searches for a shipping agent. He did not dare buy tickets in London as they could have led Lord Dalrymple to Arabella.

The first office he tries cannot help him, they are still waiting for their passenger list to fill up. But the balding clerk, eyes bulbous behind thick lenses, suggests the Black Ball Line, not much further along the quay towards the pier head, as they have a fixed sailing date for New York.

The vessel is a sailing packet, a ship of all trades, carrying mail, cargo and people. She departs on the morning tide tomorrow, a thin, creased, near-toothless teller confirms. For the right fee, forty guineas a head, they can accommodate four more passengers.

Richard is glad he has Dalrymple's wallet, as his gold is almost exhausted from settling his London expenses. He hopes Mrs Jones finds the coins he slipped into her half-empty teapot before bidding her and her extended family a fond farewell.

Epilogue

S tanding at the stern of the *James Monroe*, Richard steals a surreptitious glance at Arabella, still decked out as a maidservant. Mbikwane is below decks with Jamaica Jim, doubtless making friends in steerage.

'No darkies in the cabins,' the purser had insisted with casual contempt. Richard knows better than to explain Mbikwane is an ambassador. Better they draw no attention, raise no suspicion, and reach the other side of the Atlantic anonymously.

Richard unfolds a newspaper he bought from an urchin at the foot of the gangway. It is *The Morning Post*, a London daily, dated four days ago. It might have travelled with them on the mail coach.

He is studying the back page when Arabella gasps. He peers over the paper to see her staring wide-eyed at the front page. With her forefinger she indicates the lead article.

He turns the paper to read the headline. He has to squint as the whole page is covered in small print, each article butted beneath the previous one. 'Peer found dead at home. Suicide suspected,' he reads on, 'brother expected to inherit title in the absence of offspring.'

Richard smiles at Arabella, whose shock is dissipating.

'Seems your brother-in-law made good on his promise!' he

suggests, unable to stifle a laugh. Arabella is smiling now, her white teeth bright against her black clothes. Their giggles intertwine, deep and high, loud and demure, startling the gulls circling the wake. The sickle-winged birds call back with their own mocking laughter.

'So, there's no one coming after me!' Arabella exclaims. A fish jumps free of the ocean's surface, its scales silvery as the sky. A gull swoops, cruel yellow beak open, neck outstretched as it arrows towards its target, a split second too late.

Richard hugs her against his side. She winces slightly but does not pull away. He takes a half step along the rail. Month piles into month in his head. Another one likely spent before they disembark in New York. He thinks of his son and his wife. He thinks of Napoleon and Shaka. In the whole time he was on English soil, he never once felt he belonged. His England remains two hundred years away.

THE RICHARD DAVEY

CHRONICLES

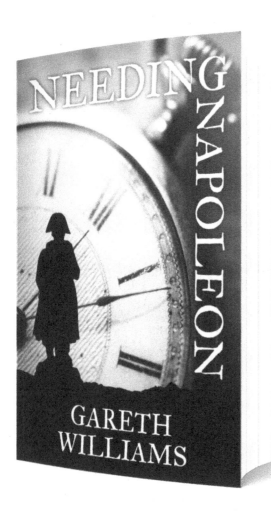

NEEDING NAPOLEON

Available in paperback and as an ebook

Paperback ISBN: 978-1-914913-21-1
eBook ISBN: 978-1-839784-19-4

SERVING SHAKA

Available in paperback and as an ebook

Paperback ISBN: 978-1-914913-53-2
eBook ISBN: 978-1-839784-70-5